NORTHFIELD BRANCH
847-446-5990

CITY
OF THE
UNCOMMON
THIEF

CITY OF THE UNCOMMON THIEF

by Lynne Bertrand

DUTTON BOOKS

DUTTON BOOKS

An imprint of Penguin Random House LLC, New York

First published in the United States of America by Dutton Books,
an imprint of Penguin Random House LLC, 2021

Text copyright © 2021 by Lynne Bertrand

Map art copyright © 2021 by Francesca Baerald

Visit us online at penguinrandomhouse.com

Library of Congress Cataloging-in-Publication Data is available.

Printed in the United States of America

ISBN 9780525555322

10 9 8 7 6 5 4 3 2 1

Design by Anna Booth

Text set in Minion Pro

For Hans

EX LIBRIS
Errol Thebes

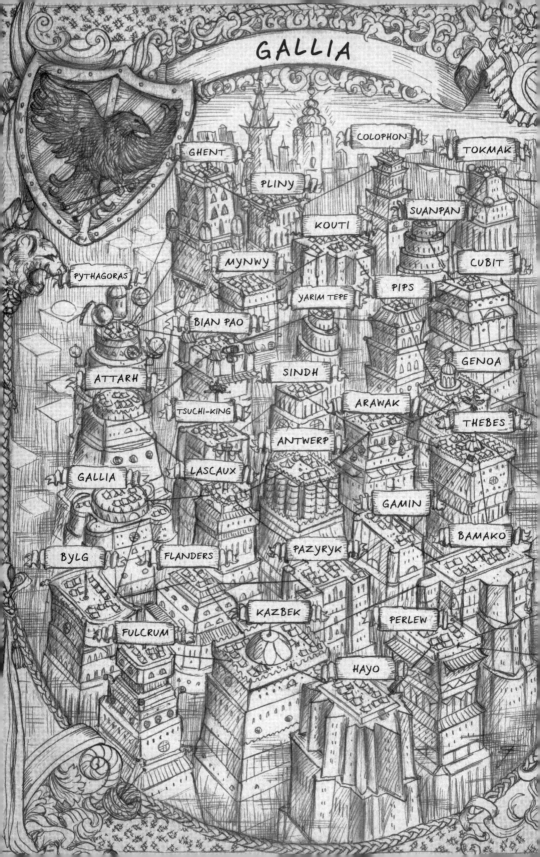

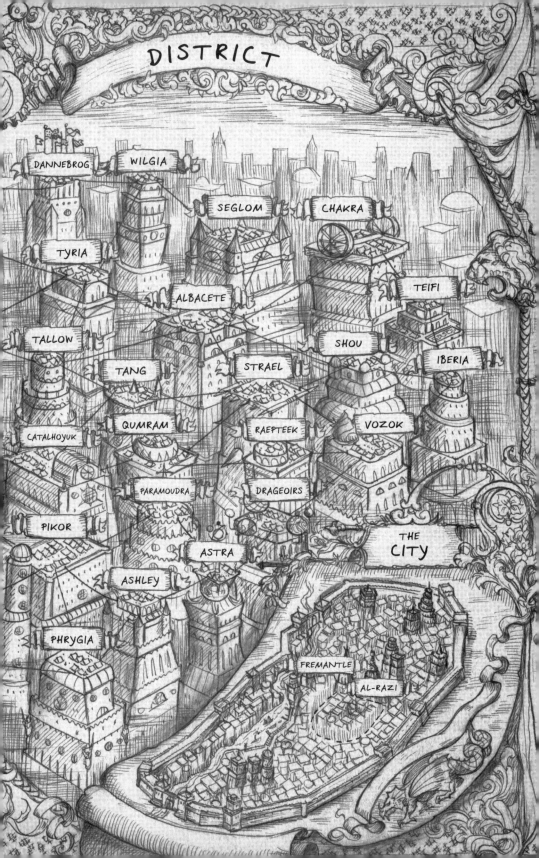

ELEMENTS OF THE CLOCK AND CALENDAR

THE BELLS OF THE DAY

NOCTIS: MIDNIGHT

FESTIVUM: ONE O'CLOCK

SOMNIUM: TWO

CRUSTUM: THREE

PURGAMENTUM: FOUR

EPISTOLA: FIVE

PERFECTUM: SIX

ERRATUM: SEVEN

GRANUM: EIGHT

SANGUIS: NINE

SUDORE: TEN

LACRIMAE: ELEVEN

MERIDIANUS: NOON

LIBRI: ONE

TEXO: TWO

PARIO: THREE

EFFIO: FOUR

FORCTIS: FIVE

ANIMO: SIX

RADIX: SEVEN

JOCUS: EIGHT

DULCIBUS: NINE

TUMULTUS: TEN

IN SACCI: ELEVEN

THE DAYS OF THE WEEK

IDEM 1 • IDEM 2 • IDEM 3 • IDEM 4 • IDEM 5 • IDEM 6 • IDEM 7

THE MONTHS OF THE YEAR

WINTER	SPRING	SUMMER	AUTUMN
BOREAL	FAOL	PIOGGIA	SHAMAL
RHAGFYR	HLYDA	LANGESONNE	MISTRAL
HORNUNG	ZEPHYR	GAMAN	GANSO

THE GUILD TOWERS
OF GALLIA DISTRICT
AND THEIR EXPORTS

ALBACETE
NAVAJAS

ANTWERP
LACE

ARAWAK
HAMACS

ASHLEY
DITTY BAGS

ASTRA
ASTROLABES

ATTARH
ATTARH

BAMAKO
DOHOLS

BIAN PAO
FIREWORKS

BYLG
BELLOWS

CATALHOYUK
MAPS

CHAKRA
WHEELS

COLOPHON
SPINDLES

CUBIT
WEIGHTS &
    MEASURES

DANNEBROG
VEXILLA

DRAGEOIRS
PLANETS

FLANDERS
DAMASK

FULCRUM
BALANCES

GALLIA
BARRELS

GAMIN
LOCKS

GENOA
BOBBINS

GHENT
WOOL FELT

HAYO
FLAILS

IBERIA
VIHUELAS

KAZBEK
BURKAS

KOUTI
CHESTS

LASCAUX
FLY-LINES,
ROPE, RIGGING

MYNWY
MONMOUTHS

PARAMOUDRA
FLINTS

PAZYRYK
CARPETS

PERLEW
FISHING NETS

PHRYGIA
TOQUES

PIKOR
GRAIN SACKS

PIPS
DICE

PLINY
BESTIARIES

PYTHAGORAS
FORMULAE

QUMRAM
QUILL INK

RAEPTEEK
BEADS

SEGLOM
SAILCLOTH

SHOU
INCENSE

SINDH
BUTTONS

STRAEL
FLETCHERY

SUANPAN
ABACUSES

TALLOW
CANDLES

TANG
PLAYING CARDS

TEIFI
CORACLES

THEBES
KNOTTING SPIKES

TOKMAK
KNOBS

TSUCHI-KING
CRICKET ROOMS

TYRIA
DYES

VOZOK
SLEDGES

WILGIA
WILLOW BASKETS

YARIM TEPE
KILNWORK

CITY
OF THE
UNCOMMON
THIEF

I DON'T DREAM and never have. I hardly sleep. Lately I bide the nights by choosing names for each ship in a vast fleet. The names come to me from what sky I can see through a square cut in the roof of my tent. *Taygete, Ye-Ji, Bellatrix, Al-Uqdah.* I was at work on this list, long after noctis on the thirteenth of Rhagfyr, with a quill in hand and my head lamp dimly lit. An east wind harassed the tower roofs and strained the tent flaps and tethers. One of the bog-pot doors must have pulled off its hinge and was banging against the jamb. Odd Thebes lay next to me, lost in sleep.

"What was that?" I said.

"What was what?" he mumbled into his pillow.

"Someone just called for you."

"'Tis naught." He rolled away from me. "Who would be out in this larceny wind? No one."

I pulled wools and a tunic from the heap of our clothes and slipped out onto the roof. The bucket fires were cold and the iron tower was slick with ice underfoot. I stood at the edge.

A minute passed before someone called again the bard's name: "Odd Thebes." I shone my lamp into the abyss. Twenty feet out and ten down, on the plank between my guild tower, Lascaux, and our neighbor Gallia, sat a runner so ragged I barely knew him.

"The bard ignores me and sends a mere muse," he called, squinting into my light through a billow of steam. I had to wipe my hands of sudden sweat, for I had never seen a plank so deeply bowed as this one, certainly not under the weight of one runner.

"The outlaw returns," I called back.

A gust of wind dispelled the steam, and now I could see that the weight bearing down on the plank was not merely the runner's but also that of the colossal beast upon which he sat.

"What is *that*?" I said.

The runner studied the animal beneath him, as though he was as surprised as I was to find it there. It was a hoofed creature, easily the weight of seven guilders, umber-furred and broad in the chest, with a pair of branches jutting from the sides of its head and more of that steam huffing from velvet nostrils.

"That," he said, "is another. A nother." He was struggling. "An *other*." The mere emphasis on the word caused the plank to tremble. In one hand he held a pair of sticks—tamping rods or lapidary files, I thought, or marlinespikes. With the other hand he removed a flask from his pocket, then uncorked it with his teeth and spit the cork into the abyss. "Tell me something," he said, taking an unsteady swig. "Given the choice, would you rather be Sisyphus or Theseus?"

"It's the middle of the night," I said.

"Would you prefer to drown in the hands of a fiend or be devoured alive?"

"That depends. Are we out of arsenic?"

"I'm asking a real question. What would you do, if you were me, the irfelaf son of a high-ranking guildmaster, in a city quarantined by fear?"

"I would think twice before I filled my head with whiskey over a mile-high abyss," I said. "On the back of a sheep on an ice-rimed plank. And insulted the only help within earshot."

"It's a stag," he said.

Something moved at the edge of my lamplight. The runner and I both turned to look. A skin-and-bones foundling crouched at the edge of Gallia.

The runner flinched and blurted something in his ancient guild tongue and, to my horror, hurled the sticks at the foundling. He may as well have dropped a whole new stag onto the stressed plank. The cedar split with a sickening crack. The stag scrambled for purchase in a spray of splinters and ice but slid backward, with the runner gripping its fur. They fell into the abyss.

Then? Then. That foundling leapt out onto what remained of the plank and ran toward me. Did it not see the splintered end? The nothing air? It dove straight down, grasping at the darkness.

From inside my tent the bard called out, "What was that?"

"Um—"

There came a shift in the column of air between the towers, and I stepped back from the edge for what came next.

———

This isn't my tale, and I won't be accused of thieving it from the bard. But as I have a script of my own, I'll tell this bit more. I kept a wad of that umber fur, and a feather, too. I'm sure there are cities in the world beyond our wall where, every day, guilders find such relics caught on a fence or blowing about in the street and can't even bother to pick them up, common as the beasts are who wear them. But here, in towers devoid of animals of any kind, fur and feathers are the irfelaf, "all that remains." I keep them in my tellensac. For similar reasons I name a fleet of ships I do not own to sail on oceans I have never seen.

PART I

BE WARNED. A fragrance rises from this ink. The recipe is equal parts blood, gall, sewage, tears, the spit of a dying bard, and the soot from a sputtering head lamp. This day has not gone well.

Homer would never find himself here, squatting on a ledge in an earthen shaft, scratching plot on a scab of parchment with a quill yanked from a chicken's ass. I'm glad for him. Let him ply his trade on the other side of the wall. Homer, Ovid, Virgil. They're all there, no doubt barding together around a blazing fire, unfurling high tales of heroes and Olympians. I'm sure they have no trouble keeping a safe distance from their own plots. So glad for them. I fling all my good wishes to them from my pit. However, for any tales that occur on this side of the wall and that involve a shafted bard, there is Odd Thebes. Despite all of my best efforts, I am he.

The scratches of this plot begin with a game of cards, a felony theft, and a pair of missing pelts on the roof of Thebes. It was the fifth of Ganso.

Five of us were well into a round of maw in Talwyn's tent when our roof master, Marek Thebes, called us for body count. I abandoned a perfect hand to grope my way across the flat expanse of our roof in the cloud that had lain thick as a kitchen sponge on us and stinking of fish all week. Our clothes were sopped. I could see nothing but white—not the yurt, or the earth below us, not one of the 999 other guild towers of our city, not even the snot dripping off my nose.

Marek paced inside the yurt. He felt an evil lack. Felt it in his teeth, he said. We counted ourselves off and found his teeth to be correct. There were merely fifteen of us. The two who were missing were pelts from a group who had come up that morning. Marek dispatched us to find them.

New runners always go missing. How can anything prepare them for that first full day on a tower roof? And yet there are so few places to hide. On Thebes: seventeen tents, seventeen trunks, a common yurt, a tent kitchen, and the bogs. It's tempting, in the first days, to go down, to find permanent relief from the vast, too-beautiful sky in the grim tedium of the guild tower below. I felt my way to the grate and woke the hatch-guilder beneath it with a jab.

"Two runners gone!" I yelled. "Before the tufuga could even mark them. Did they bribe their way home?"

"That's a dark question to wake me with," he growled, scratching his nethers. "Look for yourself! The hatch is locked. And no pimple-faced, homesick runners paid me to slip home through it. It's a misdemeanor for you runners to come home. You'd know that as well as any."

(Actually what he said was "Foulen darky, wakken en gulder. Luket ye. Atchis locked, en naught puss-scabben geld-seck roonies fived my to slip mam-home twanen the bares. 'Tis a foul crimm for en of ye te mam-home roon. En ye nown it verily, Odd Thebes, bester than te rest, as ye'v trine it for your own salf thryce that once't yar." But if I laid out every actor's mother tongue, every guild's language, this quill will fray before a plot rises.)

The idea of two gone runners conjured squalls in our chests. We felt the city's restless quarantine, her lack of a place on any map or calendar. Most of all—

"It's a long way down," said Ping Thebes, our cook. We were back in the yurt. Marek narrowed his eyes, but Ping shrugged. "I'm just saying what you're all thinking."

Marek paced again. "Either they pulled an Icarus or they're out gut-running and I'll murder them myself."

Someone whispered, "It's the gut run."

Marek turned to stare at Dragomir, who had come up with the two who were missing.

"The other pelts in the guild dared us to make a gut run on our first day," Dragomir said. At fifteen times around the sun, he was a human-skin map of wens, grease ponds, and tufts. Thus, a pelt. Marek's stare unnerved him and he blurted, "A gut run is a prank, uh, an attempt to sort of *acquire* an object of local value from another guild house to prove one has the, say, courage to run the fly-lines."

A muscle twitched under the stubble of Marek's close-cut beard. "I am aware of the meaning of 'gut run.'"

"Of course. Yes." Dragomir reddened.

"Why didn't you go with them?" Marek said.

The question took Dragomir off guard, as gut runs were illegal. "I, uh, fear heights," he fumbled.

"I see," said Marek. He glanced out the door of the yurt into the cloud. Everything out there was high. "It's not the drop you should fear, Dragomir. It's me."

"I do fear you."

Marek sucked his teeth. "Run the lines," he said. "Find them."

"Me?" squeaked Dragomir. "But I have yet to run even one line—"

Marek circled the fire, past Dragomir, past Ping, past my cousin Errol. He stopped at me.

"Odd Thebes. Take the pelt. Go find what's left of his friends."

I flinched. "Why me? We can't find a guild tower in this cloud, never mind two scrawny pelts. Also I had a winning hand—"

Marek hissed in my ear, "I wonder how many aces of hearts there are supposed to be in one deck of cards. Shall we find the answer under your toque?"

———

Dragomir and I stood at the edge of Thebes, our head lamps pulsing in the cloud.

He was silent. All he knew of life so far was the inside of a guild tower. Work, sleep, work. He was pale from the lack of sun. Bored from lack of plot. In guild life a bit of salt in your soup constituted a festival. A rumor on any subject from the roofs overhead kept you going for months. By the time Dragomir had rounded the sun, say, fourteen times, all he could think about was climbing through the hole in the tower roof, seeing that sun for himself. Running the infinite web of planks, ladders, masts, and flies that glistened in it. *Am I going?* Until today, an iron roof kept him down. And an iron wall pens us all in. We are a remnant civilization of a thousand locked towers striving to produce magnificent wares so a single fleet of ships can come once a year and take them—

"Where is the fly-line?" said Dragomir, waving his hand in the air. "I cannot feel it."

"Here." I guided his hand to the thread stretched over our heads and anchored securely to a mast behind us. Its other end was similarly connected to a mast on the tower to our east.

"Moth spit," Dragomir whispered.

Moth spit, rigging, flies. We had a long list of nicknames for the lines. The best was *fet-makkers.* Faith makers. Stand at any edge and fling a rag over a fly as thin as the line you could draw with a quill, and step off into the abyss. Never again would *fet* be a theory.

"I can't do this," Dragomir gasped.

"That fly is strong enough to carry you and your supper across the abyss. Even if your supper is a two-ton wheel of cheese."

"*Abyss?* Could we just call it 'the area in between'?"

"Abyss. Abyss. Abyss. Get used to it."

Through the cloud I could hear him fumbling with his pack. I pushed his hands away and reached inside the pack.

"Looking for this?" I said, holding two clips and a reel of line. "Safest thing you own. Hook the red clip to your pack and the green one to the fly. Eight strata of line and never will it snap."

"You're sure?" said Dragomir, his voice quavering.

"Aye. That's why we call this your mam-line. The mam will never, ever let you fall." I pushed the red clip onto his finger like a ring and yanked it off. The bearings in it closed fast and pinched him hard. The emergency stop. He yelped. "See? Or you can set the brakes yourself, and the line length, with these levers—" He moved before I could hurt him again. "Your mam wrote to us, Dragomir. She wants you to go slow."

"She did?" One part surprise, one part embarrassment.

"No. Of course she didn't. Yes she did."

"I'm confused."

I sighed. "Forget your mam, Dragomir. Forget your da and all your guild toys and the fifteen-year nap you've had in the tower. Today is the first day of your life!" I was stuffing the clips and the mam-line back into his pack. He was trying to dig them back out. "Answer me: Do you want to go fast or not?" He shrugged. "Yes, you do. You didn't come to the roofs to be safe. All you need"—I reached into his pack again—"is *this*." Now I was holding a yard-long lanyard of greased silk, with a Turk's head knot at each end. The runner's rag. "This is fast. Just throw this over the fly and go."

"How far down is the drop here?"

"Fifty feet. Fifty-one, tops."

"It's a mile. I heard it's a mile down."

"Just a rumor. Anyway, after fifty feet, how could it matter? Don't ever look down."

"I'm going to die," he whispered.

"You're definitely going to die. You're going to die when you're an old, skinny guilder with a bound-wife and so many worthless kelps you run out of names for them. Did you knock the crow for luck?"

"Aye. Thrice."

"So you won't die *today*. Let's go find your idiot friends."

I tossed my rag over the line, caught it in the same hand, made a bow and flourish to Dragomir with the other, and dropped off the edge. Thirty yards through the cloud I landed on the roof of Catalhoyuk with a skid. I heard Dragomir gasp and drop behind me. Silence. For a moment I thought I lost him, but he barreled into me, the color of fear. There was no going back now for him, not without running a line or walking a plank. He was one of us.

———

We were sitting on the edge of Raepteek, and Dragomir was just saying we ought to be looking for his friends instead of stopping to eat cheese, when a light cracked from the direction of Thebes and the cloud lit up around us.

"A flare?!" he cried, while I pried him off my arm. "Wait! Who found them? *We* were supposed to find them!"

I licked my fingers. "Five uurs says it was Errol Thebes."

"Ten!" he said. "Ten uurs says it *wasn't*! Marek sent *us*!"

"If you insist." I shrugged. "Ten uurs. I'll go to twenty, if you have it."

———

Marek had dispatched Errol before Dragomir and I had even left the edge of Thebes. *Of course* he had. Everyone knew he would. And within ten minutes Errol had found the missing pelts. Or, rather, he had run into their taut mam-lines, pinched on the fly between Ghent and Pliny.

———

The kelps in Thebes House used to whisper the names of heroes when Errol Thebes passed them in the halls of the tower. *Achilles. Parsival. Jack.* Most often, *Bee Wolf.* They were referring to Beowulf, the warrior in that story we have from the other side of the wall: broad in the face and chest, and unkempt, with long, dark red hair. Whenever I caught the kelps carrying on about this, I reprimanded them, for there was no such description in the text. But they just touched Errol with their cold little fingers and laughed at me and whispered, *'Tis him.*

Errol plucked both mam-lines. No response. He pulled out his own mam, clipped it to the fly, pinched the brake. Anyone could see the problem. Those two runners had leapt from Ghent House, with a sloped fly across an eighty-foot-wide abyss to Pliny. Cold fell while they were midair, and the cloud rimed on the line. They forgot everything they knew about braking on ice and slammed into Pliny like twin hams. They were tossed backward, up the fly, *bragen ofer earsas*, as my mother would say. They dropped their rags. Their green clips gripped the line. But they lost control of the reds, and five thousand feet above the street, they spun off the reels. Eight strata down they slammed the end of their lines. The common term for a drop like that is a "screamer." Roughly, they'd been hanging four uurs in a frozen sky.

Errol yanked the first line, setting himself and everything else twanging on the fly. From far below him in the cloud came panicked begging. He wound the line around his belt to haul up the human luggage on the end of it.

This runner was a thin pelt, his face frozen in a weird grin. His chest was iced in his own heave, his leggings in piss. When he spoke, the standard greeting of the roofs came off his blue lips in a spray of spit: "SSSSsssstay high."

"High," returned Errol, man of many words. "I'm going to let go of you now and you'll slip down the fly and wait at the edge of Pliny." But the runner would have none of that. He clung to Errol, too terrified of life, death, and everything in between, to let go. "We'll have to leave your friend down there if you don't let go of me," Errol said. The runner shook his head no. Errol said, "All right. We'll do it your way." The runner closed his eyes in relief.

I could have told him closing his eyes around Errol Thebes was a mistake. Errol curled a fast fist and threw a punch. There was a *crack* and the runner's eyes took a brief tour of the inside of his skull and his body sagged. Errol said, "Wait here."

The second body came up blue-black and motionless with a cold, hard jugular. Errol strapped the body to his back and cut the mam-line from the fly. As he was adjusting the dead weight, he heard a grinding sound behind him. The first runner had come to and was gnawing his own mam-line between his teeth.

"If that breaks, you'll drop!" Errol shouted at him.

"I can stand on the cloud," the runner said, continuing to gnaw. "Watch!"

"Stop! Your brain is rimed!" But there was a sickening *pop* of teeth as the line snapped, and the pelt disappeared, spiraling down into the cloud.

The great bee wolf clenched his fist around his own green clip and slashed the fly half a foot from where it pinched. If the clip could just hold him to the severed fly, he could dig that runner out of a cloud while they both were falling. Chances were none in a million.

Errol flipped upside down, flailing at the air for any piece of that free-falling runner. The severed fly was pulling him sideways toward Pliny. The dead pelt was shifting maniacally on his back. A sky full of nothing. More nothing. And then? A thread slipped past his cheek, fine as a strand of his own hair. Errol grabbed it, wound it around his hand, and turned to take the force of the tower.

The three of them crashed against the south wall of Pliny: Errol, the dead runner, and the live one. The green clip on the severed fly-line blew into pieces and they slid down the side of the tower, tethered now to nothing but each other. For two strata they fell. Three, five. They were coming down out of the cloud, and Errol could see the full length of Pliny and the earth a mile down. His elbow slammed against a knob of some kind and he grabbed it and they all came to a fright stop. Dangling. Errol heaved the live runner up and hung him by a loop on his pack on the knob—the heel of an iron lizard with the legs and mane of a lion. Such was the humor of the bestiary guild.

Errol's right hand was bloody. The fingers of the left had come out of their knuckle sockets. He put the hand between his knees and twisted hard to snap his joints together.

"You're inthane," said the runner, lisping through broken teeth. His eyes flitted to the thick human form tied to Errol's back. "I only wanted a gut run. I never thought Seppo would—"

"Die?" supplied Errol.

"They'll drop me for that, won't they?"

"If dropping you is the right thing, let's get back to Thebes and face it." For reasons I cannot even now explain, this terrifying statement calmed the pelt. They climbed the side of Pliny, over the iron herd that adorns the tower from which animal forms and disguises are exported, and flung themselves onto the roof.

When the bee wolf and his pelts arrived at Thebes, he shot off that flare from the yurt. Dragomir and I came in on the flies to do absolutely nothing. And I was twenty uurs richer. I never lost, betting on my cousin.

Stolen Goods

THE PELTS WERE SURNAMED, like the rest of us, after our guild house. Faisal Thebes was small and sharp. His chin, thrust forward, ended in the first ragged hairs of a goatee. He spat blood from between chipped teeth while Errol unlaced him from his pack and wrapped him in blankets.

Errol untied Seppo Thebes's body from his back and carried it to our medic, Grid. She laid the body down. Thick-shouldered, it was, with a big head and small eyes. Grid dragged everyone's sacks from our tents and piled them on top of it, then crawled into the tomb she had made and wrapped herself around the corpse. Dragomir asked if this was the time to begin Seppo's going-tales, but someone said to wait.

Time has a way of folding in on itself. I can't say if it was five minutes or an uur before the dead pelt was wiggling his fingers in front of his eyes like a baby who has just discovered that he controls the far reaches of himself.

In a high voice Seppo moaned, "I am blinded. The light is needling my eyes. Cold, silver handfuls of light are strewn up there, everywhere, jabbing me."

Errol followed Seppo's wide-eyed gaze into the sky. The cloud had frayed and gone. "That's the sun," he said.

Seppo gave a half laugh and winced with pain. "So bright, it hurts," he said.

"You get used to it," said Errol. "Welcome back."

———

With the cloud off us, I could see the bucket fires across the roofs of the city. Ten thousand fires blazing on a thousand roofs, with yurts, tents, and guild flags silhouetted against the sky. It always reminded me of a massive army camped across the ridge of mountain range. I had read of such things.

Thebes's runners settled in around the bucket fire. Petroc, Siwan, Jaromir, Sa'id, Yael, Ping, and Emem. These were the third-years, all of them deadly dull, studying for apprenticeship exams. Grid, Talwyn, Errol, and I were the second-years, by far the ablest. Mirembe, Eluned, and Dragomir were the first-year idiots. And now that Faisal and Seppo had survived their first day, so they were with us, too.

Grid stood with her hands on her hips staring at them. She herself was something to stare at: a lanky runner with white-blond hair, and scars we called lightning blooms. She said it made her a better medic, to have been hit by storms early on.

She made Faisal yell as loud as he could while she snapped his nose back into place and packed rags up his nostrils. She made him and Seppo lift their shirts. Their chests were bright black where their pack harnesses had crushed ribs. She bound them in linen strips and a firepit paste of comfrey root. I was trying to read but it was distracting to me, to watch her touching them.

"Take these beads to kill the pain," she said, handing them water. To Seppo she added, "You'll lose that small finger on that left hand by next week, but the rest of you will stay." Seppo's mouth opened and closed in horror.

Grid turned to Errol, who was restringing Faisal's mam-line reel. "Tie those two in their tents tonight or the beads will make them wander off the edge."

"Aye," Errol said. He didn't look up.

"Don't think I don't see you, Errol Thebes," she said. "Your face. Your hands. Did you forget again that iron towers are hard? Get out of that tunic and I'll rub camphor into your joints."

Errol shrugged. "I'm fine."

I cleared my throat. "You can give *Odd* Thebes a rub. I feel a great deal of pain in this area." I pointed to my lips.

Grid rolled her eyes. "There is no cure for you, Odd Thebes."

"Plenty of curing, going on in here," I said, holding up my book.

"Ovid's gossip again?" Grid said. "Aren't you sick of love scenes yet? Don't you have a rag to grease?"

"He can't be reading," Faisal said. "The book is upside down."

"You've forgotten, that's how he reads," said Grid.

———

Behind us we heard someone suck his teeth. "Will they live?" said Marek Thebes.

"Yes. So you can murder them now," I said, hoping for drama. Faisal and Seppo stared at their feet. Marek asked how many ribs had been broken; Grid said it was five, between the two of them.

"Well, that will render them useless until we get through Beklemek. And Faisal's face? How did all that wreckage happen?"

Faisal looked away. Runners who went mad were risks. And a runner who obstructed another's rescue stood to be punished.

"He and I disagreed," said Errol, "on how to save his friend Seppo."

I snorted, but Faisal slumped in relief. Marek spit into the fire. "I'm sure there is more to that story, Errol Thebes. And equally sure that only Odd will ever get it out of you." Errol was silent. Marek turned to go, then paused. "Out of curiosity, Errol Thebes, do you *remember* how to call for help?"

Errol's hands worked at Faisal's reel bearings. "I believed I could save them both if I brought them in fast," he said.

"That is riveting information, but it was not my question," said Marek.

A smile played behind Errol's eyes. "I do remember. Aye."

"Excellent. I'm relieved to hear it. Someday it will behoove you to use *that* skill."

———

When Marek was gone we took up the work of Thebes's roof: rags to grease; herbs to grind between mortar and pestle; scripts to memorize for plays we were staging; lists to make of the morning's chores; shatranj moves to inflict upon one another; guild exams for which to study.

There was, on the roof of Thebes, a particular mix of circumstances that was an elixir to all of us. A snapping bucket fire was part of it, and the math of sixteen runners and our roof master, all in. The noctis—that is, midnight—stars had not yet risen above the wall. And Ping Thebes, our cook, passed bowls of roasted hazelnuts out of his mysterious roof kitchen. Nobody ever said it aloud, but we relished the times when we were all here, and our talk ranged from the tasks in our hands to issues of love and all its lesser forms. This was that kind of night.

It was that kind of night until, that is, Faisal stood in front of Errol, drew himself up, and began the conversation that would change our lives forever.

"And anyway, as Marek said, you shouldn't have come for us, Errol Thebes. If you hadn't interrupted, we'd have got up to the fly and come in on our own." We all snorted at Faisal's bravado, to which he added, "And by the way, we still plan to beat you in the Long Run."

Seppo groaned from where he lay, still under the bedrolls. "You are brain-rimed, Faisal Thebes. I was dead on the lines till Errol Thebes came for us. We can't possibly race with all these wounds."

Faisal kicked Seppo. "I've waited all my life for that run. We'll all go against one another. You and I will win it. We've won every race in the guild."

"Don't be a fool," I said, keeping my eyes on my book. "The Long Run is no kelp's footrace up the stairs of a guild tower. To be the first to tag every roof of this vast city in one night—Marathon House to Athens—well, every runner in the race will be sweating blood. You two look like a sale on body parts. You'll be lucky if you can brush what's left of your teeth by Winter Ship."

Faisal glared at me. "Odd Thebes will only drop out of the Long Run like he did last year. Everyone is counting on it."

I shut my book. "I didn't *drop out*. I was wounded."

"Ah. I remember now," said Faisal, his tone falsely soothing. "We heard about it down in the guild. You wounded your—what was it?—your hair."

A shudder of laughter ran around the fire, and Errol coughed into his shoulder.

"*Scalp*," I said. "I wounded my scalp. I was in the sack for a week. Anyway, how did this news reach the guild? Is there no roof thick enough to contain gossip in this city?"

Faisal grinned at me. "And now you won't run again, in favor of not reinjuring your scalp?" Everyone was laughing now.

Seppo said, "I'm *not* running."

"Don't be a kelp, Seppo," said Faisal. "Think of it. The prize can be anything you want. Anything. Remember that oily little foundling who haunts the edge of the laundry? You can have it!"

"That was for your ears only!" Seppo said, his eyes flitting nervously to Errol's.

Errol said, "Look around. Do you see any foundlings here?" Seppo shook his head. "That's because they're foul thieves. With a iosal stench. If you run the lines fast enough to win that race, you can have anything or anyone. Why would you want a foundling?" He handed the restrung mam-line reel to Faisal, who tossed it in his pack.

Faisal cleared his throat and said in a silky voice, "Did *you* take anyone you wanted, Errol Thebes? When you won the Long Run last year? In your very first week on the roofs?" Errol reached for Seppo's reel to restring it. I waited. No first-year runner had ever before taken the Long Run. "What would be the point of running again," Faisal pressed, "if you already got what you wanted? This year you can just leave the winning to Seppo and me."

Silence.

"Yes. What prize did you claim, Errol Thebes?" I said. "A guild house? But, wait. You have that already. Girls? Money? The first choice of apprenticeships in the city? What could the son of Margaret Thebes, the most prestigious guildmaster in this city, possibly need or want? We'd all love to—"

"You should be able to guess, Odd Thebes. We've spoken of it together for as long as I can remember."

Faisal kicked the bucket fire into a spray of sparks, and we all jumped. He said, "Did you not hear me, runners of Thebes? Seppo and I will win! The whole guild awaits our victory down below."

"Congratulations, then, in advance," said Errol, handing Seppo his reel. "A word of advice? Remember to stop this time when you get to the end."

Faisal went to the edge to sulk.

"Speaking of prizes," I called, agitated as I was with Faisal about the scalp thing, "what was your trophy tonight?"

"What trophy?"

"You two ran a gut run, did you not? I just wondered what object you stole. Or did you forget the point of a gut run?"

Faisal narrowed his eyes at me. "Nothing," he said.

"You went all the way to Pliny and took no flag? No tooth, no claw? Not even some woolies off a runner's clothesline?"

"We forgot," he said.

"That's a shame! Nothing to send mam-home for the other pelts? Dragomir says there was a challenge—"

Seppo said, "Actually, we did find something."

Faisal kicked him. "Shut up."

"Ow!"

"What was it?" Errol said.

Faisal shot Seppo an irritated look, but he reached for his pack and pulled a leather sheath from it. The sheath looked like a navaja case, the simple kind to wear on a belt. But its hinged lid was barred, a cage constructed to restrain the object inside. Faisal turned the knob, flipped the lid, and slid a felt cloth out of the case. He unrolled the cloth.

I burst out laughing. "You stole knotting spikes?"

"We thought it was a dagger," said Faisal. He handed Errol the cloth and its contents, a pair of thin black-iron sticks, each eight inches long, tapered on the ends.

"You thought knotting spikes were a dagger," I repeated. "Yes, it's a common mistake. No, *wait*. Errol Thebes, remind me again, what does Thebes Guild produce? Because I always forget."

"Cnyttan spican," Errol said, giving the ancient name. He was distracted by the spikes.

"Right! *Knotting spikes*. Cnyttan needles. Famous the world over for making socks, right? And sweaters! There's a gut run for you. Such courage this took. Well, don't worry, we can never have enough knotting spikes here at Thebes. Where we *make* them."

Errol slid his fingers up the length of one spike, feeling for burrs. Fast, he pulled his hand away and put it in his mouth. I felt something in my chest, a kind of fluttering that was not without pain.

"Put them away," I whispered, suddenly unnerved. His finger was bleeding. "I said, put them away. Where did you two get those? At Ghent House, or right here in Thebes?"

"Neither," Seppo said.

"Nobody would want these for knotting," Errol said, wiping the bloody spike on his tunic. "Too heavy. Too coarse. They'd put rust on the wool. Did you go to Bian Pao? Maybe they use these to tamp fireworks."

"We got them at Fremantle," said Seppo.

The entire circle of runners turned to stare. I was sure Seppo had misspoken. But Faisal pointed. One district away, Fremantle House and her neighbor Al-Razi towered over the rest of the city, some thirty strata higher than any guild around them. Al-Razi was lit by bucket fires and runners' lamps. Fremantle, seat of the city's government, was a dark shadow with one light at the top.

"Fremantle is our rival, right?" Seppo said. "We got these from a room on the top strata."

I had never seen Errol so stunned at anyone who wasn't me. "You went *inside* Fremantle?" he said. "To the top and in?"

Seppo nodded. "That one light at the top," he said (we all certainly looked), "is the window of a room with a hundred lamps in it. More, even. So bright it was blinding."

"That window," I said, "is the regnat's quarters."

Seppo looked back and forth between Errol and me. "What?"

Errol rolled the spikes in the cloth. He rubbed his face in his hands and asked the two runners if anyone at Fremantle had tried to stop them. Seppo said no. He said the roof and the room were both empty, and the case was on a table under the lights.

"You lie," I said. "You both lie."

"No. It's all true," said Seppo. "We thought you'd be impressed. Short of the fact that it's knotting spikes. Did we do something wrong?"

Errol laughed. "You bested us! For a year and a half, Odd Thebes and I have been crawling up the flies to Fremantle, trying to grab a pair of wools off their clotheslines. Guards, everywhere. Now you two just run up there on your first night, slip right *into* the guild, and take a pair of knotting spikes off a table. What were the chances?"

"It was more of a desk, actually," said Seppo.

"Whatever it was, it was insane. And a felony." Errol grew sober. "Of course you do realize what it means."

"What?" said Faisal.

Errol and I exchanged glances.

"We'll have company tonight," I said.

"Nobody saw us!" Faisal argued. "They'll never know we took anything!"

"Similarly, I was alone when I wounded my scalp in the Long Run," I said.

Seppo shifted. "So it's war?"

"It's always been war between Thebes and Fremantle," said Errol. "Tonight, it's battle."

Faisal shrieked and said he didn't want battle and couldn't we throw the spikes over the edge?

But Seppo said, "Can I have them?"

Errol slipped the cloth and its contents back into the case. "You don't want Fremantle in your tent."

Faisal burst out, "Please! I didn't have anything to do with this! Seppo took them! I was waiting down on the ladder. I didn't even touch Fremantle!"

We all looked at Seppo, the recent corpse who had single-handedly infiltrated the weapons arsenal.

"I know," he said. "I don't look like much."

"Why would you want an old pair of spikes?" Errol asked.

But he didn't need to ask.

Home was the Thebes tower beneath our feet, 151 strata of work and life. Our families, our old friends, workrooms full of familiar guilders carving and forging spikes such as these, but finer, the best in the world. Most of those people were born in that tower, and most would never leave. We were above them all now. Daresay, we missed them. For most of us would never return to Thebes. I swear, if we dumped out every pack, we would have among us a bucket's worth of knotting spikes. Errol looked at me and I shrugged. He handed the spikes to Seppo.

Caput Mortuum

"I WANT NOTHING TO DO WITH THIS," Marek said, rising from the table in the yurt, his pack and tent slung over his shoulder. "Nothing. I'm staying at Mildenhall tonight to negotiate my apprenticeship. If I were to be associated with this mutiny you have just described, I'd lose hope of a contract."

"We had hoped you'd help us," Errol said.

"*Nothing* to do with it."

"It would be a tale to savor when you're living down in a dull guild," I said. "Getting thick around the middle."

"*Tidy,*" said Marek. "Every toque on its peg by morning. Errol, the roof is in your care."

I bristled, for I was at least as competent as my cousin.

Marek paused before he stepped out of the yurt. "I mention in passing that the guilders of Thebes have sent us several buckets of caput mortuum in the ash bins, for disposal. Also, it looks like rain."

Errol and I looked out at a clear winter sky.

"*Buckets,*" Marek said. "Buckets and buckets of rain."

We grinned, even Marek, and he was gone.

Errol and I enlisted Thebes's runners, who rigged black buckets of water and of caput mortuum on lines mounted high over the usual planks and lines coming onto Thebes tower. We set trip wires that would spill the buckets in pairs—water from one, mortuum from the other. Then we removed ourselves to neighboring Bamako House and pitched travel tents between our friends' tents there. Errol was the last off Thebes; he lit a lamp in every tent and a fire in the yurt. From across the plank, Thebes looked like a busy roof.

Caput mortuum is the powder residue of iron processing, a byproduct of the forging of knotting spikes. In combination with water, it stains everything it touches an indelible, deep purple.

———

We were in high spirits as we stood with Bamako's runners that evening to join all the runners across the city, all home on their roofs, to sing down the sun as usual in a round that began at Cairns House at the west wall and ended at Visby at the east. *The earth is in darkness like the dead*, or some cheerful dirge from the other side of the wall.

Careful not to trip the purpling buckets, Errol and I met for sausages and cider on the plank between Thebes and Bamako. All the towers in the city were massive structures, rising into the clouds. But Fremantle was a behemoth, nearly twice the size of Thebes. Home not only to the regnat, she housed the weapons guild and nearly a thousand guilders of master skill in metallurgy and smithing. She had no runners. Instead, her staggered roofs were patrolled night and day by armed guards. And yet our youngest runner had crept up a ladder, slipped through a window, and taken a pair of iron spikes off the regnat's nightstand. Oh, aye, Fremantle would come our way tonight.

There was the slightest grin on Errol's face as he warmed his sore hands around the canteen of cider.

"What?" I said.

"Finally," he said, "something to do."

TALWYN WAS NOT SINGING.

I sat up.

It was past dawn, with a gray sun leaking through the vents of my travel tent. Talwyn Thebes was always the first of us, up and out for the rising of the sun and the singing. I came out of my tent to listen. There was only the wind. I sat on the cold roof and spoke through Errol's tent flap. I asked him, yawning, whether the roofs had already sung, whether Fremantle had come for the iron spikes. How had I missed it? I could smell Bamako's cook burning our breakfasts, I said, and we ought to get up and have pokerounce before it was charred beyond recognition. I slapped his tent with the back of my hand. "Hey. Are you up?"

From behind me Errol called my name. He was standing at the north edge of Bamako, staring over the abyss toward Thebes. I rose to repeat with some agitation everything I had wasted my breath saying to his tent flap, but an unsettling sight caught my eye. A book lay open on the edge of Thebes's roof, thirty yards from us, its bone-colored pages fanned open, blowing one way, then the other.

"Aren't you going to get that before it—" As I spoke, a gust of wind swept the book off the tower. The book rolled over and over in its plummet to earth. It was Ovid.

Like a man waking to consciousness, I took in the rest slowly. The plank to Thebes was half gone, where Errol and I had sat last night. It jutted from the edge of Bamako but came to a burned end half across the abyss. Smoke and flames billowed from heaps of rubble on Thebes's otherwise empty roof. I spun around. All the other guilds were in place: Gamin House, Perlew, Phrygia, Catalhoyuk. Runners had gathered at those edges.

"Fremantle, right?" I said. "What, they removed everything from our roof and set fire to our trash?"

"Look again," said Errol.

It was worse. The yurt had collapsed, its scalloped edge flapped in the ashes of a fire. Our oak table, our lines, our seventeen tents that we each had made with our own hands, Ping's kitchen, our guild banners, our trunks, the massive black-iron cookstove, the bog stalls, our food, our rain barrels, even our flies and the buckets of caput mortuum were burning in that rubble. What fool would burn food in a quarantine city?

"No one sang," I said stupidly.

The runners of Thebes had come up behind us. Grid pointed. Xerxes, the massive iron crow that had hung from a chain on the yardarm at the top of our mast, had been cut loose and dropped on his back on the fire heap. As we watched, his wings drew back in the heat, and his head twisted toward us, as if to seek from us some answer. Errol rubbed his hand over his face.

"Are you *crying*?" I said, fear gripping my innards.

I was relieved beyond measure to hear someone sucking his teeth.

Marek opened his mouth as if to say something but stopped himself. In the end, "I suggest we order out," he said. "Ping, send word to Derbent for dinner. Talwyn, ask our good friend the roof master Itsaso Bamako for a crossbow. Hello? *Talwyn?* Are you with me? Grid, check Seppo's ribs. Odd, find a quill. We have lists to make." And then to himself he said, "*Tidy*. Did I not say, 'tidy'?"

When Talwyn returned with a bow and bolt, Marek knotted a fly to the bolt and shot it hard into the mast on Thebes. He crossed, hand over hand on the line, to what was left of our roof. We followed. We rummaged through the ashes. We stomped out the small fires, threw soot-blackened pots and silverware where the kitchen had been, and marked our old tent sites so we could toss Talwyn's blackened flute, Ping's ruined apron, and the charred remains of game pieces, soup bowls, and tent stakes into their rightful places.

Two runners from Lascaux arrived on Marek's temporary line, bringing with them a pack heavy with the tools of their guild. They would supervise the splicing, worming, and serving of new lines, restoring Thebes's connections to its neighboring towers and the rest of the city.

We were heaving the stove back toward what used to be our roof kitchen, lifting and dragging, when I looked back at the fire and saw Errol. He had wrapped his hands in his tunic and was pulling the iron bird from the blaze.

I went over to him. "We need your help."

"This is not the end of this," he said.

He could have meant that it would take us forever to restore the roof to our home. But he didn't mean that. There was something to fear in that dawn and we both knew it. I was afraid even to know what it was.

FIRES WERE STILL FLARING at midden in the rubble on our roof when we saw a procession of the regnat's scribes, guards, and flag corps wind its way down and across, from Fremantle to Thebes.

The torchbearers dropped first off the lines, so many I lost count after four dozen, their lamps spitting wax and pulsing with white light. Then came the rustle of regal heraldry. Then, a fleet of guards, so heavily armored and armed, with a pair of swords across each back, that their rapid drops onto our roof sounded like a barrel of forks rolling down the stairs. A trumpet voluntary. A battalion of scribes. Finally, the regnat's palanquin, a half ton of gilded ivory, was lifted from the lines and set upon a damask rug in the center of the roof. Layer upon layer of furs were removed from on top of him and cataloged aloud—*Pribilof fox, Tasman stoat, Bengal tiger, Makkovik seal*. I was surprised after all the care he required that the regnat could stand on his own.

He wore a full tunic of white bearskin, with the head of the bear pitched backward in a silent roar. He was pale and heavy, with fine yellow hair and restless eyes that lingered now upon Talwyn, then Eluned, then Grid. Fifty orbits? Sixty? I couldn't say. His courtiers were all so much older than we were. Their age and their excessive display was an oppression. Even factoring Marek's twenty-four years into the mathematics, we were on average seventeen. And everything we owned was gone. I wanted them to go. I kept this thought to myself, assuming the regnat had come, albeit awkwardly, to care for us in our grief.

He had not.

His guards dragged Seppo from our ranks, bound the pelt's frostbitten hands and feet, and hauled him, screaming in agony with his broken ribs, to the edge. The chief scribe read from the scroll of law, announcing the felony of a plunder of the regnat's guild, a crime punishable, like any plot against the regnat, by death.

Never before had I seen Marek kneel. "Your Honor, the theft was a mere gut run, which, as you know, is a tradition of the roofs, intended to build courage and camaraderie among runners. We are able to arrange the return of the knotting spikes, and to amend the return with a pair of the finest quality made in Thebes—"

The regnat dismissed Marek with a wave of his gloved hand. "He must die. I don't write the law."

"Technically he does," I whispered.

"Poor Seppo," said Ping.

Seppo looked over at us. He was paler than his own teeth. Would we really be emptying his tellensac tonight and pouring out his tales? It was only his second day on the roofs and he was about to be tossed, by two armed guards he had never seen, over the edge.

And then came the voice of the bee wolf.

"Your Honor! I beg an audience!" Forward Errol strode and bowed, no beggar at all. "The runner Seppo Thebes has been charged with a crime he did not commit. In failing to contest your scribe's accusation, he is acting out of a noble but misplaced sense of loyalty. To me. *I* was on a gut run, as I have been nearly every night this year in the direction of Fremantle. I took the iron spikes from a table"— Errol's hesitated—"more of a desk. From your quarters." I was stunned. This was a direct challenge.

"The great Errol Thebes." The regnat's words hung slippery in the air. "So much for the noble winner of a Long Run. Sooner or later, every foul act on these roofs can be traced to one or the other sons of Margaret Thebes."

Errol lifted his chin, as though the regnat had hit him. "I was a kelp. I hardly knew my brothers."

The regnat snorted. "Margaret Thebes raises felons. Fenn and Rip Thebes thought they were a gift to the city till they were—"

"Killed?" I suggested from behind the crowd.

"Dropped," said the regnat, glancing in my direction.

The scribe leaned over to the regnat. "Your Honor, Seppo Thebes is known to have committed this crime. If this other runner claims to be the thief, the law requires evidence."

Seppo watched as an armed guard clumsily unlaced his pack and flipped it out on the roof. There were errand lists, a water canteen, half-eaten snacks. Anyone could see even Seppo was surprised.

Errol didn't wait for the guard. He removed his pack, reached into it, and pulled out the two spikes.

"Sheath!" screamed the regnat. "Sheath them! Where is the cage! Guards!" The guards flung the regnat into the palanquin and threw the skins onto him. They were on the lines in less than a minute followed by the entire court in tumult.

We stood, stunned. Had some assassin appeared?

Marek untied Seppo, who fell into Errol's arms.

Eight Fremantle guards returned at dulcibus to arrest Errol Thebes and retrieve the sheathed spikes. We were already stretching a goatskin tarp over the frame of a new yurt in a spitting drizzle out of the east when they arrived, and we told them the truth: Errol Thebes left when they did, and he was nowhere to be found. The unit returned to Fremantle empty-handed. It is worth noting that all of those empty hands were purple.

A Night Visit

THE REGNAT FINED THEBES a month of our income for harboring the fugitive whom we weren't, in fact, harboring. Marek paid the fee from his own accounts. Fremantle's investigators arrived on our roof the next morning before dawn and stayed, interrupting the rebuilding of the roof to interrogate us all. On Marek's orders, even Seppo stayed true to Errol's lie, that he had stolen the spikes. Seeing as we didn't know where the iron spikes were, we had nothing else to hide.

On the second day after the sacking of Thebes, the regnat fined Marek again. He issued orders to every guild in the city, offering a year's salary for Errol's capture. Alternately: death, for harboring a fugitive who plotted against the regnat. But no news came. More guards arrived at Thebes, to set up a watch at every corner of our roof. I wondered whether the regnat would revisit the thought of dropping Seppo, to lure Errol in. I kept the idea to myself.

During those first days of Errol's absence, I felt an inexplicable soreness in my chest, as though my ribs had been broken like Faisal's and Seppo's. I could not breathe without pain. I woke many times to the sound of the beating of wings, a sound I had never heard before, as the city is devoid of beasts of any kind. I made frequent trips to the reconstructed bog pots to hang my backside off the tower and read. It was the one place where the guards would not follow me.

That is where I was, in the middle of the night, when I heard someone in the next stall.

"Have you never heard the expression 'Piss or get off the pot'?"

I knew his voice better than I knew my own. "In faith?" I laughed. And then in a whisper, "You cannot be here. Fremantle is everywhere."

"Are you ill? What are *you* doing in here, half the night?"

"The regnat's guards are on us, and you are a fugitive, and you have nothing better to do than ask after my intestines? Where have you been all week?"

"Do you miss me?" he said.

"I miss you doing your own chores." Errol laughed and I grinned in my stall. "How did you get past the watch?"

"No one would expect me to come up through the pots."

"I'm going to be sick. So when are you turning yourself in?"

"Never."

"*Never?* What does that mean? Where will you hide on these roofs?"

"What would you have done, if you were me the night the regnat came?"

"Well, I certainly wouldn't have saved Seppo and Faisal in the first place. And I would have let the regnat drop Seppo."

"Obviously. I meant, what would you do with the spikes?"

"Throw them over the edge. They're junk."

"The regnat doesn't come out on the roofs for junk."

"Look at the wound on your fingers. I can smell it festering from here. If the iron wounds skin, it's junk. Anyway, why do you care? We have so many spikes."

"Maybe the black-iron spikes are something else."

The reference to the black-iron spikes chilled me like the names of certain weapons do. Like Skofnung, the famed sword that shrieks in battle.

"What do you mean by 'something else'?" I said. "What purpose could two short spikes serve, but in knotting?"

"I think they're *uncommon*."

I burst out laughing. "This is a quarantined guild city. You're joking, right? You are only longing for what you can never have. Uncommon tools belong to worlds outside the wall. What, like a flying rug?"

"Why not?"

"*Pff.* You're just bored."

"Why would Fremantle care about junk iron?" he said. "And why would the regnat drop Seppo?" I had no answer for that. Was the regnat embarrassed to be caught off guard? That didn't explain the screaming. *Sheath them!* In truth, I didn't want to think about whatever it was that could terrify a regnat.

"Well then," said Errol. He was silent for a while, the kind of silence in which one of us was waiting for the other to catch up.

"Just, don't tell me you still have the spikes."

"Fine. I won't tell you."

I closed my book. "There is no place to hide anything on these roofs."

"Does *prinsessen paa aerten* mean anything to you?"

"The princess and the pea?" I burst from the bog, tore across the roof, ripped open the flap of my tent. Under my sack in a heap of laundry was the sheath, with the two spikes inside of it.

The guards watched me run back to the bog pots. They thought I was sick. Errol put out his hand. I pulled the case from under my shirt and feigned the hand-off. But then I held the case too high, too low. Why? I was furious, that's why. If I had been caught? What then? There was some other reason I couldn't name. And by the way, was it just sleeping on the spikes that made my chest ache?

Errol tired of this kelp's game. He grabbed my hair and shoved my head into the bog pot. I threw the sheath at his feet.

"Don't you want to know what happens next? What those iron spikes really are? You, more than anyone? The *bard*?" He let me up.

"I should tell those guards you're here. *Nothing* happens next," I spat, wiping my face. "You give them back, is what happens. Otherwise they will track you down. Small city. Big wall."

"I need someone to hold them while I find out what they are. Someone who has nothing to lose."

"So that's why you're here? Odd Thebes, at your service: nothing to lose?"

"No. I'm here because you know everyone. *Everyone.* Find someone who will hold them for me until I know what they do."

Feh. Was it his face? His constant, irritating honesty? How did he *do* that?

"Fine," I said. "Yes, I know someone. But you won't like it."

JAMILA FOUNDLING WAITED IN THE RAIN on the edge of the roof at Samoa House. She was sopped. Rain dripped from her chin and soaked her ragged tunic. Her gray leggings clung to her skin and rivulets of rainwater dripped down her shins, off her bare toes, into the abyss. She sipped rain from her cupped palms.

"It's just water," I said. "It has no flavor."

"It tastes strongly of seven."

A line of first-year runners waited under a tarp behind us to be tatued with the mark of their guild. If I wasn't with a foundling, I would have been under a tarp, too.

"Whatever you say."

Certain words carried, for Jamila, the scent of almonds or wet clay or civet grease. Sounds were sopped with ochre and indigo. Rainwater was sharp and tasted of seven.

I handed her the sheath from my pack. She sniffed it, listened to it.

"Don't ask me any questions," I said. "Just hide that in the morgues."

"Till when?"

"There you go with a question," I said.

"Whatever it is, it reeks of blood."

"It's not blood. It's made of iron," I said.

"It's made of mayhem. And it isn't what it was."

"What is that supposed to mean? It's nothing. They're nothing. Put them away."

"Nobody notices what's out in the open," she said, setting the sheath in her lap. The rains had been driving down on us all day. I'd been sweeping it into barrels since sanguis. I was in no mood to argue with a foundling. I took a book out of my pack.

The girl behind us had hair down to her waist, divided into a thousand braids. I pushed up my sleeve to show off the marks on my forearm: the standing crow of Thebes from my first year on the roofs, and the flight wings, added on the first night of my second year.

"Do the towers always sway like this in wind?" she said.

"Like what?" I got up and perched at the wet edge. Jamila rolled her eyes.

"Does the tatu hurt?" the girl said. I squeezed myself onto the bench next to her.

"Not at all. Really. Half a bell and it's over. Well, except, just be glad you're not from Catalhoyuk. The mark, right? They put a whole map of the world on your arm. Seas of red." We were both quiet for a bit and I added coolly, "I do wish they knew where to put this city on that map. That's blood worth shedding." When she was still quiet, I said, "I am guessing that you're from Catalhoyuk."

"Yes."

Samoa was a busy roof, with unusual living arrangements due to the nature of its export. On the north side, master guilders, apprentices, and runners lived side by side in tents. On the south side, two dozen box-shaped yurts divided the roof into workrooms. A runner led us to one of those and held the tent flap open. Inside were a pair of stools and an oak table, stained with ash. An apprentice tufuga came in, with a red rag tied around his bald head and a red shop apron. He was tatued on every visible surface and likely, I whispered to Jamila, the surfaces that weren't. He saw where my eyes rested, and he put his hand on his guilder's paunch defensively before he settled in across from Jamila at the table. He reeked of cabbage.

From the first tap of the mallet on the needle-rake there was pain. Jamila stared at a spot on the floor, but when the tufuga struck bone, she flinched, knocking his ash bowl off the table. A cloud of black smoke rose around their ankles. The tufuga made a face, went out, and came back with new supplies and a rag for the blood. He dipped the needles in new ash and the work began again—*batat, batat*. A familiar voice spoke from the doorway.

"Odd Thebes. You've kept me waiting." Errol hadn't changed his clothes since the bog pots, six days past. He glanced at the foundling. "What's this?"

"I don't think you've been introduced to Jamila," I said.

"Odd, are you coming? We have an arrangement."

"This *is* the arrangement," I said.

"But you said—"

"That I would find you someone with nothing to lose. This is the someone."

"A tufuga?"

"No," I said. "Again, this is Jamila."

Errol's eyes rested on the naught mark branded on Jamila's neck. "A foundling? Foundlings are thieves. Where are my—" I pointed at the sheathed spikes in her lap. His eyes widened. The tapping hit a nerve and Jamila bit her lip. Errol said, "Couldn't it get a master to make its tatu?"

The tufuga stiffened and said, "I beg your pardon. I am two years in Samoa."

"That qualifies you to explain why we are about to watch it faint."

"I don't faint," said Jamila. "Offend the tufuga again, though, and I'll leave here with a one-winged crow."

Errol looked at her in surprise. The tufuga covered a smirk with the back of his hand.

"Actually she can't afford to pay a master's fee," I said.

"The *guild* pays for tatus," said Errol.

"Not for a foundling." I was surprised I knew something he did not. "*You're* paying the fee; she's handling that package for you. This was the arrangement she demanded." I was relieved the tufuga kept his eyes to his work, for he might know the fugitive.

Errol looked at Jamila now with interest. "A demanding foundling," he mused. "And why would a foundling want a guild mark?"

Jamila lifted her chin. She was soaked, but there was a length and shape to her that Errol would have considered extraordinary if the naught brand didn't nullify it all. Black hair, tied in a knot to keep it out of the tufuga's way. Eyes as black as her hair. I'm sure Errol was trying to find her deficiency. He was well within his rights to look over a foundling, but it was beneath him to question.

The apprentice was outlining the beak of the crow. He looked up at her. "We have beads for the pain," he said.

"I do not require them."

Errol sighed, agitated. "It should just think of something to get its mind off the needles. Let's go, Odd. Get the package from it and let's go. This is not what I expected."

Jamila was wet, cold, and sore. I felt pity for her. "I'll meet you later," I said. Then, because I was embarrassed to care about the welfare of a foundling, I held up the book I was reading. "An excellent passage."

"Suit yourself." Errol pulled up his hood and left through the tent flap. I was still wondering where he could possibly be going when he returned with a stool, rainwater running from his coat. "An otherwise dull night," he said by way of explanation.

Jamila put the rag to her lip, where she had bitten it. "Read to me, Odd," she said. "Or let's play a game."

"Picket?" I said, reaching for my deck of cards.

Jamila wiggled the fingers of the arm she couldn't otherwise move. "Can't play cards," she said.

"Another game, then," I said.

We went quiet, brooding. Errol stared at the sheath in Jamila's lap—surely, I thought, annoyed. But then he said, "What was that game you made me play all the time, Odd? Rats or Boils. When we were kelps. Remember?"

"You made me, too, Odd Thebes," said Jamila. "You used to say I had to play 'in the language of the people who put the tongue in kiss.'"

Errol looked at her, amused, and said to me, "Does it even know what that means?"

"How do I know? But the game is not Rats or Boils. It is *Préférerais tu*. It means, 'Would you rather.'"

"Whatever the name was, it wants to play," said Errol, pointing at Jamila.

———

I dug through my pack for a package of waxed parchment. "Préférerais tu—"

"Cut it out, Odd. Play in the common tongue," said Errol. "Is that peen tong? Did you get that from Ping?"

"*Naturellement. Tres bien.*" I unwrapped a slab of brown sugar candy and took the first bite. "Would you rather, let's see, pluck out your left eyeball or lose your right thumb to frostbite?" I knew Errol was watching me, wanting that sweet.

Jamila closed her eyes and made two fists to make her thumbs disappear. "My eyes," she said.

"It's either the *left* eye or the *right* thumb," said Errol, sighing. "This promises to be a dull game."

"Doesn't matter," said Jamila.

"Yes it matters. Close one eye. The correct one," he said.

"I still say my eye."

"It will regret that," said Errol to me. "It needs both eyes if it's getting that tatu to run the flies."

"I'd lose both eyes before I gave up even one thumb," said Jamila.

"You'll fall, then."

"I live in the morgues in a constant night. *You'll* fall, without a thumb."

"Aye, well. Then I shall meet you on the streets."

"I look forward to it," said Jamila.

I threw up my hands. "Excellent. Fine start! Here's another. Who would you be—Sisyphus or Theseus?"

Errol groaned. "Are you going to drag out all the old questions?"

"Of course. They're the best."

The tufuga lifted his head. "Where would we come in, in the two tales?"

I was surprised he had been listening at all. But I humored him and said it would be the standard entries. Sisyphus is rolling the boulder up the mountain for the first time, for all infinity; Theseus has just entered the labyrinth. He can smell the rotting bits of virgins stuck between the minotaur's teeth.

"I'm Theseus," called Errol.

"It was the virgins, persuaded him," said the tufuga. He winked at Jamila.

"Not at all," protested Errol. "I've always wanted to have a look at that minotaur. Scratch him behind the ears as men outside the wall do with horses. Tame him. I'm fond of beasts."

"How would you know anything of horses or minotaurs?" said Jamila.

"I just know. Anyway, like the tufuga said, Theseus had a *girl*. Great, big—" Errol hesitated in the middle of a two-handed gesture on the very edge of lewd.

The tufuga looked over and raised his eyebrows.

"A great, big ball of string. Remember?" Errol said, reforming his hands around an innocent, imaginary ball.

"*Mais oui,*" said the tufuga. "The string led Theseus out of the labyrinth."

"I'm Sisyphus," said Jamila. "I'll outlast the rock. Grind it down to sand and be free of it."

Errol snorted. "Somewhere out there, Sisyphus is still rolling a rock up an infinite mountain. Whereas Theseus already escaped." He reached for the slab of peen tong, and I handed it to him. He bit off half of it and sucked on it for a moment, thinking. "Saved everybody."

"Thanks to his girlfriend," I said. "And the big—"

"String," said Jamila, in a husky whisper. Errol sat back and nodded his head in appreciation. Jamila reached to him for the sweet. To my surprise he gave it to her.

———

Curse at your roof master or run the lines naked. Shave yourself bald or be chained for a week on a plank. On we went in this cheerful repartee, while a crow took shape on Jamila's arm. The game relaxed the tufuga. Here and there he asked to see the crows on my arm and Errol's, to compare ours with the mark he was making. Once or twice he looked up and seemed to be considering what his own answers would be to my examination questions.

After a while, when I paused too long to think, he offered a question of his own. "Préférerais tu," he said, "to give up talking, or dancing?" I doubted whether the tufuga did much of either of those things anymore. I imagined dull nights and a frumpy bound-wife waiting in his bedchamber.

Errol said, "I'd like Odd to give up dancing."

I laughed, faking offense. "I am an excellent dancer." I raised my hands high, snapped my fingers, and rolled my hips against Jamila. *Me voulez-vous, bébé?* I took the stub of the brown-sugar slab from her and put it in my mouth, knowing Errol would never have done such a thing. Foundlings are contagious.

"I prefer you to *stop*," she said, pushing me away with her free hand. Errol laughed.

"But I must have you," I said to her.

"I'd like Odd to give up *talking*," Jamila said and shivered. Errol laughed again. She had surprised him.

The tufuga stepped out. He returned with a bucket fire and set it next to Jamila. "And would you prefer to live in silence, or darkness?" he said.

We all three closed our eyes and sank into the warmth of the new fire. We could hear Samoa's runners returning to their roof, calling in for dinner. *Marius, safe in! Remy, in!* Someone was laughing and we heard a roof master explaining the knotting of a chain sennit to a pelt outside the wall of our tent. Grill fires snapped and a tuber popped softly on one of them. Above those sounds came the perpetual *essing* of rags on silk fly-lines, the pounding of runners' sharps on the planks, the steady rain. The city pulsed, through the guild towers, through our bodies. Who could ever give that up?

On the other hand, who could give up the sight of the high roofs? Every morning I came out of my tent, excited to know what the sky would bring. There was nothing inside the guilds that could compare to that glorious horizon. That web of flies, glistening over the city in whatever colors the sun offered that morning. I longed for that sight every day, and dreaded the morning the roofs were done with me and I would be called down into a guild.

On all our behalf, I called "muet"—*silenced*—in the tradition of the game. "The tufuga wins all."

"But I am only half done with this crow," the tufuga said. Jamila flexed her fingers and looked at me cross-eyed. She shivered again.

Errol took off his overcoat and tossed it on the floor. He sat back down, stretched out his legs, and crossed his arms. The tufuga studied him for a moment and I wondered what the man would do if he recognized the fugitive. There was that insanely huge reward. And a punishment for not—

"Would you rather be trapped inside a guild forever with all your friends," said the tufuga, "or escape from this city tomorrow but never see anyone you know again?"

"Trapped," I said, and then regretted having laid down my cards so fast. "Well, I would have books."

"And gossip," said Errol, grinning. "Odd's two essentials."

Jamila laughed. I made a face at her.

"And you?" said the tufuga.

"I'd be gone before you could say my name."

The tufuga threw him a skeptical glance. "In truth, Errol Thebes? And what would your mother say to that?"

I looked fast at Errol but he registered no concern. "My mother would say, 'Here's your hat, whatever your name is.' "

Jamila chewed on her lip. "I don't think so," she said.

Errol studied her. "Really. And what do you know of my mother?"

"Brilliant guildmaster. Foolish in love. Married a monster—"

"Don't, Jamila," I said.

"Three sons, any of whom could have run Thebes with their little finger, but two are gone and the third, I think, will drop as well—"

"Stop," I said, motioning her down with my hand. "Stop it, Jamila."

"She had one other man but he left her, too—"

Errol rubbed his face, a fugitive again.

"Foundling, stop," I whispered.

"Actually that's about right," said Errol. "Except there was no other man. My mother is faithful, if nothing else. And I am better than my brothers. One would hope."

The tufuga was watching the two of them, his hands still. "But what is your answer?" he said. "Trapped or free?"

"Trapped," Jamila said. "With the other foundlings."

"Sisyphus pushing the rock," said Errol.

"Grinding the rock to sand," she said. "I stay, out of love."

"Whatever you want to believe," said Errol. "Fine. Here's one, speaking of love: With which poet would you rather spend the night—Ovid or Hesiod? What is your name again?"

"Naught," she said, pointing to the sign on her neck. "Nothing. Nil. Zero."

"Her name is Jamila," I said.

"For clarity," said the tufuga, "do you mean spend the night? Or"—he lowered his voice—"*spend the night?*"

"There is no distinction," said Errol. "*From the time the sun goes down over the west wall of this city until dawn rises over the east*—this is a binding contract between two runners on the roofs, encompassing all or nothing that happens in a tent through the night."

"A ridiculous law," I said.

Errol ignored my opinion. It never bothered him that the city's ancient rule stated that if you overnighted in a tent with anyone, you were bound to them for life. He gestured to Jamila. "Does it even know who Ovid is? Can it read?"

Jamila snorted and said, "*Quae dant, quaeque negant, gaudent tamen esse rogatae.*"

I grinned and translated for Errol: "Whether they say yes or no, women like to be asked."

She had bested him. "Ovid?" she said. "He's obsessed with getting anyone into the sack. Whereas Hesiod just wants to get his work done before he dies. I can read. I can also fart, same as you."

Errol put his hands up as though to ward her off. "You offended me. I've returned the favor."

"Offended? I told you the truth. Which no one dares to do. Speaking of which, I choose Hesiod."

"Hesiod?" I said, coming for her. "*Hesiod?!* What about Ovid? Plenty-of-time-for-rest-when-you're-in-the-grave Ovid? I-clinged-her-naked-body-down-she-fell Ovid?" I was grasping for any quote I could remember. "Hesiod?! Hesiod is a hack! What would you want with Hesiod? He was *born* old!"

"He's lonely. You can smell it in every word," said Jamila.

"See? She would take Hesiod because she pities him," said Errol. "Hesiod knows that. He is . . . strategic."

"No," said Jamila. "I would take Hesiod because Ovid is insubstantial." Had she said *Ovid*, or *Odd*?

I realized, at that moment, that no one in the tent was talking anymore about Ovid and Hesiod, and I wondered how long we had not been talking about what we were talking about. I stood up. "Fine, then, let's have it. Who would you choose, Jamila? Who, in this tent?"

The tufuga wrinkled his nose as if my question smelled foul. Errol had a grin on his face, a grin I had seen a thousand times on him when we were kelps. *Want to race?*

"I'd take him," Jamila said, lifting her chin.

"I'm honored," said the tufuga. "You're a great beauty, but I'm already bound."

"So, not a choice." I pressed my finger into her shoulder. Errol watched me touch her. He never had touched a foundling, for all he knew. I pressed hard. "Which of the two of us, then, Jamila?"

Errol shifted, pretending to be bored. "This is more than you should ask of it," he said, his eyes on her. "It will never have this choice in life."

"Who do you think you are?" said Jamila. Errol stood now. No one talked to him that way.

"I'm the one sparing you the embarrassment of having laid out your hopes in a game. Or, how did you put it? I'm telling the truth."

"You're only sparing yourself," said Jamila. "There is air in this tent. I may choose the air if I find nothing else suitable."

"Nothing suitable?" Errol laughed. "You think you can do better than Errol Thebes? Or even Odd Thebes?"

"That will depend on what you become."

"You're bold, for someone who can hope for nothing."

"And who has nothing to lose," she said, and that silenced him for a moment.

I was still waiting for her to speak my name, to choose me. *Odd Thebes*. I mouthed my name at her.

But Errol was in her face now and something beyond mischief played in his eyes. "If you insist on choosing, then will it be the rising third son of a powerful guildmaster? Or the chatty ne'er-do-well behind me, whose idea of heofon is any girl or any card game? Is that so difficult a choice?" She was trapped in the tufuga's chair. A piece of her hair slipped out of its knot and hung in her face. Errol pulled it away and held it between his fingers, pressed his hand to the back of her neck. He bent down so that he was a breath from her, his eyes on her mouth. My heart pounded in my chest.

The tufuga protested, "I cannot work like this. I must insist—"

"Shut up," said Errol. Then, to Jamila: "Which of us is it?"

Jamila touched the rag to her lip, nonchalant. "Neither of you is fearless," she said.

"I fear nothing."

"Not even a bogle?"

Errol recoiled as if she had spit on him. "What do you know? Let's have it."

"And you don't know what love is," she said.

"What could you possibly know about me?" I may as well have been invisible.

"I know you sat there while I froze tonight. You threw your coat on the floor. You didn't hear a single thing I said."

In an exact replication of the tufuga's voice, he said, "*We have beads for the pain*." And then, affecting Jamila's own voice, he replied, "*I do not require them*."

Oh yes, he had heard her.

Errol touched the tip of his tongue to his bottom lip and she saw that. I was sure everyone could hear my own heart flailing like a hammer. She was *mine*. He grinned now, not the child at all but the warmonger. But when his thumb played on her chin, Jamila turned her head away.

"*Muet*," she called. "I cannot choose."

But he whispered in her ear, "The choice is not yours; it is mine. Get all thousand tatus, you still won't belong in high places. A foundling belongs nowhere." He took her rag and wiped his hands. He removed a thick wad of uurs from his tunic and threw it at the tufuga. "For the crow," he said. And then he looked at Jamila and said, "Anyway, Odd can't dance."

He turned and strode to the tent flap, grabbing his coat as he went. He turned and threw the thing to me. "Wrap the foundling in that," he said. "I don't want it." He disappeared into the driving rain.

Jamila stared at the door, her fingers tight on the sheath in her lap.

"*Et voilà*," said the tufuga, spreading his hands wide over Jamila's forearm. "The crow flies."

An Odd Assignment

MAREK THEBES CALLED FOR ME at crustum. Three in the morning.

"Did I wake you?" he said. It was the seventh of Boreal, three weeks since the tufuga. Winter was full upon us. He sat at a new table in the new yurt on Thebes's roof, a stack of paperwork towering at his elbow, and an untouched tart steaming on a dish on top of that. Rug-beating north winds buffeted the yurt and twitched the flame on his lamp.

"Wake me? Are you jesting?" I said, pulling wools over my leggings. "I was polishing the silver." I slumped on a stool in front of him. "May I?" He nodded and I reached for the tart.

"So, Odd Thebes. You know what Ship is," he said.

"Of course. It's a party," I said, my mouth full. "Is this dried plum?"

He cleared his throat. "Ship—that is, *Winter Shipment*—is the arrival of the fleet. The river gates open on the north wall, the gate used just once every year. And then a fleet of ships sails in with a year's worth of raw materials, food, and fuel from the north. Later that same day a year's worth of our work leaves through the southern gate. So, in short, every export and import, all on one day."

"Aye," I said, swallowing. "And *then* a party. Huge one."

"Our lives depend upon Ship," he pressed on. "It is the high point of our year, our only connection to the world outside that wall."

"*And* a party," I said with a grin.

He stared at the table. "It is the *work* I am interested in discussing with you this morning, Odd Thebes."

"Fine. I concede the party is secondary. Chronologically."

He sighed, as if he'd regretted knowing me. Then he continued to carry on about how we never even know the day the ships will arrive. How the fleet never rises over the horizon earlier than the middle of Boreal, and yet it must come soon after that, for the river freezes at the beginning of Rhagfyr. How, knowing it is coming, but not when, we prepare early and remain prepared. How we must do vast amounts of paperwork—shipping forms, banking forms, cataloging the whereabouts of every item that leaves the city and every one that enters—and then must run everything where it needs to be, all on that day—

I leaned back in my chair and yawned.

Marek stopped. "Am I keeping you from something?"

"With all due respect, Marek Thebes, there are a thousand guild houses, all of which I can name for you by export, guildmaster, roof master, strata, fathoms. I speak twenty-three local tongues fluently, and the rest well enough to get myself someone to kiss. Additionally I was born in this city, like everyone else here, and I've been up here on the roofs two years. How could I *not* know what Ship is?"

"I'm never sure you're paying attention, or that you care about the work we do here. So you know also about the export log I am charged with compiling?"

"Mm. Lot of work," I said. Ping appeared with another tart on a dish, for Marek. I waited for him to go, then said, "Are you going to eat that?" Marek waved it away, and I took the dish.

"The log takes work, yes," he said. And then he told me all about how in one day he visits the fifty-two roofs of guilds in our district to collect their export estimates so we can organize rooms in our storehouses and barter for space in the cargo holds of the ships. "Meeting the guildmasters in this ritual is a privilege," he said. "This is the only time they come out. All year. And then I am up till noctis, compiling their numbers, and that is interesting as well. And of importance." He studied me.

"Riveting," I said, licking my fingers.

He sighed. "I was going to ask Errol Thebes to fill out the log this year."

"Errol Thebes? Who is that? Do I know him?"

"I've been called to Fremantle today, to meet with the regnat concerning a missing runner. Errol. The regnat thinks I know where he is. Don't tell me, if you do."

"He's in my pack, in small pieces," I said. I had seen neither Errol nor Jamila. Jamila lived deep in the morgues of the guild. Errol—who knew? Gone? Caught? Dead? *Chatty ne'er-do-well?* He had been my best friend.

"Meanwhile, all of Thebes's runners have work to do, except that I noticed"—he looked at the roof log—"that you put down here that you will be working in your tent today."

"Accounting," I said, putting my hands up defensively, failing to mention a private tournament of maw I had scheduled for myself with the runners on Bamako.

"Well, you'll have to get back to that tonight. I'm having you do the export log this year. Today. Or actually—" He looked out the door of the yurt at Berfrei. "Right now."

"Me?" I said. "Why me?"

"It's a simple form," Marek said, reaching for a thick envelope. "The guildmasters will"—he paused—"they'll *probably* like you. You're good with languages."

"Am I expected to do this alone?" I said.

"Your friend Dragomir is also apparently working on accounting." Marek turned the log around so I could see that Dragomir had made a ditto mark under my entry. "You may take him."

"No thanks," I said. "He slows me down."

Marek winced. "Odd Thebes, how did you ever get called to the roofs?"

"What do you mean?"

"You know what I mean. How did you become a runner?"

"Same way as everybody else," I said. But that was a lie.

Coracles

THE TOWERS SWAYED HARD IN THE WINDS, straining the lines and flinging me around like a kelp's toy. Here I was, forced to run myself ragged, doing Errol's chores. The only redeeming thing about the day was that Fremantle's guards, who followed me everywhere, decided that the rogue runner would not try to contact me on such an auspicious errand. Or perhaps they didn't want to be out in such weather. Neither did I.

Cwym Teifi was young for a guildmaster, thirty times around the sun. He was tired and sallow, with dye-stained fingers and long hair that he had tied back like a runner's. He had to yell to be heard over the gusts: "Cwym Teifi, *yn eich gwasanaeth.*"

I yelled back, "Right. Fine. Odd Thebes, at your service, too. I'm in a hurry. Let's use the common tongue."

Cwym's expression fell. He stepped away from me toward the hatch full of guilders behind him. They were jammed in the door to the roof like pale herring just to see the sky for ten minutes. Through their ranks they passed a huge blue bowl, easily the volume of three bathing troughs but light enough he could balance it on two fingers. Cwym made as if to pass it to me but I just stared at it.

"Soup tureen?" I said, with my quill over the form.

"*Cwrwgl,*" he said. "A coracle. She is a boat." Again he thrust the bowl toward me but I kept my hands busy, writing *coracle* on my form.

From behind me a familiar voice ordered, "*Take* it from him, Odd Thebes."

"Quantity?" I said.

Errol Thebes pushed past me and grabbed the coracle in his hands as if it were a gift to him personally. "Look, Odd Thebes!" he said. "This beautiful craft, she is strong as the sea itself and yet so fine you can see through her, like mica! She weighs less than your quill." I stepped back in surprise at the sight of him. This was not the disheveled runner of the tufuga's tent. He was lean and angular, and his hair was plaited like the thick manes of warriors we had read about as kelps.

"Cwym Teifi is showing you his best work," he said, skipping the friendly greeting. "Take a minute to admire it. *See it.*"

"What I *see* is that someone is still struggling with the definition of hiding." I put the date on my form: viiB. The seventh of Boreal.

Errol turned back to the guildmaster. "Stay high," he said.

"High," said Cwym Teifi. They tilted toward each other in a slight bow.

"*A gaf i roe cynnig arni?*" said Errol.

Cwym brightened. "Of course. Yes—we'd love you to try it."

I flinched. "But it's a boat. And we're on a roof."

"But look," said Cwym as he grinned. He gestured to two of his runners, who rolled back a tarp to expose a square pool of water half the size of the tower's roof. The runners' tents from that roof were set on the banks of a lake.

Errol grabbed the paddles from the runners, set the coracle on the waves riled up by the wind, and tumbled awkwardly into her. The bowl skidded across the surface of the water so fast I thought we were about to watch Errol slip over the edge of that tower. But he flapped the paddles and spun the boat and whooped into the wind. "This is marvelous! I am sailing on top of the world!"

"Sailing implies the use of a *sail*," I called flatly.

Cwym roared, "Try to tip her, Errol Thebes! Try as hard as you can!" I was jarred that the guildmaster knew it was Errol Thebes in that coracle. But Errol seemed not to notice. He stood unsteadily in the little craft, put a foot up on the rim of the bowl, and stepped down hard. The rim slid into the water but came up again so fast Errol fell backward into the boat. Cwym erupted with delight.

Errol's voice was high: "Odd! You see? This is splendid, is it not? You must try her!"

I tapped my quill on my paperwork. "Quantity? And it is made of—what? Abalone?"

"She *looks* like abalone," replied Cwym. "But she's parchment dyed with indigo, laid over fine wicker." He pointed to the line on my form that called for a description. "This one's the color of my bound-wife's eyes, so we call her Maggie." He grew sober. "The real Maggie left me for the morgues three months ago. I am left with the infant she carried. Our first."

Errol lifted his paddles. "How on earth were you able to lead the guild into Ship, with a bound-wife passing?"

"The work is a relief. I dread the quiet of night most of all."

"Aye," said Errol. "And how will you manage the wait, in Beklemek?"

"I can't bear the thought. Send me news from the roofs, will you? That will be distracting, for I was a runner long ago."

The guilders waiting at the hatch could not get enough of Errol, the way he was talking to their beloved guildmaster. You could see it in their faces, waiting to see what he would ask next. That was the disappointment I felt from Teifi when I first got here: They were all waiting for someone who cared, and all they got was me.

"Quantity?" I held my quill over the form. "Six coracles? Something like that?"

Cwym Teifi shook his head. "Six? Nay. We have two thousand."

I looked up from my papers. "Two *thousand*? *Dwy fil o cwryglau*? Are you serious?"

"In all colors. We could make more than that, but the regnat will only take so many." Cwym pointed to the line on my form for the tax. "And tell the regnat I have thirty-eight foundlings for him. They'll come when we send the coracles." He added, "Truth is, I haven't chosen them yet. I hate that part."

When we left, Cwym Teifi nodded to me and said a terse thanks in the common tongue. And Errol? Cwym held Errol in his arms like a rising third son.

———

Errol trailed me across the lines from Teifi to Shou. With flourish, the wizened guildmaster there, Diaochan Shou, opened a trunk lid on what appeared to be a heap of broom handles. Errol reached for one and asked, *May I?* in her guild's tongue. "*Wo keyi?*" Diaochan grinned with the one tooth left in her gums while Errol lit the pressed powder on one end of the stick with his flint. The wind bloomed with the fragrance of cedar. As the flame reduced itself to a steady light, it revealed ornate carvings in the wood. The rough broom handle was actually an intricate trough, a tiny winding river with trees on its banks. As the ember moved down the river of tamped incense, minuscule redbirds lit up in the branches of the trees. The first stand of trees was cedar (so was the first uur of incense, Diaochan said); the next was witch hazel; the next, pear; and so on.

"So the fragrance marks the time of day," Errol said.

Diaochan was delighted with him. She laid a thread of hemp, with a tiny brass bell tied to each end, over a bend in the river and held a brass bowl under it all. When the ember reached the bend, the thread burned and broke, dropping the bells into the bowl with a clamor.

Errol laughed. "A private clock with an alarm!"

Diaochan Shou put her hand on Errol's shoulder and smiled up at him.

I wrote: *Fire hazard*.

———

As we crossed the lines I mumbled under my breath, "What did you do, memorize 'May I?' in every tongue? In the wyrm-slayers' tongue, in tongue of the Three Kingdoms—?"

"You yourself taught me."

"I did no such thing!" But then it came to me. In Langesonne he had wanted a list and I had written it all out for him on a scrap of palimpsest: *Mag ik? Puedo?*

Mogu ya? I wrote "May I?" in every language spoken in the district. "I thought you wanted all those lines to use on girls?"

The last time I saw Errol make such a face I had bet him that I could swallow my own hand.

———

He plucked the vihuelas at Iberia House, shot my own quill at me from a bow at Strael, sampled eight tiny *theobroma* planets at Drageoirs. He chose Saturn as his favorite for the glassy rings of sugar and cardamom. Fifty houses, fifty-one—

"Rumor has it you've fallen from the towers," I said, panting, as we crossed the flies toward the last stop, Pliny. "Aye. Or that you were abducted by raiders from outside the wall, or the galaxy. Or by some girl. You're a legend, Errol Thebes. But now as I am doing all your errands, don't you think I have the right to know which rumor is true?" I was in excellent condition, but I had to stop more than once to bend over to fill my lungs with air, from the effort of keeping up with him. "Everyone knows this disappearance of yours has nothing to do with knotting spikes anymore. Stirring up drama. Look at you today, risking both our lives for no reason at all."

"I came today because it was necessary."

"How were you necessary? I was doing the work."

"You were doing the *paper*work. But I knew you would forget that these people work in dark isolation all year, building the most beautiful exports on earth. Their work is full of—how would *you* put it?"

"Boredom?" I said.

"Longing."

I shrugged. "So you admit the iron spikes are a ruse, an excuse to get away from your life, away from your mam."

He was exasperated. He said, "If you are so convinced, then turn them in. You know that iosal foundling. You know it has them."

I hesitated, trying to figure out why I hadn't thought of such a thing myself. All I could say was "But they're yours."

He laughed. "That's irony. Odd Thebes has sudden ethics, and I am the thief. In truth you know I'm right. The black-iron spikes are uncommon."

I waved my hand in dismissal. "The Long Run awaits us. And Winter Ship. And the glorious party. And girls. You have robbed me of these high pleasures, Errol Thebes. We had a plan, and now I am alone."

I turned to the Pliny House guildmaster, who was waiting to register the mass of feathered paper dragons his guild had produced this year. The man shouted in my ear, "The master guilders wish me to express to Errol Thebes that we will be glad to harbor the fugitive when he tires of running."

"Death!" I said loudly, irritated. "Are you all glad about death? And don't you think any one of the guilders in Pliny would turn him in?"

"Sooner their own sons," said the guildmaster.

Errol bowed to the man.

I turned to Errol, agitated. "*May I, this*? and *May I, that*? That was all strategic! You're just kissing their backends because you need allies."

Errol grabbed my collar. "Here's everything you want to know. I am running the path along the top of the wall every night. During the days, I am asking every guilder who will come to the hatch, What is the origin of the black-iron spikes? No one knows. I find more information in my dreams. I sleep in empty tents during the day. It's that simple. Today? I suspected you would not understand the importance of the work of all these guildmasters or the significance of your job. I was right."

I looked down at the wall that surrounded our city. It was half the height of our tower and the width of forty guilders standing shoulder to shoulder. It was a quarter mile from the closest tower. I couldn't imagine how he'd get a line out there to run it. Plus, the wall was nearly thirty miles, the circumference of the city, so long it curved with the surface of the planet. And he expected me to believe he was running it every night?

"It's more likely you were abducted by a girl," I said. "Aye, it's always a girl." When I turned around, he had disappeared.

WITH WINTER HARD UPON US, the city's exports now filled the storehouses along the river while our food had dwindled to a few sacks of rice and a bin of tubers in the cavernous pantry of every guild and roof kitchen. The city moved full speed ahead toward total depletion.

We observed this annual hardship in the ironic tradition of our ancestors, by forming a holiday around it. We called it Beklemek—*the wait*. While Beklemek was a holiday of unspecified length, it had a specific beginning on the Ides of Boreal, with a feast to finish off every dreg of food in the city.

Inside the towers, Beklemek came as a relief. Guilders had been working around the clock to fill their export quotas. For them, the feast was a tired meal scraped from fry pans, followed by a round of baduk to satisfy the kelps before everyone fell into exhausted slumber. The roofs, by contrast, were in high spirits. We had worked as hard as the guilds but work came easy to us. On Thebes, we rehung Xerxes, the iron crow, which had been reforged after the sacking of our roof, and tied red pennons around his chest. We invited Bamako's runners to join us, all dozen of them, for they had shared their food and wood with us since the fire. We also invited the six runners of the wheel-making Chakra House. We sat elbow to elbow and ate from lavish dishes Ping created from the same rice and roots the guild kitchens below us had no doubt burned to a crisp. Soufflés and stews, puddings and flambés. When the meal was gone, we slept in heaps around the yurt fire, and stoked the flames with the last of our wood.

At dawn we emerged to watch a thousand roof masters take their places in a sober vigil on the north edges of their towers. They trained long-lenses on the north gate, through which was a mountain gorge they would see when the gate opened. From that gorge our river flowed, and on our river a fleet of ships would sail into our harbor.

The daily practice of singing the sun up and down was suspended for Beklemek, and a halt put to nonessential errands. No bells rang. We pulled blankets around our shoulders and returned to the yurt, where our breath made clouds in the frozen air. For the first time in our year there was no work to do. Dragomir ran outside and pretended to eat the iron mast out of hunger. He wanted to get a laugh but he froze his tongue to the mast. We made him tell his life story while we heated spit in our hands to free him. When Marek Thebes returned from Beklemek meetings at Fremantle he reported that diversions had been planned in every district to fill a week of waiting. This did get a laugh. The ships always came after a day, two days at the most. The mood was high.

———

On that first night after the Ides, we joined a district tournament of picket at Tang House. The stakes were not laid out in kisses: winners with winners, losers with losers. I was curious to watch Dragomir lose to Sa'id on purpose in order to have a chance at Grid, who appeared to be fumbling a hand at the next table and losing to Marek. Grid never lost at deck games, though, except to me. I would have warned Dragomir but the circumstances were too amusing. To their credit, our roof master and Dragomir made the most of that kiss, dragging it on longer than any I had ever had. And we all made the most of the next morning, with no fleet on our horizon.

All day and late into the second night of Beklemek, we cut up old clothes and skins that had been sent up from the guild, and fashioned them into costumes for the party of Winter Ship. Sixteen elaborate disguises hung in the yurt when we were done, lacking only Errol's: Helen of Troy, Menelaus of Sparta, a djinn, a bolt of lightning, Achilles, Patroclus, a she-goat such as one was described in Pliny's field guides, a bonnacon, a white bear (with a fanged bear mask from Pliny House), a troll, a wild boar, an E-minor chord, Sir Parsival (most excellent Knight of the Round Table and Purveyor of the Grail), a master chef, Brunhilde, and a foppish fleet commander with a toy ship foundering on a ring of high waves about his hips—a weird lifesaver, held up by a pair of suspenders. No one said a word the next morning when the real fleet commander did not appear under any disguise.

On the third night we ran the lines to Teifi House, to throw ourselves in the rectangular sea of the coracles guild. I had proposed this idea but, now that the time came, I regretted it. We had read a thousand books that included men and women who swam in every imaginable sea and river, but no one had ever taught us to swim. So we crowded into the water and stood, shivering, then clambered out and wiped the water off with our tunics. Inside our wall, we were the strongest civilians; outside we would barely survive. Further disappointment in the morning: no ships.

By the fourth night, we were anxious with hunger. We stayed home for a night of petit jeux, the games we had played as kelps: forfeits, botticelli, charades, and the like. Each of us drew a specific instruction from a bin: Talwyn had to play with her eyes closed. Sa'id had to sing every word. I was required to lie, but no one could tell the difference. Here was a lie: The ships arrived at dawn.

On the fifth night we played flying disc games across the city under a waxing moon and then hung the long hamacs from the flies and slept the night dangling in the winds under the lines. Seed pods hanging lightly over the earth. Speaking of dangling in the wind: There were no ships in the morning.

Fremantle devised a distracting challenge for the sixth night of Beklemek. Every guild had till a random trumpet blast to build a lorry from whatever materials or exports its guild produced, and to race the lorry on the lines. That night the heats of those races filled the sky. Chakra House took the prize with a frictionless spinning wheel from which all six of its runners hung, three on each side, as the wheel ran along the lines. This insane run was the idea of Siwan Chakra—not our Siwan, but another. This feat caught Grid's eye. I noticed later that she was wearing Siwan's toque.

The races invoked a late-night discussion back at Thebes, of the regulations Fremantle imposed. Dragomir quoted verbatim: *Precept the Twelfth: The reckless, high-speed racing of lorries or cargo buckets on the fly-lines is considered the sole purview of the third-year runners, who shall be reminded,* cadavera innumera.

They all turned to me for the translation. I swallowed some ice I had broken from the rain barrel. "Lots of corpses," I said.

The first-years wanted to know how many of the rules we each had broken, in our time on the roofs. Marek objected, but Talwyn interrupted him to say that she had been the one in the month of Langesonne to remove Marek's tent, intact and with him asleep in it, from Thebes's roof and to re-suspend it from the lines over the river. I had never seen Marek laugh till that moment, his sharp teeth flashing. He had credited Errol Thebes and some of his old friends from Perlew for that prank, and had spent all his nights retaliating against the lot of them. He regarded Talwyn with new admiration. Marek's laughter was read as a general amnesty, and it induced a spate of confessions. We lay in each other's laps around the yurt, braiding each other's hair as our mothers used to do. Seppo said he wished he had never seen Fremantle, for it ruined everything about the roofs to have Errol gone. Dragomir proposed pranking Fremantle for the month of Rhagfyr in memory of the felon Errol Thebes.

"Assuming," he added, "that any of us survive Beklemek." Marek sent Dragomir to his tent for that grim remark. There were no pranks in the morning, or ships.

On the seventh night, Gallia House, the seat of our district, took down its yurt and tents, and set up one great tarp that held off the snow, to host an evening of *Beste Bat,* which meant *one more.* It was a night of odd talents. A runner from Arawak House could repeat any sentence spoken to her in perfect reverse, *rettel rof rettel.* That Catalhoyuk runner I had met on the roof at the tufuga's, the one who now had a tatu of the bloody map on her arm, drew on a cheroute and blew smoke through her ears. A runner from Ghent could bend over backward and sit on his own head. One from Gallia sang a song by herself in three-note harmony.

A Kazbek runner shot an arrow from a bow and hit a bull's-eye at the other end of the roof; he used his toes to do this, and stood on his hands. Grid offered to call up the dead but we pretended not to hear her.

For my part, I announced I could translate from any guild tongue to any other, and found myself in the middle of a proposal—a pair of runners from Albacete and Arawak, binding themselves together in what felt more like panic in the face of starvation than an act of love. Someone made the joke that any marriage would probably be better if the members spoke two different languages. The roof master bound and dropped the couple from the plank off the north side of the tower and hauled them up. The girl's ribs had broken in the drop and her new husband vomited. We were all unnerved until someone thought to call for a tune in honor of the new couple. Talwyn got out her fiddle and we danced, light in the head and on our feet. The gavotte she played was my cousin Errol's favorite, a tune to which we had often, as kelps, danced in the kitchens. As I turned near the edge with Grid, I watched Marek stepping with Itsaso, the roof master of Bamako House, their hands together and raised high. I was light-headed and kelpish and found myself in a strange state of missing Marek although he was right there in front of me. Roof masters were chosen like apprentices; they rarely came from the guilds whose roofs they led. Which meant that, although Marek had been living on my roof long enough to have known my cousins Rip and Fenn, I knew nothing about him. Just then he looked over at me and I felt our frailty for the first time.

This frayed night, these silly games, were the last of what we had prepared for diversions. On the eighth morning, there were no ships.

MAREK STOOD SOLITARY WATCH that morning while the rest of us slept past sudore and well into evening. Without fire to melt ice, we slaked our thirst by sucking on bits of frozen water we chipped from the rain barrels. We knew that soon after the high places froze, so followed the low, and ice would make the river impassable for ships. We pulled extra toques onto our heads and burkas over our wools. When Ping discovered a crate of slime onions he had thrown under the stove we cut off the rot and sucked on what was left. Dragomir said he felt like he had swallowed a crate of nails.

The days passed in a smear of gray hunger and exhaustion. By the thirtieth of the month of Boreal, we had gone without food for fifteen days. We were wasting weight.

Marek sent me to Fremantle on that morning to deliver Thebes's body count. He made me wear a mam-line as he knew I would faint on the way. "Tell them Thebes contains now only four hundred twenty-one guilders, fifteen apprentices, eighty-nine kelps. Three elders have died since Beklemek began, their bodies sent to the guild morgues. And tell them"—here Marek hurled his quill over the edge—"seven foundlings are gone from the unnumbered throng. We have fifteen runners on the roof, plus myself. One of my runners is too ill to rise. We could put feverfew to good use."

Marek would not let us look when he brought seven burlap sacks up and rolled the foundlings over the edge. Five were small—the size and weight of tiny kelps. Two were our size.

We told no stories that day, gave each other no lessons in knotting, rehearsed no lines for any plays, and did not study. I stayed in my sack in my tent, trying to stop shaking.

———

The next day we moved the stone to Rhagfyr, and it was a new year. The sun arced lower in the sky and snow came. My tent sagged and dripped during the day, froze into a solid triangle at night. Marek Thebes shoveled the paths himself and came around to our tent flaps in the mornings, whispering tendernesses.

"Get the hel out of bed, Odd Thebes."

"Why? Is there hope?"

"You worry about your breath. I'll worry about hope. Do I have to come in there and drag you out like a kelp? Do I look like your mother?"

"A bit. Yes."

"Come out here and say that." I didn't care that he was trying to cheer me.

"I don't want to come out. When did they reverse the flags?"

"In the night."

"I hate it." He did not answer. He hated it, too. "We ate a fool's meal, that Beklemek feast. We would still have food if we had meted it out—"

He was into my tent in a split second, his face in my face. "We were never fools. You know why we did it," he said, his teeth bared.

"I forget. Tell me again."

"We can't tell the damned ships when to come," he said. "We're at the mercy of a fleet of strangers from a world that walls us in. And so we hold that feast and eat everything we have because it is the one decision we have agency to make."

When had my ears begun to ring? They hurt so much. "But—" I put my face in my hands.

"But what?" he demanded.

"Was one of those foundlings Jamila Thebes?"

"I don't know," he said. "I could not look."

WHEN MAREK WAS DONE WITH ME, I drew a leather pouch from my runner's pack. Embroidered shoddily by my mother with my name and a pair of dice, this tellensac contained the relics of my life so far. I spilled it out on my bedroll and picked from among a half dozen folded wads of paper a scrap of old parchment. My fingers were shaking. On the scrap were written six lines of poetry, in an alphabet that looked like red threads dangling from a tiny clothesline.

I was nine times around the sun that year, living on the nineteenth strata of Thebes House, the guild of my birth. I was the same age as my cousin Errol, as always. At that time he had begun to work with the master guilder Wahid Thebes, learning to run his mam's guild. With Errol gone, all of our "mutual" friends disappeared, and even my own brothers and sisters would not play with me. I was younger than they were; I should have known better than to beat them at maw and take their uurs. More than once they chased me down the guild halls, yelling, "You are nothing without Errol Thebes! Your name came from none of the books! And no one wants you!" Even by guild standards they were an unaffectionate lot.

I fled from them on one such night to the guild library, on the 151st strata, knowing they were far too lazy to climb 132 flights just to dislike me in person.

The library was silent, its lamps extinguished for the night. I crossed to the corner where Homer's tales were shelved, running my hands over the scrolls and books. Long before even our oldest guilders were born, someone or something had discarded the motherlode once contained in this room, which spanned the entire top strata of Thebes tower. So many shelves were empty. I wondered often what books and scrolls had been discarded and why. Still, the irfelaf, the remnant, the treasured last bit, was more than sufficient for me. Thousands of volumes, all full of news from the world outside our wall, had been kept: tales of men who were fauns from the hips down, of tiny guild cottages built out of sweets, of trolls living in exile under drawbridges, of wars against beasts with multiplying heads, of uncommon swords whose glint would kill a man. Of all the hidden passages and secret strata, this was my favorite place in the tower. I removed Homer from a shelf and sat breathing in the thick smell of parchment and leather and tale.

Next to me, a human form shifted in the shadows. A high-pitched voice screamed in fright, and I realized the voice was my own. When I fumbled to light my lamp I was mortified to see I had been frightened by a mere kelp of my own size and age. She sat in a chair with a scroll in her lap, her finger pressed on a line of red-inked text.

"Ye dinna friten me," I said, my heart pounding in my ears. "I yelled te friten thee."

"Oh. And I am terrified," she said flatly. She had black hair and blacker eyes.

"Who are you?" I said, my back still to the wall. "And why are you speaking in the common tongue? You're no one I know."

"I'm no one at all," she said.

"*Feh*. Was that a riddle?"

She pointed to the naught brand on her neck, an empty circle. "I'm nothing," she said.

"Foundling," I whispered. I had never seen a foundling. "You are not allowed—I—could throw you out of this library."

"You could try."

I hesitated. If I tried to take her on she would probably thrash around and bite me. I said, "If I felt inclined, I would do it, here and now. What is your deficit? Something must be lacking or you wouldn't be a foundling. Is it your eyes? They're strange. Show it to me. Is it your mind?"

"I was found by Margaret Thebes herself," the foundling said. I was young but not too young to know that my aunt, the guildmaster, kept strong ties to the foundlings.

"Found where?"

"In a trash bin."

"So you lack a mam, then," I said.

"Aye."

"And a da."

"Aye." Foundlings were forbidden to lie, but this one, my first foundling, certainly wasn't forthcoming.

"And why are you sitting like that, with your feet up in the air? As if there's an invisible footstool? Are you a dullard?" I said.

The foundling sighed as if I was the stupid one. "All I want, at this moment, is to lower my feet," she said. "But I'll not do it. When I am past thinking I can endure the hardship, then I will lower them. Much later. Do you understand?"

I had no idea what she was talking about. I just said, "And what? You read that scroll so you can stop reading it later?"

"The light spills off these six lines of text, and pours down my fingers," she said, as if such an explanation made everything clear.

"That," I said, "is my lamplight pouring down your fingers." I craned my neck to see her scroll. I wanted to know what those six lines said. The words were nothing to me but tiny pieces of red thread dangling from a clothesline. I said, "That is an idiot's writing. You should read something else."

"This is the only text I allow myself to read this year."

"*Feh*. Then you should also read that scroll over there on the table. Look at it. It is written in your tongue, see? Aren't you dying to know what it says?"

"Yes. I am. That is my point in not reading it."

"Well. And I will not tell you what it says, for I am extremely busy." I strolled over to that table and casually picked up that other scroll. Of course I wouldn't tell her what it said, for I could not read it if our two lives depended on it. I knew only my own language at that time, and the common tongue. I sat down next to her, though, and pretended to read that scroll, laughing at what I imagined were key plot turns in it, pressing certain words of feigned interest with my finger. "Ah," I said. And occasionally, "Aha!" I went on like this all night, making myself comfortable in a heap of cushions while the foundling kept her feet just off the floor, her thigh muscles spasming. I forgot my wastrel siblings. I forgot my cousin Errol Thebes. This foundling had my attention.

At the end of the night I said, "I'm going home now to my kin. I order you to go home to your—bin." I had worked on that rhyme all night and regretted it the moment it left my lips.

"Make me," she said. She stood up.

I dropped the scroll and eased myself around her, heading for the door. "That's an excellent tale, in that scroll," I said. "I'm sure you'll sneak in and read it, after I am gone."

She said, "Incidentally, you were reading it upside down."

I yelled from down the hallway: "I always read upside down. For the challenge of it!"

The next night, I crept back to the library and discovered the foundling in the chair with her feet up. I arranged myself in the chair next to her, expending a great deal of time finding a thick footstool to shove under my feet, and pretended to read yet another scroll in the letters of her language. I even remembered to turn it upside down.

After this, I went every night to the 151st strata.

Nobody missed me. My own mam, who worked in the guild kitchens, failed to notice I did not appear from meals. She had no idea I spent my time pretending to read the flourishes of a foundling's alphabet, trying to imagine what it was like to be unimportant.

I knew little about foundlings at that time, only that for reasons too complicated to explain to us kelps they were required to move in separate hallways from ours and to sleep in the morgues. At night they crept along the edges of our workrooms, spilling our pisspots out the vents, and scavenging whatever food we had dropped on the floor. They owned neither quills nor paper, beds nor clothes. They fashioned tunics from our rags. They did not wear tellensacs, as they had no stories worth telling. I once overheard my father say at one of his card games that the guilds paid taxes, to the regnat of Fremantle, in foundlings. But my father had reeked of whiskey, and I had corrected him in front of everyone, saying taxes were paid in the most valuable thing the guild had, and only a fool would think that was anything but uurs.

One night I held the foundling's scroll in my hands and stared at it until my eyes crossed and the letters lifted off the page, shimmering with some kind of light that poured off onto my fingers. I rolled it backward and forward. Finally I turned to the very back of the scroll and found, attached with old bookmaker's thread, a list of letters of her tongue and the common tongue, the sounds they made, and a key to the meanings of various words one could find in the text: *hija* for "seed" and *simhah* for "lion." In two uurs I spoke a sentence in the language of red curls of thread, and the foundling informed me I had demanded to eat her cat. By Langesonne that year, I read a poem in the language of the red threads and watched in surprise as the foundling wept.

The foundling would never herself read more than the six lines of poetry from which light poured down her fingers, but I didn't ask her permission to read aloud to her, and she didn't protest. As I had found with her scroll, I next found a primer for the language of Ovid. *Amo, amas, amat.* After another month in the library I could read my favorite bard aloud in his mother tongue. I sat next to the foundling and let Ovid pour onto her. After that I poured Hesiod, in his tongue. Luo Ben, in his. I poured the writings of the nameless scribes who tailed Beowulf and Siegfried. And then, and on.

Often, when I read, the foundling repeated my words silently, her eyes closed and her lips forming the shapes of sound. I moved my chair to sit across from her and lifted my book so that, from underneath it, I could watch her do this.

From time to time the foundling would disappear for several nights, and I was afraid my drunken father had been right, that my foundling had been paid in tax to the regnat. I would go to the library and wait for her, for I would have this or that to tell her or some new scroll I had found to read to her. Eventually she always returned.

One night she asked, "What do you smell when I am here?"

"Nothing. Sheep skin from the scrolls," I said. "Iron and gall, in the ink."

"Can't you smell me?"

"Cardamom in your hair maybe." If she expected poetry, she would have to look elsewhere. I was only nine.

But it wasn't poetry she sought. To her I smelled mustily of quills. Ovid's prose tasted thin and yellow in her mouth. Hesiod was heavy and fleeting, like firewood. The bread I gave her sounded of drumming. The number three, in any language, felt like a sharp pinch. She had long suspected she was alone in these ways and I told her to keep such things to herself, or the guilders would throw her off the roof.

"But then who would clean their pisspots?" she said. "No one." She was quiet for a long while, then said, "Why are you coming to the library every night?"

How much did I want to tell her? "My da named me after someone in the books. I need to know who it is.

"I see. And why are you learning all these languages?" she said.

"You wouldn't understand."

"Feh," she said. "As if you are too complex for me?"

I told her I was learning the tongues in case the wall came down and we opened the city to the world.

These explanations had once been true, but they were lies now. I came here to be with her. I learned the languages for her. Could she be trusted to know that? To know that I left my guild and my city every night, on sky-worthy carpets woven for me of alphabets and runes I had learned for her?

Definitely not.

She said, "Well. You do talk a lot. I'm sure you would have a lot to say to anyone outside the wall."

"How do you know how much I talk? You never see me anywhere but here."

"I see you with your cousin and all those kelps who want to be with him. Today he said merely ten words and you said more than three thousand before epistola."

"As if you watch me from the walls and keep count," I said.

She made her voice sound like mine: "'I call that I am playing Beowulf today! No, *me*! Errol is always Beowulf! Listen, you felons and thieves. My great-grandmother was from Camelot and that is only five leagues from Geatland—'"

I put my hands over my ears. "Stop. I hear myself. Stop now."

"That was just the first thirty-two—" she said.

"Stop."

She smiled at me. "I love listening to you talk, Odd Thebes."

This stunned me. My whole life, my family just told me to shut up: my father, my siblings, even my own mam. I said, "And somehow you know my name, also. So I must know yours, if a foundling even has a name."

"Find it out for yourself," she said. And she closed her eyes and slept, with her feet in the air: the skinny, impermeable one.

I was outflanked. So I did what any man would do in my situation.

"Well," said my mother, later that night, wiping the grease from her hands and leaning against her cookstove. "You have met the great Jamila Foundling. Margaret Thebes found her in a scrap bin. Sent her to be raised with the found-lings in the morgues. Which was a good thing for them, as Jamila Foundling steals food and blankets for them, and once a month or so she is called up to the guildmaster's quarters to explain why the foundlings are dancing on the caskets again, to fiddle music, and flute, which she teaches them."

"Foundlings are filthy, are they not? And contagious."

My mam laughed. "This, from my son who refuses to bathe."

"It sleeps sitting up," I said.

"Aye, well. For a month Jamila Foundling refused to open her eyes. And then for a fortnight she went everywhere on her hands. And then she would not touch the floor at all. Leapt from the rafters over our heads. She is what you might call *mul-heafod.*"

I don't know where my mother got that word, mule-headed. There were no living animals in the guilds of this nameless, placeless city. Skins. Feathers. Wool. Bones. All the parts of former animals. But nothing alive. How would my mam know how a mule's head acted? And can you blame me that, from then on, I as-sumed a mule head was a glorious thing—a winged horse, or some kind of fairy.

———

As I lay in my tent on the roof of Thebes, eight years later and nearly seventeen times around the sun, on the first night of the new year with six lines of stolen po-etry from a torn scroll pouring light on my fingers while I was dying of starvation, my mam's words were a relief to me. The foundling who could walk on her hands for a fortnight and dance on death's luggage—such a mule head would survive Beklemek.

A FEW WEEKS AGO we had been high with excitement over Beklemek and Winter Ship. Now our bellies were concave. Breathing was our one chore. I woke in the night, licking the iron roof under my pillow.

Grid came around each morning. "Are you making water?" In faith, I had no spit, no tears, no piss. What could she do, but give me a larger ration of water from ice she had melted under her body in her bedroll in the night?

Marek put Dragomir in my charge, and Faisal, too. He was too busy to notice if they fainted or lost faith. What could I say to them? The three of us were barely alive, lying side by side each night in my tent, exhaling foul stenches from empty innards.

On every roof and in every guild the scene was the same. The city was being driven to its knees.

——

On the fifth morning of the month of Rhagfyr, I rolled out of my sack, thick with coats and hides and joined a line of Thebes's runners at the west edge. Marek was not there.

Grid carried Emem to the edge because he was too weak to walk. Emem had a lens and was watching something on the earth. A black form, some shadow fathoms and fathoms below us, chased a smaller form through the streets and to the river, a narrow ribbon of silver we could see between the towers. We had never seen a beast before, save once, in a far-gone time. The smaller one was panicked, angling back and forth.

"*Isan. Nnwoon,*" said Emem, unaware he had reverted to his mother's tongue. Everyone looked at me. "He says they can walk on the water."

"Emem, no," Grid said quietly. "They are running on ice. We are iced in."

The first shadow was faster and it overcame the small one.

Emem said, "Wait, where did it go?" But no one answered.

I lay in my bedroll late into that night, running my fingers between the ribs under my shirt, wondering where Marek was and where Errol was. Wondering where I would be when I took my final breath and who would be left to tell my going-stories. I had thought it would be Errol Thebes and he would rest me in my mother's bed. The thought of this undid me, and I laid my elbow over my face and ached with homesickness for my own self.

———

I lay half sleeping, restless, in my tent like that.

"Odd Thebes," said a voice at the flap. "Are you awake?"

"I'm up. Yes. Just finishing some astronomy calculations. What is it?"

"Are the kelps still with us?"

"What kelps?"

"Dragomir and Faisal."

"Marek—is that you? There's ice on the river. Where were you this morning?"

He did not answer but rather whispered, "Emem has—" He could not say it. "Emem is gone."

"*Gone* gone?" I said.

"Aye. We've lost him."

Emem was gone? Nobody was gone! Nobody died at eighteen! Emem knocked the crow every morning! How could he be gone?

I pressed on Faisal's shoulder. He yawned and asked if it was time for breakfast. *Aye*, I said. Let him dream. But Dragomir would not wake. I shook him. I pinched his cheek hard enough to bruise it. I leapt out of my sack and jumped on his chest. Nothing. I put my face next to his and blew a great hot gush of foul breath up his nose. His eyes opened, the stone-cold look of a corpse.

"Odd Thebes, you are beyond all help," he said.

I fell back into my sack with my heart beating wildly. I cried out, "Both pelts are with us still."

"Would you come out?" Marek's voice cracked. "I have Emem's tellensac."

"Of course. Yes." I laid my head back on my pillow. "What time is it?"

"Crust," he said. "By the stars." Three in the morning. Festivum, somnium, crustum.

"So early?" I said. I thought of the baker's bell for a long while—of bakers, and bread, and how when we were kelps we used to steal precious white flour from the kitchen and spew it at each other and pretend to be fire-breathing wyrms. I thought about all this until I could not remember what I was thinking about and I forgot Marek outside my tent and sank into sleep.

"**THERE WAS ONE GRIM WINTER** the ships didn't come," said Marek. I sat up. How long had I been asleep? Was he still talking to me? "I only know of it from hearsay," he went on. "None of us were born yet. First they ran out of food and fire, then water. They reversed the flags. They burned the lines. And then they ran out of restraint. Few survived. This will be that winter again." He was outside my tent.

A new voice, lower and muffled, said, "We have sufficient lines to drop to the street, to go for food. Why don't we ever consider that? You and I could go."

"No," said Marek. "There are terrors on the street far worse than starvation."

"To die of starvation is also a terror," said the other. "Ask Emem." Marek was quiet. "What is it, on the streets, that we fear so much that we agree to be kept locked in these guilds for all of time?"

"You don't want to know." That was Marek's voice again.

"I do want to know, Marek Thebes. You might even say we are all dying to know."

Marek answered tersely, "What I do know, I am unwilling to say, even to you."

"Are they going to burn the lines?"

"Yes. At dawn. The fire will melt this ice. It will buy us a day of drinking water. I don't know what purpose that serves—" Marek paused. "I cannot tell all these going-stories." He stopped, overcome. Finally he cursed and said, "I dread the stench of silk ablaze."

The second speaker said, "Don't let them burn. Wait one more dawn."

"You're a dreamer," said Marek. "Margaret Thebes is burning the workbenches to keep the guilds warm. The whole guild is packed into the dining hall."

"Tell her to wait. Tell her that's an order from Fremantle." The speaker scrambled to his feet. "Or, as she's my mother, tell her I asked her to wait. They're looking for me. I must go."

I untangled myself from the bedding and came flying out of the tent. It was snowing hard. Errol was already on the fly. I ran after him, stumbling across planks and fumbling with lines laced with ice for three roofs before he heard me. He turned to face me on some plank at some tower I no longer recognized. I took a step back. He was lean from starvation, like all of us, and there was a danger about him.

"Stay high," he said. I barely recognized his voice.

"I plan to," I said, panting. I spat blood. "What are you—a ghost? Rumor said you were dead."

"An exaggeration. Are you all right?"

"Look at me. The answer is in front of you. I'm a thousand years old. I'll be dead tomorrow. Where have you been? What are you doing here?"

"I came to ask Marek to go down to the streets with me."

"Why didn't you ask me?"

"Will you go?"

"No. Don't be ridiculous."

"Well then. Can I rely upon that foundling to keep the cnyttan spican safe?"

"What—? Nobody is thinking about those stupid knotting spikes anymore. Stop!"

"Someone is thinking about them. Guards tracked me yesterday from Fremantle."

I threw up my hands. "Emem is dead. The whole city is starving while you and the regnat squabble like kelps over a pair of knotting spikes."

"The regnat isn't starving. I saw him on his roof. He is thicker than he ever was."

"He—what?" A fat regnat in a starving city? I was too sick with vertigo to think. I said, "Are you leaving again? If so, this is the last time we will speak."

We were silent for a while, and then he shifted. "No, it's not the last. I will be everywhere. I'm coming to hear Emem's going-stories. And to watch the Long Run. And to the Winter Ship party you and I planned to attend together. Tell me your costume so I can find you. Are you Homer?"

I looked at him, incredulous. "You're joking! There won't be a iosal party. And no Long Run. By the end of this week the city will be a morgue."

"Still I'm asking. What is your costume?"

I stared at him blankly. "I—I cannot remember."

"Fine. Be that way. Then I won't tell you, either. And you'll not know me." When I shook my head, confounded, he said conspiratorially, "You know this is my only chance to find that kitchen girl."

There was play in his voice. I threw my head back and groaned. "Wait—not Kitchen Girl!" And now there was play in my own voice. "You haven't spoken of her once since we came up to the roofs. I thought you didn't love her anymore."

He laughed, and we were together in this now. "How could you say such a thing? Kitchen Girl is everything. *Everything!*"

I sniffed. "I see. And here I thought those iron spikes were everything. And how will you even know which girl she is, should you meet her on Al-Razi? Considering it was pitch-black in that kitchen and you never actually saw her."

"*You* know who she is. I could ask you anytime."

"In faith, there were many names carved on the underside of that table. Easily a thousand pairs. Also, wads of chewn-up mastiche." I shrugged. This was an old routine of ours. "Whatever. Maybe I know, maybe I don't." I kicked at the edge of the plank. "Incidentally, if I could have told you who Kitchen Girl is, would you have given up everything, just to have her?"

"Yes. Of course," he said. "Why?"

I paused. "Well, girls seem to like that. The giving-up-everything thing."

Errol's eyes darted to a point over my shoulder. "Stay high," he said, and he was gone.

I was run down then by two Fremantle guards. They didn't want me; they wanted him. I was left clinging to the underside of a plank.

Back in my tent, lying in my sack, I wheezed with laughter. The whole city was trapped in a high and ancient quarantine. Starvation was upon us. The river was ice. Fremantle was coming for Errol. And there he and I had been, out on a thin plank, speaking of death. And in the middle of all that, Errol had managed to conjure the image of a party and a girl, and his conjuring was better for me than bread or water.

Ships

ERROL DID NOT COME to Emem's going-stories. Marek called us into the yurt without notice, and the stories had been quick.

The two pelts were asleep, one on each side of me: Faisal and Dragomir. They were fifteen. Old enough to run fly-lines a mile over the earth, to apprentice themselves to a guild for life, to be bound and wed, to father kelps, and now to hear the going-stories of their friend. Let them dream.

In my thin state I hallucinated the faraway voices of men shouting orders. Their voices were small and they yelled in the cadences of a language I didn't know. My disoriented mind could twist languages. Guilders? Were there guilders on the roofs, come to burn the lines? I sat up, the tent spinning. A hallucination of sound, I told myself. Was I dead? Was this heofon? Please tell me the afterlife was not three stinking runners in a rancid tent.

Faisal sat up. "What?"

Not even in a hallucination could I summon what came next. The tower shook so hard I thought it would collapse with the gongs of the bells of Berfrei tower. I had forgotten the sound of bells. Faisal and I clutched for the tent, for Dragomir, for anything to hang on to. Then came the wild clamor of more bells from the compass points—Athens at the north wall and Marathon at the south. Visby and Cairns were answering.

I was knocked over by the two pelts, and then we all three were swept up in a mob of runners and carried along off the edges, over the lines, all running the flies toward the towers along the harbor.

I found Marek at the edge of one of the Makhazin storehouses. He handed me his lens. The fleet of ships was below us, so enormous it filled the river from the north wall to the south, the hulls so heavy with supplies that river water and thin slabs of ice sloshed over their decks. Their crews were lowering the sails and fixing the hawsers to the quay bollards. Fires burned in the lanterns in their rigging. Easily three hundred sailing ships. In the early light, the crews were already unloading and, from a mile above, runners were dropping lines to hoist firewood up to the flies in canvas tarps as wide as our yurts. The harbor smelled thickly of the pitch of fir kindling.

What a morning that was! Barrels of herring rising into the sky. Thousands of sacks of cornmeal. Tarps heaped with salsify, pignut, cassava, breadroot, tubers—swinging and rising on pulleys over the harbor. One longship had to be unloaded, two enormous cheese wheels at once, one from port and other from starboard, or the vessel would have foundered. Barrels and casks came up out of the holds, filled with wheat, cubebs, hard sausage, dates, rock salt, saffron, walnuts, galangal, sorghum, honey, olive oil, on and on and on. The sky ripened with clouds of spikenard and cinnamon dust.

Marek Thebes wiped his face with his hands and turned to us. "There. What were you worried about? Petroc, gather the first-years. They'll need to see this done. Odd, get a quill and parchment. Really? Are you barefoot? Ironic to die now, don't you think? Slipping on the planks? Go get sharps. Do I look like your mother?"

"Quite a bit. Yes."

"Well, she's a lucky girl."

An Odd Remedy

I WAS TRYING TO FIND A SOCK under all the filthy bedding in my tent.

"Odd Thebes. Come out of there. Ping is down." It was Dragomir.

"What?"

"Aye. He fainted in the yurt."

"And?" I said, one sharp in my hands. "Name one of us who hasn't fainted twice already this morning."

"He's going to die, Odd. The ships are here but Ping is dying." Dragomir pushed my tent flap aside. "Can you go any faster?"

The circle of runners parted for me and there lay our cook, bundled in wools at the first bucket fire with the first wood. We all looked like stick figures but he was particularly gaunt, working to breathe. Grid knelt by him with a cup of melted snow.

"Odd Thebes," she whispered. "Ping has given up."

"But the ships are here," I said. "He's a cook. Give him, I don't know, something to boil."

"He won't drink."

Ping's eyes shifted balefully toward me. He whispered, "Odd Thebes. What do you make of this?" He stopped to draw a breath, his sides heaving with the effort. "I even had my plan. But now I am going."

I looked at Grid. "You're the medic," I said. "Do that thing that brought Seppo back from the dead. What do you want from me?" I had begun to walk away through the circle when it occurred to me—"Wait, did you just want a going-story?" But Grid shook her head and shifted uncomfortably. They were *all* staring at me now. I realized that they had called me because Marek was not here and Errol was not here, and I was the closest thing they all had to the two who could talk a runner out of dying.

"Fine," I said. I pressed my way back to Ping and squatted next to him. "I forget," I said. "What *was* your plan, anyway?"

Ping closed his eyes and shook his head.

"He hasn't the strength for this," Grid said. I took the cup of water from her and drank it myself. She frowned at me.

"What was your plan, Ping?" I demanded.

"I was to be bound," he whispered. "Bound to Ella Gallia after Beklemek."

"So—that's *now*."

"Aye. I am to apprentice in her parents' guild. To make barrel staves." He opened his eyes and rolled them. He coughed hard and lay back. "Tell her I loved her, Odd? Tell her I loved . . . her *eyes*."

"Feh. Don't be ridiculous, Ping," I said. "Everybody loves everybody's eyes. Is that really the message you wish me to bear?"

Grid kicked me and Ping flinched. "Say anything, then. You're the bard." His voice was raspy. "Get it from one of your books."

They were all watching, waiting for me to do something.

I got up. "Write your own iosal poetry," I said to Ping. Then, to Grid: "I don't know what you want from me. I have to look for my left sharp."

Every runner standing in that circle would have flung me off the edge at that moment, but Ping whispered something and I turned back to him.

"What did you say?"

"The way she licks her fingers after she eats what I cook for her. I loved that."

"That's good. That's something. But you'll have to give me more than that, to take to her."

"Talking with her hands, lively as she is," said Ping. "While she washed my dinner pots." He winced. "I loved that. And I will miss hearing of her day." His voice broke, and he coughed into a rag Grid held for him.

"This is much better," I said. "This will please her. You'll need to give me more, though. The poor girl's got to go her whole life in a locked guild on whatever sentiment you form here and now."

"Her two big—uh—turnips get me—uh—"

I put up my hands and a rumble of laughter rolled around the circle.

"I get it, Ping. I'll clean that up for you. '*Dazzled by your beauty, excitement rises in me.*'" Everyone laughed now, even Grid.

I sat next to Ping and sighed with as much drama as I could muster. "Well, and how I wish I *could* tell all this to Ella Gallia."

"What?" Ping turned his head to look at me.

"Well, I don't want to trouble you, but—"

"Trouble me with what? Is she all right?"

"Haven't you heard?"

"Heard *what*, Odd Thebes?" He grabbed my leg.

I pulled a piece of parchment from my pocket.

"What *is* that?" Ping said. He reached for it, but I flicked it away from his fingers.

"It is not good news," I said.

"Tell me!"

I admitted to Ping that I had gone through his mail this morning. He was near death, after all, and, well, everyone knows *me*: I like to know what's going on. I looked around at the runners in the yurt and demanded to know why anyone didn't tell Ping what was in this letter. They all stared at me blankly, as if they had no idea what I was talking about. Which, of course, they didn't.

"At any rate, it says here, 'Dear Ping Thebes, I am writing to you in dismay, et cetera, et cetera . . . I am at odds with my guildmaster, et cetera, et cetera . . . Ah, here it is: 'My guildmaster promised in Langesonne to bind me to another runner. I did not know of it when we made our oath, you and I. All this past month, I thought we would not live through Beklemek. Now that we will, I regret that I shall never see you—blah, blah—I am binding myself to another, et cetera . . . I remain yours forever, Ella Gallia of Gallia House.'" I looked up at Ping. "So you see—"

"What's his name?!"

I studied the paper. "Do you know someone named *Phineas*?"

"Phineas?!" Ping squealed, like someone had stuck him with a pin. "Phineas Thieus? He makes forks! They promised Ella Gallia to a *fork* maker?!"

"Now, now. Everybody needs forks. Let's not poke fun." I looked at Grid. "I'm sorry. My timing is foul."

Grid was staring at me as if I had just turned inside out.

Ping was up on his elbow, gasping. Wasn't it obvious to everyone that Ella loved him? *Aye*, we all said, it was obvious. He hacked and fell backward. Didn't everyone know for a year they were going to be bound? *Yes.* A violent spasm overtook him, but he ended up on his knees.

"Of course Ella wants you," I said, picking at some lint on my tunic. "But there are connections in these guilds. Politics. It isn't always love that binds us. Anyway, you obviously aren't well, so everything will no doubt work out for the best."

"'Not well'? 'Not *well*'! Get me up, Grid. And get a fire going in my ovens. I need a meat pasty. No. A *tagine*. She likes a tagine. Get me some salt cod. How long does a cook have to wait for a salt cod around here?"

———

Grid followed me back to my tent with her hand on her hip. She demanded to see the parchment, which I produced from my pocket. It was a list of chores Marek had given me.

She sniffed skeptically. "*What* am I supposed to tell Ping when he finds out there's not a letter?"

"How is this my problem?" I said.

She laughed.

"Ping doesn't want to go down into the guilds. He doesn't want to make barrel staves for the rest of his life, with his bound-wife's father breathing down his neck. He wants to cook. But that isn't my problem either."

"Right," said Grid. "Who's Phineas?"

I shrugged. "I made it up. Which is to say, I stole the name from Ovid. From the tale of Andromeda."

"Then who's the fork maker named Phineas Thieus."

"No idea. Somebody Ping knows. A coincidence."

She shook her head, confounded. "So 'Phineas' was a stab in the dark?"

"Yes. And no." And now I grinned. "Ah. So there is something even our death-defying Grid doesn't know. I shall savor this moment." I stared at her until she shifted uncomfortably. "Ping is *male*, Grid. Any male name on earth would have brought him back from the dead."

"Brilliant," she said.

I had only ever wanted a kiss from Grid Thebes, better yet an uur in the sack. Hard to explain, but her approval was more satisfying.

Exports

IF ANY RUNNER touched any part of any ship or any sailor, a cry would go up and the fleet would weigh anchor, still loaded with a year's worth of our provisions, and sail south. Every year, at least one runner attempted to escape the city in this manner; anyone who saw it had to cut the runner's line before all was lost. Today there were no such idiots. Every last runner worked high in the frigid winter air, a mile over the fleet on rigged lines and pulleys to pull up everything they had brought us. Within half a bell after the gates had opened for the fleet, there was wood to burn in every tower. Flints were struck by thin and shaking hands in a thousand guilds and on a thousand roofs, and plumes of smoke rose as they had before, from guild vents and yurt roofs. Ovens roared into service. The first yeast of the year arrived in kitchens, and the first flour, salt, and olive oil. Before Berfrei tolled erratum, dough was rising in pantries all over the city. Everything else went to storehouses—every ounce of food and drink and every raw material we needed to begin a new year of work—all to be meticulously sorted and meted out according to the time and day of the calendar. It was snowing again. We shoveled and threw on more coats and kept on.

By midafternoon, we began to lower our exports to their decks. From our district alone, for which I had done the paperwork: abacuses, astrolabes, attarh, balances, barrels, beads, bellows, bestiary wares, bobbins, burkas, buttons, candles, carpets, chests, coracles, cricket rooms, damask, dice, ditty bags, dohols, dyes, fireworks, fishing nets, flails, fletching, flints, fly-line, formulae, grain sacks, hamacs, incense, kilnwork, knobs, knotting spikes, lace, locks, maps, monmouths, navajas, planets, playing cards, quill ink, sailcloth, sledges, spindles, toques, vexilla, vihuelas, weights and measures, wheels, willow baskets, wool felt.

IN THE LATE AFTERNOON, with the ships loaded and the winds driving snow sideways across our roofs, we stretched out around Ping's fire. We gouged chunks of sweet butter out of crocks and dropped them into hot tea, dredged them out on our fingers and poured honey on them, dipped them in theobroma powder and sucked on them. We ate doughy bread as it came out of the ovens, and fell into one another's laps—sticky, shaking with exhaustion, delirious.

We sang the sun down for the first time since the start of Beklemek—thousands of runners, our voices new to us. It was a shanty we sang in a round:

> *The wind it blows from east-nor'east,*
> *our ship will scud ten knots at least,*
> *the purser would our wants supply,*
> *so while with life we'll never say die.*

From far below us came the sounds of pulleys again, the great iron gates of the south harbor lifting, the whistles and bellows of ships' captains, urging their crews to tack into the blizzard to escape our heinous walls before nightfall. We came out to watch them go.

I wished, at that moment more than ever, that we had never seen the foul pair of black-iron spikes. Without them, Errol would be here, singing. I hated the thought that they waited in the depths of this tower, in the foundlings' hiding place, to do whatever work they were forged to do.

Marek brought me back to the present, for he was pacing the edge, delivering an elaborate malediction regarding those hated ships and their free sailors—a curse on their mothers, their rigging, their king, their rats, their private parts.

"Careful," Grid said. "We might need those ships in a year."

He turned to her, teeth flashing rage. "I'd gouge out their eyes with their own marlinespikes, given the chance. Do you know why the ships were late?"

"Ice?" she said. "Weren't we iced in?"

"No," said Marek. "The ice was thin still."

"Floods?" said Ping.

"A battle upriver?" said Talwyn.

"No."

"It was a girl," I said.

Marek spun around to look at me. "Who told you?"

I shrugged. "No one. Everyone. It's always a girl."

Marek could barely spit out the tale, so bitter he was. Apparently the pilot of the fleet had a sister in the first port where the ships all anchored to collect the last of our provisions. The pilot mentioned to the fleet captain that his sister was something to see, as much as Helen. Every ship in the fleet had weighed anchor, loaded down with our food and supplies. It didn't matter that the captain was a bound man already. Or that a whole city was waiting, starving. Weeks he spent, searching door to door to find that girl while his ships bobbed in that port, while we wasted away in a city blotted from all maps but his. They finally realized the girl had long ago left the port town for parts unknown.

Now I was the sober one. "Who told you this?" I said. "No one but the regnat speaks the language of those ships."

"The regnat. The regnat told a guard, who told Itsaso Bamako, who told me. It was confidential." Marek shook his head and looked across the fire at me. "This entire city was nearly lost because of a girl. Odd—how did you know that?"

I shrugged. "Like I said. Ask Menelaus. Or Paris, for that matter. Sigurd. Lancelot. Odysseus. Artemis. The Robbing Hood. Ask anyone. It's always about a girl."

BEFORE OUR SONGS HAD CEASED TO ECHO in the abyss, packages arrived at every roof, one for each runner. At first the objects inside the packages appeared to be flickering lanterns. But in fact each one was an invitation in the form of a tiny scroll enclosed in a flame-shaped capsule carved of garnet, once more encased in translucent soap, cast in the form of a lamp. The soap had been scented with the oil of cypriol. After three weeks of frigid cold and starvation, the thought of a steaming cypriol bath in a sky of driving snow was more perfect than we could have asked.

Each scroll read:

> *The honor of your presence is requested by the*
> *esteemed guilders of Al-Razi House on this night*
> *of the departure of the fleet at Winter Shipment*
> *of this unknown year, that we may convey on*
> *behalf of the Masters of the Guilds of this*
> *city our Gratitude to the Intrepid*
> *Runners without Whose Daring the export of All Guild Work*
> *and the import of Sustenance would not have been*
> *Possible.*

Al-Razi. Al-Razi was the one guild tower in the city that had been built as high as Fremantle, her great neighbor to the east. While Fremantle was a massive shadow over the city, Razi was gorgeous, a veritable sky full of light turrets, bonfires, and flags unfurled. Al-Razi's exports in any year filled the cargo holds of ten ships of the fleet, with bricks, flakes, crocks, bins, barrels, and bars of soap of every fragrance and shape imaginable. As kelps, we used to scrub in our troughs with little Al-Razi schooners that smelled of the salt sea or creamy white sheep that smelled of lanolin.

For runners, Al-Razi was more than the soap makers' guild. She was the queen of parties, and tonight was our night with her.

We were called by the beat of a sky full of dohols—ceaseless booms of the drums, a beating too loud to allow for human speech, a pulse to which our own hearts adjusted. Every roof extinguished its fires so that Al-Razi shone alone against the stars.

In the yurt on Thebes we changed into the costumes we had made on the second night of Beklemek. These transformations were so thorough that, if we had not painted and adorned one another, we would have thought we were among strangers.

We unfurled Thebes's red silk banner, emblazoned with Xerxes, our crow, and a pair of crossed knotting spikes, and ran the flies. Runners from every other guild tower were doing the same.

It dizzied me to stand at the walkway on Al-Razi's 160th strata and look up into the clouds at her. She rose another fifty strata above that, and to our amazement, ladders ran like streamers up the sides of the tower and led even farther to a temporary loft suspended in the sky, easily twice the width and breadth of Al-Razi's own roof. Dozens of kites flew under its canopy in the rising heat of a blue fire. Insane swings hung from its corners into the abyss. Snow fell on us as we climbed the last ladder. The flakes lit upon glassy spheres of soap blown from cannons mounted somewhere below us, freezing and bursting in the winter air over our heads, spewing mica dust on us till we shone. We set Thebes's banner in the mount reserved for us on the north edge and whooped like kelps, giddy merely to have arrived. For once, beauty out-towered the grim weapons and bureaucracy of the regnat.

———

I closed the visor on the helmet of my costume and set a red plume in the crest.

A throng of thousands was already dancing on the loft, rising and falling to the surge of the drums: heroes, damsels, nymphs, trolls, djinn with their lamps, a set of shatranj pieces, a dozen plagues, hags, Titans, ogres, contortionists. Among us were fire swallowers and aerialists. A fortune-teller said I would find love tonight. Outnumbering all others were the beasts: werebears, steeds, hares, satyrs, rossignols, wildcats, crickets, foxes, peafowl, bears, bulls, mountain goats, wildcats, bonnacons, minotaurs, oxen, unicorns, eels. Costumes sewn and built of real skins and wool, antlers, horns, tails, and hoofs gotten from Pliny House. Beasts from a world none of us would know whirled in a wild play of predator and prey as far as the eye could see.

Over the drums a single ney-player blew into her reed and a lonely pitch rose. A cheer went up, so thunderous I thought Al-Razi's magnificent silk city would collapse. From out of the cheering came more music, as the other players joined in from surprise points all over the tent. Thebes's runners danced in a circle, fully aware of our legendary wildness. Marek roared and flipped backward and leapt over our heads. He danced on his hands in his freakish troll costume. Runners from every roof joined us. The music was infinite and everywhere, and I lost my bearings entirely. We were one, and the sky was full of us. Burn the lines? The memory of Beklemek disappeared in a puff of glitter. There would be other nights to die.

———

The city's cooks and bakers had been busier in their kitchens than we had been on our roofs, and now sent up everything from grilled sausages to cakelets festooned with perfect candied images of every guild mascot. We were so hungry, and there was plenty to eat.

Sometime after noctis, Grid pointed over my shoulder and said, "Look, Odd. There must be a girl for you in that pretty mob."

Excitement rose in me. There were the muses, exactly as I had always imagined, each one a beauty with gossamer wings. When the music stopped, they curled their fingers and beckoned. I looked behind me.

Grid gave me a shove. "Go, before they change their minds."

I adjusted my plume and swaggered toward them, wishing I had oiled my armor. I lifted the visor. "Is there a muse here I can invoke to dance?" They laughed in harmony and made a production of making me guess which of them was which of the nine muses. When I said, "You're short by one! Where, pray tell, is the muse of the dance?" their eyes strayed to something over my shoulder.

I felt a hand brush the back of my neck and a voice said, "Sir Parsival! What troubles you?"

She was gaunt like I was, from starvation, but with a shape gloriously, precisely, mercifully unlike mine. She was tightly wound in a toga, with gold sandals knotted in Xs up her long legs and her tresses in a huge crown sennit of gold on top of her head. Her eyes were the blue-black of the night sky. Her lips, the red of hot sun on the iron wall. "Terpsichore, I presume?"

She arched an eyebrow. "There is one way to be sure."

Oh, I did want to be sure. I grabbed a chalice of rosewater from a merman and presented it to her.

Up until this night, I had practiced a kind of solitary existence on the dance floor, a flailing, twitching, jabbing, hips-forward bit, with my eyes closed and my feet flying over my head. This muse knew what she was doing, so I had to modify my routine, by which I mean I kept my eyes open. I was moving around her, sweating in full armor. I started to remove a gauntlet from my hand so I could touch some part of her and was trying to decide which part, when someone backed into me, hard.

I turned to find that I was staring through my visor at the broad back of a Fremantle guard, with the standard-issue sheaths forming an X across his back. He moved as though to draw both swords at once.

"A Fremantle silverware drawer has trespassed into my space!" I yelled from under my visor. Anything to amuse a muse. But when the guard turned around, the grin disappeared from my face. Fremantle's guards had come tonight in primitive black iron, the most harrowing metalwork wrought by that guild. "Warmonger," I whispered, unable to stop myself. The helmet was a black cylinder. Where a face would be, there was a narrow row of vertical bars, the guard's eyes and teeth white behind it. A beast staring out at me from a cell.

"Name?" the guard demanded, his voice an echo in the chamber.

"Isn't it obvious? What with the grail?" Terpsichore and I both pointed to her drink.

"Guild?" he said.

"Thebes House," I said, less jovially.

"Thebes," he said. "Home of that runner. The felon."

"Aye. And five hundred others who *aren't* him. I am one of those." I reached for Terpsichore, but she had turned to her friends. "I haven't seen Errol Thebes in weeks."

"Is that right?" said the guard. His teeth frightened me. I had just lied to him for no reason. "We've been told he's here tonight."

"You would have to order the removal of all ten thousand costumes to find him." I glanced over the throng. "No one would turn him in."

"Aye. The roofs are surprisingly loyal to him. Some call him a legend." I felt ire rising in me.

"The allegiance can't be a surprise to you," I said. "He's a guildmaster's son. Have you met Margaret Thebes? Allegiance to her is not really what you would call optional. Or to her son."

He studied my face from behind his helmet's bars. "He seems to have allies. Everywhere the fugitive goes, no one will tell us whether he has been there or where he has gone. What does that have to do with his mother?"

"Try this. If he was a foundling, do you think anyone would harbor him?"

I had given him something to think about. He said, "Rumor says he is sacrificing his own future for the future of the city. You're laughing. Is that humorous?"

"Sacrificing what for what? There's no need to fix this city."

"I see."

"We survived Beklemek, if that's what you mean. It's over."

"And the fact that you citizens are locked in your towers?"

I spread my hands. "So we may as well dance." *Where was Terpsichore?*

"We have heard the fugitive believes the uncommon knotting spikes have some power to release the city from a kind of captivity."

"What?"

"The spikes are uncommon."

"Please. Tell me the regnat doesn't believe that. There's nothing uncommon about a pair of junk spikes or about this dull city or our lives in it. Heroes don't come from places like this. Errol Thebes, especially. He grew up farting and belching like the rest of us. If he wants to be Beowulf, there's a bog pot on Thebes that needs a new hinge in the seat. I'm sure we'd all appreciate the hero who fixes that."

The guard paused. "I imagine Beowulf farted at least once." We both laughed at the thought of the great Beowulf passing gas, and I felt an affinity for this guard. I could be frank with him.

"If you knew Errol Thebes like I did, you would see it. He thinks too much of himself."

"It was our impression he was hidden by his beloved friends, certainly by the runners on his roof."

I shrugged, my armor creaking. I bowed in mock obeisance. "I'm forced to love him." The party had moved away from us, and I was distracted by the absence of the muse. My own words made me restless, suddenly. A poison concocted of jealousies and partial truths. At least no one but the guard had heard me.

"'Forced'?" he said, so low I could barely hear him. "Perhaps you would like to see him dropped." I looked at him in surprise. "Could I count on you to give him up?"

"No. I mean, yes. If I only knew where he was—"

"Could you lure him, then?"

"Lure?"

"A friend would know how. I don't think you know Errol Thebes at all."

"What? I know everything. Ask me anything. I just saw him yesterday!"

"So you *lied*—" He shoved me backward.

"No!" I had to pretend I had tripped but I was down. I was scuttling around, trying to get up. Armor is an absurd idea. "Leave me alone—"

"We know who you are. You're the bard of Thebes," he seethed. His helmet was pressed to mine.

"How do you *know* me?" I grabbed at the air trying to find anything to hold.

When had we come this close to the abyss? His hand was on the strap of my breast-plate. If he let go, I would be gone.

"Which do you prefer?" he demanded. "Are you friend or foe of the runner Errol Thebes?"

"Whichever answer will save me!" In a panic, I threw up my visor and grabbed for his legs. I thought we were both falling, but he pulled me back in a shriek of metal and I fell into his arms.

"My hero," I said, panting. Terpsichore was coming toward me through a pack of wolves, and a crowd had gathered.

And then.

Then the black-iron guard, with his back to the crowd, facing only me, reached up and tipped his visor back. I felt my mouth open, then close, but I uttered no sound.

"Parsival, am I right?" said Errol Thebes. "Grail knight? Pure in heart." He dropped his visor and disappeared into the crowd, leaving me at the edge.

IT GETS WORSE.

From a distance I watched him work his way around that party. In that iosal disguise he danced with Talwyn, Grid, Mirembe, Eluned. I wondered whether those girls had any idea who was judging them from under that disguise, or how they would feel if they knew that he was only measuring them against his memory of a girl he had once met in a night kitchen.

I resented that he had let that false interview go on so long, forced me to say all I had said. I turned my back on him and talked with Terpsichore. Talked and danced. Recklessly I put up my visor and kissed her in a way I had never dared to kiss any girl. She touched her tongue to the inside of my top lip, and my body lit up like a flare.

"Do that again," I murmured.

I wanted to forget Errol Thebes. In faith, I wanted to forget Odd Thebes. We danced on and on.

Marek, his voice full of odd cheer, made merry with someone in the crowd. I turned away from Terpsichore, curious to see what could elicit such glee from our grim troll of a roof master.

Jamila Foundling was barefoot on the dance floor. She had plaited her black hair in tight rows, exposing the naught symbol on her neck. She was thin as thread, after Beklemek's starvation, dressed in the drab gray wools of a foundling. I had never understood Marek's interest in Jamila or in the other foundlings who came to the roof of Thebes. Roof masters went where they were assigned and as a rule had little contact with the underbelly of guild life. But I was as thrilled as he was that she was here. I felt loneliness lift at the sight of her.

The muse raised her chalice in high spirits. "You should dance with her! Go ahead!"

"What? No! I don't know her. I just . . . Why is a foundling here?" I said. "It should stay in the morgues."

Terpsichore laughed. "*Costume* party, right? Unless, wait, are you the real Parsival?"

I had never seen Jamila dance. Suffice to say, there was nothing gray or dull about her, despite the rags she wore. If I couldn't hear the music, I would have felt it from watching her move. Here was this foundling, dancing in the open at a runner's party, uninvited, unwelcome. *Nobody notices what's out in the open*, she had said. At the moment nobody could do anything *but* notice her.

When had I crossed the floor? How had I gotten next to her? I unhinged my gauntlets and dropped them and put my hands on her hips. She looked up at me, velvety with sweat in the cold winter air. I could feel the bones under her skin. I ran my finger inside the belt of her leggings. My mind exploded with the feel of her body in my hands.

"Odd Thebes, the Grail Knight," she said. "How many pages have you turned?"

I put my visor up. "You knew me?"

She put her hand inside the sleeve of my armor and swayed her hips playfully in rhythm with mine. I ached with longing. I danced, my body moving with hers. All the chaos in my head, my agitation with Errol, my idiotic efforts to keep the attention of that muse, were gone. I pulled Jamila to me and kissed her.

She pulled away and wiped her mouth with the back of her hand. "Ow," she said. Everyone around us had their eyes on me.

"Ow," I said. "What were you thinking?"

She backed away from me and into the Fremantle guard, who stared at me with his white eyes from behind those bars.

"Stop harassing this runner," he said to me.

"I'll harass anyone I want," I said. I wiped my mouth. "How dare you protect a foundling from *me*?" I grabbed the bars of his helmet and yanked the white eyes close. "From one knight to another, *Cousin*," I whispered into his cage. (And, oh, I must defend myself here. I had already been fooled once on this night.) "How to lure Errol Thebes? Just put any damsel into distress and he'll come running." He and I glanced at Jamila. "Aye. Even a thieving, contagious damsel foundling."

Jamila's eyes went wide with surprise, or more likely pain, now that I think of it. Terpsichore said something I can't remember at all and pulled me away.

And here it comes.

Three strides from Jamila and that blackguard, I stopped in my tracks. I looked back at the two of them, and then ahead of me. A second guard stood twenty yards away, at the archery range. His visor was down, but I could see that he was chatting with Marek Thebes. Marek reached to a waiter's platter and took an eyroun from it, one of those sweet almond desserts piped into an eggshell, and handed it to the guard.

I pointed stupidly. "*That's* Errol Thebes! Over there."

Terpsichore pushed my hand down. "Of course it is, but maybe you should keep that quiet."

I whipped around and saw that the other guard—the one I had been so sure was Errol, the one I had just told to put a damsel *in distress*—oh, he had the edge of his dagger at Jamila's neck and was scraping the naught brand. Jamila was twisting from his grip.

SHE MUST HAVE TRIED to get away from that guard. Jumped from the loft to the nearest fly, to head for the safety of Thebes. But there she hung, utterly still, in the middle of the line. Stalled? Why wouldn't she just drop the makeshift rag and go, hand over hand. *Get over the abyss, across that fly.*

Runners had gathered at the edge of the Al-Razi. I could hear a frantic search for lines to throw her. Someone said, *Just go.* She shook her head no.

I saw the reason. There stood the real black-iron guard, where Jamila's fly met the loft of Al-Razi. He had slipped his sword around the sheath of the silk, leaving nothing but a thin core of invisible thread. Even silk had its limits. Any movement now on the line—if she just shifted to grab the fly itself—would snap it.

Jamila saw me at the edge of Al-Razi and mouthed, *Get help.* The force of just that much motion caused the fibers near the cut to pull farther apart in a spray of moonlight. The crowd gasped. Halfway across the abyss, Jamila dropped silently, two feet more. She was the lure.

There came the sound of a scuffle in the mob and a yell to get out of the way. I was run over by a Fremantle guard, charging full-on, jettisoning the swords from his back, the knives from his belt, his gauntlets, the visor of his helmet, as he built momentum toward the edge. Bee Wolf. No one in this city *ever* leapt untethered from an edge. Even as I write this, I feel my pulse throbbing in my hands. Halfway across the abyss he crashed into Jamila. The shred of her fly-line snapped. Fremantle was one strata lower than Al-Razi tonight. Still, too far. Fifteen feet down, fifty out. Chances were none in a million.

When they hit the roof, they lay still in the snow. She stood up; the crowd cheered from Al-Razi.

Errol walked to the edge of Fremantle to pull up the broken fly. He had never seen such a thing. He examined the break and saw what I had seen: the clear cut of blade work. He turned fast, for now he understood—

He knew her, this foundling who stood before him, holding his helmet out to him. He had played a game of preference with her in a tufuga's tent, and she had known more than she should have, about him and about his mother.

"What did they pay you?" he yelled.

"Pay me?" She wiped blood from her face.

"Was it your freedom? Did you exchange your freedom for this?"

She saw the guards coming down the lines from Al-Razi, coming from all around the roof of Fremantle, running toward the fugitive. She said, "*Wiltu hem to ganganne mid thu?*"

"What?" Before she could say it again, the guards were upon him.

"*Wiltu? Wiltu hem to ganganne mid thu?*" She was yelling it now. She pointed to the edge, speaking his mother's mother tongue.

He looked at her as if she was insane, and then he, too, looked to the edge, to the abyss. He understood then, and shook his head no, as the guards bound his hands and forced him down, with his face in the snow. He struggled for a moment but there were so many of them. He looked up and yelled at her: "*Gea.*" And she turned and ran. No one cared about the lure now, or cared what she did next. They had their fugitive. The foundling was nothing.

The regnat's voice boomed as he emerged from Fremantle behind his torch-bearers, his guards, his pennons, and furs. A scribe was speaking into his ear, telling him everything. The scribe had his arm around one particular guard, who lifted his visor and, from across the abyss, gave me the gladiator's thumbs-up, for I had just made him the regnat's favorite. I turned my back to him, terrified that everyone on the loft had seen that gesture.

The guards stood Errol up, to face the regnat. Instead he turned and looked at Al-Razi. He found me in the crowd. I don't know what he was thinking. He had no idea what part I had in all of this. Still, I kept Parsival's visor down for I was sure he would see the guilt on my face.

"TELL THE WHEREABOUTS OF THE BLACK-IRON SPIKES," yelled the regnat. "We are all ready for the truth." Marek had led the movement across the lines so Thebes could stand with Errol.

"Yes. I wonder about the truth," said Errol. "What is the value of those spikes? What is their power?"

"You are owed nothing," the regnat seethed. "Least of all, answers. I protect this city. You attack it."

Errol's eyes settled on something. I followed his gaze down and saw Jamila, alone on the north corner of Pitcairn. Errol turned to the regnat. "The spikes are mine now. They go where I go."

The scribe said, "The spikes are not on him, Your Honor."

The regnat paled. "Well, the devil can have you, then." Or had he said *double*? "And so you shall drop. Here are the lines. Which do you prefer?"

"I don't understand."

The Fremantle guard stepped up—the regnat's new favorite. "Fremantle offers a one-in-three chance. A choice." There were three massive coils in a hut on the edge of the roof. These were nothing like the silk and iron flies; they were old-fashioned hemp, thicker than a finger. "Only one is shorter than the distance to the earth. The other two lines are fatally long. We change them daily." He was enjoying this. Errol nodded matter-of-factly, as if the guard were describing a banking errand. The guard said, "Which do you prefer?"

Marek was standing next to Errol now. "The third and second are the smallest heaps of coil," he said. "One of those, perhaps—"

Terpsichore whispered, "Take the first."

"With all due respect, I'll take the first," Errol said.

Marek nodded. "What shall I tell your mam?" he said.

"Tell her to send me some soap," said Errol.

"And where is your pack? We will have going-stories to tell. We'll need—" This was unbearable for Marek.

"My tellensac? Xerxes ate it."

Marek laughed grimly. "The iron crow? On Thebes? But you've been gone—" Marek's mouth twisted and I realized he was trying not to weep.

"Thebes is home," said Errol. "And always will be."

"Stay high, runner," Marek said.

"En ye, also," Errol said.

With ten thousand witnesses, the guard yanked Errol out onto a plank that led from Fremantle into thin air. He pulled the navaja from a leather sheath on Errol's belt, thought about where to put it, and dropped it down the breastplate of Errol's own armor. A joke? Or was even the guard nervous? I couldn't tell. There was a commotion in the crowd and a tufuga was brought out—the same one who had tatued a crow on Jamila's arm. He was in his nightclothes and red in the face, carrying a bucket of coals, sizzling in the snowfall. I had no idea why he was here, but Errol knew and removed the vambrace that protected his forearm. The tufuga approached him gingerly across the plank. He put on a thick furnace glove and flinched and whispered an apology as he pulled a branding iron from the bucket, but Errol grabbed the iron and pressed it on his own arm, above the beautiful crow with his outspread wings. There was a hiss and stench of burnt skin, and the tufuga gasped and pulled the brand away.

Errol turned his arm for the regnat to see. *Utlaga*, it read. Outlaw. The tufuga reached into his bag to bandage Errol's arm, but the guard shoved him away and asked what would be the point of that.

Errol put on the helmet, strapped it under his chin, and let the guard bind his wrists. I kept waiting for some sort of mutiny. Were we afraid they would throw all of us, too? Did we accept this as the natural order of the roofs? But this was Errol Thebes! Three guards dragged Errol's chosen rope out onto the plank. The bitter end of it was bound in marline, dyed an ominous bloody red. A guard ran it through the hook on the fly above the plank and harnessed Errol to it.

The first blow of the axes made us cry out. Talwyn shouted, "Idiots!" and Ping wept in Grid's arms. Five more strokes and the plank gave. The message was so final. *We don't want you.* Errol slipped on the plank, slid into the abyss.

The rope spun off its wheel, a mile and a half of hemp, give or take. I put my hand on it and let the friction burn, punishing myself for guilt that sat like a knife in my ribs. After an eternity the line jerked to a halt.

There was no movement. *Would* we see the movements of a single human being on the other end of a rope that heavy? The guards began to roll up the line. I dreaded the idea of what would be dangling on the end of it, how my cousin would look, crushed by a blow with the earth. A similar thought must have occurred to the regnat. He must have known that thousands of runners would finally turn on him if Errol's body came up broken.

He yelled, "Cut the line." The guard threw his rag over the fly and went out to the middle to saw at the hemp rope that held whatever remained of Errol Thebes.

———

When everyone was gone, I glimpsed a movement on the roof of Pitcairn. Jamila. She walked to the edge and dropped the sheath where Errol had dropped. I remembered then what she had said to him. In the ancient tongue of our guild, a language no one but Thebes's own runners would understand: *Wiltu hem to ganganne mid thu?* Do you want them to go with you?

At first he hadn't understood. And then he hadn't wanted to think what was about to happen to him. And then, *Gea,* he had said. Yes.

What I witnessed next, I cannot explain. Jamila leapt from the edge of Pitcairn. She used no line. No plank. I screamed, helpless to stop what I thought was a fatal act. Before I even knew my own mind, I was leaping for a fly to get to her. But a few moments later she appeared on the roof of Djibouti, having dropped a very long way. She leapt from that edge, threw herself off. Again, no rag. No line. Her grace and certainty in leaping exceeded anything I had ever seen. She hit the side of Pliny hard and slid down the wall, sliding and scraping until she caught herself on some small ledge, scaled the wall, dragged herself onto the roof. I lost sight of her.

I arrived first at Thebes and watched her come in. Bruised and bloodied by towers, she came up over the edge. She said nothing to me as she passed.

She knew what I had done. She and that muse Terpsichore and the black-iron guard. I watched her pay the guilder a bribe for passing down into the guild, lift the hatch, and drop into Thebes.

Jamila Foundling did not care whether it bloodied or broke her. She did not care if she fell one strata or ten. Never again would she rely upon a runner or any plan a runner had made or any line a runner had tied or cut.

PART II

THEBES'S RUNNERS MILLED ABOUT in the yurt, stunned by what we had just witnessed. They spoke of irrelevancies: where Sa'id had stacked the kindling from the ships; whether Seppo had left his hoofs at Al-Razi; whether the snow on the streets could cushion a runner from a fall of more than a mile. I was sure they were making small talk so I would go mad and blurt out the one relevant fact: that it was my advice to the guard that had killed their prince.

Marek blew into the yurt and set Errol's pack on the table. He had retrieved it from the iron crow.

"Settle in. We'll be here till dawn," he said.

We fell into restless heaps around the yurt fire. Grid, next to me, was wiping her face on the sleeve of her lightning suit. She looked away when she caught me staring. How could I stop from staring? I had never before seen her cry.

Marek set a kettle on the flames and steeped a remedy of strong herbs he'd make for us when we were sick.

"Stay high." He raised his cup.

"High," we said.

His eyes found mine across the fire. "I have never understood how it happened that you were called to the roofs, Odd Thebes." I felt the blood drain from my face. "Tonight, I believe I will come to know."

He poured out Errol's pack in front of us: a water sack; three ma'amouls wrapped in parchment; a brake clip; a pair of heartwood knotting spikes; a copy of Pliny's *Natural History*; a heavy copy of the laws of the city; three balled-up errand slips; and a small linen bag, embroidered plainly with Errol's initials and with the crow and crossed spikes. Errol's tellensac. Marek passed it to me across the fire.

"No." I put my hands up. But he waved away my objection.

I spread my rag on the roof, put the tellensac on it, and reached to loosen the cord. With my fingers on the knot I met Errol's her-ongean for the first time—his gone-presence.

How to explain? It was an old habit of Errol Thebes's to tie a kitchen knot in this cord. He got the idea from the footnotes of a ship's cook in a book we read once. To detect the work of a common thief in the galley, she would tie her own knot—a kitchen knot—instead of a standard reef knot. Any sailor thieving from the rations would miss the ruse and tie a reef knot to close the bag. They looked alike unless you paid attention. An alarm of sorts. Like that cook, Errol had possessions to guard.

I loosened the cord and spilled out the handful of relics: a three of spades; a sliver of glass; a charred twig; a black-stained wad of muslin; and a baidaq piece from a shatranj set.

"I can't believe he kept that iosal thumb," I murmured to myself.

"So you know his stories," Marek said.

"Of course. Our stories run together—" I put my head back. "Don't ask me to do this."

"Odd Thebes." In my name was the command.

"Talwyn knows him well. Grid. Ping. They all grew up with him."

"He was your cousin," said Grid.

"He was your *best friend*," said Talwyn.

"I hate you all." My eyes watered. I was sure they only wanted me to use those relic tales to spin a line and entangle myself in it. And yet I didn't want to listen to some other fool tell my cousin's stories. I knew him better than any of them did, and I am the bard of this tower.

Fine.

Fine, then.

"*We sitton on thone hrofe usseran huses ond onginnon tha gangende-yeddu Errol Thebes, se the is—*" I began, in the ancient tongue of Thebes House. "We sit on the roof of our home and begin the going-stories of Errol Thebes, who is—" My voice broke as I searched in vain for an end to that sentence.

Grid moved to sit behind me and wrapped her long lightning-flash arms and legs around me. "*Bewrecen*," she whispered in my ear.

"*Bewrecen*," I said gratefully. Exiled. It was better than any other word I had conjured: *crushed, dead, devoured.* "Listen, Errol, as you rise up—" My voice cracked. "One by one your tales will lift you from us."

This was the way runners wanted their going-stories: around a fire, from a bard, and with no end in sight. I leaned back against Grid. The runners lay, too, with their hands resting on one another. They drank of Marek's remedy as they drank of mine. They wanted the irfelaf. The remainder. Whatever I still had of Errol Thebes.

IT WAS A LONG WAY DOWN. Errol ignored the sick feeling that his feet were coming up through his intestines and the urge to curl into a ball to prepare his bones for impact. The towers were a blur in the falling snow. His wrists were still bound.

He could never climb fast enough to remedy the problem of—what had the guard called it?—*a fatally long line*. Still, with the wind whipping, he dropped the navaja into his bound hands, from behind his breastplate. He cut the binding on his wrists and slashed pieces of his tunic and stuffed them into his mouth and into his helmet, to brace his spine.

The street was coming up at him, coming so fast, looking impossibly small—tiny white pools of moonlight spilled on brown wetness. He closed his eyes.

It took so long to fall. There came a colossal screaming in the rope, and he felt the crushing force of the harness on his ribs and heard himself yell out, the air punched from his lungs. And then he was flung upward, weightless, thrown at the sky. Now he was plunging again, and then again back up. Finally the line was still. He dangled five strata over the street, shaking, his mouth thick with blood.

The problem was ironic. The rope had not been too long, but too short.

The line jerked. Errol flailed. Far above, the regnat's guards had begun to wind the rope up. He rose till he was eight strata from the earth and rising fast. If he came back to the roof alive, they would drop him with no line.

His hands shook as he fumbled for the rope over his head. Sawed and hacked and yelled until finally a few strands of frayed hemp held his weight, and he slashed those. He plummeted ten strata, staring up into the sky. At some unbearable speed, he hit the earth.

The world spun. He watched the rope and harness twist above him, the clips clinking, disappearing up and up into the falling snow. In a moment the rope reappeared, and he knew they had cut it. It was falling like a great serpent attacking from the sky. He knew if it had landed fully upon him, it would crush him. His last conscious act was to hurl himself out of its way.

The Twig

"THE BURNT TWIG, FIRST," said Grid.

"Fine," I said, picking up the fragile char of wood I had spilled from Errol's tellensac. I drew in my breath and wandered around in my mind, looking for the beginning of a thread of a tale.

We import fleece and tallow from outside the walls of this city, and bristles and gall and down, I began. Even this yurt we inhabit now is sewn of the skins of former beasts. But we lack a single complete animal in these towers. A silence pervades this city. Aye, nothing clatters on hoofs down our halls, or howls or rises on beating wings into any sky.

When I paused to consider whether this beginning was overly dramatic, they all looked at me with nothing more than expectation, so I went on.

Errol Thebes felt the lack more acutely than any of us. Even when he and I were three, I would find him in his rooms in the guildmaster's quarters, tracing with lead the drawings he found in books and scrolls, of lions and cockerels, wyrms and deer and winged horses. His tracings became drawings. His drawings grew in complexity. The walls of our quarters teemed with wild things.

I once found him weeping at his wall in our room. This was later. We were maybe seven or eight times around the sun.

"Heft ye lost at maw?" I asked him. No, I shall tell it in the common tongue: "Did you lose at cards again? Your face is sopped."

"Nay," he said, shaking his head.

"Then what?"

"I will never know equus," he said.

"Equus?" My mind ranged for the translation of that old word. I looked at the wall and saw it. "A *horse*?"

"Aye. I'll never even see one, never mind hold one in my arms or tame it or ride on its back holding its mane."

"A horse is what you're sobbing about? You're the guildmaster's son. How bad can it be for you?"

He shrugged his small shoulders. "I would rather have the horse."

"Are you insane?"

"Aye, so the rumors have it. And nay."

Such were the beginnings of Errol's longings, for, as you all know, beasts were not his only deficit.

When his brothers were dropped from the roof, his mam, the guildmaster Margaret Thebes, had sent her last son, Errol, to live with my family, her sister's kin. I followed him nightwise and knew his secret, that after Mam slept, Errol snuck out to wander the halls of the tower. Down he went to the woodshops, where he buried himself in wood shavings and could sleep. One night, I kicked the shavings and woke him up.

"We all know you're better than us. Too good to sleep in our quarters," I said. "Do you have to rub it in?"

"I miss my brothers," he said.

"They're gone. Dead and gone."

He pointed to a beam where Fenn and Rip Thebes had carved their names. Even their vandalism was héafodstede. Sacred.

"Don't you hate them for being *utlaga*? Wicked outlaws? For leaving you behind?"

"Aye," he said. "And nay."

One night the master guilder, Wahid Thebes, known to us as Woody, discovered Errol in his shop. The kelp was running one of the woodworkers' planes along the edge of a bench, producing a thin curl of ironwood. When Errol realized Woody was watching him, he hid the blade behind his back.

"I won't have you whittling the furniture down to a toothpick," Woody said. He had hands as broad as dinner plates.

"Don't throw me out," said Errol.

"Find me any reason not to."

"I've no place to go in this guild. I'm lower than a foundling."

Woody grunted. "You're the guildmaster's son. The whole tower is yours."

"Nay. Margaret Thebes is grievous. My cousins hate me, save Odd. I miss my dropped brothers. The aunt is weary. The uncle frightens me." Errol's voice went so quiet I hardly could hear him from the hall. "And my own da is extinct." Woody ran his big hands over his face. He barely ever spoke to kelps. Errol kicked the workbench. "Also I will never see a horse or any beast, jammed forever as we are, in this tower."

Woody grunted again. "First you will learn not to carve excuses. Second, you'll not thieve from me." He reached out his hand, and Errol produced the stolen plane. "Third and fourth, you will bathe and eat. I won't have you smelling like a fart in my shop. After all that, I'll teach you about wood."

———

A shipment arrived from Albacete House, two dozen glistening knives Woody laid out on a workbench. A choice. He was surprised, delighted, to watch the kelp point instead to a knife on another bench, to Woody's favored blade, with its perfect edge and worn leather haft. Woody instructed Errol to use the navaja to free any creature from any scrap of ironwood or heart pine he could find in the shop.

"I left a fold of muslin at my bench," he said. "Bandage the wounds you inflict on yourself. The midwife will sew you, when it comes to that. And I've set a fire in the oven, which you'll keep stoked with your errors. Look at some scrolls or books to remember what beasts look like. Any of my apprentices can show you how to carve an eye without gouging it out, a tail without lopping it from a rump. Sit here at my bench. When you do finally carve some fair approximation of a beast, a month from now or a year, I will teach you from there."

My heart leaps even now, to think of this offer. Woody Thebes was second in this tower only to the guildmaster. He oversaw the work of the guild. He never ate with the guilders, played cards or danced with us, listened to our gossip, or even attended the guild meetings where work shifts and apprentices were assigned. If he slept, it was in a bed none of us could find. He was known within the city and, rumor had it, even outside the wall, for his uncommon skill. What I—what any of us kelps—would have given to be taken into his tutelage, we did not own.

Woody turned to go, his broad shoulders filling the doorway.

Errol called out, "I'll give you a stag, Master Wahid."

"Overreaching," Woody said. "The antlers will snap off in your fingers. The ripples of the chest will be surgical mishaps. Half the apprentices who begin with an antlered beast can salvage nothing more than the form of a wild boar with a misshapen head and stub legs. When the boar also fails to materialize, half of those can reduce the wood to a serpent. Even a stiff spike of a serpent will be a trick for a kelp of eight."

Errol bristled. "A guildmaster's son should be able to carve a stag."

"The guildmaster's son will be a skinny, old, dying man before he begins his training, if he sets impossible tests for himself."

But Woody Thebes had no idea how fresh those beasts were in Errol Thebes's heart. The kelp, his little feet dangling from the rungs of Woody's high stool, sat at that bench all day and night while Woody was gone to oversee the forges and the workrooms. Twice, food arrived on a tray from the guild kitchens. Twice, Errol ate nothing—well, nothing but the ma'amouls, for he had an insatiable sweet tooth.

The apprentices working their shifts down the hall were mad with jealousy. *They* had not come to Woody until they were fifteen, and even then their parents had had to pay, and they had been required to carve scrap beasts on their own time, in their own quarters. Not one of them came close to Woody's workroom, never mind his own bench. In faith, all them now rather hoped Errol would appear at their benches for help, so they could work him over and send some diminishing gossip about him up to the shops. But all was quiet in that workroom. So they gave themselves false errands that would take them, instead, to him.

They stood at the bench and stared, gape-mouthed.

Soon enough, a different sort of gossip buzzed in the tower, and the whole guild began to file past Woody's door to see this thing for themselves. When Woody Thebes himself returned long after the somnium bell, he pushed through a crowd.

"Begone, you foul things," he said. To himself he muttered, "What? Have they never seen blood before?"

There was no blood. The room was neatly swept, and a tidy fire burned in the stove. A thick pile of sketches lay on the workbench. The drawing on the top of that pile was a rendering of the joint between the skull and the antler of a red deer, with a tuft of fur indicated. Woody held the page in his big hands. He could not help but feel pleasure rise in his chest. None of his apprentices appreciated the work of drawing their carvings beforehand. Across the room, on a shelf, something like movement caught his eye. A tiny wild boar trotted across the shelf—not literally, of course, but in a posture so real Woody Thebes swore he heard the racket of tiny hoofs. A snake was coiled around the boar's neck, an ornamental collar, the diamonds in its scales tinier than heads of pins.

Woody heard a murmur and looked behind him. The kelp was asleep in the corner on the floor, wrapped in Woody's own ragged work sweater. He had something in his hand.

The heart-pine stag was so tiny the master could close his fingers around it and make it disappear in his palm, and yet it gave the appearance of massive bulk. Its legs were spread wide as though to support the heft of its chest and antlers, which rose in a flourish over its noble head and splayed over the shoulders and tail. Woody set the tiny stag down on the bench. "Level," he whispered. The beast surveyed the room as if it owned them all.

"Look at you," Woody said softly to the kelp. "You are more even than Rip or Fenn."

" 'Tis not your place to judge," a woman's voice boomed behind him. Woody flinched and turned to see Margaret Thebes blocking his doorway. "He will not rise, Wahid Thebes."

"You've always been iron on him," said Woody. "He will make an able apprentice, even this early. Look—"

Margaret took the stag as though to admire it, but crushed it in her hand and threw it in the fire. "I'll not lose another son," she said.

"You'll lose Errol Thebes either way," said Woody, a muscle twitching in his jaw. "A guildmaster's son rises. You knew that at the start of this—"

"He'll live with my sister."

"That's a fool's judgment. Your sister's a rag of a woman, and she's got nothing but the drunken husband. From Heimdall the liar to Odd the eavesdropper, they do half an uur of work a month. Errol Thebes will be neither a guilder nor a runner, raised by that lot. He'll amount to nothing."

"That is precisely the point."

"I won't stand for it. We've made a bargain, you and I. You've already robbed me once, and you won't have another chance."

Margaret raised her hand fast to hit him, but he grabbed it. She hissed, "I'll drop you and the kelp if you speak of a bargain again."

Oh, but he was her match. "I am caged in this guild with you, *Guildmaster*. The only pleasure I have is to raise this kelp, who can already free a beast from a scrap of wood. Drop me if you will. I'll relish the quick freedom before I meet the earth. But let him rise. You owe it." I gasped, in the hall. Could anyone talk to the guildmaster that way? "Get out," he said.

"If you'll have me gone," said Margaret, "let go of my arm."

Woody reached into the fire to remove the pieces of the stag. He pressed his fingers on each point of the broken antlers, to extinguish tiny flames. In a low voice, he said, "Forget what you've heard, lying there awake, Errol Thebes. No doubt your cousin in the hall will remember it for you. Fetch our breakfast. Your nights belong to you, but your days are mine now. I'll raise you to run this guild. This guild is yours if only you live long enough."

Purgament

CONCEALED IN THE BROWN MURK, in the stench of the streets, Errol lay still. He was a runner of movement and high air, accustomed to the sway of towers, to the force of clean winds. He spat the bloody cloth from between his teeth, wrenched the black-iron helmet off his head. Blood returned to his legs, and that hurt. The armor shifted on his skin. His broken ribs expanded, and that hurt. He knew neither what day it was nor how long he had lain in purgament. He heard bells ringing, a mile overhead, before the world went dark again.

The Shard

"THAT BIT OF GLASS," said Talwyn.

I accepted another cup of Marek's elixir and held it to warm my hands. "The shard," I said, "is a story of what did *not* happen."

Thebes Guild contained more than a hundred kelps when we were young. We ran as a mob: were fed, whipped, and worked as one. Guild life lacked the quotient of drama we required, so we lived through tales from books and scrolls, acted them out from epistola to dulcibus, reviewed them in our sacks, arguing over which of us was Parsival or Jason or Odette till we fell asleep. Our grandmothers did not refer to us as boys or girls. We were just *wuscbearns* to them. Dear little ones. And we were just kelps to our mams, and we were all Icarus and we were all Helen, and we stepped easily over such borders that would soon be silken screens and then iron walls.

"You be Icarus today!"

"Naw. I been Icarus all week and I've a bruise on every bone to show for it."

I was conjuring Talwyn and Ping, from when they were kelps. Everyone was laughing. So I kept it going, our childhood selves—

"Hey all! Sa'id Thebes won't get out of the sack if he isn't Robin Hood."

This was Faisal—

"Fine. Tell him to bring his own felons."

This was Ping. Do I need to name them all? You get the idea. I was going around the fire—

"And I shall be Lancelot and I shall be wild for Helen from Troy."

"That's rot, Grid! Lancelot was wild for Gwenhwyfar."

"Not after he rubbed his eyeballs on Helen."

"Then Odd Thebes shall be Helen, to rile you."

"Nah. Odd has to be Homer or we forget the gruesome kissing."

"Fine. So Eluned will be Helen. And Talwyn will be the faithful Penelope and she'll wait twenty years for Odysseus to stumble home from refusing to look at a map."

"Forget it! I wouldn't wait twenty seconds for any of ye foul wens."

"Lucre and rot, Talwyn! Be Mabh, then, and wait for none."

"Aye. I am Mabh. And in that state I'll gallop night by night, through lovers' brains and then they'll dream of love."

"Quit it, Talwyn. We didn't start yet."

"And Errol Thebes is Beowulf again."

"Feh! I just saw him, quill to the page at Woody Thebes's, and he demands we make him Daedalus the Inventor. And make me the bee wolf."

"Naw, Odd. Errol must be Beowulf, for he is the only one who remembers to go back for the dying warriors and to unfurl the flags. And you cannot be Beowulf, for you are Homer on all shifts."

"Feh. Give him a iosal horse, then. He says he'll be Beowulf if you give him the horse."

"There wasn't a mount in *Beowulf*. Tell that iosal news to Errol Thebes."

"Shut it, Faisal. There wasn't a ship on the beanstalk last month, nay, but we hauled it up the stalk, didn't we? Aye, because you all said you always had to have your ship with you, even on a dry bean."

We all were laughing now, at the kelps we had been.

These tales of ours unspun for days and years, stopping only when our mams and das called us up to be thrown in a tub or a sack.

One day, when we were pretending to be Beowulf and the Argonauts, Errol sent me down to storage on the thirteenth strata to find fletching feathers for the archers' arrows. We were fully nine now, the two of us.

I was alone, the dim light of my head lamp flickering in the storage rooms. I opened a closet and reached past crates and cartons for a box in the back.

I screamed, for a skinny, horrifying creature startled me from the back of the closet. He was nearly my size. Bony and angular. Short on chin, with a hurricane of black hair over bead eyes and an enormous nose. He stared back at me from the neck of green robes as baggy as my own. I reached my fingers toward him. He reached for mine. When we touched, I smiled and he smiled back broadly, with great black gaps between his teeth. Have I mentioned his nose?

In the yurt, my fellow runners all laughed. For they knew I was barding, likely embellishing, and they knew what was coming.

"Are you the bogle of Thebes Guild?" His lips formed words when mine did, but he was silent. I had my fingers up against glazing. Was this a portal to some other world? I brought my knuckles up to rap on the glass and stopped, for his hand did the same. I moved my fingers and watched his same fingers move as mine did.

"No! Feh! It is naught but my own self!" I yelled. I turned up my lamp and he turned up his. "*No!*"

I had never seen a mirror before. None of us had. By decree, as long as Margaret was guildmaster, there were none in Thebes. So we lacked a way of seeing ourselves. Except here was this mirror someone had forgotten. I moved closer to the glass to see who I was.

All along I had thought I was a wild thing. A warrior! With fervor in my face, the great chest, my powerful limbs, and the play of my hips in the knife belt I slung over them. Every morning, when all you kelps cast Errol as Beowulf over and over again, and I was yet again the bard or Helen of Troy or some nameless Argonaut, I thought to myself that it was just charity on your part. Charity toward Errol. He never bothered to order his men around as I would do. He didn't yell or carry on the way captains ought to. I had always told myself that you secretly thought I, Odd Thebes, should be Beowulf, with the wild-haired, warmongering look about me. Terror of Grendel, I had thought. Terror indeed. There was this huge nose in the middle of me. No wonder I was Homer on every shift.

I looked behind me at Grid, who was braiding my hair, and said, "I am able to tell this story now, by the way, for the midwife told me when I left for the roofs that I am now taller than all of you and proportional in every way: big nose, big hands, big feet, very big—"

To which Grid whispered, "Mouth."

In front of the mirror, I thrust my jaw forward and made muscles in my sinewy little arms. This is what I was doing when Errol found me. His hand lay on the hilt of Fragarach, his lie-sniffing sword.

"We thought ye lost at sea, Odd Thebes," he said. "What bogle has caught ye?"

"Nothing! Nothing caught me."

"Then where are the fletching feathers?"

"In some cursed box."

"What are you staring at? Wait—is that a mirror? But mirrors are felonies in Thebes—" He came toward it.

"There's just this one and only mirror," I said, blocking him from it. "It's mine. I'm in the middle of pillaging it."

"I must see it."

"No. You mustn't."

"I just want to know—do I look like my brothers? Or my gone da? Or like you, even? We're cousins, so perhaps—"

"*No.* No, you don't look anything like me," I said. "You don't look like anyone." He tried to see over my shoulder into the glass, but I stood on my toes. "You have to pay. Are you carrying a thousand uurs with you?" He shoved me aside. I yelled, "Here's the truth! You have wens!"

He put his fingers to his face. "I don't *feel* wens."

"They're flat. And blue."

"I want to see them. It's better to know."

"Fine! Fine. Take your chance, then. Go ahead. You are no Bee Wolf. You're a foul thing. But don't worry about it. I will still be your friend, pathetic though ye are. And wen-covered."

He studied me now. "You're lying to me, Odd Thebes. Why? Consider yourself. Ye look like—"

"Grendel, I know it," I said. "I've just seen myself."

"Not Grendel. You're the spitting image of your da."

I stabbed at him then, with my wooden dagger and he unsheathed Fragarach fast and hit me full in the chest with the broadside. I doubled over, the breath robbed from my lungs. I kicked him between the legs and felled him. We rolled around on the floor, slapping and punching each other till we were winded. Finally we stood up, both of us stunned and gasping. He turned yet again to look into the mirror, but I grabbed Fragarach from him and crashed the sword hard into the silvered glass, which shattered into a thousand pieces. He grabbed my shoulders and swept his foot under both of mine and dropped me to the floor, pinning me on jagged shards.

"Ow?" I said.

"What is this about?" he said.

"Nothing. I'm not Slyngel. I'm not my drunken da or any of my brothers. You're hurting me."

"Who are you, then?"

"Who's asking? Who are *you*?" I demanded.

"Errol Thebes, of course. Your cousin. The guildmaster's son. Brother of dead men."

"A kelp with his da gone missing," I added, digging into him.

"Aye. Long gone," he said. "And you?"

I closed my eyes hard. The picture of that creature in the mirror would not leave me.

"Feh. I don't know. Let me up."

I marched ahead of him for thirty strata. Back at *Argo*, I threw myself in with the rest of the oarsmen, pretending to row up the forty-third strata of Thebes. We were fools. Beowulf never rode in Jason's flagship. And what was Errol doing standing in the bow like that, with his foot on the hull, the flags unfurled in the dead air of a guild hallway?

If he *had* seen himself, he would have been unbearable. The strength of him even then. The warrior, he was. Or the warmonger. All that's left from that mirror now is this shard of silvered glass, too small even to see his whole eyeball. A fragment of his own self. He never knew the whole of what we saw when we looked at him.

THE PAIN OF INHALING with broken ribs was worse than any pain he had read about in books. He couldn't actually remember anyone describing that. Maybe they all did and he ignored it. Wet ice had crusted on his face. He was so cold he could not feel the difference between his own skin and the black-iron armor. He lay back and stared up into the abyss. He could hear the steady rushing of wind. Or possibly that was the river.

The Remains

THE BLACK-STAINED MUSLIN held the shape and form of a human thumb and had the smell of blood-iron and amputation about it. Faisal picked it from my rag by its frayed edge. It was a fearful thing, and the tales that seethed around it frightened even me.

"This relic is a *maso-swefn*, a snaring dream," I began. "If you ask me who did it, at the end, I'll tell you I don't know. Judge for yourself."

When Errol Thebes was seven times around the sun, a rumor circulated like a contagion in the tower that he was haunted by a bogle. One by one, his possessions were going missing. Most disappeared never to be seen again, but some—some were found. He lost his pillow from off his bed. Days later the sopping wad of it was dredged from the bottom of a vat of wood dye in the shops. A pair of his lost leggings were found tangled in the gears of the guildhall clock. His quills were found jabbing through the bedding under a guilder recovering in the midwife's quarters from a furnace burn. The rumor of a bogle held the place of a serious concern that the sole remaining heir to the tower was a danger to us all.

It came in fits and starts. More than once, Errol begged me to admit the fact he thought everyone was keeping from him: that he had a wen deep in his mind that was the cause of his troubles. How else but by some slippery tumor could he explain his forgetfulness or, worse yet, the mischief he caused, unaware of himself, in the guild? I assured him he was healthy, for I had interrogated the midwife.

When we were coming back from work one night, Errol questioned the men playing cards in the halls outside my family's quarters. Had they seen the thief, making off with his things?

"It's that handsome bogle of yours," one of them said, discarding into the pile. They all laughed, all but my father, Slyngel Thebes, who squinted at Errol as though he could see more or less than what was there. Da was always on the whiskey.

"Has hoofs," he slurred.

No one in Thebes had ever seen a bogle. We lived in towers made of stone and iron. We had no ghosts, fiends, frights, changelings, or such, and nothing to fear but a dull guild life stretching on and on and on. Still we had books, and we had nightmares. In mine, the bogle was a squat, grinning, leathery little mistake with foul mischief in its fingers. Hoofs, fangs. It would lie in wait with hectic eyes under your bed, or make you appear to have boiled your own pillow in a vat of dye. I preferred the idea that Errol had a tumor.

Margaret Thebes was the only one in the guild who dared speak publicly of any of this. Errol was our prince but he was just her kelp. For one guild meeting, Errol arrived half dressed. Margaret bellowed at him, "Are ye so thick now as to have lost your tunic yet again?" He was nine.

"Aye," said Errol, his voice barely audible over the sounds of five hundred guilders staring.

"Do without, then. *Cold*, you might for once remember where you forgot your shirt."

"Yes, Mam."

"See all these guilders here?"

He turned. "Aye."

"Look at their hands."

"I see them."

"Ask these guilders, with their hands worn by labor, if they're glad to waste a precious day's work, sewing fine tunics so you can cram them into the bog pipes." I was standing next to him, feeling for once at an advantage, to have the other sister for *my* mam. He was desperate not to cry in front of them all. "Ask them!" she yelled.

He stared at the floor. "Will ye waste your precious work on me?"

Who knew what to say, caught between the guildmaster and her kelp?

"You're just like your brothers. I can't bear the sight of you. Wild things and reckless. Does Wahid Thebes permit you in his woodshop, half naked like that?"

"Odd lends me his tunic," Errol said.

Margaret shifted her glance to me, as if seeing me for the first time. "You're Odd Thebes," she said. If I wasn't Odd Thebes, I would have been now, such was her command of that guild.

"Aye, Mam."

"Gudrun's kelp."

"Aye."

"Give him your tunic," she said. I pulled my tunic over my head and handed it to Errol. I crossed my spindly arms to cover my skinny kelp chest. "You're a gossip, Odd Thebes. Why must you tell other people's stories?"

The question flew at me from nowhere. I blurted, "I wish I were Beowulf sometimes. Odysseus. The Robbing Hood. Or anyone else. But I'm always Homer."

Her laugh was unfriendly. "Homer had no stories of his own."

"Yes he did."

"Tell us one." My mouth opened and closed. Margaret waited, knowing full well I had nothing on Homer. "You are the gossip who's inventing the rumors about Errol Thebes."

"No!"

"Half the guild says so." Margaret was silent for a long while. "Truth is slippery. Whoever tells the story decides the truth. Odysseus could have been a fool for all we know. Homer *made* him. Who can check his facts? You want that power, don't you?"

"No!" Yes, I did.

She said, "Leave Errol Thebes's story alone."

I hated her from then on. I didn't care about her wasting-grief over the loss of two sons, the shame she carried of a bound husband who had done something so final that his name was blotted from guild records, or why she protected and punished my cousin in equal parts when he was the sole remnant of her family. Why was I so important suddenly, that she would take me on in front of the entire guild? Then it occurred to me. She wasn't mad. She was afraid. She was afraid of a story.

During Beklemek of our tenth year, a bony foundling appeared at our door to report that "a tellensac marked with the guildmaster's son's initials had been found in the"—here it hesitated—"in the luggage." Gudrun Thebes gave Errol a mam-look.

Neither of us had ever been lower in Thebes than the seventh strata. We had never seen the so-called luggage, which was the foundlings' polite term for the trunks that had once served to hold guilders' possessions but now held the guilders themselves. We were going to the morgues.

Foundlings lined the tunnels to watch us pass, hiding behind cloaks and blankets. The morgues branched off in the halls in every direction; guilders from a thousand years were entombed above and below us. I was shaking. I would never rid myself now of the realization that the whole tower was little more than a mass grave with a remnant population living on top of it.

"Why didn't the foundling just bring the tellensac to you?" I whispered behind Errol.

"It can't touch what belongs to the guildmaster's son," he said. "Foundlings are contagious."

"More contagious than this place?"

"Aye."

"What's the penalty if he touches your things?"

"Death."

"And what if he touches *my* things?"

"Death, also, seeing as you are related to me." I was filled with a sense of my own importance.

I took a step back when the foundling opened the trunk. The tellensac had been stuffed between the waxy fingers of the corpse, with the two items that had been in it by then—a shard and a twig—spilled on the floor. The body was folded into the box. The lips had pulled back from gums and teeth.

"How did you know the tellensac was here?" I said to the foundling. I was trying to calm myself while Errol picked his relics off the floor.

"I sleep on this trunk," he said, gesturing to a rag that was his bedding. "One night I found it unlocked."

"Who would do such a thing?" I said.

I had meant, *Who the hel would sleep on a coffin?* but the foundling said to Errol, "You must have an enemy. Would you want me to get that for you? I could use a rag. If you fear death—"

"I fear nothing," Errol said. He grabbed the sac from the dead guilder's hands and the twig and shard from the floor and bolted for the tunnel. Seconds later he and I stood panting on the landing outside of the midwife's ward.

"For someone who fears nothing, you run fast," I said. The blood was pumping so wildly in my ears I thought I was only imagining a woman's voice around the corner of the wall.

". . . must allow the kelp his mischief, his bogling of himself," she was saying. "Hiding his tellensac down there in the morgues. He knows his tales belong there, secrets and lies as they are."

I turned to Errol. "She's talking about *you*," I said, alarmed. But Errol put his finger to his lips.

"Secrets and lies," she said again. "I should drink—aye, you're right—and forget it. But if I go on the whiskey, I lose my skills. I regret the day he was born." She stood to my right with her back to me, working at something on her table.

I was watching her so closely I failed to see the guilder on the other side of the midwife's ward till a voice rose in a puling slur, "*Bulluc stertep, bucke uertep, murie sing cuccu.*" I nearly leapt out of my skin. It was my da, Slyngel Thebes, slumped in the midwife's birthing chair, his thin neck bent under the weight of his porous slab of a nose, singing: *The bull stirs, the stag farts, and we sing cuckoo . . .*

"Was that your da?" Errol whispered from behind me.

"Nay. Some drunk." I pushed him away, mortified.

"Meanwhile," the midwife droned, "I vowed to keep my mouth shut while she has Woody Thebes train the unsteady kelp to lead us."

"Ah yes, the hoofed one," my father slurred. He caught sight of me then. "Feathers," he whispered. Did he know me? Was that a grin or a leer on his face? Just then Errol came around the corner, though, and Slyngel Thebes heaved himself up and yelled, "Look! Hoofs! Speak of the beast!"

The midwife turned fast. "Errol Thebes! Odd! Damn! Have you heard all that I said? Please dinna tell! Please! I'll drop for it!"

We weren't going to tell anybody anything. We ran again, faster than we'd run any guild stair race, and reached the nineteenth strata before we even exhaled. I slammed the thick wooden door between our quarters and the hall.

Errol punched the stone wall. "I will show her 'unsteady'! I will creep down to her rooms in the night and jab her with a knife. And everyone will think it was your foul da that did it." I thought he would hit me for being the son of my da, but he collapsed on the floor with his face in his hands. "Tell me what to do, Odd Thebes. You know me better than anyone. Am I bogling my own self?"

"Definitely not!" I said, although I was unsure. I sat next to him. "Here's the truth. On her deathbed, your mam will admit she was the very bogle stealing your things and pressing them in her kelpie diary." This was meant to sting him for what he'd just said about my hideous da, but the idea of his mam, severe as she was, pressing anything in a diary made us both laugh.

The bogling hardened him. By the time we were twelve, he could argue with anyone on any subject: the precise height of the wall that surrounded our city, the presence or absence of gall in ink. He was glad when arguments turned to fistfights.

Still I would wake in the night in our shared quarters and find him standing up in his bedroll, sopped in sweat.

"Again a nightmare?" I was half asleep.

"Again it felt real." He was wide-awake.

His drawings frightened me. One sketch showed the head of the bogle, with the jaws pried open on a stick. The mandible had burst from the gums, with teeth budding in spirals around the bone like eruptions from a wound.

One night I woke to the sound of my mam whispering outside the door of our room.

"So much of his life is lost," she said. "It's no wonder the kelp forgets where he puts his things."

My father belched. "You haven't two bits of brain to rub together, Gudrun. He forgets nothing. You know it's no fairy bogle haunting Errol Thebes. Your sister herself brought this on. That fiend of hers haunts this tower—"

Mam slammed a cup down. "You'll be spending the night in the library again," she said, "if you have so much free time as to use it counting my brains."

When I left for breakfast in the morning I stepped over my da splayed on the floor in the hall, sleeping in the slick of his own drool.

"How you and Mam managed to breed nine kelps together, I have no idea," I said. I never told anyone the thought that occurred to me at that moment: Slyngel Thebes himself was never far from my cousin.

Errol burst into the Great Hall one morning, demanding to know where someone had put his tool chest. He was fourteen by then: a pelt and volatile. Across the table from me, my brothers Heimdall and Ragnar, older than we were by a decade and well into their careers as idiots, exchanged mocking glances.

But my mother came flying down the stairs from the guild kitchens. "All is not well!" she screamed. "There be summat in the ovens!" It was an odd thing to say. There was always something in the ovens. Everyone in the hall raced to see what had frightened Gudrun Thebes. My eyes stung at the oily smoke that filled the kitchen.

"Gudrun, were ye baking the tool bench?" one of the guilders said, waving black smoke from the open oven.

Mam's voice was shrill. " 'Tis not my doing! Why would I?!"

Errol slipped through the crowd and grabbed his precious navaja from the oven, so blazing hot it hissed as it seared his skin. His tools were laid out on the oven racks—chisels, planes, a bevel—their edges glowing in the flames, their wood handles turned to ash.

"Woody will kill me," he whispered.

"Why would you do this, Errol Thebes?" screamed my mam. Errol backed away as though she had hit him. "I mean to say, who would do this to you?"

"Why don't you ask your hardworking bound-husband?"

Mam flinched, but there indeed was my father, huddled under the bread table.

"That fiend!" Da shrieked and we all leapt at the pitch of fear. "See it!" He jabbed at the air with his grimy finger. "Lurking in this guild all these long years. Look at it! Look! I will CATCH IT! I will make it face its undoing. Why will none of ye look?!"

I turned to look behind me but saw nothing.

Well, that is not exactly true. I told myself that the shapeshift in the hall was the play of lamplight or some guilder leaving the scene.

"You're mistaken, Slyngel Thebes," Gudrun said. "'Tis but Errol Thebes standing here, and not a fiend."

"The hoofed one? Where?"

"Right in front of you," said Mam. "You're pointing right at him."

"What? No! I'm pointing to—" And then Slyngel actually seemed to see Errol. "I cannot bear it!" he said, sobbing. "I cannot be the one who knows what I know! Look at him! Look at all of you! With your tusks, fangs, udders! Covered with fur! Leave me alone!" He tipped his flask over so a drop leaked out of it onto his gray tongue. He flung the empty thing down the hall and ran after the clattering of it. Such was the chaos that was my father.

Heimdall spit on the floor. "Slyngel Thebes is sopped, Mam. And Errol Thebes is a fool who can't tell the difference between his workbench and an oven."

Errol came down on Heimdall out of nowhere, with the force of a sledging hammer, pounding him in a fury of fists. By the time three furnace guilders pulled Errol off him, Heimdall was so bloody and swollen he looked like the bogle in Errol's drawings.

Margaret Thebes summoned Errol to her quarters that night. I shadowed him.

As if wasting gold and guild work on Errol's absentminded foolery wasn't bad enough, she said, the guild was now frightened of him. If he could think of nothing better to do than burn his tools, attack his fellow guilders, and upset the fragile order of a guild tower, she would have him confined.

"More confined than I am already?" he said.

I took a step back, for Margaret was frightful. But Errol moved toward her. He had nothing to do with the bogling, he said. In fact, he had begun to keep his belongings in a locked trunk, and gave the key to me every night for safekeeping. The lock showed no signs of tampering. Still his clothes, drawings, books, his tellensac, and now his tools themselves continued to disappear. He had sprinkled talc on the floor to track the bogle, even if it was his own trail, but never were there footprints.

He pulled a scrap of parchment from his pocket and thrust it at her. "Suspects," he said.

Margaret read the list aloud. On it were the names of all the guilders in Errol's woodshop (except, of course, for Wahid Thebes), the apprentices who worked alongside him, my brothers, my sisters, my own mam who had taken him in, Slyngel Thebes, all of Errol's friends, and finally me, Odd Thebes.

"I'll thank you for leaving me off your list," said Margaret.

"It can't be you," Errol said. "Everyone knows you stay as far from me as this quarantined guild tower allows. You spend all your time talking to the iosal foundlings."

Her eyes narrowed. "Watch yourself, Errol Thebes. You're at an edge."

"So are you," Errol said. "Don't summon me again until you know more than I do."

I thought Margaret would eat his eyes for such audacity, but something had frightened her. When Errol had mentioned the lock undone without a key, the lack of footprints in the powder, she had steadied herself with a hand on the table. I should have told Errol, but I was wounded by the appearance of my name on his list of suspects and didn't speak to him for the better part of an uur.

———

Back on the roof of Thebes, at the runners' fire, Marek had gotten up to pace the edge. I was distracted by him.

"I warned you," I said. "It's a long thread of a tale."

"Not just a thread. A knot. A serpent tied in a tight knot," he said.

"I can leave it untold. There are other relics."

"No."

"You doubt my telling."

"No."

"What bothers you, then?"

"Errol would be with us now if this had been solved."

"Nay. This tale was kept in a locked guild."

"Aye," Marek said. "Similarly, Errol's possessions were kept in a locked trunk."

From then on Errol and I haunted Thebes's halls, on the prowl for anything that took the shape of his fear. After one such night we returned to the nineteenth strata to find a throng of guilders crowded at the hall door to our very sleep quarters.

"There be summat carrying on in your room," Mam said when she saw us. "What have ye hidden in there? A girl?"

"Never," I said. "Well, I mean, not so far—"

"They think it's Cerberus."

We heard a crash on the other side of our door. The mob stood silent, waiting.

"It's the bogle," Errol whispered to me. He put his key in the lock, held up his lamp, and shoved the door open. "Show yourself!" he yelled.

The laundry guilder beside me was the first to scream. A fierce, black blur shot from our room as if from a catapult, hissing and slashing with claws and fangs as it passed my head.

The hall was chaos. I was thrown against a wall. Most of the mob fled. A half dozen guilders cornered the beast and pinned it with brooms. One beat its head with a shovel. Errol plunged into the crowd throwing guilders out of his way. I thought he was going to join the killing. Instead he pulled the leather belt from his leggings as he ran. "Draw back!" he yelled. When they withdrew their brooms, the beast lunged. Errol was faster. He yanked the animal by its tail with one hand. The beast whipped around with unnatural speed and sank its jagged teeth into the belt Errol held in his other hand.

"There, now," Errol said, to a hall gone silent. "Everyone step away."

No one needed to hear the order twice.

Errol dragged the creature through the crowd to our rooms on the strength of its own grip on the belt. The guilders cleared their throats and murmured as we passed. They were embarrassed for having delivered such a beating. None had seen a beast of any kind before.

We calmed the beast, which is to say I stood on a chair reading the volume of Pliny's *Natural History* and his descriptions of all the beasts of the world, while Errol scratched under the animal's chin.

"*Stille,*" he said. "*Stille, wael-geuga.*" Hush, little wild beast. Finally Errol pulled its fangs out of the belt and washed the blood from its head. With its mouth closed and its fur no longer standing on end, the beast appeared significantly smaller than when it was trying to murder us all. It was the size of a soup cauldron. Its eyes were black beads on a long, flat triangle of a head, with a black nose at the tip and a stripe of pure white between its ears. As it limped around the edges of the room, its claws clicked on our stone floor.

"Pliny says here, fangs are typical of the beast known as *catoblepas,*" I said. "Which carries its head down, as this animal does. 'The catoblepas will prove the destruction of the human race,' Pliny writes, 'and all who behold its eyes will' "—I turned the page—" 'fall dead upon the spot.' " I looked up from the book. "How are you feeling?"

"We already beheld its eyes," said Errol. "And apart from the wound you received from running into a wall, we're fine. What does Pliny have to say about bears?"

I thumbed through the pages. " 'There is magical poison in the brain of the bear that, if drunk, induces rage in men.' "

"Aye. We saw the beginnings of rage," said Errol. "Does he mention the stripe?"

I read down the page. "Nothing here," I said.

"I wish there were drawings. What do you think? An infant bear, with a stripe?"

"Absolutely. Here we have a perfect specimen of a striped infant bear." Errol nodded, as if I were serious. But I said, "How, in the towers of a quarantine city, would I know what a striped infant bear looks like?"

Errol held out small things for the animal to inspect: a lock and key, a handful of quills. No doubt he was testing for a bogle. But it made no sense that this wild creature, now licking the salt sweat from his fingers, could pick a lock and find its way to the kitchens, fire up the ovens, and set two dozen chisels on fire.

We sat with the beast all night, under the spell of its otherness. We wanted to know its stories, how it had gotten into our walled city, climbed up the long stairwells of an iron tower, and chosen our room.

"The beast wants to speak with us," said Errol.

"Aye. But it lacks an alphabet," I said.

"Or we lack its alphabet," said Errol. We were all three silent as the animal curled in Errol's lap, its head tipped sideways. The pain seemed to be eased by Errol's fingers working the fur over its neck and shoulders. The beast slept.

After a while Errol said to me, "When it was afraid, the striped infant bear attacked everyone. It came after me, though I was helping it, as fast as it came after the guilders who delivered those blows."

"Aye. I was there. I saw the whole thing," I said.

"It clung to the belt in fear," Errol said. "Its own fear made it possible for me to trap it."

"Aye," I said. "I was there. I can see you're a fine trapper, like everything else you do."

But he said, "No. I have become like the beast, out of fear. I am so full of fear and rage I cannot separate friend from foe."

I sat up. "In faith—"

"You don't have to disagree. I know it to be true," he said.

"I wasn't going to disagree."

I awoke in the night. Errol was cradling the beast. The animal was spasming, as we had seen guilders do after a blow to the head, and then it lay stiff.

When my mam came to bring breakfast to us, Errol fell into her arms and wept. He would never see another beast again, he said, or feel that wildness that had inhabited our quarters for one night. I had never seen anything like this. Mam carried the striped infant bear away, to be thrown from the roofs like the carcass of any foundling.

In the chaos of that night, no one noticed an old woman wandering in the morgues deep under Thebes. She was a tunnel knocker, a useless old foundling whose name, when they looked it up for the death records, was Durga. The younger foundlings who happened upon her carcass found her wounded inexplicably, a hairline incision in the chest, still wet and badly bruised, as though someone had opened her chest with a rough blade, put something into her ribs or taken something out, and tailored the seam. The tunnel was strewn with the things she had been carrying. A certain foundling with whom I was acquainted made me look at the body when they carried it up to be thrown off.

"Foundlings die all the time," I said.

I didn't tell this part, but in that odd moment, I was trying to ignore the sensation that I could see the striped bear curled up next to that murdered foundling.

"Foundlings die all the time, aye, but your da never made it a point to attend a foundling's death till now." In her hand was my father's whiskey flask, broken at the neck, sticky with blood.

After the striped infant bear, Errol was different. He began to run the flights of the guild tower. Half the night, up and down, down and up. I could hear him passing our room. In the mornings he went to work with Woody.

The bogling did not end, but it had a new effect on him. He was humbled by it and had a new understanding of fear. He had a new respect for the guilders' endurance and their work, and he asked questions and talked to them in new ways. The guilders began to like their prince. On the first calm evening in our bunks in seven years, Errol said to me that he would either lead the guild or be called to the roofs. Either future would be acceptable.

I was changed, too. Whenever I smelled Slyngel Thebes coming toward me in the stairwells, I took a turn so I would not have to see him or to ever ask him what he had done to a tunnel knocker with the jagged edge of a flask.

Then? Then.

A month before Errol was called to rise to the roofs, Margaret Thebes descended to my family's quarters and told me to fetch my mam.

"Gudrun, you and that foul man and your pack of idiots are moving. Gather your things," Margaret said. Margaret did not belong on this strata. We were beneath her in every possible sense of the word.

"Why? But we didn't do anything wrong!" Mam said. Then she looked at my brothers and their girlfriends, my sisters and their men, lying in a room full of unfinished chores. We were lazy and we were multiplying. "Nothing that I know of."

"I am not moving you *down*, Gudrun. Rather, up."

"But we didn't do anything right, either," Mam said.

"Cease talking," said Margaret Thebes.

I should have wondered why Margaret Thebes would give our slouching clan the finest quarters of the tower, on the coveted 130th strata. But I didn't care. Errol and I would now have a room big enough not only for beds but for desks and workbenches. When he left for the roofs, I would have it for myself. I ran up and down the 111 flights from our former rooms, dragging our old chairs and beds as fast as I could, lest Margaret change her mind.

On my last run down to the old rooms, I was stopped short by a strange sight. A pack of foundlings was moving into our former quarters.

Foundlings?

They were my age, all of them. There was no mam in their midst and no da. I had to look twice because, I swear it, I thought one of them was Errol. He had Errol's build and gait and his head of dark red hair, although the foundling's hair went all the way to his waist.

I was still standing in the hall staring at these facts, when Margaret called that same foundling into the hall. I stepped back into the shadow of the stairs.

"So you've moved in. Good. If anyone tries to harm ye, Feo Foundling," she said, "merely tell them you are my son. Aye, tell them you are the son of the guildmaster Margaret Thebes. Yell it if you must." She paused. "You may even say you are Errol Thebes if you think it would help."

"Mam?" said the foundling, confused. Who, on this strata, could mistake him for Errol? But for him, to question her sanity would be a step over the edge of a tower roof.

There was nothing insane in Margaret's voice that day. I am a bard and a translator, able to hear a script's worth of desires and intents buried in the pitches and draw of even a single word. When Margaret ordered Feo to masquerade as her son, I heard the distinct timbres of fear and regret.

That night I awoke with Errol's salt-sweaty hand over my mouth.

My father was mewling out in the hall. "I don't care what ye say! I will not drink that! Dinna bite me! Nawww! I see swine and rooks and stinking rats when I don't have the whiskey. Give me the whiskey!" There were the scuffling sounds of a struggle, and then Slyngel was gurgling and spitting and coughing.

I pushed Errol's hand away and got up. "He's just drunk. Stay here." I went through the great room of our new quarters and flung open the door to the hall. Someone or *something* ran like a shadow up a wall. It shot down the hallway. My father lay sprawled on the stone floor in a pool of black liquid.

"Locking me from my own fine quarters, are ye, then?" he said, wiping his chin with his sleeve.

"Stop bogling Errol Thebes," I said.

"What? Nay! *What?* I must see him—" His eyes darted down the hallway.

"Come back when you're sober. Which is to say, never," I said.

He craned his neck to look over me. "He's here, then?"

"Errol Thebes wants no part of you."

"It's my last chance!" He ran at me. "For I've drunk that poison—"

"Of course you have drunk it. You always have drunk it." I moved to shut the door, but my father lowered his head and rammed into me. I was surprised as much by the fact that he had done *anything* as the amount of force with which he had done it, and I threw him across the hall.

"I'm ashamed of you!" I yelled.

He was up again and coming at me, his eyes flitting to the open door of our quarters. "Which one of my nine demons are ye?" he said. "I have drunk too much of the double's vitriol to see—" Had he said devil? Or double—?

"Ragnar," I lied. "I'm your son Ragnar Thebes."

"Not the one everyone calls Odd? That one would help me."

"No. I'm not Odd."

"But you're feathery—"

"Stop it! Stop with the feathers! I don't have feathers!"

"Sh!" He stopped and listened over my shoulder. "I hear him. Is Errol Thebes coming out? I must tell him. I must." He looked straight at me. "I must warn him."

"Fine. I'll warn him," I said. "I'll warn him you're here. But he already knows it."

"No!" he panicked. "I'm not the one to fear!"

But I slammed the door on him and bolted the lock. For a long while Errol and I lay awake in our bedrolls, listening to Da's fingers playing at that lock.

The night was not done with us. We were awakened before the next bell by an echoing in the walls, far below us. Someone was running up through the north wall of our tower, in one of the hollow, stone-and-iron passages foundlings use. They came our way, passed our strata and our rooms, then we heard them above us, one of them screaming and begging: "I am the guildmaster's son! The guild-master's son, I tell you! The guildmaster is my own mam!"

We lit our bed lamps.

"I am right here, am I not?" said Errol.

"Aye," I said.

"Who is that, then?"

"I don't know," I said. That was a lie. I knew exactly who it was.

Higher the pitch rose, full of a fear I had never heard: "What are you doing to me?! Let go! No! Stop! I am Errol Thebes himself!" I heard the clatter of hoofs in that wall. (And how would I know that sound, having never heard it before?) The screams grew fainter above us until, finally, silence.

When Errol appeared in the hall for breakfast, guilders eyed him like a ghost. He and I ate breakfast alone. Margaret Thebes called him into her quarters.

"We're done," she said. She was pale.

"I don't understand," said Errol.

"You don't need to," she said. "I am guildmaster and I say we're done. There will be no more."

Feo was gone. The rest of the foundlings in our old quarters moved back to the morgues where they felt, in a twist of irony, safer. The quarters stood empty, and remain so even now, having been the temporary home to a raging striped infant bear and, for one night, an insane foundling.

Errol threw his old list of suspects in the fire in our room. He told me that Feo must have been the one bogling him since he was seven. Not Slyngel, not the infant striped bear, not me.

I shrugged. "No tumors, then?"

"I never thought a foundling would have the courage to bogle me," he said. "Can you believe the audacity? The last thing it stole was my name. Did it really look like me?"

"Aye. He did. He was older. Thinner, as you might suspect, with his being a foundling and you being, well, you."

"To look like the guildmaster's son, yet to have none of my privileges, must have driven it over the edge."

Errol's explanation did not fit the particulars. Men did not scream for help on the way to a suicide. And I did not tell Errol that his own mother had urged Feo to steal that identity. I myself needed to be done with the whole business.

He and I visited our old rooms on the nineteenth strata one last time, to see what was left of that night. When he picked a human thumb off the carpet, my stomach heaved. The nail of it was outlined in blood. A white bone—well. Errol wrapped it in a strip of muslin and put it in his tellensac. I pointed out how disgusting this was. But Errol said Feo's thumb would remind him forever not to trust a foundling, prone, as they were, to jealousies.

I saw my da that night, the great Slyngel Thebes, staggering into the stairwells, holding his right hand in his left, protecting that amputation wound.

I didn't have to worry that Errol would ever see the nine-fingered Slyngel. My da lost his sight that same night, and his liver hardened like a scroll wedged up under his ribs. From the door of the midwife's rooms, I watched my brothers drag a keg of whiskey to the dying-bed so Slyngel did not have to see the end coming, or hear it. He had no tellensac, no going-stories he wanted Mam to tell. It was the third night of the month of Faol—spring somewhere outside the guild but winter in it. They folded him in his trunk, poured the last of his whiskey on him, and sent him to the morgues.

Truth is slippery. Here's everything I know: The bogling ended after Feo was gone. Slyngel was gone, too. Errol Thebes left for the roofs a month later. He was stronger for all that had happened to him. A runner of extraordinary endurance for all his time running the stairs. A guildmaster's son who actually loved his guild and its work and its city. A bogled kelp who had risen, fearless.

ERROL THEBES HELD HIS HANDS OUT to his sides like a baby learning to walk. What time of night was it? Or was it night at all? He felt an impulse to reach for a rag, to run a fly and get away from the pain. There was no rag. No fly.

In the wan moonlight he could see the plank that had fallen with him. The force of the fall had driven it into the earth. Frozen in the purgament of the street next to it was something that glinted of black iron. He pressed at the iron with his navaja. Kicked it. It was the hinged lid of the case that held the iron spikes.

"Maso-swefn," he said. A snaring dream. He remembered that foundling and its betrayal of him with those guards and then its insane question: *Do you want the spikes to go with you?* As if he would still live after it had lured him in. Yet, here he was, alive. And here was that iron case, and those spikes.

From somewhere behind him came the faraway crack of voices and laughter. Utterly disorienting. Errol staggered to the edge of the alley, following the sounds.

The telling of this is a snaring dream for me, too. What do I know of the street? Nothing really. The rubble of fountains, a shingle with the hint of past lettering. A foul system of feral canals, carrying in their ebb and flow the irfelaf of what was.

Over the sounds of the laughter came a loud *thwack* and again, louder. The shadows of two creatures jerked and leapt in the light of a fire at the end of an alley. Men. They were men! They were agile. His age! One of them was beating the dust from a rug against the wall of the tower. Or not a rug. A belt or a strap. The other was bent around some object in his arms—a sack, perhaps. Errol leaned against a wall, dizzy. He was still in armor. His first thought—and this is no bard's embellishment, not this time—was gladness at finding runners on the street. He would help them with whatever it was they were doing.

When the strap hit the wall, it appeared to shudder. Errol squinted. The two men were laughing. They were calling out each other's names: "Dete!" "Clegis!" This time—*thwack*—the strap recoiled with such speed that it wrapped around the wrist of the one called Dete, and he screamed and shook it off.

"Look at it, Clegis! All a mess of its parts and still trying to come at me." Errol was close enough to see the two of them were scarred with worm tunnels. A third figure shifted in the play of the fire. That one was thin and lanky, pale as a disease, taut. Hair wild as a spill of soot ink.

"Finish up," that pale one said, a vacant voice.

"Aye, Jago," said the other two.

The strap was not a strap. Errol knew it now. It was some kind of asp, and Dete had it by the tail. And the sack was not a sack. It was a writhing kelp, a girl, and she must have just stomped on the one called Clegis, for he roared and grabbed his foot. All Errol could think was the snake must have bitten the girl, and now the girl was wounded and crazed and the runners were protecting her.

The girl was the first to see him. She caught his eye and shook her head no. Again the snake hit the wall and the girl cried out and there was a fan-shaped splatter of blood. The snake hung from Dete's hand, bobbing its wounded head, disoriented. Dete spun the snake over his head like a rope, counting the revolutions of it—"One! Two! Thr—"

Errol bent over and picked up a cobble from the street. He threw it. Dete crashed into the muck and leapt up, spinning to see what had hit him.

You have to remember who Errol was and where he had come from. He thought—I can barely write it—that those three would be ashamed of themselves. That they would forge a fast apology and tend the snake's wounds or lay it in some narrow, decent grave, and do right by the girl. This is what he thought. He was from a high place and he did not know.

In that pause the snake swung in an arc, threw its jaws thrice-wide on some secret hinge, and set its fangs into the white of Dete's wrist. The air filled with pulse blood. The snake shot into the air and was a blur, and gone. The girl bit Clegis and too was gone.

Errol stumbled backward. He flailed around a corner, down a set of cobbled stairs, sliding in the frozen armor. They were coming. He ran stupidly, clumsily. Finally he stopped, tipped his head back, turned. Dete slammed into him, felled him, pressed his face into the street.

"Dead end. As it were," said Jago, approaching. "Who have we here?"

"A runner," said Errol, "like you."

"He's the Green Knight, Jago!" yelled Clegis. His breath reeked. "You can tell it by looking at him."

"Silence, Clegis. Or I'll find the square inch of you that's not already a lack and suck your blood out of it. Name?"

"Runner," said Errol.

"Anonymous Runner. And from what guild hail ye?" Jago demanded. When Errol refused to speak, Jago said, "Dete, make a study of that, would you?"

Dete broke the armor at the elbow hinge, wrenched off the sleeve and the gauntlet.

"Branded an outlaw. Recently," Dete said. "Before that he was second-year Thebes."

"You must also be runners, if you know the marks," said Errol. Errol's eyes settled on Jago's forearm. A piece of leather had been sewn to him, with the first-year mark of Lascaux on it, a silk moth. "Where did you get that—"

"Hel has no tufugas," Jago said. "So we help ourselves." He pointed at Errol's crow. "I like that one for you, Dete." Errol tried again to get away but Dete caught him. Jago said, "'Tis a rare privilege for us, your visit. We will do well by you." He pulled a kitchen knife from somewhere behind him.

Errol's head was spinning. "This armor is excellent black iron, and you may have it, as a gift from me."

"'*Have it*'?" said Jago. "This is my street. The rope that fell with you is mine. The armor is mine. The plank is mine. You are mine."

Errol reached into the pocket of his belt. In a swift move he crouched low and wielded the navaja. Dete and Clegis burst out laughing.

"I am guessing," said Jago, "you learned that from a book."

"And you? Where did you learn to mistreat a kelp? From what great hero? From what book?" Errol tossed the navaja up and caught it, turned it in his fingers.

Jago scraped at his lip with the edge of his filthy fingernail. "There are no kelps on the streets. That girl Sitembile, least of all. There are no heroes, either, unfortunately for you."

"But, Jago," said Clegis. "You are our hero, mine and Dete's. You saved us from Utlag!" Errol ducked away as Jago kicked Clegis hard in the teeth.

"Don't mock me, ever," Jago said to Clegis.

Clegis was down, fumbling at his mouth.

Errol tried again to run but Dete grabbed him from behind; Errol slashed a red bloom across Dete's cheek. Dete was punching his face, and he felt his body fold under him like pieces of a broken chair and he was staring up at the three of them.

For a long while Clegis and Dete pulled and cut his armor off him and took the wools he was wearing. They uncurled his fingers from the navaja. When he struggled, they knelt on his broken ribs. He did not tell them that he saw from far down the street the figure of that kelp watching him in the shadows. He was ashamed that she would see any of this. No kelp should see it.

Jago squatted beside him. Errol could not take his eyes from the silk moth that had been cut from someone's arm.

Jago followed his gaze. "It'll be easier for me to take that bird on your arm if you're not alive for it. Clegis, let's show some mercy."

Dete dragged Errol to his feet, and Clegis moved uncertainly toward him.

"What sort of mercy is this?" whispered Errol.

Clegis pressed the navaja hard into the side of his gut, piercing skin and driving the blade up under Errol's ribs. Errol staggered into Clegis's arms. And then it was done. Errol stared at the blood running in a rivulet from his own body, and willing himself not to fall.

"That will take a day," said Jago. "We'll wait with you."

Errol bent over, trying not to slip away. "What have I ever done to you?"

Jago laughed. "Done? Look around you. You left us here, to fend for ourselves."

"Me?" said Errol. His voice sounded so far away in his ears. "I have never been here. I don't even know you."

Bells were ringing far away.

"Ah," Jago said. "Nine bells. Dulcibus. Time for sweets. I wonder what we are having for dessert on the roofs." Errol was sure he was hallucinating. There was that girl again. This time she was running toward him, in a little mob of kelps with sticks and their fists raised, and howling.

Jago flinched. "Relentless. Let's go. Dete, you're a foul mess, with that wound on your face. We'll get rid of this trouble and come back for that crow. Let's make sure he doesn't leave."

The rest happened so fast. Errol thought Dete was coming for his guild mark. But Clegis held him down and Dete took Errol's foot in his hand. He sank the blade into the sole of it and wrenched the foot to jam the rest of the blade into the street. Errol's vision diminished to a single point and disappeared. His body was cold and reeked of sweat and a kind of meatiness that came from his own muscles. He was pinned to the earth, and he felt nothing.

MAREK TOLD ME TO WAIT. He left the yurt and trudged through the snow to the grate at the center of Thebes's roof. The grate swung up on its hinge and Marek disappeared into the tower.

When Margaret Thebes was angry, the guilders could hide from her. When she was exacting, they worked harder. But her twisted sorrow filled the tower like a disease and was more frightening than any wrath. I thought she would order Marek thrown off the roof that night in an effort to jettison the news he brought her. Fenn and Rip were gone, and now Errol. A lesser man would have put the news in writing.

When the guilders returned Marek to us, they also sent late supper, an offering so rare I had never seen it made before: three immense cast-iron pots containing potatoes boiled to sludge; sausage blackened in the ovens; leeks sopped in oil. On any other night, we would have mocked their food, which looked like they had boiled up their socks. But tonight we were thin from Beklemek and ragged from the loss of Errol Thebes. The meal from a low place made us feel like kelps again, held up to the sky on the strength of the towers in which our parents forever toiled. We held our scalding bowls in our hands and devoured that meal.

Ping studied the two remaining relics. "What is that?" he said.

"The baidaq," I said, picking it up and rolling it in my fingers. "The pawn from a shatranj board. The relic of the kitchen girl."

"Kitchen girl?" Ping said. "I am the cook. Yet I know nothing of a kitchen girl?"

Every guilder in Thebes wondered what Margaret would do—I began—with the news that Errol was called to run the roofs. Any other parent would have laid out a feast for the guild in their son's honor. Margaret was silent and refused to leave her quarters.

Gudrun Thebes threw the mam-party. She made eyrouns for him, his favorite sweet. We all brought gifts. Mine was a stolen copy of Pliny. Woody Thebes appeared from nowhere, with his gift: a shatranj board and all its shahs, ruhks, faras, baidaqs, each meticulously hand-carved from two colors of heart pine. How I wanted that board. The black ruhk was crowded with minuscule archers. The shah's crown was a perfect, tiny cage in which a thrush was perched on a bar with his head tossed back in song. Errol was grateful. But I knew he wanted something else. He was waiting for *her*. At midnight I woke him to say she had come. He came out of our room, pulling his tunic on.

"I've come to pay what respects are due," she said.

"Aye. Thank you," he said.

"Don't thank me. Wahid Thebes said you would run the guild. So that's what I expected. You are a disappointment."

"I was called to the work of the roofs, Mam. Only you could rescind that offer, and you didn't. I promise to return."

"And did I ask you to return?"

"No, Mam." His voice was as small as a kelp's. She had diminished him yet again. Now she stepped aside. A foundling who'd been concealed behind her dragged a sack across the floor and let it fall at Errol's feet. Why, I wondered, did the foundling appear to be embarrassed?

"Is this a gift for me?" said Errol.

"Aye. 'Tis the best of its kind," Margaret said.

Imagine my cousin Errol opening, in front of all of us, the first gift he had ever received from Margaret Thebes, the wealthiest guildmaster in the city. Imagine him wondering as he untied the sack if there was something in that bag that could account for a mam who avoided even the sight of him.

And now imagine our quarters filling with the scent of a hundred bars of rose soap.

"Your brothers had a reek to them," Margaret said. "I gave them this soap to cut the stench. In fairness to you, I must give it to you as well."

I had been jealous of him a moment ago, with that chess set. I was not jealous now.

To Errol's credit he managed to thank the guildmaster, to say how useful a gift soap was. But as soon as she left, I found him cutting the bars into shards with his navaja and feeding them into the drains. Back in his bedroll he lay, reeking of roses.

"She has no idea how to be a mam," I said.

"She could read a book about it," he said.

I laughed. "What do you want to do?"

"Well." He paused. He was grinning. "I've the hunger of ten men."

I hesitated, then laughed as well. "Aye," I said. "And the darkness calls to me."

He was already up and running. "I feel the need for a blind feast! Will ye join me?"

This was an old exchange between us. A code. We scrambled out of our family's quarters and around the corner into the hall, our lanky arms and legs flailing as we raced down dozens of flights to the guild kitchens, knocking each other out of the way. Howling. All to find the kitchens with no head lamps, to make a feast for ourselves from what we could feel in the pantries in the pitch-black kitchen of an iron guild in the dead of night. A childhood game. A pelt's feast. A wild errand. Always we left the cooks to clean the huge and wasteful mess in the morning. What could they say? He was the guildmaster's son.

As he ransacked the shelves and oven, making what smelled like saffron fry-tour, I sank my hands into a bowl of eyrouns.

"Errol Thebes!" I called.

"Dinna wear out my name."

"Catch!" I threw an egg hard where his voice was and heard it crack against the wall.

"Was that my eyroun, which your loving mam made for me?!" he said.

"Aye, it was! And—?" I said.

"And you'll lick it from the floor before we're done here!" He was laughing. He found the remains of the egg on the floor and threw the mess back at me.

"Come on now. Is that your best throw?" I mocked him. "You'll be falling from the lines if that's all the strength in that weakling arm." I had Errol's full attention now and I could forget he was leaving me behind for the roofs in the morning. We pelted the shelves and pans and each other and stuffed ourselves with whatever we didn't hurl.

Errol's mouth was full. "Aht. Sat oo?" he asked. And then he swallowed. "Is that you, Odd?"

"Who else would it be?" I said, licking a peeled egg and dipping it into a ceramic crock of what I hoped was sugar and not lye powder.

"Is this you?" He paused, holding his voice steady. "Is that you, touching my shirt?"

"What are you talking about?" I said. "I'm over here. At the table. Aim for my voice. La-la-la-la-la!"

"Then who is *this*?" Errol said.

A chill ran up my spine. There was a scuffle and the sounds of a struggle. My heart raced. What frights were left to haunt us tonight of all nights? Slyngel was a month in the morgues. Who else could it be? And *why*, in a guild kitchen run on flames, could I not find a single iosal flint to ignite a lamp?

In the hallway someone began to play a fiddle. Playing a dance I knew, a ga-votte. What was next? Acrobats? Fire-eaters? I shook my head, trying to make sense of such a thing while the sweetness of the tune filled the kitchen like the thick scent of those almond eyrouns.

"And now there's a hand in mine," Errol called out, his voice cracking like a pelt's. "Odd, someone is pressing me to dance." I felt the movement of air as bodies spun past me. "Odd? This is a gift from you, isn't it? My favorite tune!" His voice was full of pleasure. I reached out to catch them, whoever they were, but caught only the rush of air in their wake.

I felt for an egg on the table next to me and threw it hard. "What if that's the bogle? What if it intends you harm?"

"Do you intend me harm?" he said. Then, "Hey!" and he was laughing. What was someone doing to him?

"Fine," I said petulantly. "Fine. I see. Feh. In that case, does she have a friend?" But they were not listening to me. So I left them there—Errol and the kitchen girl—and knocked over an anonymous fiddler in the hall as I stumbled back up the unlit stairs to our quarters alone.

A long while later, Errol returned and flung himself on the bedroll. On my own bedroll I sat cheating myself at solitaire.

"On your last night in the tower, on the night before you leave for the roofs, you leave me alone for so long that I am an old man," I said. But he did not answer. "Will there be offspring?" I said.

"We danced, only. The gavotte," he said. "She is the dawn star. She is all of the stars."

"When was the last time you saw even one star?"

"Never."

"Then don't commit poetry."

"She kissed me," said Errol. "I must know her, Odd Thebes. Who is she? Where does she work? She must be from some strata in this guild."

I rolled my eyes. "Obviously she is either a bound guilder, wed to someone she hates, or she's ugly as a fart. How else to explain her cover of darkness?"

"I don't know her name, I only know the sawol in her chest."

"Her soul? I think you mean her tits."

"Shut up, Odd Thebes. The kitchen is héafodstede now," Errol said.

"Sacred? I shall bow when I enter and belch. And did the kitchen girl leave a shoe when she ran from the ball? Your little Aschenputtel?"

"We were barefoot."

"Then how will you ever find her?"

"We carved our names, in the dark, on the underside of the table."

"Ah. Excellent idea. With a million other pairs of names no one can read."

"Aye. And we swore not to look, until we meet in the kitchen again someday."

"A logistical nightmare. As reliable a tool of detection as the shoe left by the cinder girl. A twelfth of the world would fit into such a shoe, not including small men and boys."

"I gave her a black faras piece from Woody Thebes's shatranj set."

I made a gagging sound. "What! You *what*? You broke up the new set?"

"I had to."

"Black is *me*! You gave my horse to the ugly, married Kitchen Girl?"

"You can use a quarter-uur piece in its place. Anyway I'll be gone tomorrow to the roofs, and you'll be here alone in the tower. So there will be no more beating me at shatranj."

"I hate you," I said. "For leaving me for a girl, before you even leave me for the roof."

"Well, and I hate you for staying behind with that girl in this guild house," he said. "I have just enough time to pummel you, to keep you from coming near my faras."

He launched himself from his bedroll and landed on me. I bit him. Straightaway my brothers yelled from their quarters that the two of us should just kill each other so they could live in peace. But we lived and fought on, marking Errol's rising to the roofs with a night of warfare.

When I pretended to sleep, later, I watched Errol put the black baidaq into his tellensac. Barely had he known her. Known her? Could he pick her out in a crowd?

Yes, well. I read all the same books he read, and I grew up on all the same tales of King Arthur and all of those idiots. I know what he was thinking. He was thinking that, if the kitchen girl was the faras, then he wanted to be a mere foot soldier in her service. Her servant. Her slave. Her pawn. Her baidaq.

"Why didn't you give her the queen?" I said.

"The queen is of no interest to me. The horse has always been my favorite."

"That explains why I always beat you at the game."

"That, and you move the pieces when I am not looking."

Two years later, on the sixth of Ganso, when the roof of Thebes was sacked by Fremantle, the shatranj set Woody had made burned in Errol's tent. All except for this baidaq piece, this pawn in my hand. Well, yes, and somewhere in Thebes Guild a girl is carrying a black horse.

———

When I was done with this going-story, Ping stirred and said, "*In* Thebes Guild or perhaps *on* it. Isn't that right, Odd? Kitchen Girl could be any one of the girls who came up after you two did. It could be Talwyn here. Or Eluned. Or Mirembe."

All three of them shrugged, knowing, as I knew, that they were not the one.

Birth-Night

THRICE THE BELL STRUCK from High Berfrei—flat and echoless, damped for the night. "An, twa, pri . . ." Errol was shaking. He waited for feower, hoped for it.

"How can it be only the baker's bell?" he slurred. "Bakers, fakers, undertakers, law breakers, matchmakers. Will the sun never rise on this city?" He tried to turn over to find warmth, but his foot was stuck and he couldn't figure out why or on what. The foot must have been numb by then or he would have remembered. He tried again to roll over, to sleep, to find that kitchen girl again in his dreams. But pain spiked in his shin. The night was evil cold; sweat had frozen in his hair, on his shoulders. "Odd Thebes," he said to me. "I have done the math. I am seventeen times around the sun. Would it be so much to ask, on my birth-night, that you light the bucket fire? Ideally before my body freezes to the roof."

I did not reply, for I was not there. No one was there. Errol Thebes stared at the lack of me, and then, slowly, at the lack of a bucket fire, the lack of his sleep-sack, the lack of a tent. I wonder how long it took him to realize his clothes were gone.

A grin spread over his face. "Well done, Odd Thebes," he said. "I deserve this. Well done."

On any other night, in some higher time, it would have made sense to think what he was thinking: that I had crept into his tent while he slept, worked him out of his sack and wools, hauled him across the roofs, drooling and mumbling state secrets, tethered him by a foot to some fly, and winched him into the sky with makeshift pulleys. This is what he thought, for he had played that same small-uurs prank on me on my birth-night, and on every runner on the roof of Thebes. And on those sacked-and-plundered mornings we, each of us, had awakened disoriented, only to find ourselves bound, naked, suspended by a silk thread so high we could see the arc of the earth. Our finest wares on display for every roof to see. Crowds. Applause. Cheering. Certain formerly private things never to be forgotten.

"Oh, aye," Errol said, grinning. "I definitely deserve this." He rubbed his bound hands on his face and laughed. But his laugh was cut short, for the moon shone on his palms, which were wet with blood.

He sat up so fast he pulled at the muscles all the way down his spine and legs, and cried out at the pain in his foot. He reached to rub away the pain and found the blade of the navaja, driven through his sole and into the earth.

He became aware that, from behind a heap of rubble, the snake was staring at him, unblinking, licking the air between them. It was the color of fire and it, too, was wounded. They studied each other until finally the snake withdrew into nothing. Errol lay with his face in the sop of the street till the tower bells rang feower.

Purgamentum. They were heaving the trash from the roofs.

The Three of Spades

FROM THE EAST there came singing and I realized, disoriented by my own barding and the timelines I had spun, that Visby was rising and we had survived our first night without Errol. I tossed the relics back into the bag, counting on the sunrise for a distraction.

"Wait," Faisal said, turning back. "One last tale. What about the playing card?"

I yanked the cords tight on the bag. "Playing card?"

"The three of spades."

"I can't remember the story."

"But you said you knew all his tales."

"I was mistaken."

"'Our stories ran together—' Is that not what you said?"

It was unheard of, not to tell every tale in a tellensac.

"Let me see that," said Sa'id, reaching for the bag. He loosened the cord and pulled out the card. "Think, Odd. The three of spades. Not much value there. It must be some sort of code."

"I'm sure you're right," I said. "There! We're all done." Marek was staring at me.

"Or perhaps," said Talwyn. "Perhaps the card was given to him by Woody Thebes? Errol would cherish anything Woody gave him. Woody or you, the two he loved most—"

I shrugged. "I hardly think he had favorites." Did she have to carry on like that? Did I not feel the guilt enough already?

Marek took the card from Sa'id and pushed it across the roof to me.

"There is nothing so constant in guild life as a playing card," he said. "So useful in relieving the tedium of these towers. In a sense its value is immeasurable and yet, look, it weighs hardly anything." He caught my eye this time and I flinched. Without breaking his stare, he said, "Ping, make us some breakfast, will you? If we require this last tale, we should offer more sustenance to Errol Thebes's bard."

Errol Thebes's bard. Was that a promotion or did I just vanish completely?

Ping obliged and cooked breakfast for us: waffres and thick tea with butter spiraling in it. It can't have been an uur since we had eaten the guild stew but we were hungry again.

The other going-stories in that tellensac had been hard enough to tell, but this one was impossible. In those others, there had been players onstage. Errol and Woody or Errol and the rumor-mongering guild tower or Errol and Kitchen Girl or Errol and his own stunning reflection. The three of spades was Errol and me.

Under other circumstances, this would be little more than a tale of a long and uncommon friendship. Now it was a snake I was being forced to conjure and then hold in my hands until it writhed and bit.

"I think, I *think* this spade is from our first day on the roofs—" I began, as if I didn't know. My voice was quiet, barely audible over the sounds of 999 roofs of runners singing up the sun.

Errol Thebes could never win at any game—not shatranj or thimblerig or dice—as you all know from having beaten him and taken his money since you were kelps. But he lost with particular magnificence at games of the deck. Maw, piquet, ombre. Conversely and for reasons involving mathematical skill, highly refined strategy, and a complex understanding of the guild mind, I generally win.

"Also you cheat," Grid whispered.

On the morning Errol rose to the roofs, he and I were packed and waiting in our quarters for the order to come to the 151st strata. We played a round of maw on our trunks and I beat him for old time's sake, but neither of us cared. He was rising and I was suddenly rising with him. My luck had turned in the night, and we could be together for three more years. An infinity.

"But tell me, Odd Thebes," he said in high spirits. "Now that you will have a thousand roofs' worth of runners to challenge you at the deck, and I will be the dull cousin you never bother to play anymore, what *is* your strategy? How do you always win at these games? You can trust me to keep trade secrets."

At first I refused. Why would I give him any more advantages over me than what he already had? But he carried on about it, and in the end I said he could bribe me with his copy of Ovid.

"You want to know? Fine," I said. "I'll tell you. The face cards? They weigh more than the rest of the cards in the deck. The kings are heavier by an infinitesimal fraction than the queens, and both are more than the jacks. The numerical cards can be sorted by ink weight in descending order. Red? Red pigment is lighter than black, which sorts the ranks in half. And there you have it! Simply put, I have memorized the weights. I draw a card from the stream and know what it is before I turn it. What? Yes, I'm brilliant indeed. Give it a try." Errol weighed a card in each hand, like a balance scale. "Can't you feel it?" I whispered, a conspirator in my own ruse.

"I think so. Yes," he said. "This one is extremely heavy." But when he turned that card over it was the three of spades.

"There! You see? It weighs more than that deuce!" I said. "You, Cousin, have sensitive fingers for this."

"You really think so?"

"Of course. *And . . .* if you study card weights your whole life, as I have done, in many years you'll be able to tell exactly which cards your opponent is dealt, even facedown, by how heavily they land upon the table."

"I hear it already," he said.

Feh. Was he really buying this? *Weigh the ink?* With my eyes closed, even now, I couldn't tell the difference between this three of spades and a whole suit in my hand.

Errol spent the next uur playing with that deck, dropping cards facedown, comparing in two hands the weight of the lean one-eyed jack with the stone-heavy hatchet-bearing king.

The absurdity came to an end when a messenger finally came for us. When we passed our trunks up and stepped from the stagnant guild into high air, the furthest thing from our minds was a hand of cards.

It was the month of Hlyda. We were fifteen. Pale as lard. The sky was so big we staggered around, squinting in the sun, losing our balance on this swaying, monstrous tower. Guild flags billowed from the masts of every house. Lamps, pennons, and laundry caught the wind from every yurt and tent line as far as our eyes could see. The legendary Marek Thebes was our roof master. Every time he turned his back on us, Errol and I laughed at our great luck. Here, finally, we were! Finally! On top of the world! With the infamous runners of the city, who worked harder than even the guilds did, stayed up all night for nights on end, pranking one another and putting on glorious plays and running the lines in the light of a moon we had yet to see. The great web of silk fly-lines was more vast than we even *we* had imagined. We raced over to knock the mast of the iron crow Xerxes, aching to be part of every tradition we had grown up hearing.

At that moment Errol sobered. "Where"—he pointed—"are the crossed needles, the knotting spikes, that belong in the crow's talons?"

Marek shrugged. "Those have been gone for years."

"Who took them?"

"Suffice to say I know where they are. It's the crow that's the luck."

"So—stolen," said Errol.

Marek sucked his teeth, judging whether to give the answer. "Your brother

Rip, when he ran the roofs, lost them in a round of maw on Gallia House. He was notoriously unlucky at cards. If crossed spikes are important to you, the guild can reforge a set."

"Forget about it," I said. "It's not important to us."

"Yes it is," Errol said. I couldn't believe he was going to make this an issue. What bothered him was that his own brother had lost that game and marred the enduring symbol of Thebes.

We dropped the subject. Marek had brought the two of us to the edge of Thebes. We were 151 strata, 900 fathoms, to the earth. More than a mile. Bamako, Phrygia, Gamin, and Catalhoyuk swayed in the high winds, throwing shadows against us. We couldn't see to the street, at the bottom of the abyss.

Marek pointed to Bamako House. "The specific breakfasts you requested in your paperwork await you there. It will be the best food you ever ate."

Errol grinned at me. "You first," he said. And then, for the first time, "Stay high."

I put my rag over the line, over my head. Just that small maneuver set me off-balance. My hands sweat like spigots. A dozen runners waited behind me to get on with their errands. It would be better to die, I thought, than to lose courage here and be sent back down into the guild. With my fingers clenched so tight on that rag my nails were cutting into my hand, I let myself fall from the edge. I slammed my tailbone hard. I was thrown into a bounce and was going down too fast, utterly sure half the rag had slipped from my grip. Or maybe the line snapped, how would that sound? *"Here's good luck to the quart pot and luck to the ballymow—!"*

"You're not dropping, Odd!" Marek yelled. "Don't sing!"

Even with all the gossip everyone tells you, no one ever thinks to mention that the flies are invisible when you look up at them from underneath, into the shimmer of sun.

"The fly is there!" yelled Marek.

"I'm going down!" I yelled. I had come to a stop and was dangling in the pit of the line. "It's too thin!"

"We brought Xerxes in on that line. Two tons of iron."

"Was that wise, do you think?" I screamed. "Could you have frayed the—"

Marek lifted the Thebes end of the line high with a y-stick and I slid across the rest of the abyss, opening my eyes in time to watch my nose crash into Bamako. My sharps stuck to the tower. I yanked my foot and the left sharp came off, and I watched it spiral out of sight. Marek trotted across a plank, climbed down the wall, got me into a pair of dry leggings, and up we climbed.

Errol had requested drageoirs for breakfast—theobromas in the various shapes of the planets. He swung his rag and turned to look at the runners behind him with a huge grin. Grid kissed him for luck. He turned and leapt. He whooped when he hit the pit of the line and swung his feet up so he flipped over the fly as he was vaulted onto Bamako. The runners cheered from every roof around.

After we ate, I made my way hand over hand back across the line to Thebes. Errol had gone his own way.

When he returned to Thebes well after sundown, he stopped at the crow. He unstrapped his pack and pulled out a huge pair of ornamental spikes. He climbed the mast, shimmied across the yardarm, and dropped down a line to jam the spikes back into Xerxes's talons.

I came out of my tent.

"So that's where you went. Thieving the spikes from Gallia House so everything can be perfect."

"There was no thieving. I won at maw," he said.

I hesitated. "I don't believe that for a second. You're terrible at cards."

"Not anymore. *Obviously.*"

"What do you mean?"

"Why do you have to ask, Cousin?" His voice dropped to a whisper. "I used your secret."

"*What* secret?"

"You know. Ink weight. The high cards weigh more than the rest. And on down the line. I could wager my life on it."

———

I returned the three of spades and the rest of the relics to Errol's tellensac. I couldn't remember when, in the telling of that tale, I had begun to shake. Or when Grid had drawn her lightning cloak over my shoulders.

"Impossible," I whispered.

"What? The card trick? He was just lucky," she said.

I nodded. But I wasn't talking about the card trick. It was Errol who was impossible. It was his unflagging belief in me, so huge and absurd that even my lies became truths in his hands.

We were done here. He was gone. His stories had taken him from us. I put the card in the bag, tied a reef knot in his tellensac cord, handed the sac to Marek, who would present it to Margaret Thebes, and removed myself to the solitude of my tent.

"*HERE'S GOOD LUCK to the quart pot and luck to the ballymow!*" Errol's singing voice pitched wildly as he fingered the hilt of the navaja. His foot had swollen around the blade. "*To the quart pot, pint pot, gill pot, half-a-gill, lilliget, ben, ben-mow!*" He wished for Grid. He shifted the blade in the swelling and then cursed and pulled it hard. Yelling now. Not singing. When it was done, he looked at the blade in his hand, forgetting that he knew better. *Don't look down.* He slid backward into nothingness.

———

He woke. He pulled himself out of the cold sewage and pitched his body forward on two hands and one foot. The streets were dark again. Or dark, still. He could feel the river's presence before he could see it. Along the banks he saw the glimmer of an eye of a man gnawing on some creature that was still writhing in his hands.

Errol lay on his belly on the bank and felt for the water, drank it, and dragged himself down into the shallows. The muck and rot of the banks smelled of eggs and bread mold, but the water itself whirled under a thin crust of ice, and rushed and smelled of cloud. He let himself be carried out. The cold current stretched his ribs and made his muscles itch in a terrible way. Out farther, it swept him downriver and he then felt his body scrape against sand. There he lay, half in the water and half out.

More than once, men on the bank stood and watched him, out on the sandbar. They waded into the shallows. Finally they turned and went back. Errol drifted like a corpse, and slept.

———

He dreamt that our mams came to him, scrubbed him with soap that turned the river red. He dreamt that the foundling reached out to him, and he watched her tatu rustle its wings and fly off her arm. He dreamt of one other woman, though he did not know her. She was sinewy and tall, with unwieldy hair knotted on her head and tipped eyes. She was the age of a roof master and shouldered a bow and quiver. She had pulled her skirts up through her legs and twisted them into her belt. She pressed ointment into the wounds under Errol's ribs and on his foot. The grease frothed hot and white like a pot boiling over into the river, and in his dream he begged her to stop. A half dozen long, silver snouts pressed into his face. Lank beasts and cold furred. Even on all fours they were nearly as tall as the woman.

They splashed in the water and shouldered one another out of the way to sniff Errol's breath, the part in his hair, his armpits, his nethers. He lifted dripping fingers to touch one of them, but the beast tensed and pinched a low growl from black lips.

"Roban! *Sitte!*" ordered the woman. The wolf yawned and feigned interest in something else.

"*Nu,*" the woman said. The wolf sat *now.*

Errol whispered, "*Beorht Roban.*" The woman looked down at him in surprise. The competence of her hands made him want to tell her everything. "I fell down" was all he could think to say.

"I watched you. And then you saved the snake. Saved me from getting involved. You're lucky. I thought you were dead."

Why was she pinching his foot? The current ran bright red with his blood.

"Right. Yes. I'm feeling very lucky."

———

He knew it was morning, because when he woke on the sand, the sky was brown instead of black. He was alone.

"I've fallen from the towers and lived," he said to no one. "Been beaten by thieves and lived. I can find some clothes and food and fight them off if they come back. There have been none of the terrors the guilders fear; only humans, and I've seen the worst they have to offer."

As I've said before, he was naive.

The Khazarite's Journal

OUR STORIES RAN TOGETHER, Errol's and mine. I was as gone as he was, when his tellensac tales had been told. Back in my tent I emptied the contents of my own tellensac, swept my hand through the relics, and reached for a folded page torn from the journal of a Khazar horseman.

In the late summer of a time he recorded only as the Year of Ardabil, the Khazarite vexillographer Amman Busir set off on an expedition from Balanjar to Sardinia, intending to settle once and for all a dispute with his master silk dyers over the exact meaning of the word *azure* by pointing to the Tyrrhenian Sea. The expedition ran off course, first in Balanjar and then in the Carpathian Alps. It ended prematurely in a tempest on the Marmara Sea, which was neither azure nor, unfortunately, shallow. Busir's journals were later found, stained with salt foam and ale suds and worked over by rats, in the floorboards of a pub in Cairo.

An unknown number of years later (fifty? five thousand? How could I ever know?), I was a first-year runner on Thebes. Around a bucket fire one night, a runner from Dannebrog House challenged my skills with a vexillography journal, a copy of that original from Amman Busir. This one was worn thin from constant use in Dannebrog for reference. The breathtaking drawings of flags and pennons were instructive, but none of the guilders in that tower could read or speak the ornate language of the text anymore. (Most guild translations, like guild cooking, are a grim affair, with glossaries too rudimentary to describe anything more than your boot size or how to find the bogs.)

What did I care about the work of Dannebrog, or all those flags and pennons they designed? Not at all. But I was obsessed with the remnants of alphabets. I talked the runner into lending me the book and promised I would do my best to translate it in a month. Dannebrog's guildmaster got wind of my offer and presented an incentive: *two* months' salary if I could really do the job.

Amman Busir arranged his runes like rows of fishing hooks on the page. His was like no other language I had seen or heard. I pored over the text, using repetitions and references to illustrations to unlock the codes within the hooks. Dannebrog was delighted with my first scribbled returns, for the writing ascribed new history and artisan vision to the designs of flags. I was delighted, for although Busir wrote mainly of his constant search for silks and pigments, in so doing, he wrote also of his travels to every known settlement on earth. In such uncommon writing I escaped my quarantined tower.

I made not only two months' salary but nearly a full year's pay, for there were more volumes than one.

I never told Errol Thebes, or anyone else, about this work. It was mine. All mine. Plus, there was one entry, unrelated to those around it, that I kept to myself—

"My men came undone this morning," Busir wrote, "as they rowed our expedition barges downriver toward the west wall of the ancient guild city of a thousand iron towers. An unwitting course."

Imagine the first time I had turned to that page.

"The shadows of the wall and the towers behind it slid cold over us and froze idle chatter. Were we in a trance? Why did we not we stop to portage? The brisk current carried us through an arch in the wall, an act that placed us inside the city where an internal harbor flowed into a series of narrow canals and along shadowy streets. We were, that morning: twenty men, eleven stallions, three barges.

"We paddled in silence, but for the river dripping from our oars and the shifting of our horses. We tilted our heads back to take in the infamous guild towers from which magnificent wares are exported. [Busir's exact expression was "monstrous wares," which I translated as "huge" or "magnificent", for he certainly meant a compliment to the grand size of our guild products.] These guilds were not the squat and buzzing work-hives we have seen in our expeditions over other folds of the map. Rather, enormous black-iron stalagmites, a thousand of them, each an eruption from under the earth, each rising insanely into the clouds, behemoths of proportion. Each tower sways in sky winds we cannot feel, pings and creaks under its own heaving weight. Each emits an occasional spray of smoke or squirt of filth from orifices we cannot see. One is covered with iron beasts that cling to its turrets and ledges. The air reeks of excrement and of blood.

"With long lens and this journal in hand, I lay on the barge while we moved downriver and sketched what I could of the banners on the roofs—ten thousand pennons and silks in charges and tints that took my breath away. Reds that broke my heart. A blue deeper than any sea. And designs whose perfection made my own look like a child's scribblings. I have sketched them here. In all my travels I have never seen such glory unfurled in any sky.

"My men were not interested in silk, for the flags on every roof were hung upside down, a sign of a city gripped by plague or by mutiny or—if I can judge by the world's use of this place—by abomination.

"I have been followed before by felons on the road. I know the shiftings and shadows of trackers. We were at a disadvantage here, on the water. My men whispered their own names backward, a fool's incantation their grandparents had taught them, to render themselves invisible. The stallions rolled their eyes in fear.

"Something watched us. I felt its presence. I cannot describe it except to say that there was a force of some intention coming behind us. We paddled hard for the south gate and found it closed. We saw a man moving along the river—not a man but something like one. Its joints bent in both directions. We used our oars to hammer the stiff levers from a small arch in the south gate. Unlike the gate, which was broad and high enough to accommodate a dozen warships in full sail, this arch was too small for anything but one of us at a time. We leapt into the water and through that door, left behind our barges and our stallions floating helplessly upon them.

"Tonight we made camp a league downriver from the iron city, high in the mountains. I smell the city on me, a filth that cannot be scrubbed away with soap. I regret my cowardice. It cost me my horse and companion, Ardabil. I am unwilling to describe here the screams of the horses in full panic, and, worse, the morbid silence that followed.

"It is too dark to see the towers and the wall from where I sit, but the roofs are lit with fires. Even from this distance I can see men leaping, flying, between the towers. Either I have lost my mind or they have."

———

For the thousandth time, I willed Busir back down that mountain, back to my city. Why did he not describe that folded map of his in more detail? Hint at his where-abouts on it and, therefore, hint at mine? With Errol gone and a morbid silence en-shrouding our roof, nothing could distract me from the weariness of not knowing where we are, or when we are, or who we are. But these three pages torn from the journals were all Busir wrote of the city before he discovered a high pass through the mountains and was gone.

I returned the pages to my tellensac. I was the only one to know about them. But if Errol had survived the fall, he already knew the fear of eleven slaughtered horses.

A Pub Squall

IN THE REEDS at the edge Errol lifted his foot to find a scrap of a submerged tent twisted around his ankle. He dredged it from the water, scraped the river ice from it and wrapped himself in it, like a kilt. Whatever thin starlight there was, was drowned in the torrents of rain. He was not alone and hadn't been for a while.

"Who's there?"

There came no answer, and this was the fifth time he had called. But a sudden scuffle and then someone hit him in the back, and he was dragged out of the water, up an embankment. Through the streets. Down a flight of stone steps, and tossed, sprawling, into a room underground. He got to his feet in time to see his captor turn for the stairs, the skeletal remains of human grime with thick yellow nails and more gums than teeth. "Another one from the river," the grime called over its shoulder.

The mob pressed in on him. Forty of them, maybe? They smelled of sweat and grease and ale, the familiar attarh of guilders at day's end. A small man was hurrying over. "Lookit! Lookit what Pollux fished from the river! Roof treasure! Not a foundling, no. A runner! Stay high!" With the familiar smells of work and a greeting of the roofs, Errol thought he had been dragged here to safety. But then that street fighter Jago stepped out from behind the barkeep, and from behind him came that other one, Dete, still crusted with the blood from the snake bite.

"You were dead," Jago said.

"You were mistaken," said Errol. The crowd murmured with laughter.

The ceiling was low and hewn of dirt, a reversal of the floor, with reed roots dangling from it and bolstered by wet planks wedged between it and the floor. It sagged under the weight of the river.

Errol said, "What are you doing here, the two of you, in public with decent people?"

"Decent?" Jago laughed. "Look again."

The barkeep grinned, a thin pair of lips pulled back over peg teeth. "I am Null. You be—?"

"An outlaw," Errol said.

"He's an exiled runner from Thebes," said Jago. "He owes Dete a guild mark."

"I see. Well, Thebes, how it goes in this place is Dete here will finish you. All you must do is stand for it, long as you're able to stand. You won't do harm to him or to these fine patrons who have paid to see it."

"Finish me at *what*?" Errol said, glancing around the room. "Are we to compete?"

Jago rubbed his chin in amusement. "Are you really such a fool? Guess again."

"I assume you wish us to wrestle. But anyone can see a fight would be unfair, as he and I are both wounded." A shudder of laughter moved through the mob again.

"If you won't fight," said Null, "Dete maybe will have some luck, then."

Dete grimaced at the insult. He thrust his hand in his pocket and tossed open a navaja.

"That's my blade," said Errol, keeping his voice steady. "I left it on the street. If this is a test of knife skills, I'll take my own knife and he can find his own."

" 'Knife skills'?" Null yelled grandly to the room. "And that, my friends, is the fine lips of one of them sky runners you watch from your box seats in hel. Shall he have a knife?" Null turned to Errol and shrugged. "You heard them. They'd rather ye die. To be one blade short in a pub squall is forfeit for trespassing in the streets."

"And what's the forfeit for murder?" said Errol. "And will he pay it now or after he's finished with me?"

Null laughed. "Fine looks and a brain! Shame, really, trading all that for ugly old Dete."

Dete had had enough of Null. He charged at Errol, who grabbed for the blade and felt the edge slide across his palm and heat his hand with blood. Errol swept his foot under Dete, dropped him to the floor in a clatter of elbows, pinned him with his face to the dirt and an arm behind his back. He twisted the knife from Dete's fist and held it to his throat.

"I read this in a book," Errol said. "We're done here. I've bested him." But Dete was grinning, and Errol turned in time to see a woman behind him. She held a plank high. Before he could understand, she brought it down on his head.

Dete was standing over him, kicking at his head to return him to consciousness. His knife was gone. "Will you all murder me?" Errol groaned. "Does it really take more than one of you?"

"They want to see you fight," Dete roared.

Jago pointed to Errol's wounded foot. Dete stomped on it. Errol roared and leapt up limping and charged with his head down, crushing Dete's ribs. They stumbled into the mob.

"Remember! Remember, Thebes!" Null laughed. "You mayn't harm our beloved Dete!"

Errol pummeled Dete's broken chest. Dete dropped to his knees. Errol stood gasping, waiting for someone to call the fight over. Was a man not down on his knees? But Dete was up again.

Over the cheers, Null yelled, "Halloo! Lookit! For Thebes! Here comes a weapon!"

Null shoved a girl toward him. She was Errol's own age, pale, thin. Her hair was cut short like a kelp's; it fell over a bruised face.

"Never seen a woman before, Thebes?" said Jago. "This is Sabine."

"Does she have some weapon for me?"

Laughter.

Null grabbed Errol's right wrist and the girl's left, spit on his bar rag and bound them together with a wet knot.

"She's the weapon," Null said.

"How is she a weapon—?"

Jago crossed his arms. "More of a shield, really," he said.

Dete threw a hard fist at Errol's broken ribs. Errol threw his right hand up fast to stop the blow. That reflex yanked the shield into the way. She took Dete's fist full to the jaw, and she was down on the floor.

"An outlaw!" yelled Jago, triumphant. "See! No heroes on the roofs. I told you!"

Errol pulled the girl up, steadied her. She spat at him. "Go ahead. Keep on with your fight. Get this over with."

"I didn't understand! That won't happen again!" Errol yelled, shoving her behind him. Dete came at him this time, grabbed his left arm. With the arm held out straight, with a shove and swipe of his foot, he dropped them both. Errol heard the sucking sound of his bones twisting out of the shoulder joint and he howled with pain. Before he could reconsider what had to be done, he threw himself backward against the floor, to set the joint. He got up, delirious with pain, flailing his free fist anywhere it would go, keeping Sabine behind him. Dete came for his ribs, pounding.

Null called out, "There's your hero! Nobody in the history of this illustrious place saves the shield!"

A man in the mob yelled, "Kill Dete!"

Dete spun in a spray of sweat. "Isn't anyone here for me?"

Out of the corner of his eye, Errol saw Jago hand Dete the navaja.

Now Dete grabbed Errol's throat with his left hand and pressed the blade against it with his right. Errol went down on his knees, the girl—*Sabine*—with him. The room was chaos. Cheering and banging chairs on the planks.

In this moment Errol knew he would lose. The point of the blade was cutting him now.

He would lose because he was fighting as we wrestled on the roofs: fairly, and without intent to wound. The bodies of runners were too precious to squander. But here in this foul room under the river, wasting was the whole game. If he didn't change, he would die, as would the girl.

Errol wedged his free hand between his throat and the blade. He could feel the navaja cutting him again. He gripped Dete's blade hand and turned the fist and the knife toward Dete. Errol's fingers were blue. Dete was crushing his windpipe with his other hand. Errol could no longer hear the mob calling for death. He couldn't see. His vision was going black. He could only feel that he had Dete's right fist in his hand and he knew the navaja was there, and he drove the blade fist into Dete's ribs and dragged it sideways, with no mercy. None. Then he let go and fell back.

Dete released his grip on Errol's throat and leapt into the air, hopping and kicking in a panicky dance. He thought he had won. But the girl on the floor was staring up at him, and Errol, too, was staring. And the eyes of the mob were fixed on his chest. Dete looked down and saw the great gaping wound in himself. He pinched the skin with his fingers, as he had seen men do on the streets to stanch their own bleeding.

"Jago?" he said, his voice sounded like it came from some other room.

Jago spit, "You're finished, Dete."

"But—"

Null said, "Ah well. You'll not be cleaning up after yourself, then?" He grinned.

Dete fell backward into a woman, who shoved him away. He rocked forward, his toes clumsily turned in, and fell onto Errol and Sabine. "Day," he struggled. He ground his teeth together, for now he was feeling the pain. "Stay."

Errol was shaking. He said, "You want us to stay with you?"

Dete grabbed Errol's hair and yanked him close to his mouth. "They tell gone-tales at the end, up there on the roofs."

Errol hesitated in the chaos, then said, "*Going-stories?* Yes, we do. We tell going-stories."

"Tell mine."

"I don't know you," said Errol. "The teller must be someone who knows you."

"Do it!" screamed Jago. He was barely human now.

"You tell it, then, Jago, if you are his friend," said Errol. "Come over here and hold him at least." Jago did not move.

"You tell it," whispered Dete, his teeth red with blood, his breath thick. "Use your own story. No one will know."

"It doesn't work that way."

"Tell something about me."

"Listen, Dete, as you rise up—"

"Up," said Dete, sucking in air as pain gripped him. "Is that what they say? What are the—" He cringed. "What are the odds that I will rise up? Same as Null's ass, I expect."

Errol snorted. "Are you making a joke?"

Dete spread his lips in a red grin.

Errol propped himself up on his elbow, with the girl bound to him. What story to tell? What did he know? Not his own tales. They did not belong here. He reached for something else—

"'The road was stone-laid, the path directed. The men together. The war-burnie shone, hard and hand-locked. The bright ringed iron sang in the armor, when they to the hall in their war-weeds at first approached—'"

"Is the burnie their river?" whispered Dete.

"Aye," whispered Errol. "The armor shone like a silver river. And we think the war-weed is their spears."

"Go on."

"'Sea-wearied they set their broad-shapen shields against the hall's wall. War-armor of men; their long spears stood—' Dete, are you with us still?"

"Tell it," mouthed Dete, his eyes open in a stare.

Someone behind Errol said, "Tell it." The room stood silent now, waiting.

"'Ne'er saw I strangers, so many men, with prouder looks—'"

Errol knew the bee wolf's tale from memory in the common tongue and in the tongue of the bard Anonymous. He could have gone on and on.

Dete's throat-rattle sounded. He grabbed at Errol again and pulled him to his face. "Geddout," he whispered. "Get away from Utlag."

Null kicked Dete in the head. "State secrets," he said. He reached into his apron, pulled out a rusted piece of a mirror, and put it in front of Dete's mouth. Errol watched the mirror steam from Dete's breath. Errol smelled the river again and turned to see where the smell was coming from. He saw a furred black snout come around a low doorframe. Then a broad, round head and small ears. The beast found Dete in the crowd, stared at him.

"What is that?" said Errol.

"My fillg—" Dete said. "Fil— My bear. Come to fetch me."

Null held Dete's mouth shut and pinched his nose.

"No! Stop! You felon!" yelled Errol, shoving Null's hand away. But Dete was gone, and the mob was cheering.

Errol struggled to his feet. He tore at the knot from the girl's wrist and pushed through the room to get out, but Null grabbed him. He raised Errol's fist. "Any who bet on this one can come get what's owed. And don't rush all at once. I'll not have all hel brekking loose in my place."

High Poetry

I LONGED TO BE RELIEVED of the burden of the gone-prince: to find my way from grief to relief, solitude to festivity, darkness to light. I decided, in short, to get myself a girl.

Thebes offered nothing. Talwyn preferred solitude. Mirembe had laundry. Siwan was with Petroc. Yael wanted a nap. Grid wasn't interested in men, least of all me. Eluned was down with a vile, snot-producing, rag-sopping allergy and, anyway, she also said no.

By festivum I would have done anything to get away. I found the hatch-guilder asleep on duty below his grate. I picked the lock and slipped past him, down the iron ladder and into the guild tower. I was looking for a kelp named Odd Thebes.

The tunnels of the guild were claustrophobic to me after two years in an open sky, and smelled of cooking grease, armpits, and wood dust. I found my way through halls of the 151st strata to the library, lit a lamp, and sank into my old leather chair to wait for a girl.

My tales were Errol's tales. Was there not a single one that belonged only to me? I spilled my tellensac, seeking a relic from the years I spent here. It was a page torn from Anonymous.

I was eleven times around the sun, old enough to eavesdrop on my brothers' exploits in the lesser forms of love. One morning, I was reading King Arthur's tales over a plate of frytour when I overheard Ragnar tell Heimdall that he would gladly fling himself on the tines of his fork for a night in the sack with the new apprentice Augustina.

"Don't bore *me* with this," said Heimdall with a yawn, who was already bound at twenty-three. "Bore *her*. She is sitting right there."

Augustina had just been shipped to Thebes from the guild house Bacalhau. She was as strong as any of my brothers. She had a mesmerizing overbite and fine hair on her arms and her upper lip. She laughed in a husky low voice that had the attention of every male in the hall.

"I can't speak to her," said Ragnar. "She won't understand me."

"No one understands you," said Heimdall.

"I mean, she doesn't yet speak the common tongue."

"So? Make Odd Thebes tell her," said Heimdall.

"Odd Thebes?" said Ragnar, looking over at me as if he had never seen me before. "What does he know?"

I placed a marker in my book and strolled over to Augustina, who was surrounded by her new girlfriends. She raised her eyebrows—*sim?*—and I nodded my head in the direction of Ragnar. *"Você é tão bonita, ele quer morrer,"* I said. You are so beautiful, he wishes to die.

Augustina smiled gloriously at me, then at Ragnar, and said in that velvet voice, *"Quer comer comigo?"*

I looked over at Ragnar. "She wants to know if you wish to eat with her."

"Tell her I wish to eat her," said Ragnar. Heimdall blew soup through his nose, laughing.

I turned to Augustina: *"Deseje comer . . ."*

"Don't actually *say* that, you fool!" Ragnar scraped back his chair and landed on me hard. I was about to take a beating when Augustina did me the favor of laughing. And all her girlfriends laughed. And then she crooked her finger at Ragnar and called him to her, and he got off my head.

"Hoje à noite?" I asked her on the idiot's behalf. Tonight?

"Sim," she said. Big smile.

Ragnar lifted me onto his shoulders and paraded me down the hall, his tuneless singing echoing off the stone-and-iron walls: *"This is my worthless bro-ther, my worthless little bro-ther!"* I agreed to translate his first meal with Augustina for a fortnight of his salary. If that seems exorbitant, I extracted an extra fee for eleven years of oppression.

The three of us met in the library—Ragnar, Augustina, and me—where I would have at my fingertips all the volumes of complex expressions of love. I even tore this page from one of the troubadours of Augustina's tongue in case Ragnar was insufficient. It was something about the parallel exuberances of spring love and birdsong, et cetera.

Ragnar: Tell her my favorite color is blue.

Me: *Minha cor favorita é azul.*

Augustina: *Minha cor favorita é azul também! O mesmo lindo azul dos seus olhos, minha querida!*

Me (yawning): Blue, too.

Ragnar (jaw hanging open): What are the chances?

Ragnar did not have to fling himself on any silverware to get what he wanted. With such a vast set of mutual interests, they went directly to the main one. Their kisses were wet, with tongues and hands pressed into service in ways I had thought I was the first to imagine. It was all utterly disgusting to me; however, I forced myself to watch.

Over time the word got out, of my skill as a translator. When a cook in Colophon House needed to know which jar was the poison sumaq and which was the secret ingredient of za'atar, labels, jars, and recipes would be carried over the lines and down into Thebes for my consideration. When the Lascaux fly-mongers uncovered a fid in deep storage, it was sent to me, along with a marlinespike and the directions for forging the one and turning the other, for I alone could read texts that had long been dry-docked on their shelves. A midwife called for me when a new apprentice refused to come out of her quarters in Flanders. As it happens, the midwife had offhandedly said the apprentice shouldn't be embarrassed about a rip in her tunic. I told her *embarazada* meant "pregnant" in the tongue of six guild towers.

Thebes guilders began to think that I, who could decode their city's languages, could also make sense of *them*. They hauled their tired selves to this chair in the library and begged me to interpret their waking fears, their rogue dreams, the tangled lines of their tales. Why Petra will never speak Sa'id's name, why Ciaran wears pieces of black yarn tied around her fingers. I didn't expect to be so interested in such yammering. And yet these stories were as compelling to me as the tales I consumed day and night in the library.

One night at supper I said offhandedly, "Pay a quarter-uur, anyone? And listen to what Emile does at dulcibus every night." The first coin clinked into my cup. Within a minute my cup overflowed with uurs and the table was full of company. I began in a stage whisper, "He writes a letter and stuffs it in the kitchen drain, hoping it will reach his sister in the street." And everybody was listening, even Emile, who was ninety-one times around the sun and had outlasted three guildmasters.

I never had to waste another day in a guild workroom.

"Have you no scruples?" Errol once asked me, as I poured the nightly contents of my bard's cup into a hole in the floor of our chamber. "Turning a profit on the guilder's private, miserable tales—does it not seem wrong to you?"

"What is a scruple?" I said. "Can I eat it? Will it keep me warm at night?"

THE STEPS OF A GUILDER IN THE HALL yanked me back to the present. I squatted in the corner behind the writings of Hesiod, where no one ever went. The guilder trudged into the library and sat at a table, twenty feet from me, unhurriedly relighting a lamp. It was too dim to see but I heard him retrieve a book from the shelves, flip through the pages of it, toss it aside, and get up to search for another. And another. This went on and on. After two bells, I was crossing my legs, afraid I would piss on the floor.

The guilder said, "I'm not alone in this room, am I?" It was a woman's voice.

Reluctantly I said no, but, at that same moment, a new voice said the same no. That speaker leapt from a beam in the rafters, lit upon the table, and dropped to the floor.

"Trespassing," said the guilder. "Foundlings are not permitted in the library. Not permitted to read. Not permitted to eat from the same tables as the guild. I see you're observing guild law with all your usual reverence."

Jamila took a bite of something. "If I had known you were coming, I would have brought enough for you."

The guilder snorted. "You knew I was coming here before I thought of it myself. Sit down. If I wasted my time trying to enforce guild law on Jamila Foundling, I'd have to hire someone else to run Thebes."

To run Thebes? I had never once seen Margaret Thebes in the library.

Jamila took a seat at the far end of the table and set her book down. "What brings you here?"

"I've come to save the guild," said Margaret. "Yet I can find nothing I need in these books and scrolls. There is nothing about a pair of iron knotting spikes. Iron swords and daggers, aye, and war hammers. All manner of weapons. But the lowly tools that bind us together are absent in the texts, unlike the exalted tools that tear us apart."

"There was a spindle," said Jamila. "In the tale of—"

"Everybody knows about the spindle." Margaret made a dismissive gesture. "On a spinning wheel that pricked the maiden's finger and induced a hundred-year sleep. By definition, the spindle was a weapon."

"Same with the distaff of Zeus's fates." Jamila was smiling, I could hear it in her voice.

"Yes. Same. Clip the thread of fate and die," said Margaret. "That's a weapon if ever there was one. The regnat insists I have a pair of black-iron knotting spikes that belong to him. They consume his thoughts. If we cannot produce them, we will be required to pay."

"How much?"

"The question is not how much, but whom," said Margaret.

"He can't have even one foundling," said Jamila. "Pay him double, in gold."

"We can sit here in the obscure safety of a guild library in the middle of the night and carry on forever about how I will stand in the way of a regnat. Here's the question: *Do* I have the iron spikes, foundling? Are they concealed in this tower somewhere?"

"No."

"Can they be retrieved?"

"No."

Margaret leaned back in her chair. "Errol Thebes was dropped three nights ago. It is rumored you were there."

"He asked me for protection," said Jamila.

Margaret looked away. "It's more than a mile to the earth from the top of Fremantle. If by chance he survived the drop, the streets murdered him before a bell." Margaret was strident but her voice broke on her own sentence, and she put her hand to her mouth. "How could you ever have protected him from the regnat?"

"I wasn't there to protect the runner. I was there to protect the spikes."

"I see. And did you?"

"Aye. I dropped the spikes with him, to the streets."

Margaret pushed her chair back so fast I jumped. "What purpose could that possibly serve?"

"Errol Thebes believes the tools to be uncommon. It appears the regnat believes the same. Of the two, I trust Errol. The spikes were unsafe here in the guild."

"Nothing seems to be safe in this locked iron tower, despite my efforts," said Margaret. She was quiet for a long while. "And about the word *uncommon*. I ban the use of that, from here on. We both know there is nothing uncommon within the walls of this city."

"Then what were you seeking in the library tonight? Information regarding a set of common knotting spikes? I doubt it."

Margaret sighed. "Five hundred men, women, children, and a throng of foundlings depend upon me to sustain them. I am a leader in a city that has fallen into oblivion. So I must always consider all possibilities. If the iron spikes are uncommon, what property could they possible have?"

"They're sharp. They wound."

"They are *spikes*."

"They're aggressive." Jamila had had her hands in her lap under the table. Now she held them out to Margaret. Even in the dim lamplight I recoiled, for I could see they were covered with cuts, some of her fingers wrapped in rag bandages.

Margaret reached out to touch Jamila's fingers but then withdrew. "Perhaps someone should teach you how to knot."

"The spikes reek of mayhem, Guildmaster. Of human flesh and marrow. Of the pelts and feathers and claws of beasts. More so, they sound of two forgings, not one."

"What were they first?" Margaret said.

"I doubt it was a spindle."

"Your imagination is big enough for the whole guild, foundling. Still, I am aware that your senses are attuned to things no one else can taste or smell or hear. Tell me where your mind wanders on this subject."

Jamila turned her book absentmindedly in front of her on the table. She said, "What do you recall of the tales of fylgias from cold places?"

"Fylgias," Margaret Thebes repeated. "Something to do with beasts."

"Aye. Fylgias are uncommon beasts that appear as an animal shadow, to help under duress, to fetch their person at death. An *other*. Such incidents of humans and beasts bound together, one a reflection of the other, exist in nearly every language in this library."

"Tell one."

"From the north, a fierce bear relieved the warrior Bodvar Bjarki when Bjarki was too weary to go on in battle. It was thought to be the warrior's other. Also, the kelp Thorstein Uxafot had a fylgia, again a bear, which he tripped over constantly, unable to see it himself."

"I see no connection between a pair of junk knotting spikes and the fylgias from outside the wall," Margaret said. "Those scents on the spikes could as easily be from the iron. From the wool. We have no beasts in this city."

"We had one beast. That striped infant bear Errol and Odd Thebes found in their quarters," said Jamila.

"An anomaly. A dead anomaly."

"There was another anomaly in Thebes that night. The tunnel knocker Durga. Died that same night," said Jamila.

"Foundlings die all the time."

"Feo would agree."

"Stay away from that thought, foundling."

There was a pulse of silence in the conversation.

Margaret pulled the stack of books to her. "It would be better if we used our time to figure out what those black-iron spikes were made of, what iron was used. Considering I am the guildmaster of Thebes, I could surely assign some apprentice to forge a pair of junk spikes and give those to the regnat. How would he ever know? Here"—Margaret set her hand on a thick volume—"in this book we read of a narrow chain as fine as a strand of thread, which restrains the insane wolf Fenrir. The slurry contained a cat's thunderous footfall, a length of bear sinew, the roots of a mountain—"

"—the breath of a fish, the spit of a bird, and the beard of a woman," said Jamila. (She knew the tale of Gylfi from memory.)

"Nothing impossible in that list," said Margaret. "I have seen plenty of women with beards in this guild."

Jamila opened the book she had been reading on the rafter. "Here we read of a crescent sword smelted with the skin of a pale green dragon who *tripped* into the furnace." (This was the thick and meandering tale of *The Three Kingdoms*. I had read it to Jamila when we were ten. The dragon didn't trip; he was murdered, but this was a constant dispute between Jamila and me. I realized Jamila knew I was in the room.)

"You see?" said Margaret. "All we need is a green wyrm."

"Just send a runner for it," said Jamila.

"I'm serious," said Margaret. "But if the spikes are in any way uncommon, I need to know their power. Is there nothing written of the black-iron needles, in all these scrolls and books?"

Jamila paused.

"You're required to speak the truth, foundling," said Margaret Thebes.

"There is no mention of the black-iron needles in the text of any tale," said Jamila.

I shifted behind Hesiod, my knees aching from being folded up here for so long.

"Then what do I hand to the regnat tomorrow?"

"Hand him the truth. Tell him I dropped his needles when Errol Thebes dropped. He can have me. I can be the first and last guild tax—"

"I'll pit my guild against his whole city, before such a day," said Margaret. Then, shifting: "I can't have guilders scrubbing our bog pots."

Jamila re-stacked the books in front of Margaret. "It would be an interesting war," she said. "Thebes against Fremantle. And when Errol returns, we have the spikes as a weapon."

"Do you truly believe, Jamila Founding, that those simple spikes do anything other than knot?"

"I'm sure of it."

Margaret shook her head. "What is it in us that makes us hope for uncommon things? Things that make us rise or fall: daggers, spikes, swords—"

"Men," said Jamila.

"Tell your meaning," said Margaret.

"You know my meaning, Guildmaster."

"You trespass," Margaret whispered.

"Perhaps a trespass of yours has put this guild in danger. Perhaps you know something of men and beasts."

Margaret stood up fast, as if to come at Jamila, but it was an act of flight, not fight. "In the end, the common things must suffice, foundling," she said. "Guilders work. Foundlings scrub the bogs. Needles bind. Swords tear. And men leave. There is nothing uncommon in this city. I hope Errol Thebes is dead. We both know he is safer that way." Again her voice broke. In the dim silence, they faced each other. Margaret said, "I am insulted to think that the two of you would assume I know nothing of the runner behind Hesiod's writings. I would expect little more from my sister's son, but from you, Jamila Foundling, I do expect more. I suggest the felon return to the roof before my guards arrive."

I crashed out of the bookshelf and stood in front of Jamila. The last time I saw her, I threw her as bait to the guards of Fremantle. Now she took a deep breath, taking in the smell of me. We were kelps again. And then I ran.

Spoke

WE USED TO PLAY A GAME in the halls of Thebes, whenever we found ourselves banded together to run some guild errand on an unfamiliar strata. *Spoke*, we called it. Two mobs of us would stand face-to-face, our backs to the walls. With mere words—a *spoke*—we had to frighten our opponents into running. One side would start by calling out *Death!* pitching the word as iosal as anyone could do at eight years or nine. But the ridiculously high kelp's voice would only set everyone laughing. And then we were off. *I eat* kelps! Or *I come out only in the night! Bloody knives! Darkness! Teeth! Infinity!* Back and forth we hurled frights of minor proportions. The opposing team would shake and clutch at one another in the interest of drama, but hold its ground. I could frighten some of our opponents with the word *foundling*, and I knew all its translations from the other guilds—*zwerver, paria, utlendinger, bezdomen, inimirceach, flygtning, ionnsaigh, satan*. Stray, outcast, stranger, homeless, immigrant, fugitive, intruder, enemy. One side might find itself accidentally in the clutch of real fear by the opponent's humming the tune for "Good Luck to the Ballymow." Of course we always dragged up the tales we read in the library and flung those words about—*demons, doubles, wyrms, felons, witches, Cerberus*. Still we did not run, for in truth we expected the inhabitants of the library to remain there—more so, on the other side of the wall. The obvious exception was the library word that frightened us soundly for, despite our parents' disclaimers, we were aware that a bogle had somehow gotten out of its page. One night we were in some forgotten hallway, more or less in murk. A stranger must have heard us playing the game and thought he would give us a scare.

Rare! we heard him whisper. We went fright quiet, huddled at our two walls. And then: *I see you.*

A MAN STOOD BENT OVER, with his arms plunged to the elbows in a trough. The trough was long enough for bathing. Barrels had been placed under it to shore it up at table height. He was swarthy, built like a furnace, and the room was too narrow and too low for him. His curly hair, his white overshirt, his white pants were sopped with black water, such that he gave the appearance of a guilder doing a reckless job of his laundry. Errol had been dragged down a tunnel and brought here, by Null. He was trying to forget the mob in that pub who had rubbed Dete's blood onto their faces.

Null said, "Utlag. This is that runner from Thebes who fell from the sky." Errol saw only the man at the trough.

Something shifted overhead. The ceiling was so close Errol could press his hands on it. A muffled voice in it said, "What is that?" The voice, the first sound of it, gave him the sensation that the foul contents of a pisspot had been drizzled down his neck. He studied the ceiling till he saw the whites of two eyes studying him through a pair of holes.

"Stay high, Utlag," Errol said.

"What is it?" the voice said again.

Null leaned over to Errol and said, "Give a name."

"Outlaw," said Errol. He could hear his own pulse in his ears.

"Murderer," said Utlag.

"Yes," said Errol, unblinking.

"A murderer from Thebes. Regret! Nothing is ever simple from Thebes. We bring you here; you murder us." The voice was two pitches at once, as though the larynx had suffered some trauma.

"No one in Thebes would order two runners to fight to the death."

"You have the fool's enthusiasm for guild life," Utlag said. "Speaking of fools, Stewart, let's have a look at ours."

Stewart pulled two thick handfuls of hair from the trough, hair that, Errol realized as water flooded over the sides and barrels, was attached to the scalp of a man. The head and chest of the man came partway out of the water, the color of indigo dye. The man disgorged water and gasped. He lifted his eyes to stare at the holes in the mud ceiling. Tired eyes. He was young. "Are we done now?" he said.

"Not quite," said Utlag and then blurted, "Impatience!" Stewart pushed the head back underwater. Utlag said, "I lost money on the fight."

"With him?" said Errol, pointing at the water. His hand was shaking.

"No. When you murdered Jago's man."

"His name was Dete," said Errol.

"He should have won."

"You should have bet on me," said Errol. He could not take his eyes off the water.

Utlag made a clicking sound. "Null bet on you. Null! Why did you bet on a iosal runner from Thebes? What do you see in him?"

Null shrugged. "All them look the same," he said. "Sheep and foul dogs. This one was different."

Errol had no idea what Null was talking about. He glanced at the door and wondered how far he could get if he started to run. He said, "Are you going to let that man up?"

"Why?" said Utlag.

There was a struggle under the water.

"What is your plan for him?"

"What is *your* plan?" said Utlag.

"To stay out of that trough," said Errol. Again Utlag clicked, and Errol understood the clicking to be laughter.

"Turn around," said Utlag, who then blurted, "Necessity! What do you look like!"

Errol made a face. He began to turn, holding his arms out to the sides like a kelp.

"Do you know what a kardunn is?" said Utlag.

"Everyone does," Errol said.

"Not anymore. No one."

"It's a beast from outside the wall. A single-horned forest animal, hoofed, a cousin of horses and goats but rarely seen, possibly related to the qilin. In some texts kardunns are referred to as licorns or unicorns. Noble animals."

"You're a kardunn," said Utlag, his voice greasy with pleasure. Errol was sure he saw Null roll his eyes. "What is it like to be loved? Tell us."

"Don't mock me," Errol said. "What are *you*, that you hide in the ceiling like a foundling?" Stewart turned to Errol for the first time and shook his head no, almost imperceptibly. Fair warning.

"I'm an uncommon thing," said Utlag. "I'm a rare form seeking rare forms. A griffin. A bonnacon. A kardunn."

"I am a monster," said Errol.

A voice spoke from the hall: "He's a coward."

"Don't lurk in doorways, Jago," whispered Utlag, then blurted, "Boredom!"

Jago stepped into the room, bowed awkwardly to the ceiling, and said, "I'll take on this runner. You'll see what he is. A cowardly rodent."

"Watch this," said Utlag. "Are we done, Stewart? Is the fool gone?"

This time, when Stewart lifted him out, the drowning man gasped and reached to put his bound hands on Stewart's hands. There, on that blue arm, was the flying crow with crossed spikes and the brand of an outlaw. "Who—?" Errol said. He stopped. "What did he do to be in there?"

Utlag said, "A reasonable question, Rip. Tell this murderer what you did."

"Rip?" Errol whispered.

The man sputtered, "F-f-f-failed."

"You failed to *what*?"

Panting. "To guard the spican."

Ten years, it had been, since Errol had heard his brother's voice.

"Spican?" Errol realized he was yelling. Lowered his voice: "You mean spikes? What sort of spikes?"

"*My* spikes," said Utlag. "Where could they be lost? It is a walled city."

"I'll go. I'll look again. I'm begging," whispered Rip.

"Don't beg, Rip," said Utlag. "This won't take even a minute. Jago, over there, will watch you drown. And that will inspire him to do your work."

Errol thought this: There are three men who would surely stop me. I could fight them, then haul Rip out of the water. But Rip couldn't run. His hands are bound; no doubt so are his feet. Never in any book was it written like this, where the hero was an idiot and no one was playing by the rules. Then he wondered to himself, *How would Odd handle this?*

"I'll get them for you," he said. Everyone in the room turned to him. He turned his back on the hole in the ceiling and spoke to Null, as though Utlag did not exist. "Neither of those two will ever do the work you need. Not Jago, and not that one in the water. If Jago knew how to finish anything, I would be dead. Which I'm obviously not. And if the fool in that tub was worth his pay, then the iron spokes—"

"Spikes," Utlag said from above.

"Whatever," Errol said, shrugging. "Whatever they are, they would be here. Tell me what they are and I'll get them for you by tomorrow. The noctis bell."

Jago glared at Errol, but Utlag groaned in pleasure and said, "Curious. How? How would you get them?"

Errol looked up at the eye. "It's simple. I am a runner from the high tower roofs of this city. I run errands. I am, unlike your staff, reliable."

Utlag clicked. And then screamed, "Do you think I'm the fool? The regnat sent you! *Suspicion!*"

"He dropped me, if that's what you mean. He wanted me to die."

"Rip? Tell me who this is, this murderer from Thebes. He's obviously here to save you."

Rip searched Errol's face.

Errol could not give Rip the time to think. "You have no idea who I am, do you? Of course you know me. Of course he knew me. And I knew him. He was the guildmaster's son. I served him breakfast every day. No. See? He can't remember. None of Margaret Thebes's sons ever cared for anyone but themselves. Drown him. I don't care. Just give me anyone who knows the streets and I'll have the spikes for you by tomorrow. And for this? I want the money that was in the pot today when I won my fight. It was two hundred thirty-seven uurs."

The room was silent. Utlag finally said, "I think, perhaps, scorpion. Well, the abbot will be glad of it. Stewart, be done with Rip. And, Null, take Jago to gaol."

"You mean, take the runner to gaol?" said Null.

"No."

Jago cried out and tried to run but Null was unnaturally fast, and in a moment Jago was gone.

Utlag said, "It's all very well to choose a time, but we don't observe the roof's timekeeping here. The unrelenting bells. It is more accurate on these streets to keep time in increments of pain. Let's start with Jago's pain. He will be kept in gaol until you come to the scriptorium with the iron spican."

"What is the scriptorium?" said Errol.

"It was the house of tales once. Now it's where deals are dealt."

"And what's gaol?"

Utlag paused. "It's a place to meet yourself. All right. You find the spikes. Suffice to say, if you don't reappear, I'll send whatever is left of Jago to come for you. I'm sure he'll run *that* errand reliably."

"Why would you wager Jago's life? He has twice tried to finish me off. I would never come back for him."

Utlag clicked. "Oh, you would come back for Jago." Click. "You'd come back for Null. For Stewart, there. For Rip. As soon as I'm gone, you'll make some effort to save Rip. You are a runner from the high tower roofs of this city, trained to go back for every bloody, dying prisoner. Under the right circumstances you would even come back for me. I'll give you the money. Just find what is mine." There was a shuffling in the ceiling and the eyes were gone.

Errol ran for the trough and threw Stewart out of the way, grabbed Rip's shoulders, hauled him out of the water. "Stay high," whispered Errol in his ear, then threw his full weight on Rip's chest.

The Sewers

"**WHAT DID YOU EXPECT?**" said Rip.

"A table," said Errol. "Maybe even a chair."

A little band of kelps had followed them to Rip's tower, their hands caked with filth, their eyes red with fever. The journey here had not gone well. For one thing, Rip was nothing like Errol expected. He had spent the whole journey digging in the rubble for rot that he threw at the kelps and they put in their pockets. *Like some game,* Errol murmured. Then he disappeared down stairways and into grimy hovels and kept Errol waiting with the kelps outside. Errol's wounds hurt, and he could make no sense of the streets. How could people could live in such squalor? Why didn't parents wash their kelps or cover such rashes or feed them? All the women Rip greeted in the hovels were iosal, like foundlings, and after the third stop, Errol wondered aloud how Rip knew them or even if any of the kelps were his. Rip stopped long enough to remove a flask from his shirt, uncork it, and take a long swig.

"It's possible, runner. You never know."

They had come to a tower, the door of which had to be pried open with a pipe they had to dig out of the mud. Rip had forgotten this was the guild tower Thrace. Errol pointed to the golden lyre over the entry. The inner wall of the entry hall had been hacked open to expose the frayed ropes of a transport pulley. Errol climbed into the box, bending his legs up under so that his chin was between his knees. He expected to rise, but the tower had long been locked. The box bumped and jerked as it dropped within the wall. When it slammed to a halt, Errol opened the panel and let himself fall out. The floor materialized beneath his feet. He was eleven strata below the street, in a sewage main.

Rip's quarters, a hollow dug out of the earthen tunnel, was crammed with salvage: scraps of canvas blooming with mold, broken sieves, loom treadles, barrel staves, flints. Rip had cleared two narrow paths through the refuse, one to a mass of mildewed shipping sacks, the other to a sodden cushion with a heap of tiny bones on it. The place reeked of the sewer. No chair, no table.

"You can sleep over there," said Rip. "And put on these clothes. Sleep an uur. We'll have to work through the night to find somewhere to hide you in the city."

"Hiding is not my plan. I plan to get the knotting spikes." He was pulling Rip's tunic over his head. It was too small. The leggings, too. They sat on the floor and ate in silence, scraping gray meat from rusted tins.

"I didn't ask you to save me," said Rip.

Errol was licking the tin. "Well, let's think about that for a second. If I didn't come along, that eyeball called Utlag would be disposing of your soggy remains right now."

"I had a plan."

"What was it? Taxidermy? Tell me about the job you failed to do. Seems like a pair of simple knotting spikes would be easy enough to buy or steal, or even to make." He set the empty tin on the floor.

"Utlag's spikes are uncommon," Rip said. He used the word *uncommon* so casually, Errol laughed. "And it's better if you don't know about them. You're not exactly able to defend yourself."

"Don't be ridiculous. So far I've saved both myself and you."

"Luck. Your fighting is sloppy. Didn't you have any brothers or sisters up there on the roofs, to teach you to fight?"

"Brothers, actually. But they both were criminals, dropped before I was old enough to learn anything from them. And they certainly never taught me to knot."

Rip's eyes narrowed and his mouth fell open.

He did not get up or fumble with word or embrace Errol as other long-lost brothers had done in stories we had read. Rather he threw his head back and cried out, "Do all of Margaret Thebes's sons have to die before this ends?" And then he said, "You have to admit, you don't look like me."

Errol said, "I've been told that. But I've never seen a mirror."

"Again, lucky," Rip said, uncorking his flask.

———

Through the night, Errol told Rip the pieces of legends that still circulated on the roof, of two wild sons who rose high and fell fast.

"Marek Thebes loved you especially," said Errol. "He loves me because I'm his connection to you."

"He was a first-year runner when Fenn was roof master of Thebes," said Rip. "I was in my second year. Somebody owed somebody a favor, and Marek ended up on our roof."

"A favor? Marek is the best roof master in this city. He didn't need any favors," said Errol.

"You do know, don't you, that he was a foundling?"

"That's ridiculous. He came from Topfer."

"Everyone comes from somewhere. He came up to the roofs with only the clothes he wore. No tent, and no pack. He grew the beard to hide the naught mark."

"That can't be," said Errol. "What does he lack? Nothing that I could see—"

"What is your point in looking for his deficit?"

"What is your point in slandering him?"

"Not slander. I admired him. For the first week he slept in the weather till we all realized he wasn't being stubborn, he just didn't have a tent. We very much wanted him to live through winter. So we ordered skins and sewed him a black one-man tent with a chimney so he could have his own fire. Seemed to like solitude."

"He still uses that tent."

"I'm not surprised. Foundlings live frugally."

"I would have told Margaret Thebes had I known he was a foundling, and had him arrested. Foundlings cannot be trusted."

Rip looked at him with curiosity. "Why would you say that?"

"A foundling was the cause of my drop to the streets."

Rip drank from the flask. "From what I see so far, I'd wager you were your own cause."

They sat staring at each other. Errol could feel his blood pulsing in the sole of that foot, in the wound, and it was throbbing up his shin.

Rip broke the silence. "Well, Sabine liked you. The shield. I can't see why."

"I have a clever strategy," said Errol, picking up the tin again to see if he had missed anything. "I didn't let Dete kill her in the fight. She liked that."

"Well, I resent it," said Rip. "I thought she and I might have something."

"Odd once told me girls wanted to be near the three of us just because we're the sons of the guildmaster."

"Who's Odd?"

"Your cousin. He was a kelp when you went up to the roofs. Slyngel and Gudrun's last of nine."

"I don't remember him."

"Of course you do. Heimdall and Ragnar's little brother. He is my best friend. Skinny. Tall. Good company. The best card player in the guilds."

"Nothing."

"Always beating everyone at shatranj. Even you."

Rip made a face, trying to remember.

"He talks quite a bit."

"Oh, him! Odd Thebes! Aye, I remember now."

Rip turned the flask in his fingers. The warm peat of whiskey filled the room. He drank again and looked at his brother, at the foot Errol had propped over the chair to relieve the pain. The wound bulged with infection. An angry red stripe ran up the inside of Errol's calf.

"Before you pass out in that chair, what exactly were you thinking when you offered to find the spikes?"

"First a question for you. Where would you begin looking?" said Errol.

"I'd ask the hawkers in the market."

"I should think you would have done that already this week."

"Or I would ask the felons who roam the city at night."

"Why would they tell you?"

"I would rummage around in the streets."

Errol sat with his eyes closed for a while. "You haven't looked for them, have you? You have never even tried to find the spikes."

"It's not so simple as that."

"But you said that you tried and failed."

"I lied."

Errol said, "Why don't you look for them? You are afraid of something."

"And so should you be."

"But Utlag nearly killed you today. What could be worse than that?"

"Plenty," said Rip. "Some things are better left unfound."

Errol didn't have the strength to argue. "Then I should tell you that I am the one who possesses the knotting spikes."

"What?" Rip jumped up. "Where are they?!"

"I came upon them on the roof in a gut run. Black-iron, plain ones that cut my fingers when I just held them. They're in a sheath that looks like a cage, right? When I took them out—"

"Are they *here*?" Rip demanded.

"They're buried in the street where I fell."

"Are they in their cage?"

"Their sheath? Yes. That seems to be a common concern."

Rip sat back. "Did nothing happen to you when you found them?"

"You mean, anything worse than being dropped to the streets, beaten and stabbed, and dying tonight of infection in a bog room off a sewer tunnel, eleven strata under the street?"

Rip took the last swig from the bottle. "Yes."

The Attarh

I SHINED MY HEAD LAMP into the chamber whose shelves were crammed with mortars and pestles, bins and bottles of a thousand shapes and colors.

"A runner? Inside? Are you not aware this is a felony?" said the old man who sat cross-legged in the middle of the round room on a small, round rug. He was long-boned and skinny with a scrub of white hair and short stubble on his long jaw. His eyes were closed. In one hand he held a green bowl under his nose; his other hand fanned the air over it.

I unfolded the papers I had brought. "I am here under orders," I said.

"You must be vastly important." He yawned, still fanning.

"I'm here to inquire about an apprenticeship. I was sent by Marek Thebes, my roof master. Are you the attarh?"

"Shine the light on yourself," he said, opening his eyes. "Ah yes. I see why he sent you. They all think a nose will do it." He took a deep whiff of the bowl. "No, this is just not the same. Merely a distant approximation."

I shrugged. "You're busy. I'll come back."

"You may stay. Ask me all your questions," he said.

"It's supposed to be the other way around."

"Guild laws." He tossed the whole bowl into a bin in the wall. I couldn't tell if he was irritated with laws, me, or the contents of the bowl. "Well, what is the scent you need?"

"I'm not here to purchase anything," I said. "I'm here to be judged."

"I judge that you are here." I put down my pack. This was going to take a while. He took the paper from me. "Marek Thebes says getting an early apprenticeship would help you. You're not working, you're not studying. You can't seem to do anything but sleep." He looked up at me. "Why not love? That's motivation."

I laughed.

"What? You don't think an old man would remember?"

"I'm the one who wouldn't remember. I can't even get a girl to run errands with me."

"Ah. I see. How many revolutions?"

"Seventeen. Almost."

He studied me now. "Yes. Well," he said. "Seventeen is good for love. And now I think that nose of yours would be good for this work."

I put my hand up to my nose. "It's not that big."

"I didn't say it was big. I said it was seventeen. What is your real name?"

"Odd Thebes."

"I doubt that. I am really Kyphi Attarh. I blend the essences of every known animal, vegetable, and mineral from outside the way into formulae. For example, tell me: What or whom do you desire?"

"The streets," I said without a thought.

"Plech," he said. "Bah! Why do you want that? The formula for the streets. Let me see. Eight parts human suffering. Three parts turds. Equal parts, after that, of blood, vomit, whiskey, blade rust, maw worms, pus, death, death, and also more death, maggot slime, and the oil of fear. You want that?"

"Aye."

The attarh got to his feet. He was agile. "Odd Thebes," he said, "give up on your cousin."

"How do you know about him?"

"Everyone knows. But the streets will do you in. For you, I think, we need something else—"

"But—"

"I think *theater*," he said. "A theater for the bard."

"And how is it that you already know who I am?"

"Small city. Big walls."

He was circling the room, reaching into bins and bowls, shaking this and that, tipping a little into a fresh bowl, all the while calling out:

"Two parts each, oils of script parchment and iron gall ink (Get this down!); three parts, the red velvet curtain; two parts, the leather seats with horsehair stuffing; one part, the rump farting on the chair; one part, corn exploded in the fire; five, the sweat of armpits in unwashed costumes; two, greasepaint; two, wigs; one, the oil from hemp rope and pulleys. Let's say a drop each: the rushes underfoot, the smoke from the lights, the pulp in the playbill. And we cannot forget"—he grinned at me and reached for a canister on a top shelf—"a pinch of sulfur from Bian Pao, the fragrance of stage explosions."

He set a carpet for me next to his on the floor. I sat with him, with the new bowl in my hands, waving the attarh of the theater into my nose. Truth? I expected nothing. But the formula in that bowl took me back immediately to the first play I had ever seen in the Great Hall of Thebes. The guilders had put on Homer's *Odyssey*. I had loved it.

"Name the formula," Kyphi said.

"How can I? I don't know it."

"No one does. It is new. Today. Give it a name."

"Act One," I said.

"Act One! Indeed!" He crossed his arms. "All right. Repeat the entire formula to me." He crossed his arms. I was surprised to find that I remembered all he had put into it: exactly what, and how much. Then he asked what I would add and I said the smell of anticipation. "Cypriol?" I ventured, remembering the soap in the invitations from Al-Razi.

"Cypriol could work. But the oil of a newly cracked-open book would be better. Not strictly theater, but every play is the opening of a tale." He retrieved a bottle and added a drop to my bowl.

"It's perfect," I said, fanning as he had shown me, genuinely impressed with his skill.

"Well done, Odd Thebes. You are welcome to take the guild exams to apprentice at Attarh House." He grew sober then. "But I smell a longing on you that will not be satisfied here. This tower contains the mere sillage of human life, and not the life itself."

"Nothing will help," I said, sniffing at my bowl again.

"A woman could help," he said. "You'll forget everything."

"Women don't like me."

"Well," he said, tipping the contents of my bowl into a miniature glass bottle he pulled from his pocket. "Try this. Women love theater. If that doesn't work, come back and I'll bottle up some heroism for you."

"Right." I laughed, but he was serious. "What's in *that*?"

"It is the formula we discussed, from the streets. Plus one drop of the oil of valor."

"Where do you get that?"

"The antlers of rutting red deer. Which, incidentally, is exactly the same as the attarh of stupidity. Sh. Don't tell."

I turned to go. "By the way," I said. "What were you doing, when I came in? That bowl you threw away—"

"I was trying again to perfect my formula for the attarh of the roofs," he said. "But then you arrived with your silk-smelling hands and the rust scrapes on your leggings, your fresh sweat and the night air cold on your hair." He inhaled deeply. "The clouds riming the lines in ice. I miss it, still."

I looked at him in a new way. We were dwellers in the same high world. "I wish you had saved the formula you made," I said. "I'd have bought it from you."

"It's too soon. When you come off the roofs next year, I'll make it for you. All the runners want it when they go down into the guilds. It is the mainstay of my business. Meanwhile, go back to the sky. There is no attarh, not even this one, who can improve upon the real thing."

The Riverbank Yurt

RIP WAS SHAKING HIM. "Get up! It's that wound on your foot. I thought you were gone. Get up!" Errol's leg was so swollen he could not bend it. He was hotter than a lamp. Rip dragged him into the sewage main, pressed him into the storage pulley, steam coming off his face and fingers in the confinement of the box.

Errol could not remember how he and Rip arrived in the alley between Fremantle and Pitcairn. He was feverish now, and his head was full of the nightmare of the fall that ended here. There was nothing to find here. The plank that had fallen with him was gone. The rope was gone. The spikes. He also could not remember leaving that alley, slogging through canals and dark corners to the river, and wondered how he came to be standing at the flap of an orange yurt on the riverbank at the south wall, lit in the night like a white-orange moon.

"Dagmar is not to be trusted," Rip was saying. "No one goes in here. She has wolves. The place is filthy."

"I dreamt of a woman with wolves, the night in the river." Errol knew he was slurring. "There were wolves. She carried a bow."

"Not a dream," said Rip.

"So you'll prop me up here by myself, with my fever and this striped leg, and hope she doesn't eat me?" Errol leaned against the yurt.

"Don't tell her you're my brother. Whatever you say, don't say that." Rip was already running away from him to hide below the riverbank. Errol reached to pull the strap on a brass bell, but the flap opened and there was the woman. The wolves slunk around her with their rear ends down.

"I'm Rip Thebes's brother."

"Here you go, then," she said. She opened her hand and he saw a small metal tube with a red cap on it. "Break the wound open and get this into it. Deep. It worked the first time I put it on your foot, but then you went barefoot in the streets." She dropped the flap and was gone.

"That's it?" he said through the canvas. She did not reply. He unscrewed the cap. The grease inside smelled of the innards of plants. He cleared his throat and said, "Hello?" In a long while, she opened the flap. She raised her eyebrows.

"I think you should look at this," he said. He pointed at his foot.

"You cannot come in here," she said.

"You've nothing to hide. I already know it's filthy in there."

She frowned. "Where *is* your brother, anyway?" She looked over his shoulder and uttered an oath under her breath.

The wolves herded Errol roughly into the yurt, stepping on his feet, running him closer to the wall, furtively concealing low threats as panting.

"Sit," commanded Dagmar. Errol sat down. "Not you. Them." The wolves tucked their tails around their rumps and sat.

The room was larger than the yurt had looked. At its center was a great fire, and around the fire a circle of hamacs strung from the frame of the yurt. The earthen floor was strewn with fresh thatch of lavender and thyme. The air smelled of cedar smoke. Errol sat and Dagmar took his foot in her hand. "Roban, *fecce fihle*," she said. The wolf disappeared up a stairway and returned with a clean rag in his mouth.

"This will hurt." She pressed her thumb into Errol's foot to crack the wound open. A thick mass of green pus wormed its way out. Errol gasped. The pain was violence and its remedy in one. She wiped the pus away and threw the rag in the fire.

Errol reached up to touch Roban. "I wouldn't," Dagmar said. "He smells Utlag on you." She set a pot under his foot and poured the liniment into the wound. It hissed and burst into a boil. He yelled out and the wolves yipped and whined and Dagmar said something to them.

"They share my pain?" Errol said.

"Not exactly. You're a wounded animal and they'd like to eat you." She packed felt into the wound and wrapped the foot tightly in strips of the rag. When she was done, Errol put his hand out. Dagmar removed the bandage. His hand was swollen and dripping with infection. Dagmar sighed irritably.

"Your brother. Is he utterly helpless?"

"All the evidence points to that," Errol said.

Errol could not take his eyes off Dagmar. "You're more animal even than your wolves," he blurted.

"Everyone is," she said. "Is your brother in a similar condition?"

"He was nearly drowned, earlier today. Or yesterday. What day is it?"

Errol pointed to the knife wound at his ribs and she dressed that and bound his chest to steady the ribs that had broken in the fall. The smell of oils and herbs in a pot in the fire made his stomach churn. She took the lid from a cauldron. A golden puff of a pie was baking in it.

"*Cwae*," she told the wolves, who trotted reluctantly in a line up to the loft of the tent.

The pie was thick and crusted with chives. Inside were two river trout, slabs of potato, and roasted field carrots. Dagmar carried him to one of the string hamacs, set him in it, and a bowl of the pie in his lap. She watched him devour it.

"This is heofon." He wiped his face on the sleeve of his tunic. "I have never eaten fresh food. What do you call this?"

"Roban's dinner."

Errol laughed. "Did this come in on the ships?"

"Ships? No. I fish the river, farm the banks. Why are you here?"

Errol made a quizzical face and pointed to the foot. His mouth was full.

"Why are you here on the streets?"

Why did he want to tell her everything? He began with the roofs of Thebes and the gut run and the iron spikes and the sacking of his roof. He told of the foundling who betrayed him, the regnat's punishment, the fight on the street, the fight in Null's pub, the near drowning of Rip.

At the end of it Dagmar said, "So you didn't come to help."

"I was thrown off a plank. I would like to help the guilds, yes."

"And what about helping us?"

"I had no idea you were here. No one knows you're here."

The comfort of the string hamac, the pie, the salves she had packed into his wounds, the fire snapping, the smoke and fragrances of the fields, all contributed to Errol's sense that it would be all right to close his eyes for a moment.

When he was almost gone, she said, "Tell me about him."

"Him?" said Errol. In slurs and half dreams, he told her what little he knew of Rip. The father they didn't know and a mother who didn't like any of them, the rogue life Rip and their elder brother, Fenn, led in the guilds and on the roofs. Thefts and gut runs, unbefitting of a roof master and a runner. Finally, their punishment. The sewer Rip lived in now, far below the street. His interest in low women and whiskey. His failed dealings with Utlag.

———

Errol awoke with a start. The fire was out. How long had he been asleep? He leapt from the hamac, lifted the flap of the yurt to leave. But something caught his attention. On the floor next to the hamac were clean wools, neatly folded in a pile, and a pair of soft leather boots he had not seen before. On top of them lay the spikes in their sheath.

ERROL TOOK THE STAIRS four at a time to the loft of Dagmar's yurt. She was curled in a heap with the wolves in the winter air.

"Where did you get these?" he said. He was taking off Rip's clothes and hopping into these new leggings. "Turn around, will you?"

"I've seen you naked."

"Aye, but at that time you were a dream. Where did you get these clothes and the iron spikes? You're a witch. There is conjuring in it."

"Everything we need is here. I know that. If that's witchery, then yes."

He followed her down the ladder, pulling the new boots on.

"I can't understand how you sleep in this yurt without being attacked, how you survive the streets."

"I know what I am. What I can do." The wolves moved with her as if they were a furred barge on which she rode.

"I know what *I* can do, too, and look at me. I've nearly been killed twice already."

"You have no idea who you are. Watch this."

She went to a hook on the yurt wall, removed an ironwood bow, and handed it to him. He was weak from the infection, but he pulled the bowstring and sighted the door. She took out a red quiver and set it over his shoulder. The wolves watched every move.

"Stand over there," she said and she walked across the yurt in the opposite direction. "Take aim."

He set the arrow and raised the bow and said, "At what?"

"At me," she said.

"I certainly will not," he said, lowering the bow. "If you mean to insult me, you should know that I'm a good aim."

"I'm sure you are. Think of this as the beginning of our friendship."

"And the end of it, all in the same moment."

She threw up her hands. "I have things to do, then. Give me the bow. You've no more courage than your brother."

He raised the bow. "Don't move," he said. He pulled back the bowstring hard. Out of the corners of his eyes he saw the ears on the entire pack of wolves prick up and turn to him. Movement, a tautness. When he released the string, he expected to be attacked. He saw the gray figure of Roban, leaping into the air, jaws narrowly open, teeth a white streak across the room. The wolf's great head was jarred sideways by the force of the arrow and Errol thought the animal had been hit. But before the bowstring had stopped vibrating, Roban dropped the arrow and was coming for him, followed by the pack. Errol raised the bow again on reflex and reached over his shoulder for a second arrow, but she had given him only one.

"You fooled me!" he said. But just as Roban leapt at his throat, Dagmar called, *"Sitte!"* The wolf swam away from him in midair and hit the earthen floor at a gallop. The rest of the pack floated up and down after him and thundered around the yurt until they came to a stop at Dagmar's feet, panting.

"Wuldorlic," Errol said. Roban looked away from him. "That must have terrified him, the first time you made him catch an arrow in his teeth."

"It wasn't my idea," she said, taking the bow he handed to her. "Fremantle tests weapons from Strael House on anything down here that moves. Thousands, in some weeks. They killed three of my wolves. They even name the arrows, as if it's amusing." She pulled two arrows from her quill and rolled the shafts in her fingers. *Doom, Iron Rain.* "Roban trained himself to catch these, and the others followed. Wolves like to work. Now it's their idea of a fine day."

"What do you do with the arrows?"

"I keep the best ones for my own. I, too, am in constant practice, should the need arise. The rest I reforge into pots, hoes, hooks, nails, whatever is required."

"Knotting spikes?"

She laughed. "An interesting theory, but I lack skills in knotwork."

Errol suddenly remembered. "I've kept my brother waiting." She took her cloak from a peg and gave it to him.

"Will this make me invisible?" he said, stuffing more pie into the pockets.

"You read too many books. Is it not enough that it keeps you warm? By the way, you'll want to be careful with those spikes in the dark," Dagmar said.

"What do you mean by 'careful'?"

"Darkness is their workroom. Keep them in their sheath. Though I wonder if you should be reckless instead. I bet you'd be something worth seeing. It would be painful, though. You don't seem to like pain."

"Do they knit an uncommon garment? Should I try knotting with them?"

"I wouldn't," she said.

"Well, thank you. You've left nothing at all to guesswork."

"They belong in the scriptorium vault, where all this city's irfelaf should be."

"That which remains," said Errol.

"Exactly. These are said to be the last of the iron this city produced. Uncommon.

Obviously. I certainly wouldn't give them to Utlag. But if you don't, then Jago will not survive. So you've made a trap for yourself."

"Jago's no good," said Errol.

"We're all no good, outlaw. And we're all good."

———

Rip had buried himself in purgament to keep warm.

"Three bells," he said. "Three long frozen bells. I despise every inch of you."

"Here's something for you." Rip fell upon the pie like the starving man he was. "And here's something else." Errol held up the sheath and tipped the pair of spikes out of it.

Rip jumped and was fifty yards up the river before he turned to yell, "Put them away! Now! It's dark! Don't you know anything?"

"I thought you'd be glad. You might live now, right? And Jago, too."

"Glad? No. I'm not ever glad to see those."

As they stole through the streets, staying alongside the towers to hide in the shadows cast by the moon, Rip said, "Tell me all about her."

In the Gutters

I WAS PLAGUED by the sudden recollection of something the foundling had not said to Margaret Thebes a night ago in the library. Over and over I recited the lines to myself, looking for what hid there. Margaret had asked, *Is there nothing written of the black-iron needles, in all these scrolls and books?* Jamila Foundling had paused, then replied, *There is no mention of the black-iron needles in the text of any tale.*

Jamila had *paused*.

A pause, in the dialect of Jamila Foundling, was a pivot. Whatever came after it would be the mathematical opposite of the truth, and yet not a lie.

I bribed the guilder at the grate and crept back into the guild.

The library was deserted. I went to the book Jamila had been reading in the rafters, the first volume in the set of *The Three Kingdoms*, the tale that contained the crescent sword smelted from the remains of a single pale green dragon that had been shoved into the forge.

I examined the covers, stared down the shaft formed by the spine and the binding. Flipped through a thousand pages. Aside from a small, upside-down set of greasy thumbprints on one spread of pages, I could find nothing worth the month's salary I had just spent to come here. Well, of course, there were a half dozen holes my father had cut out of the book. In this library such deficits were commonplace.

I should make some attempt to explain Slyngel Thebes. My da followed the custom of the city in naming his offspring from the library books and scrolls. Names, words, ideas—anything from outside the wall had value to us. However, as with all matters in which Slyngel involved himself, his particular version was lost in the labyrinth of a drunken mind. Whenever Mam announced that she was with child, Slyngel would stagger up to the library, a climb that took him half a night, weak as he was from serving no useful function. Book by book, scroll by scroll, he worked over the collection with a blade he reserved for this purpose. His excisions were perfect, tiny rectangles. He cut any name that caught his eye. Some pages were riddled with "hollows" as he called them.

As he cut the names, he stuffed them into his socks, where they could ferment while my mother grew thick with child. When Mam issued the first bellow of labor, Slyngel bellowed, too, digging the names out of his socks in a foul-smelling roll call. In the end he gave each of his kelps the name that "provoked it," he said, "from Gudrun's innards."

I was the last of nine to be provoked, so it was impossible for me to have borne witness to the hollowing. My brothers told it to me. The name "Odd" appears in a handful of texts, mainly in the northern tales, but I knew, from having gone over and over these volumes, that never were any Odds cut from any page. Heimdall took pleasure in telling me that Slyngel never bothered to venture to the library when he heard Mam was pregnant for the last time. Upon seeing me as a newborn, Slyngel said, "The socks are empty. Well, that's *odd*."

———

I held volume one of *The Three Kingdoms* in my hands, setting my mind to wander on the subject of the warrior Liu Bei.

My father had hollowed the name Liu Bei from the center of the 389th page of the book. Ultimately he had not used that name on any one of his own children. (Least to best, we were Heimdall, Ragnar, Ketill, Bellona, Bergusia, Alekto, Megaera, Tisiphone, and Odd.) However, there *was* a Liu Bei in Thebes guild. A woodshop accountant, five years older than I was, a twitchy guilder who pilfered food from the guild pantries and hoarded it in his bench.

I opened to the page with Liu Bei hollowed out of it and stared. My vision wandered from the hole to something I had not seen before. Deep in the gutter of the book, where the two pages met, was a minuscule smear of dirt. I flattened the book and looked closely. The smear was not dirt at all. There were four tiny letters—SCIU—written in lead along the stitch line between the pages. Tiny letters, squared off at their corners. My father's hollow. My father's handwriting. A shiver went up my spine.

Sciu?

I reached for the volume containing the tales of Odin and Freya and looked for my siblings' names. There was a hole in the text where "Ketill" had been cut. And there, in the gutter of that book, across from the hollow, tiny letters spelled *ratt*. I found the same minute designation—*ratt*—where Ragnar's name had been cut. And *ratt* again, next to the hollow at Heimdall.

I whispered, "*Ratt, ratt, ratt*, and *sciu*."

Alone they meant nothing to me. Together they were abbreviations from the language, not to mention the field guide, of Pliny: *rattus, rattus, rattus, sciurus*. In the common tongue: rat, rat, rat, and squirrel.

"What did *you* know about beasts?" I growled at my dead father. What on earth did you know about anything?

I went to a shelf and grabbed a copy of *Beowulf*. I had visited this book and this page a hundred times as a kelp, jealous that Errol had a real name from a real tale, more jealous that my da had once cut that name from one page in the book, while he never managed to remove my name from anywhere. *Erol*, in the ancient tongue, meant the "earl." The knight. I found the hollow. When I pressed the book open, I saw, for the first time, my father's handwriting in the gutter. He had written *cerv*.

"*Cervus*," I said. "So there, Errol Thebes. Not a tiger or a bear, not an eagle. Merely a deer." It was foolish to feel smug about this. What was I even talking about?

I was suddenly reminded of a night in the guild tower. I grabbed the tales of Ovid, Virgil, and Apollonius from the shelves and flipped through their pages, seeking a hollow at the name Orpheus. It's harder than you might expect to find a name that is gone. When I finally found that hollow, I pressed the page open and saw, in that tiny squared-off handwriting, *Xov*. I could think of no beasts in Pliny's tongue that could be abbreviated in this manner. *Xov*. But when I looked closer I saw that only the *X* was written in ink, the rest in lead. It was not *Xov* but *X ov*, separated by a hair's space.

"Ovid?" I whispered, unsure of myself. I knew of course that it was not Ovid. Not a bard. A beast. *Pay attention*, I ordered myself. *Ovis*. A sheep.

But what was the *X*? The location of a treasure? Pliny's numeral ten? A kiss?

I was on the edge of knowing something. I was also hot. I pulled the toque off my head and pushed up my sleeves. I glanced down at my arm, at the tatu of the crow with crossed spikes in his talons, spikes that formed an X. And now I was shaking.

Why? It was because, in Thebes guild, Orpheus was not just the lute-playing hero from an ancient text. He was Orpheus—Feo—the suicidal foundling. The clatter of hoofs. The screaming leap. Mayhem. Was the *X* for death? Could I go so far as to think it was a pair of crossed spikes?

I ran through the stacks. There was another unsolved murder in our tower. Jamila had questioned Margaret about it. That old tunnel knocker, Durga, had died with a fresh scar up the middle of her chest.

I yanked the scroll of the tales of *Markandeya* from its pigeonhole and rolled it open, spun the rolls until I found a hollow in the parchment where Durga's name had been. A scroll was not a book; would there still be a hidden beast? In the margin outside of the text there was my answer: *mel*. Or rather: *X mel*.

"Mel?" I said aloud, thinking. "*Melea*? In the common tongue: badger." And, as if that whole incident had happened yesterday, I said, "So, not an infant striped bear. A badger." I shoved the scroll away. A badger, dead from a beating; an old foundling found dead with a bizarre wound. I could never forget that my father had been there when that foundling died.

"Did you murder them? Feo *and* Durga?" I yelled to no one. "Just how miserable were you?!"

I went wild now, pulling scrolls and books from the shelves and finding Slyngel Thebes's gutter scribblings everywhere, connecting guilders to beasts at the point of a gone name. Horses, lizards, beetles, cats, skunks, dogs, sheep, pigs, snakes. This went far beyond the naming of his own kelps. Every name he had cut from the tales had been used in this guild to name someone, a foundling or a guilder.

It was an insane catalog, hidden in plain sight, now that I could see it, all over the tales in the library and containing, from what I could tell, the names of every foundling and guilder in Thebes. The holes in the pages were not just a naming ritual. In fact I was no longer sure they were for naming at all. They were Slyngel Thebes's bizarre method for distracting anyone from seeing his private taxonomy hidden in the gutters.

"Were you mocking us?" I yelled. "Tracking us like beasts? Killing off the weak ones? Why record your crimes? Were you proud? Did you want someone to see this? Who on earth would ever read it here? No one! Everyone knew you were a worthless drunk. We're relieved you're dead!"

I put my hands to my face, regretting my own self.

Worse yet—far worse: I was trying to ignore something within myself: Before I got to any hollow or any abbreviation in any gutter, I myself knew what beast my father would pencil in for each guilder. How did I know? I didn't even understand the game. Also, I had never seen a live beast—save that infant striped bear, that badger.

I grabbed a copy of Shirazad's tales, flipped to the first page with a hollow cut from it. I covered the gutter before I could see it. The missing name was Dunyazad, Shirazad's little sister. I thought of the guilder I knew who had that name, a jovial, stubborn woman who worked in the shops. I whispered, as if anyone were listening, the first beast that came to my mind. Ram. I lifted my hand. *Ar.* Now I was yelling, Aries! The ram indeed. I was panicked at the idea that anything my lunatic father said or wrote could make any kind of sense to me. Liu Bei was a squirrel? Yes. Ketill was a rat? Yes! The last thing I would ever want was to be like my da. His thin leggings bagging at the knees and hanging at the crotch, his stupid card games and belching and his love for that flask.

Pause.

I sat yet again at the table and reopened volume one of *The Three Kingdoms*. What did Jamila have to hide?

I checked every hole again, and every gutter. Finally I put the spine of the book on the table to see if it would fall open to a particular spread of pages.

It did. In a very fine ink line, a line as fine as a hair, this sentence was under-lined in the text: *You are surrounded with the certainty of death if you do not yield.* The first three *i*'s in the sentence were circled, and so was the letter *f* in the word *if.* A new code?

"What is *iiif*?" I put my head on the table. "There is no such beast."

Then my heart tightened fast in my ribs. I slammed the book shut, threw it on a pile on the floor. I ran all the way up the halls, shoved the grate guilder out of the way, climbed up the ladder and out to the roofs, fell into my tent, tied the flap, and dove in my sack.

That last entry was not my father's record-keeping. There were no beasts. No holes in the page. None of Pliny's names. Someone had discovered my father's catalog. Someone had tracked his movements and his writings. Someone had left this book splayed wide-open so he would see it, no doubt on the table in the night library, likely in the same place I had just opened it myself. Jamila wasn't hiding the text from Margaret that night. She was hiding it from me. The third of Faol, commonly abbreviated iiiF, was the night my father had died.

THE AIR WAS AS THICK as the midwife's birthing room: blood and salt sweat in it. Errol pulled Dagmar's cape around him and burrowed under the hemp sacks. He was safe. Safe in his brother's warren, deep in the earth. Such fierce dreams he had had, of being pierced, of having his chest splayed open. He put his hands on his ribs. His fingers came away wet.

"Rip?" His voice was ragged.

He tried to get up but fell. He had no feeling in his legs. Something weighed him down, something so vast and immoveable, Errol was sure the earth had caved in on him. Why did it have fur?

He reached for a flint, but his hand came upon the empty sheath. And now he remembered. He had ignored Rip and Dagmar and had taken the spikes from their case. He had left them next to him on a wooden crate and wrapped himself in the cloak and fallen asleep. The lamp had run down. His hand knocked a tin off a crate. The clatter was small but it brought on a frenzy of crashes. Some mammoth force was alive in the room with him, twisting now, kicking and bucking. Errol buried himself under the sacks and covered his head. When the movements stopped, he felt again for the flint and lit an edge of the sack for light.

The great beast lay on its back next to him on the shards of broken glass, with its front legs curled like the handles of an urn, and its enormous back flanks stretched across the room. Its head was turned to Errol, and a curious, fist-sized eye stared at him. Behind the snout and the eye were the low branches of a rack of antlers.

Errol tripped and stumbled over the animal and into the tunnel.

"Rip," he whispered. He tripped over something the size and shape of a rolled-up carpet and raised the lamp. "Rip. What are you doing?"

Rip took a swig of the whiskey, drizzling liquor down his ears and neck. "Am I lying down or standing up?"

"You're down."

"Thank you." He got unsteadily to his feet.

Errol cleared his throat. "Something happened in the night—"

Rip lifted the flask to his lips but stopped and lowered it. "Yes. For me, too." He surveyed the floor of the tunnel, which was littered with new, broken things. More lamps, half books, a file. He drank from the flask. "Just so long as you didn't take the knotting spikes out of their case."

From within the room came the bellowing of an animal.

Rip narrowed his eyes. "You fool," he said, pushing Errol aside, running into the room. There, in all its magnificence, was the rump of a beast. At the other end of the room, the antlers spread like two saplings.

"What is it?"

The beast swung its head around at the sound of Rip's voice and hammered Errol in the jaw with its antler.

"It's a stag," said Errol. "I think it's a large one but I have nothing to compare it with."

"I know *what* it is," murmured Rip. "How the hel—" And then he stiffened. "Who was here last night with you?"

"No one. Not even you, apparently," said Errol.

"It was Sabine. She is unwieldy like this. Wild-eyed. Skittish. Where is she?"

"What are you talking about? Why would Sabine be here?"

"Why indeed. I'm not a fool," Rip said. "Because this stag can't be yours. It's not possible."

Errol wanted to say he had no idea what Rip was talking about. But in fact his mind returned to a nightmare, of a quick slice of an edge, and an enormous animal struggling to climb out of his ribs, wrenching open the already-bruised bones to gasp for air. Then an insane knotting, as if the skin of his chest were being torn into strips and knit together.

"Let me see you!" Rip tore Dagmar's cape from Errol's shoulders. He stepped back as though he had been hit. "How is that possible?" he cried. A fine wound ran up the center of Errol's chest. Errol stared at himself in the queasy lamplight.

"It hurts," he said.

"Well of course it hurts!" Rip yelled. Then quietly, "Of course it hurts. You're a fool. You had to have those spikes. But this is not your stag. It can't be. Because that simply is not possible. You would be empty, like me." Errol could make no sense of whatever Rip was carrying on about. Rip drank from the flask and pressed the cork back into it. "Unless, of course, she was unfaithful."

"Unfaithful? I'm telling you," said Errol. "Sabine was not here."

"No. Not Sabine. Mam."

JAMILA POURED A CUP OF TEA and left it steaming between us on the plank. The bell was somnium, but I certainly wasn't getting any sleep. I had sent for her four uurs ago, but she had ignored the summons. She finally arrived in the middle of the night, when the time suited her. Now we sat with our feet dangling over the abyss.

"What is your theory?"

"Slyngel Thebes saw things," she said.

I handed her the cup and she drank from it. I said, "Here's my theory. He murdered Durga and Feo. Tracked them like prey and killed them. Then he lost his mind entirely. Then he was murdered by someone who defended them."

"I don't think so. I think someone was after him because he was right about the beasts."

"Right about what?"

"I know what it feels like to smell and taste and hear things no one else hears. I think he was seeing fylgias."

I sighed. "Those aren't our stories, Jamila. Fylgias are from outside the wall."

"How do you know?"

"I just know. Maybe out of the corner of his eye he thought he saw a squirrel tripping over Liu Bei's ankles. Or at a footrace, maybe he envisioned a red horse galloping next to a kelp and recorded it as equus in the book. Drunk, he could see anything he wanted to see."

"No. He *stopped* seeing beasts when he was drunk. That's why he drank so much." She looked at me oddly then, and said, "Why did you just say *red* horse?"

"Are not all horses red?" She stared at me for a long while. I took the tea and stood up. "I don't want to talk about this."

"You see them, too," she said.

"I see what I see."

"What do you see when you look at me?"

"Nothing. A foundling."

"What else?"

"I see you. No, actually"—I put my fingers up to my temples—"I see—a fat rump mounted on itty-bitty wings, with big teeth and silky black hair down to its tiny little hoofs. Huge tits."

She laughed and said, "I sound like a bogle."

"I don't want to talk about it." I was sullen again.

"Fine," she said. "Then bargain for my silence with news of the roofs."

I put my head back and held out my arms and felt my body sway in the winter night, high over the earth. It was so high, that plank between Bamako and Thebes. It was all edge. Nothing tethered me to it. If I stumbled, I would fall. If I fell, thirty seconds later I would die. If I saw beasts, who cared? This was my air. This was my high place. I would not be followed out onto this plank by idiot brothers or a drunken dead father. Even my mam would never venture here. Out on this plank I was myself. A runner of extraordinary competence. Such competence that I could flip myself around this board and back up onto it and live. I could walk on my hands.

I told Jamila everything. Marek was leaving for Mildenhall the next week to apprentice, an idea that left us all miserable. Talwyn had bid early in her second year for seven apprenticeships, had gotten them all. Everyone was stupidly in love. Ping had negotiated his final contract with Gallia House; he would only move there, he said, if they let him bind himself to Ella, do his barrel work, and cook for everyone in the guild for the rest of his life. No one in their right mind would ever let Ping negotiate another contract. Grid and Siwan Chakra were training together for next year's Long Run, as this year's had been canceled unceremoniously when Errol was dropped. Faisal and Seppo were seeing twin runners from Bian Pao. Dragomir had met a pelt on Ship—Gawain or Griflet, someone from the Round Table. Most lovesick of all were Petroc and our own Siwan, hanging lights in the tent, where, as the scroll dictated, the moon and sun would meet at the dawn.

"I hate the scroll," I said. "Even if you stay in the tent by accident, even if you're just doing math, you're bound. What fool thought of that and why did anyone agree to it?"

"Petroc and Siwan agreed."

"I don't want to worry about staying or not staying in some girl's tent."

"You don't have a girl."

"When I do."

"Just don't go in her tent."

"I'll just never fall sleep."

"You're in an Odd mood. Let me guess. Some girl turned you down."

"No. Whatever. Yes."

HOW TO FIT THE STAG OUT OF THE DOOR. Whether the stag could drink water (or whiskey) straight from the flask. Whether tinned meat was poison to a stag.

"The name of him," said Errol. "That's the question."

At that moment the stag turned to look at them, hitting Rip in the chin with his antlers.

"I propose *Dammit*."

"I'm trying to remember the name of that stag who lives on Yggdrasil," said Errol. "In Valhalla. I'm sure I know it. I read those northern tales every night of my life."

"It's Eikthyrnir," said Rip.

Eikthyrnir was restless, not unlike Errol, trapped in a sewage tunnel under a thousand tons of earth.

Five Hundred Pages

SHE WAS RIGHT. I was in an Odd mood.

I poured out my tellensac in a bowl she made from the front of her tunic. I took the torn page from the bowl, and put back the rest to keep it from blowing off the plank.

"It was you who stole the last page of Parsival?" she said.

"No. Yes. I have to tell you something. Don't talk. Just listen."

She crossed her arms. "Fine. But did you also steal the six lines of—"

"Just *listen*. There is a secret to whether and when you get chosen to become a runner, and I didn't know what it was—"

"You should have asked me," said Jamila.

"Is this how you look when you're just listening?"

She rolled her eyes. "Fine. Go."

"When Errol was chosen for the roofs and I wasn't, I thought I would lose my mind. Imagine me, Odd Thebes, imprisoned forever in this tower with five hundred molding guilders—"

"Them, plus me," said Jamila.

"I didn't think of that. Anyway, I begged Errol to tell me how he had been chosen, but he didn't know. They just informed him one day that he was rising and I wasn't.

"I studied every pelt who had been called and every pelt who wasn't, then tried to guess the differences. It wasn't family connections or money that put anyone up on the roof. Good teeth, a throwing arm, knotting skills, geometry prowess, clean hair, card-playing ability, cookery, running speed, high marks, or, as we can all see from their choice of Errol, any sort of ability to sing on pitch."

Jamila laughed.

"Meanwhile Errol is sewing his tent, setting his pack in order, tying his hair back like a runner. And my mam throws that party for him, and he has three uurs to go before it's the five bell and he'll climb the ladder and be gone forever. He and I have been cousins and best friends since we were provoked from our mothers' innards. And I'll be stuck in an empty tower while he's up there in high air with ten thousand runners."

I put up a finger to stop her protest.

"At the bakers' bell, I broke into my brother Heimdall's quarters on the twenty-first strata. I woke him. With his bound-wife and his family snoring around us, I laid all the money I had earned as a translator on his bed in front of him. A little more than three thousand uurs. It was literally everything I owned, and five times more gold than he had ever seen in one place.

"'Tell me the iosal secret,' I'd demanded. Of course, Heimdall had never been a runner, but he was a guilder by then, with two kelps already born. And every guilder knows the secret because they have to know it."

"Heimdall would have told you the secret for free. To get rid of you."

"Could you just listen, Jamila? This isn't easy for me."

"Fine."

"Heimdall grinned and said, 'Odd Thebes is a worse idiot than I thought. You? Mr. Nose-in-a-Scroll? *You* can't guess the answer?' He swept all my money under his bound-wife. 'You just forfeited three thousand uurs for something I'd have gladly told you for free just to be rid of you once and for all.'

"I would have given him twice the money. 'What is it?'" I begged him.

"'Ask the Parsival question.'"

"'Parsival who?' I asked. I thought he was talking about some guilder."

"'Your favorite knight, Oddity,' he said.

"'*The* Parsival? Grail knight? Pure in heart?'

"'One and the same.'

"'From *Parsival*? I know that tale by heart.'"

"Everyone knows it," whispered Jamila.

"Sh," I said. "The tale goes like this. Parsival's uncle, the king, suffers from a curse, a foul disease that makes the sickroom reek and grown men sob—"

"I know the tale," said Jamila.

"But I need to tell it," I said. "Parsival the young squire can't imagine what to say to the ailing king. He doesn't really care, is the truth of it. So he gets out of there as fast as he can and leaves his uncle behind. For five hundred pages he horses around the countryside, having his way with girls and figuring out which end of his sword is up. Fights a slew of battles against knights too big for him. Gets beaten. In the end he makes his way back to his uncle, who is nearly dead by now in the green haze of his sickroom. *Now* Parsival feels his uncle's pain.

"'Uncle, what is it that troubles you?' he says. *Et voilà!* The king is cured. Just like that. Feh. Five hundred pages of unrelenting self-interest. One selfless, un-common question. By the time Parsival asks it, you're ready to throw the grail at his head. The curse is lifted. The king is suddenly as healthy as his own horse. The story ends.

"'Uncle, what is it that troubles you?' I said to Heimdall, blinking. 'That's the secret to rising to the roofs?'

"'Aye, in every tower from Visby to Cairns.'

"I jumped on Heimdall's bed, beating him with a pillow, ramming my head against the wall, yelling over and over, 'What is it that troubles you? What is it that—'

"'Don't ask me, Odd Thebes. You've awakened the kelps now and the bound-wife. Get out of my bedchamber before you wake the dead,' said Heimdall.

"'Wait. Must I ask an uncle? I haven't got an uncle.'

"'Any guilder.'

"Finally I understood. Every year a handful of altruistic pelts happened to ask the Parsival question of a handful of guilders. And those guilders, all of whom know the secret, reported those names to the guildmaster, and those pelts rose to the roof of Thebes.

"I jammed my foot in the door before Heimdall could shut me out. 'Tell me Errol Thebes didn't just walk up to some guilder and say, What troubles you? That would be utterly pathetic.'

"Heimdall snorted. 'Five hundred times a week. Altruism is Errol Thebes's middle name. Whereas your middle name is—' I slammed his door.

"I went to my mother that morning before breakfast in the Great Hall. She was mending a kitchen towel and I waited, knowing my chance would come.

"'Ow,' she said, and put a needle-pricked finger in her mouth.

"'What is it that troubles you, Mam?'

"Gudrun Thebes burst into tears, pressed my face to her neck, and sent me down with a note to Margaret the guildmaster, who made me sign a contract that, among other things, swore against my own life that I had no idea how I had been chosen. Three thousand uurs lighter, I was rising. Exactly like Errol Thebes."

Jamila was waiting with her arms crossed.

"Well?" I said.

"Well what? Are you done?" she said.

"Yes. Didn't you hear it?"

"Hear what?"

"I don't deserve to be here, on the roofs."

"That's what this is all about?"

"Yes!" I said. "Everyone else up here is worthy. I'm not."

"Please. Confess this to someone who cares. I'm not even allowed to read your library books. I sleep on a coffin. If I didn't steal your food, I would be dead by now."

"But I'll never be like Parsival."

"You're exactly like him. You just have one thing left to decide."

"What?"

"How many more pages do you have of unrelenting self-interest?"

Sallanen

WE WERE SILENT FOR A WHILE, listening to the bakers kneading loaves in the roof kitchens of all the guilds around us. The crews were hauling purgament to the edges, tossing it over before the mail came on the lines. For the moment I didn't care about iron spikes or my cousin or Slyngel Thebes or whether I was Parsival.

"What are you thinking about?" Jamila said.

"I was just wondering what I would look like with buck teeth." She laughed. "No really. I was wondering who your mother is," I said.

She looked up at me, surprised. "What made you think of that?"

"Well, who could ever leave you?" Jamila touched her foot to mine. "Someone must know who she is. You can't keep a *wart* a secret in this city, never mind a child. And if you found out, then you wouldn't be a foundling." I laughed as casually as I could. "And you would suit me then."

"Whoever she is, I don't want to find her. She's a horrid mother. Worse than Oedipus's mam. Worse than any of the bad mams we know. Worse than Margaret Thebes."

"Feh," I said, insulted that she had trodden over my tender proposition. "Worse than Margaret? That's impossible."

"Margaret told everybody Errol had been the ugliest kelp anyone ever raised. Whiny and fearful and always losing things. She said that when he would run after everyone with his arms up, nobody would pick him up. It was better, she said, that he lived with Gudrun Thebes."

I remembered watching my cousin Errol, listening to his mam say all those things about him. He was so small.

"Back when he was a kelp, he used to draw. Remember?"

"Aye. His drawings were all over our walls." I was willing to talk all night about Errol Thebes if I could just be with Jamila. She was lean and strong and infinite, and I wanted her. Still, that memory she had conjured, of Errol's drawings, reminded me of another post on our wall. Errol hated that the name of our city was lost. Not carved in stone or written in our books. Nobody even bothered to jot it on a scrap of parchment. So Errol posted a list on our door, for everyone to see. New Camelot, Ithaca, Nirvana, Zerzura. These were his suggestions, I suppose, if anyone was listening. Shangri-La, Valhalla. I suggested Cloud Cuckoo Land. His lists grew pragmatic. Noreia, he wrote, because we also had iron. Colophon, for the spindles. Thebes, where they farmed dragon's teeth. For the better part of one year his list ended with Taygete, after the nymph who kept charge of wild animals. On the day the regnat dropped Rip and Fenn from Fremantle, he wrote *Hel*. Weeks later I passed by the list and saw that he had crossed that out and written *Nostos*. In Pliny's tongue: a homecoming. Then *Sky-rim. Iron-forest. Roof-sea*. And so I knew he was reading *Beowulf*. Finally, on the day before we left for the roofs he finished the list. *Hrof-gestas*. From our grandmothers' tongue. Literally, strangers in the sky. Not so literally, high exile.

"And he had all these ideas for things he would build to make life easier in the guild," said Jamila. "And Margaret Thebes used to hold up his papers in the Great Hall and say, 'Would any of you actually plant a forest in a soil-less guild? Or build a hot-rain bath? Who would buy these ideas?' And nobody would say anything."

"Woody bought all of Errol's drawings."

"Woody saved him, I think."

I rubbed my neck, trying to ease an ache that had been there all week. Jamila stood on her hands, flipped upside down, passed below me, hand over hand along the plank, swung herself up again behind me and sat down. All this risk, just so she could press her fingers into the muscles of my shoulders.

"*Grazia dolce*," I whispered. Imagine that nobody wanted to be touched by a foundling. If only they knew. "Well, but," I continued, "we have seen Margaret in a different light. Do you remember when we staged *Odysseus* as a play, after the guilders did? We were kelps, five or six times around the sun. Errol was Odysseus. Talwyn played Penelope. Grid was Athena."

"You were Homer."

"Aye," I said. "I can't believe you remember that. We had slaves and oarsmen and heroes and sirens and Polyphemus and a pile of suitors and a ridiculously huge flock of sheep because everyone wanted to be sheep. We were too little to know what the lines meant, but we shouted them at one another anyway. '*What's my name? It's Nobody!*'"

Jamila yelled, "'*Fine! I'll eat Nobody last!*'"

She took a long swig of the tea. "Remember when Grid spoke the last lines of the play? Margaret was sobbing."

"Aye. 'Penelope waited twenty years for Odysseus to return home. I held the dawn for them so they could be together long through that night.'" Jamila's fingers pressed into my back and neck, and I longed for anyone to hold the dawn for us.

"All right. Enough," I said. "I will do you now." I turned around on the plank and slid her backward so she sat between my legs. I undid her plait and put the tie between my teeth, and re-plaited her hair. I put my hands on her back, and she flinched.

"I only just touched you. Did that hurt?" I said.

"No. But nobody has ever touched me before."

"Feh. Prepare for a good thing."

I pressed my fingers into each notch of her spine. Pressed my hands around her shoulders, like we runners did for one another after long days on the lines. And then? Then she was crying. And she lifted the back of her shirt and pressed my hands onto her ribs.

A moment ago we were Nobody.

"*Corona borealis,*" I said.

"What?"

"In the birthmarks on your back you have the constellation."

"You're making fun of me."

"No. All seven stars of it. The crowning jewel, Alphekka, and next to it, Nusak-kan." I was touching these marks on her.

"So there is at least one good thing about me. One beautiful thing."

"Feh," I laughed. "Are you jesting?" But then I realized that of course she was just like the rest of us. She didn't know what she looked like. She was beautiful. She smelled of seed spices and oiled flowers and smoke and hard work and suddenly I had to know, as I had that night on Al-Razi, how she tasted.

I pulled my blanket from my pack and wrapped it around us. I started to take my tunic off. "In the darkness you can be mine. On a plank. Right? So long as we don't go into a tent. No paperwork."

She pushed my blanket off her and got up fast. "I have to go."

"Wait! Why?" We were both up now, balancing over the abyss.

"Why?" she said. "Because it isn't fair, what I'm doing to you."

"What *you're* doing to *me*?"

"I seek relief."

"Me too. If you want to call it that. Wait, I don't want to bind myself to you either, if that's what you mean. You can tell all the foundlings you had a runner. That's worth something."

She opened her mouth. Closed it. Finally she said, "And would you tell your friends you had a foundling?" I said nothing. I was actually thinking to myself, *What friends?* But she said, "Go away."

"This is my roof. You go away." Oh, why didn't I just close my mouth? "You know, Jamila, I could just have you bound to me. Just like that. Nobody would stop me."

She stepped away from me, as if she were nine again and we were in the library. "You could try," she said.

"I might do it someday," I said blithely. "Iosal foundling."

She wiped her face hard now, finished with crying. "You wouldn't bind yourself to a foundling. You'd have to live in a morgue."

"What difference does it make now?" I said. "Errol Thebes is gone. I might as well live with you."

"You wouldn't survive it for a night."

I made a dismissive gesture with my chin. "I'm a runner. I can survive anything."

"You're *sallanan*."

"Unstable? Don't make me translate, Jamila. All I wanted was ten minutes on a plank."

"It's hard to imagine a less compelling offer. And now you have a hundred and twenty-two pages left."

"What?"

She turned and leapt from the plank. My heart seized in my chest. But she arced through the sky below us, caught the wall of Bamako in her hands and feet, disappeared around the corner of the tower, and was gone.

Gaol

EIKTHYRNIR SHIFTED HIS WEIGHT and exhaled in the solitude of Rip's warren. Massive stag, tiny room. This wrongness of proportion set him on edge.

Wide-spaced eyes, ruddy hair, broad chest, an arrogant lift of the chin. He and Errol looked much alike. They smelled of game and the cold sweat of high air. Rip said it wasn't possible for any such things to be true, but it was hard for him to deny what he could plainly see.

There was no way to pull the stag through Rip's narrow door without sawing off the antlers. Errol held little regard for his brother's quarters or for the purgament that seemed to materialize from nowhere even in the short time Errol had been here. But it did occur to him, as he watched Rip destroy the jamb of the doorway, and as a chilling mob of shadow creatures appeared in the sewer main, the contents of Rip's quarters would be pillaged as soon as they were gone. His brother had no plan to return.

———

I can write what came next with only the most meager detail, for I, Odd Thebes, was on the high roofs of the city when all of this occurred and later I was able to extract only shreds of scenes and never the whole thing. It is better, told scant.

———

Rip held up his lantern and pointed uneasily toward a downward slope into the mines. Why did they ever go this way, instead of up and out into the streets? I don't know. There were no passages wide enough for Eikthyrnir, Rip told Errol. It was my theory, bard that I am, that some gravity, some pull of plot, called them down.

The tunnel drove deep into the earth in the form of a spiral. The way at first was wide enough for Rip, Errol, and the stag to walk abreast, but narrowed as side tunnels branched away. They fell into single file and came to pinches through which even a kelp could not have fit, and the stag had to be backed out and a new route chosen. By the time they were an uur down, they were disoriented and could not have turned back if they tried.

Rip grew sullen. He kept asking whether the iron spikes in Errol's pack were sheathed. They were low on lamp fuel.

They came to a broad arch with a frame around it, carved with codes, the entrance to some section of the mines. Crudely hewn granite stairs led farther down. Nothing remained of the labor that had once thrived in this ancient mine, except barrows abandoned in some rush to leave, and here and there a pick or shovel left in a crevice. The passages now were filled with a fine mist of an underground river. When they came abruptly upon the water, the current was too wide to see across in Rip's light, and they could not hear each other over the torrent.

Rip yelled, "This will carry us out of here!"

"Are you sure?"

They waded into the deep and were carried fast along in the cold current in silence. Rip and Errol held on to the stag, careening around stone and slipping down water chutes. When the current gathered too much strength, they let the stag tow them to the side.

They were soaked through and cold, and moved along passages, trying to find some path broad enough for the stag's antlers or some route that turned upward. Were they moving deeper into the earth or up out of it? Was it morning or night?

A sensation overcame Errol that the shape of the body of air was larger. He slowed. Rip was behind him with the lamp, which made his own shape a shadow in front of him. He stepped forward, falling into a complete lack of stone or earth. He grabbed at air, slamming his flailing shins on a shaft of bedrock. He felt a quick jerk to his shoulders as his fall came to a halt.

Rip pulled him up and they lowered the lamp into vast emptiness of the hole. Thirty feet below lay the body of a young man, staring up at them. Errol yelled down into the shaft, but the body did not stir. Errol yelled again, louder. Rip put his hand over Errol's mouth. The man was gone and, too, the lifeless bird next to him.

A few strides from this hole there was another like it. A human form curled against the wall at the bottom of this one as well, and a sheep lay next to it, their legs and arms out like kelps. Errol yelled, "Stay high." It was foolish, an old habit. The figure shifted and yelled at them to go away. Errol held the lamp high. Shafts like this one were everywhere, as far as he could see. Like a pox. Some were covered with stone disks. Some disks had a hole drilled in the top or a set of bars. The mine smelled of the grime of dung and urine and decomposition.

At one pit, a ghoulish face appeared at the hole in the disk without warning, its teeth bared, its eyes bulging and white. The girl, his age, opened her mouth, her tongue flapping like a nightmare, her breath sick. He felt a pinch and looked at his fingers. A thick-legged white spider, the size of his fist, was clinging to him through the bars. He pulled back his hand, and the spider tore away and dropped into the shaft. The girl said they needed water, they were all waiting for water. That someone went to find the spikes and everyone was starving. Errol couldn't understand her, but he promised water and said he had the spikes with him. Rip yanked him away. "Shut up. Don't promise anything."

Then? Then. From the far end of the cavern came a slow, piercing cry, as though the air itself had been rent in two. Rip said they needed to get the stag out of gaol. It was the first Errol had heard that word.

Errol edged along the wall to see where they were going. He hid behind an outcrop of stone, then moved to a ledge and dropped to a crawl. Twenty feet down, a crude arena stood empty. It had been cut from the bedrock and enclosed with iron bars. They could make out the shadows of men dragging some silhouette along the ground. A struggle.

MUCH LATER, when I saw Errol, he could not speak without weeping about what he saw. He sat with me, his knees to his chest, hiding in the morgues from a memory he could never escape. Nothing had prepared him. No guild. No workbench. No book. I demanded, when I did see him, to know what had happened to him. I insisted until he relented.

"They dragged that cat into the arena," he said.

"What cat?" I asked.

"The blackness I had seen. That silhouette."

"A house cat?"

"It was a wild cat. Fierce. And so black it looked like a hole in the air. It took four men to haul it in. The animal was writhing and clawing at them. They caught its legs in snares and pulled them out to the sides. A cat's legs don't move that way. They don't."

"Why were they at this? Had the cat harmed them?"

"No. I don't know. They tethered it to four posts. It was struggling like a demon. Teeth and claws everywhere. The mob in the stands was cheering. I don't know why. It was just like the pub. They wanted something to die. And then—" He sat silent, his hands over his mouth.

"Then what?"

"They left the cat there alone."

"*Iosal*," I whispered.

"When the bell went off, the mob started to throw things at the cat, over the bars. Purgament from the roofs. Rot, rusted metal, anything they could find."

"I don't understand."

"And then one of them pulled out a crossbow and a bucket full of bolts."

"This is low—"

"Aye. The first bolt from that archer hit the cat in the thick of the back leg. The cat went down, tangled in the tight tethers, and got up again, struggling. Howling, but more like a kitten, although what do I know about kittens. All the while they were cheering. Hitting it in the face and the head. I was so fixed on the cat that I didn't realize there were men behind us. They were running around to the shafts of gaol and prying the lids off with sticks, dropping a line in, grabbing anything, anyone, still alive. A beautiful dog, a goat, that sheep I had seen. There was terror in those animals and those foundlings in the pits. All of them were crying out, for one another's sake. As we watched, the men dragged those animals into the arena, threw them at the cat, and then cheered as it tore into them, even bound as it was. And then came Jago."

"That fright from the streets? What was *he* doing to the cat?"

"No. *No.* The opposite. Listen. He was outside of the bars, running at the bars, jerking and screeching and trying to get them to stop. When that archer started to pull the string to lock again, Jago raced to attack him. Too late."

"This is that same Jago who told that fighter to murder you in that pub?"

"Aye."

"He wanted to *save* the wildcat?"

"Aye. When it was finally over and they'd cut the ties on the cat, they opened the gate and Jago went in there."

"Was the cat dead? Was it?"

"You would think. But it dragged itself across the dirt, straight to him. Even then, that archer put another bolt into the cat's flank, right on top of the first. The power of it threw the cat ten yards. Jago leapt onto the cat to protect it and the cat was on him, pushing its face into his face. I thought the beast was biting him, killing him. But it was struggling to climb into his arms."

Suddenly I realized—"It was his cat, wasn't it? It was Jago's cat! What do you call it? His other, his fetch."

"His fylgia. Aye."

"Did it die?"

He shook his head. "It wasn't meant to die. That archer was a perfect shot. The bolts could have hit anywhere—heart, skull—but they were aimed for the leg. One after the other."

"But the other animals were all dead. Why not the cat?"

"I have no idea."

The two of us sat in silence, rendered kelps. I could see no way this tale could end, never mind end well.

"There's more," he said. "You know how it is in dreams when something happens and you see only a fragment of it? Someone walks through the dream and vanishes? I know I saw the regnat walk through the mob."

"That cannot be. What would he be doing in such a place? No."

"He was there."

And then I asked the most obvious question. "How did you rescue them, Errol Thebes? What did you do?"

Errol flinched as though I had hit him. "Nothing."

I was silent. Stunned.

"Jago saw us. He was on his feet and running toward me from inside the cage. He climbed the bars without realizing he couldn't and pressed his head through them. Screaming at me, 'Stay high! Stay high.' Mocking. He turned and pointed to the cat. Two shafts jutting out of its back end. 'Look at what you did!' In truth? I ran. The mob was coming for us." Errol made a helpless gesture. "Look what I did, Odd."

A Going-Story

ERROL AND RIP RAN HARD, following the stag. When the echoes of the stag's hoofbeats stopped, Errol thought he had been separated. But when they rounded a corner, there was Eikthyrnir, staring through the bars into a pit. Errol took Rip's lamp. A young woman looked up at him. Her arms were wrapped around a frail hoofed animal, red as Errol's deer. The stag bayed into the pit, and the tiny animal answered with a bleat.

"Let it go," Rip said. "By the time you get that hatch off—" The stag turned and with one kick from his hind hoofs, he sent the stone cover crashing against the walls of the cavern.

How little the two of them weighed, the girl and her doe. Together they were lighter than his pack. Rip pulled them up and took the doe, and they were running again. Errol noticed the mark on her forearm of the guild Albacete.

"You must keep talking. Stay with me." She was so frail. "I wonder if you made my navaja. You're from Albacete?"

"No. We're foundlings here. I paid for the mark."

"Why are there so many foundlings here? What offense did you commit?"

She ignored him. "Go back for my brother. Promise me."

"We'll go together, you and I! Tell me all about him. Tell me his name."

"It's Arthur."

"Like the king!"

"Aye. He's half my age. His fylgia is a white dog."

"And what's your name?"

She was quiet for so long he thought she hadn't heard him. She said, "I can't remember."

They could hear the mob in pursuit, pouring through the tunnels above or behind or in front of them, it was impossible to tell. When Errol turned to listen, Rip was setting the body of the doe on the stone floor of the tunnel.

Rip glanced over Errol's shoulder at the girl. "She doesn't need to get to the river now."

"What? Yes she does. She's coming with us."

I must pause to fathom what my cousin was doing here. He was trying to find his way back onto the pages of a tale he could understand. He had to save *someone*.

"I won't leave her."

"Her fetch is gone."

The girl reached for Rip, who took her from Errol and held her. The stag was nosing the tiny body of the doe.

Rip moved in and out of the shadows of the tunnel, singing an old tune from the guild nursery. *"Slippen ye, en 'tis a darky night but a gude night and a soon-rising sun—"*

The girl said, "I'm not ready—"

"We'll do this together," said Rip. "I'm here."

She touched his face. "I wish I had known you," she said. "I'm leaving before I'm ready."

Rip let out a little laugh. "Aye, well. If this helps at all, I'm not worth the staying."

Errol grabbed the girl's foot. "What are you talking about? We can take her if we go now—"

Rip set her on the floor of the tunnel and knelt over her.

"Too cold," Errol protested.

Rip kissed her, and fiercely. Errol may as well have been invisible. He watched as the girl put her hands up to pull him in and make of the kiss an infinity. Rip said, "Once upon a time there lived a young woman. Too young for such troubles as she had known—" His tears were falling on her.

"What?! Stop it, Rip!" yelled Errol. "Don't tell a going-story! She is still here with us!" But the girl put her hand out for the deer, whose body lay next to her.

"She was breathtaking, with a young whitetail as her fetch. And a little brother we'll find. I promise *my* heroic brother over there will find him. The young woman could have anything she wanted. But all she really wanted in the end was a frog—" The girl laughed, gasped, and was gone.

"Was that for you, or for her?" Errol growled. "We could have saved her!"

Rip put up his hands, then dropped them. "The doe was gone. The fetch. The fylgia. No one can live long after that."

The stag was grunting, showing the whites of his eyes. They saw what he saw— the lamplight of the mob flickering from up the tunnel. Rip stood where he was, staring at the granite of the tunnel's ceiling.

"Where are you?" he roared. He kicked at the wall. He threw himself against it. "Are you somewhere in this place? Was she not worth saving? Is there no one here worth saving? I am calling for help!" Errol was confounded. Was Rip yelling to Utlag in the ceiling of a tunnel? To the mob? Was he calling for Marek? Errol could make no sense of it. Nor can I.

———

The first of the mob appeared around the corner, and in the chaos of it, Rip and Errol and the stag were crashing into stone walls, tripping over rubble, stumbling so fast into the mist-filled tunnel they had already gone over the bank and head-long again into the river before they heard the sound of it.

———

They nearly drowned in the current this time, kicking to stay high in the water, gripping the mane of the stag. They squinted into brightness and knew it was the moon.

Any relief for having seen it was short-lived, for beyond the opening of the tunnel, beyond the edge of the river, there was nothing but sky. Two rivers collided in high air here: the underground current of the mines and the overground river that ran through the city. Rip turned to swim against the current.

"We can't go back!" yelled Errol. "We jump!"

"No! Look at the drop!"

Errol was thinking of Roban, Dagmar's wolf, who could catch those arrows that came at his pack from the roof of Fremantle. He dug the fingers of one hand into the mane on Eikthyrnir's neck and clutched Rip's shirt with the other. With a scrambling of legs, the stag set his back hoofs on the ledge of stone. He recoiled and leapt straight up, high into the moonlit spray. Errol felt his feet go out behind him. They hung in the sky for a moment and then began to drop; they could see, far below, the river and the south wall, so tiny it all appeared to be a minuscule map of itself.

"*Here's good luck to the quart pot, and luck to the ballymow!*" Errol bellowed. He looked over his shoulder and saw Rip's eyes closed, his teeth clenched. Errol kicked his brother and began the song again, louder: "*Here's good luck to the quart pot—!*"

Rip yelled back: "*Good luck to the ballymow! To the quart pot, pint pot, gill pot, half-a-gill, lilliget, ben, benmow!*"

If the stag had not leapt away from the ledge, they would have perished in the field of stones below the falls. If he hadn't hit the iced river first, the other two would have hit it like *aegru on flett*, as my mam would say. Eggs on the floor. Rip and Errol came up gasping and panicked and fumbled to the banks to drag themselves out.

The stag was nowhere to be seen.

Eikthyrnir had let himself sink down and farther down, until his hoofs touched the sand at the bottom. He swam there for as long as he could, his great legs pumping, his lungs churning bright bubbles in the moonlight. Then he rose in a silver torrent of river water, his broad chest aching with grief and with joy.

"FEH. My sawol is bounded by this roof. Do you know what I mean? As though my soul is the precise shape of the roof of Thebes? A rectangle of the same dimensions. I am imprisoned by this place."

Faisal and Seppo nodded sagely and then burst out laughing. Faisal said that it was lucky we didn't live on one of the triangular guilds or I would wound myself on my own pointed soul.

Marek came over to tell me to cut it out.

"Then write me that order for fresh fly-lines," I said sullenly. "I'll go see that girl."

This went against Marek's grain. He wasted no money on errands invented to keep runners busy. But he must have calculated that, if it was between my soul being a rectangle all night and my meeting up with a girl, a girl would cause less trouble for everyone. "Back by purgamentum," he said, handing me the slip. "I don't want to be looking for you in someone else's tent at sunrise."

"Nobody else gets a curfew. You sound like my mam."

———

Terpsichore, that muse from the party at Al-Razi, was from Lascaux House, where they make flies for the roofs. Rags. Mam-clips. All of that. I loitered, waiting until she came in off the lines with her friends. They were runners now, not muses. They had recovered from starvation like the rest of us and had the look of strength about them. She was absentmindedly knotting a clove hitch in one hand.

"I was wondering when you'd get here," she said. I was admiring the silk moth on her arm, the guild mark of Lascaux.

We ran the lines for cod kulebiake on the edge of Derbent House. Late, we danced at a party at Chakra House. I asked her if she thought I was a murderer, for what I had done to Errol on Fremantle. Apart from Jamila and the foul guard, she was the only one who knew about it.

"Murderer? I think the regnat played that role. Errol himself has to take some part. The stolen spikes, the black-iron ruse. He set himself on a course. You were the fool in a plot that required a fool."

I waved my hand in dismissal. She hadn't heard all the foul things I had said to the black-iron guard I didn't know was Errol.

She showed me a letter the Lascaux cooks had found, sewn into a sack of lentils that had come in on the ships. In three dozen languages someone had written, *I can help with what troubles you.*

"Help with *what*?" I said.

We came back to Thebes and I found that Parsival helmet buried under the clothes in my tent and put it on.

"A relic game?" she said.

"Maybe later." My voiced echoed in the helmet.

"Maw?"

"I'll only beat you."

"What, then?"

I looked out of the tent flap, into the night sky. "It is a little-known fact that when Venus rises over the wall, the first one to see her gets to say what happens next."

"And?"

"And I have seen her."

There was play in her voice when she said, "And what happens next, in this lie of yours?"

I pulled off the helmet and kissed her, is what happened next. And she pulled off her shirt and kissed me back. She was better than anything I had ever imagined, and let me pause for a moment to say that I had spent the majority of my time imagining. I was unable for the first time in known history to form a word. Maybe that's why I ran.

No Reflection

THEY FLUNG THEMSELVES ON THE RIVERBANK, their hearts flailing, and so did the stag, rolling around on his back, kicking dirt and snow into the air. They were south of the towers, on the banks of the river at the south gate.

Rip reached into his pocket for his flask and said, "Here's to Eikthyrnir. And to you. Where the hel did you come from?" Errol pointed to the roofs. "I mean, did you hear yourself in the mine? 'We'll jump!' Like it was nothing. You're like those knights you used to carry on about all the time when you were a kelp."

"You're from the same places I am," said Errol.

Rip shook his head. "I would have left everyone in gaol."

"We *did* leave everyone in gaol." Errol sat up. "What are you drinking? Give me some of that, will you? Or will you lie there having the whole thing while I die of thirst?"

Rip handed the flask over and Errol put his nose to it and handed it back. "Smells of fire."

"Tell me you've never had whiskey," said Rip.

"A fool's drink, on the flies. I prefer the juice squeezed fresh from a cloud."

"Kelp." Rip grinned at him. "*Lytling.*" It means "baby." Errol grabbed the flask back, swallowed a thick mouthful from it and sat up, coughing. "Slow down, right? It's not mother's milk." Errol felt the liquor melt his innards.

Errol raised the flask. "To my hero, my gallant brother."

Rip flinched. "In my defense," he said quietly, "I had not seen the pits of gaol."

"But you knew about it. You knew what we would find there. They're all foundlings, aren't they, in those pits?"

"And the children of foundlings. And their children. It's been a long time."

"What were they doing to Jago, in that arena?"

"They bet on the winner. Like your fight in the pub."

"No. It was different. It wasn't a fight to the end. Something else was going on there. I keep wondering, why did that foundling with the spider say they were waiting for the spikes? Did she mean these spikes? In my pack?"

"I have no idea," Rip said.

"And what foul thing were you doing to the girl?" Errol said. "Kissing her like that."

"I listened to her. Instead of carrying on about the way things ought to be."

"If that was told in a book, you would sound like a fool."

"There are no books here, Errol Thebes. No bard to make sense of what is happening here. And certainly no heroes. We are off the page."

———

When Errol awoke on the riverbank, Rip was gone. It was nearly dawn. He waded into the shallows. The stag followed. A woman stood in the river, out farther. He couldn't see her face in the waning moon, but the low pitch of her voice gave her away, as she called to the wolves who were fishing on the far bank. He could see her reflection in the ripples of the river, and the moon's, and the reeds'. He was just wondering why he could see no reflection for the stag when something shifted in the reeds. His brother crouched there, watching Dagmar.

Errol's thoughts turned to that foundling he had met on the roof of Samoa, and the game of Préférerais tu they played that rainy night. The tufuga had asked if they would prefer to be trapped in the guilds, or escape the city forever. He had said escape, but he would do anything to be back in the guild towers, safe from what he knew now.

A Guest

HIGH IN A TOWER at the northeast corner of the city, the abbot Lugius made tea. By his own decree, this was the one chore he performed, for no one in the scriptorium could get it right, not even the monk Nyree, who kept a close eye on him and in other ways knew everything she should and probably more. The precise color of the flame, the weight of the tea leaves, the length of the steep. The abbot's red damask robes swept around his ankles as he moved.

He was tall and lean and tight, with vacant eyes. His teeth were long and so yellow after all this time that they were nearly green. His hair was thin, and he always told Nyree to tie it in a knot on the top of his head like she did for the monks.

This was on his mind: He had kept the fleet captain waiting two miles upriver for four days. Utlag, who crept in the hollows and could only be found when no one wanted him, was keeping Lugius waiting. And two of Utlag's rogues, Rip and some new exile from the roofs, were keeping Utlag waiting. And so the fleet captain was waiting and the fleet was at anchor, and the world waited for a shipment that was late. And Lugius paid in gold for every day the fleet idled.

This had escaped his notice: The flame on the iron stove had frozen.

The pantry was dark but he knew it so well he required no lamp. And yet, when he put his hand onto the tea crock, someone else put a hand on his. The crock fell to the floor and cracked.

He shrieked and then aimed for a tone more commanding: "Who's there? Or am I a fool?"

A voice answered in some ancient tongue that sounded and smelled of rain and was lost on the abbot, who could never remember the language of his grandmothers, so the voice continued in the common tongue. "I am there. And I am here also. As to whether you're a fool, that is up to you."

"You surprised me."

"You finally hit the high A for which you've been aiming, since you were eleven."

"You know very well I do not appreciate these visits. Why do you always come in the dark, haunting me. You're worse than Utlag."

"You wouldn't live through it if I came in the light."

"So you've said." The abbot's tone turned sulky. "Why are you here this time?"

"To ask the question."

Lugius sighed. "What is the question yet again? I have forgotten."

"It's the same one as always. Are you ready?"

"I was quite ready for tea. Yes. But now here's this mess." Lugius spread his hands elegantly to indicate the debacle on the floor. He knew the other could see in pitch-blackness.

"Not for tea."

"I see. What do you mean by 'ready,' exactly?"

"We both know what I mean, Lugius."

It always unnerved the abbot when that voice said his name. It was the prime work of a commanding officer to name the enemy, to own that name, and then to destroy that name. Even after all these years, the abbot still did not know the name of this other.

This bothered him: The stench of the mines had risen again. It had come up into the scriptorium and into this pantry. The abbot had had his men wall off that problem a dozen times. The reek of the beasts and men in those pits in that place they called gaol, he did not want to smell that all the time. Most of all he could not bear the scent of Utlag.

"I'm not ready," he said. "I'm not ready at all."

The frozen flame on the stove bloomed into a red peony, then shattered, and Lugius was alone.

The Bluebird

LONG AGO someone had painted a bluebird with its head thrust back in song on the door of the stone shanty wedged between the bell tower of Berfrei and Lothar.

"A pub? Right now?" said Errol. "We have Utlag waiting for us at the scriptorium, and it's half a bell till noctis and you must have yet more whiskey?"

A fire roared in the hearth and the dominant perfumes were of clean sawdust spread on the plank floors and the warm, furred smell of beasts: of skunks, ermines, rats, a thick-headed sheep, a bowerbird, a roan cow, a beaver, a parrot, a green lizard on a woman's shoulder, a gazelle, a forest bear rolled into a ball in a corner of the room. Someone had a tiny flourish of a blue fish in his water glass.

The room turned to watch the stag tip his antlers to enter and watched him work his way around the room, with Errol and Rip, to a table by the hearth. There were ten around the table. Rip introduced Errol to Trula there, the proprietor, an agile woman with gray braid down her back and a rat peering out of her apron pocket. Will Bluebird was wedged into the corner at the end of a table, his scribble of a beard sopped in his ale. A bluebird perched above him on a hook in the rafter.

"We don't have much time here," said Errol "We told Utlag—"

"*You* told Utlag," said Rip, pushing himself onto the bench with the rest. "I had no part in it."

Errol was distracted by the appearance of Sabine. She climbed onto Rip's lap, and Rip put his hands around her ribs. "Cage of the beast," he said. Trula rolled her eyes, wiped her hands on her apron, and stood up. She asked what Rip's brother would want to eat. Errol said he didn't have time for any food, and it was unlikely she would have anything he liked anyway. When Trula put her hands on her hips, he said he would have a fresh pear. That was impossible enough to keep her busy.

Trula reappeared with an ornately painted chest that she opened onto a dozen delicate egg-shaped eyrouns, powdered with sugar. She set a bowl of fruit on the table for them all—apples, grapes, and pears. He looked up at her in surprise. A kelp brought a bale of hay and tossed it in front of the stag. Rip was inhaling the foam from a stein of ale.

Out of nowhere Will Bluebird bellowed into song: "*There were three ravens sat on a tree—*" His voice rose and the pub turned its attention to answering each line with various grunts and howls: *"Downe a downe, hey downe, hey downe!"* Errol was swept up in the tune and the food, and he found himself singing with the *Downe-hey-downe*s. Someone from another table passed a junk vihuela to Rip, who set his fingers on it and eked out a bad chord; then, with a laugh, he set his fingers right and came in on the raven song in a way that lifted Errol's spirits. When the song was done, Rip smiled at Errol and raised his stein.

"Who would have thought you'd have a place like this. And friends, of a sort," Errol said, over the din.

"What do you mean by that?" said Rip.

"Nothing. Drink up and let's go."

But Rip pressed him on it and Errol said Rip had to admit he was—

"He's what?" said Trula. She was sitting down.

"Well, you see him, don't you? Disappointing." Errol meant it as a joke.

"And you are a judge, Errol Thebes," said Rip. "And I have been in your court since you dropped to the streets. Why don't you hand down your verdict, then?"

Errol drew himself up. "Well, he does no work to speak of, except occasional failed acts of crime. He has nothing but a foul hollow of rusted scraps and junk to show for ten years in the sewers. He could have been anything, on the roofs. He was the closest thing we had to a prince—"

"I'm no prince," said Rip.

"On the streets he might have done some good. Might have emptied that foul place gaol. Might have even found our father, who must have dropped like we did, for he certainly wasn't in the guild tower." All eyes shifted from Errol to Rip. "But instead—" Errol reached over and took a long swig from Rip's stein. "Instead he lives half a life. He's afraid of his own shadow. And heights. And spikes. He won't even talk to that wolf-woman Dagmar though he's obviously all for her, with due respect to Sabine there on his lap. No food. No bed. No one in his bed. Or at least, no one who stays. Though he knows how to kiss. Ask any prisoner in gaol." Sabine laid her head on Rip's shoulder. Rip pushed her away. He put the stein up to his lips and tossed his head back. "And he's a drunk," said Errol, staring now at his hands.

"Aye, well," said Rip quietly. "We are clear now on what kind of felon I am exactly. And I believe I have been served the punishment for it."

Will Bluebird drew back in his chair and laid his eyes on Errol. "Well, I thought you were a smart one, because you are the second brother we've known of Rip's and smartness rides in the family. But you're less than I expected."

Rip put up his hands. "Stop, Will."

"You're right about us." Will ignored him. "Sordid friends. But you're way off, on your brother. To start with that issue of the half-life—"

"Stop."

ERROL WANDERED THE EDGES OF THE ROOM. He was a fool for what he had said about Rip. He regretted it. Still, it was all true. He pushed open one of the doors against the back wall and found himself in a great room with a steady blaze in its firepit. The stag followed.

"You can't bring the stag in here," said a small, firm voice. A kelp's.

"The stag goes wherever he pleases," said Errol. "And who is that, ordering me around before he knows me?"

"It's me." The voice came from a heap of blankets on a chair. "I'm huddled here. My fingers are waving." Was it the light from the lamp, or was the kelp's face as yellow as if he'd been dyed in a vat of weld?

"Are you opposed to stags?" said Errol.

"I am ill, and they make me excitable."

"Well, my stag is weary, and therefore unexciting." As if on cue, Eikthyrnir folded his legs under him, like a farm animal, and set his nose meditatively to the floor.

"He's a beautiful stag." The kelp was so hot Errol could feel the fever off him from where he sat. A little mongrel was curled up next to the kelp. She lifted her head. He reached and let the dog sniff his fingers.

"When I was your age," Errol said, "I was only sick once. It was a poor day for my stomach, but I loved it anyway." He scratched the dog's chin, then sat on the floor next to the two of them.

"I don't believe you. I hate being ill."

"It was the one time my mam ever told me stories," said Errol.

"My mam died of this fever herself, last week. She never had the time to tell me a story."

Errol felt his chest tighten at what the death of a mam meant for this kelp. "I am sorry to hear of it. But then it is a very good thing I am here, for I am considered a reasonably good storyteller on the roofs. Second, perhaps, to my cousin."

The kelp sat up fast. "You're a runner?" he said. "Not a foundling?"

"Aye. For Thebes House."

"Thebes! The crow and crossed spikes! I've drawn it a million times! Did you know the needles made by Thebes are named after animals? An animal for each size?"

"I've heard of that," said Errol, smiling. Every kelp in Thebes is required to memorize those needle beasts.

"Look! *Iw, zapir, sesmet* . . . By the way, Rip came from Thebes. Do you know him?"

"Not so well as I thought," said Errol.

"My mother used to say he was a common drum."

Errol studied the kelp for a moment, then had to pretend to cough, to keep from laughing. "I think you mean a conundrum. A puzzle."

"That's what I said. Can I see your guild mark?" Errol rolled back his sleeve. The kelp put hot fingers on Errol's arm. "The wings are perfect! The eyes, with the white light in them. I wish I had such a mark. Even Lothar House would be better than nothing. A sewage pipe. Feh. What does it say, there, under your sleeve, for your third-year mark? Is that your resting guild?"

"Not quite," said Errol. He pushed his sleeve back and the kelp ran his fingers over the raw wound of the brand.

"*Outlaw.* Must I be terrified of you?"

Errol looked at his own hands and remembered again what he had done to Dete. "Well, are you planning to attack me?"

"Not unless you're one of Utlag's men. Anyway, I rarely fight with anything but a bow, which is not a short-range weapon."

"A relief," said Errol, amused by the kelp's imagination.

"You have a scar from that stag, I see." Errol put his hand to his chest. He didn't expect a child to know about such things. "Do you want to see mine?" The kelp lifted his blanket. In the center of his fever-hot yellow chest ran an old satin scar: a seam from his belt to his throat.

"That's from the knotting spikes?" Errol said.

The kelp nodded.

"And that's your—"

"It's a dog," said the kelp, with a confiding look.

The little hound, her big brown eyes looking first to the kelp, then to Errol, wagged the tip of her white tail. When she opened her mouth to pant, she appeared to be smiling.

"I know what you're thinking. She looks like me. And you look like that stag, too. Too big for the room."

Errol laughed. "We both do a fair bit of damage," he said.

"Can you feel the thread between you?"

Errol put his hand up and touched something in the air in front of himself. "I thought it was my imagination," he said.

"Some people can't feel it. And no one sees it. It's invincible."

"You mean invisible," said Errol.

"Exactly."

"I don't understand how I got this scar," Errol said. "And my brother says the stag isn't mine."

"He's yours, all right. He looks like you, moves like you. He won't leave you. You even smell like him. He's all yours. He came through your ribs from some other world. That's my best explanation."

Errol snorted. "Look at the size of him. That's impossible."

"Clearly," said the kelp, "you have never witnessed a birth."

"No *thanks*," Errol said with a laugh. "As if you have?"

"Of course I have."

"Well, but, what I remember from the books is that the fetch, the fylgia, is the soul of a man in the form of a beast."

"Not the soul. The spirit. The soul is a sticky, foul-smelling thing. Don't look at it while you're eating, believe me. Also? The fetch is not always a beast. Sometimes it takes the form of a—" He hesitated.

"The form of what?"

"No. I shouldn't tell you. I think you aren't prepared to know."

"But *you* are?"

"I've been living on the streets for years."

"And you're, what? Eight?" said Errol.

"Nine. But that's irreverent."

"*Irrelevant.*"

"Exactly."

Errol leaned back against the kelp's makeshift bed and stretched out his legs. "Well, explain this to me, then. Some beasts are iosal. Low. And some are high, right? Is that true of the people associated with them also?"

"Who gave you that idea?"

"I've seen rats, for one," said Errol. "Spiders. A snake."

"You're mistaken," said the kelp. "Any beast can be high or low. I've seen two rats drag a blind and injured cat away from Utlag, in gaol. Why do you laugh? I'm not making a joke."

Errol sat up. "What are you doing, spending any of your time in gaol? You should not be there, a mere kelp."

Arthur sighed. "Well, we are something of an uprising, me and my men. And woman." He made a sweeping gesture with his hand, and Errol saw what he hadn't seen before, the scant forms of a dozen thin, sleeping kelps heaped on one another in the corners of the room. They and their fetches. A house cat. A fox. A fire-colored snake. A rat.

"We have nothing to lose, really. So we fight."

"It's fine for you to play at these games," Errol said. "I played at bows, too, when I was a kelp. But you must stay away from Utlag."

"Games?"

"Aye. You must play somewhere else," said Errol.

The kelp lay back on the chair, and Errol thought he had fallen asleep. "I'm sorry. I'm not much company . . ." the kelp said, his voice trailing off.

"Would you like me to tell you a story from the roofs?"

"Oh yes. Very much. I've waited my whole long life to hear a tale."

Errol could have begun anywhere—with Loki or Reynard or Sigurd or Sun Wukong or Al-Addin. He knew every story there was.

"First of all, forgive me. I've failed to introduce myself. My name is Errol Thebes."

"I'm Arthur. I suppose you could call me Arthur Bluebird."

Errol wondered how many Arthurs there could be in the pubs and streets of a city. "Well, such a name makes it easy for me to choose a tale for you. Once upon a time—"

"Wait. I wish to be prepared," said the kelp. "Is this my going-story?"

Errol's throat tightened at Arthur's businesslike courage. "No! It's most definitely not. It's your sleeping-story. No one is going anywhere here, least of all you. Now, drink my cup of tea and listen till sleep comes.

"Once upon a time, in the center of a heavy stone, in the center of a statued courtyard, in the center of a country far outside of our wall, a sword, forged of iron from deep under the earth, had been thrust, with all the might of a great king. That sword stood waiting in the stone, for all of time, for its master. Its name—for all great swords and daggers everywhere have names—was Caliburne."

Arthur had closed his eyes. But at the name Caliburne, he put his finger up and said dreamily, "The iron spikes had a name as well."

"They what?" said Errol.

"A single iron dagger forged by a smith and infested with powers greater than the edge of its blade."

"Invested," murmured Errol.

"As I said. Its name was Banhus-theof."

Errol felt a chill on the back of his neck. He said: *"Ne waes ecg bona ac him hildegrap heortan wylmas banhus gebraec."*

"I didn't understand that."

"It is from the tale of Beowulf, a warrior who broke the *banhus*, the bonehouse, the ribs of his enemy. No doubt the name Banhus-theof—thief of the ribs—was intended by the ironsmith to invoke fear."

"Nothing to fear in the iron spikes," said Arthur.

"And yet some are terrified of them," said Errol. "The regnat, for one. And my brother Rip."

"In my experience they're not afraid of the wounding. They're afraid of their own fetches."

"You know so much," said Errol.

"It's been a long war."

Errol reached behind his back and undid the strap that held the sheathed needles to his chest. He held out the needles. "You're not afraid?"

"Well, look at that! Look what you have. That's very good. If you have the spikes, this means that my men and woman can sleep through the night." Errol didn't have the heart to tell the kelp he was about to go to the scriptorium to hand those spikes over to Utlag, in exchange for some money and the street fighter named Jago.

Instead, for a long while he told the stories of one Arthur until the other Arthur slept: tales of battle and love and friendships that lasted beyond geography and time.

The fire in the hearth flickered, snapped, and burst into bloom, and the flames took the appearance of a stand of lupine and smelled intensely of that attarh.

"Is someone there?" said Errol. But there was no answer.

When he blew out the lamp and came from the room, the pub was empty except for Rip and Trula, who sat in a corner.

Errol said to Rip, "You should go to that wolf-woman of yours. Dagmar. She will have the cure for the ague. That kelp's mother needn't have died."

"There isn't enough of the cure here for all the ones who have it," said Rip.

"But Dagmar said the city contains everything needed."

"It does. The rest of what we need is up there, in the guild tower apothecaries. It may as well be on the sun."

Collateral

THE SCRIPTORIUM STAFF oversaw the low business of the streets: the exchanges of weapons for hostages; the testing of broken and decomposed objects suspected of being uncommon; the notarizing of contracts with shipping fleets. The scriptorium's conical tower stood alone at the northeast corner of the city in a fenced courtyard of windblown papers and rubble, and the broken anatomy of statues. No runners lived on the top of the tower. No flies connected the roof to any others. A narrow spiral of stairs wound around the exterior wall from the earth into the clouds.

A young monk in red damask robes, her long hair pulled in a topknot, met the brothers and the stag at the locked gate. She tied the stag to the fence, put water there, and said something to the stag that he didn't understand. She led Errol and Rip through an arch and to an internal corridor that spiraled up the tower parallel with the exterior stairs. The corridor was lined from floor to high ceiling with gilt-and-glass cabinets.

Despite all he had heard, Errol expected the scriptorium to be familiar to him—like a guild library, with the remains of a once-vast collection of texts. But the cabinets that lined the walls were filled with halberds, caltrops, flails, nooses, crossbows, maces, blades of various intent, and explosive devices. Each object bore a tag with the word *collateralis* printed upon it, and handwritten notes that Errol could not decipher.

The abbot sat writing at a desk by a cold lick of fire at the end of the hall. The monk shifted, waiting, but the abbot wrote on without acknowledging the presence of any of them.

"We will meet in the room where the vault is," he finally said, as though he were talking to his papers. "A showing of hands, signatures on a contract, and the spican will be removed from"—he looked up at his guests and put up his hands in an elegant gesture of neither knowing nor caring—"wherever you have them. The hatch to the vault is maintained at a boiling temperature with internal fires, a security measure from the time when this place was responsible for protecting the obscure relics of the guild city. I will unlock the vault and place the spican within, and we are done."

"We'll be done after I have my money," said Errol. "And after you release the street runner Jago. And his cat."

The abbot shifted the papers on his desk. "We do have what remains of Jago. I doubt you'll want us to release him."

"Ask your man Utlag. Those are my terms."

"Utlag is not a—" started the abbot. He started anew, "Utlag is not authorized to negotiate."

Errol was tired, tired from the streets, tired from his wounds, tired already of this abbot. He was distracted by something Rip had whispered on their way up the corridor, that no one must know they were brothers.

"I'm curious," Errol said. "Even the kelps in the guild towers have heard rumors of that scriptorium vault, that it contains the tellensacs of ancient guilders."

The abbot shrugged. "*Irfelaf.* Such a tiresome theme in this city. There is nothing precious. Not one sack of tales worth saving."

Errol let his eyes wander to the papers on the desk. The top page was written on parchment, in the language of all contracts, that of Pliny and Virgil and Ovid. Errol knew enough of that tongue to know *commutationem* meant "exchange." He knew enough to see that the exchange to be made tonight was not the one he had been promised.

A Mis-telling

ERROL COULD THINK OF NOTHING TO SAY to the young monk—"Nyree," she had introduced herself—who sat beside him at a polished table in the outer vault room. She was the same monk who had tied the stag to the fence, led them to the abbot, and now she was with him in a bizarre assembly of monks and street fighters, all of whom had some interest in the spikes Errol was to deliver. It was impossible to pay attention to her when Null and Pollux, the publican and henchman, carried Jago into the room in a barred crate, covered by a tarp.

Errol gave distracted replies (*the spican guild, an eternity*) when she asked him where he was from and how long he had been in the streets.

He was suspicious of her. On his way from the abbot's offices to here, he had asked her to direct him to the bog pots. She had hesitated for a moment, knowing her orders. She had taken him there and waited outside the door.

In Thebes the bogs were purely practical, and they smelled of overuse. Here, there was a long, opaline pool of perfumed salt water, with a cloud of steam over it. The knobs, faucets, and tiles of the walls had been cast and painted to appear as the branches of oak trees. A variety of birds, painted on the tiles, hid in the oak leaves. Painted fish swam in the pool. Errol found he could tap a dozen different perfumes and a dozen more varieties of soap from the plumbing. He had kept Nyree waiting.

And now, in the vault room, it was impossible for him to pay attention to her, or anything but Jago's crate.

Utlag had slunk into the room after they had all arrived, and kept on his furs and hoods although they were all sweltering under the extreme temperature given off by the door to the vault in the floor.

Had Errol seen Utlag in a corridor of Thebes, he might have thought he'd seen a guilder who had once been something to look at but was ill now and ready for the morgues. A black fluid seeped from the corners of Utlag's lips, which he wiped constantly with a rag as he sucked and gnawed some meat from a bowl the monks had given to him. His elbows bent both forward and backward. He perched on the chair next to the abbot, who kept shifting to put distance between them. They looked something like each other, Errol noticed. When Utlag caught Errol staring at him, he crossed his eyes.

"We don't get any foundlings from Thebes, in the streets," Nyree was saying.

"Why would we send our foundlings to the streets?" Errol said, still distracted. "Pardon me." Then, to Utlag, "Pass me that quill, will you?"

Utlag stopped with his bowl in midair.

"The quill," said Errol, holding out his hand.

Utlag's eyes shifted to the table, which was so highly polished it reflected the lights on the ceiling like a mirror. Someone had left a cup full of quills. Under his breath, Utlag whispered, "Conflict!"

The abbot had stopped talking, had taken an interest in this exchange. Once more Errol put forward his request; once again, Utlag would not move. The abbot sighed and reached across the table and pushed the cup of quills to Errol. "There you have it."

Nyree continued, "But we do have foundlings from Bamako House, so we get word about Thebes. Tell me about that foundling in Thebes who is responsible for the others. She educates the others from books, teaches them to fight with swords and also to dance. I've been curious. Is she merely a legend?"

"In Thebes? I know the guild well and there is no such foundling."

"I was bringing food to one of the foundlings Bamako dropped to the streets and she, in turn, relayed to me the stories this Thebes foundling had told her, of Shirazad."

Why was this monk so insistent?

"Foundlings cannot read. And they certainly don't train for war, or dance for that matter. If someone told you all the stories of Shirazad, she could not have been a foundling. And all of Shirazad's thousand and one tales would have filled a very long winter."

"It was our best winter," said the monk. "We are without books."

Errol caught the irritation in Nyree's tone. It occurred to him that she might not take the abbot's side on all matters. He studied her for a moment, then leaned over and whispered, "Why are the foundlings in gaol?"

Nyree said abruptly, "Thank you. Indeed, yes, please tell me one of Shirazad's stories." Errol felt the abbot's eyes on them.

The last thing on his mind were the tales of Shirazad, the bard who kept a murderous prince calm for a thousand and one nights.

"I'll tell one of those tales, if you don't mind my telling it exactly as you heard it."

"Do tell it. I'm sure everyone would love it," she said.

"Remember that it is exactly the same as the tale you know," he said again. "You won't be bored with that?"

"Not in the least. Go on," she said.

"*Exact.*"

"I heard you." She looked at him as though he were insane.

"The king of a faraway country," Errol began, and everyone turned to listen, "was an irritable man, with a mercurial temper and a quick finger to point." Utlag wiped his face. "A good woman came to the palace to stay with the king and queen. When the queen was doing her laundry one afternoon on the roof of the castle, which was full of songbirds and a pleasant place, the queen said to the good woman, 'Watch my jewels while I launder these clothes.' The woman laid the jewels on her little rug, closed her eyes for one moment to say her prayers, and the jewels disappeared."

Nyree had a confused expression on her face.

"So the rug was the thief?" said Utlag. And there was that clicking sound again.

"Wait," said Errol. "The king was furious about the jewels and had to blame someone. He had the woman dragged into court and accused her of theft, terrifying her with threats and finally beating her to get her to confess—which she would not do."

"Tiresome," said the abbot. "I'd have gotten the confession."

"The king sent the woman to prison. Two years later, he was sitting in his rooftop gardens with the queen, watching a crow fly back and forth from its nest in a cedar tree, clearing out last year's wood shavings and carrying in fresh. He watched, still, as the crow pulled the queen's necklace from the nest and flung it to the ground. The king cried out to the guards, 'Fetch that woman from prison so I may beg forgiveness and restore what is left of her life.' For although he was a brutal man, he liked to think of himself as just. And that was that."

The abbot cleared his throat. "Why, I wonder, tell such a story of thievery on a day such as this one?"

"I'm heaping tale upon story, as we do in the guilds," said Errol. "The black-iron spikes were stolen and returned, so we tell tales of loss to examine every side."

Nyree had gotten up and was backing away from the table. "Thank you for the telling. With all the details intact." She excused herself abruptly and said she was off to make tea.

There was a contract to sign. While Errol was waiting for the parchment to come around, he got up and went around the table and stood with Rip.

"You're an idiot," said Rip. "That bit in the abbot's office with the irfelaf, that demanding call for a quill you didn't use, and now this carrying on about Shirazad. Just give them the spikes."

"I don't have them," said Errol. Rip turned fast to him. Errol took the pen but moved the papers forward without signing.

"Where are they?" Rip said.

The abbot was droning, "And here is where we clasp hands with one another, to show we harbor no ill will. Let us rise to do that." Everyone held up empty hands, and many were hands of the streets, some still with blood on them, and all with grime.

But when Errol reached over the table to grasp Utlag's hand, Utlag did not move. "Utlag?" said the abbot. "Utlag." Nothing. "Well, all right, let's step over here by the vault instead—"

But Utlag plunged his hands over the table and grabbed for Errol. The hands were clammy and dry, and their thick fingernails dug into the wound on Errol's hand. Utlag's lips curled back, off his teeth, and he nodded toward the table. Errol looked down. He could see the reflection of the monks who flanked Utlag: the details of their hair; their robes; their topknots. He looked up at Utlag and down again at the table. Utlag's furs were reflected. The hood. But where Utlag's face should have been, there was no reflection.

Utlag made that clicking sound again and said, "Now *there's* a story."

Tangled

THE STAG WAITED, knotted in his tether in the courtyard of the scriptorium tower. When they had left him here, he tossed his antlers. But he flung the loose line and spun around, trying to see that monk again or have a drink from the bucket of water. The more he tossed, the more tangled the line got until it was around his hind leg now and he could move nothing but his eyes.

Out of nowhere, the monk came, running hard this time. She grabbed him roughly and strapped something to his hind leg with twine. She started to untangle the rope from his antlers but couldn't work the knots fast enough, so she grabbed for a blade on her belt and cut the tether. She disappeared again into the scriptorium.

ERROL PULLED THE SHEATH from where he had it strapped around his chest, and handed it to the abbot. The abbot pulled the cloth from inside. "You've lied to us."

"Likewise, you lied to me. I saw the contract on your desk," said Errol.

He hardly had time to say that much before Utlag was up on his feet, black vitriol spraying the air—"*Where are they? Where are my spican?*"—long fingers clawing.

Rip rubbed his face, tired. "Errol, don't be a fool. Give them the spikes."

"If I do, they will turn the spikes to some foul purpose. I agreed to the trade of the spikes for money." He looked over at the crate. "And for Jago."

"You're in over your head," said Rip. "Tell me where the spikes are."

"They'll kill you. That's the trade. They're taking you and giving me Jago."

Rip sighed. "Of course they are."

Errol's eyes widened. "What? You knew that?"

"Of course."

"We could have planned if you'd trusted me. I can't imagine that you would not tell your own br—"

Rip had leapt from his chair and was pointing across the table. "He is my father! *That* is my father!"

Errol did not want to look where Rip was pointing. Not at one of the monks or the abbot or even to Null or Pollux, against the wall. Out of the corner of his eye, Errol could see a grin spread across Utlag's face, his teeth seeping with black.

Rip was yelling again. "I beg you to consider all that implies! Give him the spikes!"

"A father would not drown his son—"

"And look!" said Rip, pointing at the table.

He was already looking. Rip's reflection was a collection of human parts and of parts missing. Blood pulsing. Sinew twitching at its bone. A socket without an eye.

"Half a life!" said Rip. "You see now? Go!"

With a nod from the abbot, Null grabbed Rip and dropped him to the floor. Pollux was coming for Errol.

The monk, Nyree, appeared, in the hall. Errol alone could see her from where he stood. She had a full tray of teapots and cups lifted over her head. While he watched, she slowly tipped the tray. The dishes slipped through the air and crashed to the floor in a clamor of porcelain and boiling water. He took the gift she had given him, leapt over the mess the crash had made, and hurled himself out the door. He could hear the alarm sounding.

Rising

THERE CAME THE RUNNER, sprinting toward him. Eikthyrnir was trotting already, and Errol ran alongside him as he sped across the ruins in the scriptorium yard. With an awkward leap Errol got himself onto the stag's back.

"Let's get to that river!" Errol said. But Eikthyrnir turned and stopped, facing Null and Pollux across the courtyard. His skin twitched.

"No," said Errol, yanking the stag's scruff. "Hey. *No*, I said. I'm in charge of you, and I'm telling you we are getting away from here now." He could hear Utlag screaming. Monks were pouring out of the building. They stopped to watch as the stag tilted back on his hind legs. He grunted fast—a chuckling, a dare—then trotted forward, dancing side to side, his great rump swinging, his antlers tossing. Pollux stepped toward them, a knife in each hand, and the stag broke into a gallop, thundering straight for him.

Null and Pollux ran for the scriptorium, but the stag crouched at full speed and sprang over them. He landed at the foot of the narrow stairs that spiraled up the tower.

Errol could not believe he was still on Eikthyrnir's back. They were galloping up the side of the tower. He couldn't see the stairs beneath the broad back of the stag—only the courtyard diminishing far below them and the neighboring towers.

The stag was a miracle of endurance. He rounded the last curve of the tower and galloped onto the roof. He trotted there, panting, filling his lungs with the thin air. Errol pressed his face into the stag's scruff and breathed in the hot steam.

"You're an idiot," he said, "and more stubborn than I am, if that makes any sense. Now look at our problem. There are no lines to cross, and you cannot leap this distance, and we have *that* coming for us." Utlag was screaming and hurtling his way up the stairs, hissing for Banhus-theof. The stag trotted over to the edge and looked down at him, then across the city's horizon line. They were so far from the next tower that the bucket fires on that distant roof looked like a half dozen flickering candles in the sky.

Errol said, "No. *Eikthyrnir*. No. *Nyet. Nei.* Whatever language you speak, we are not jumping—"

The stag trotted to the north edge of the roof and turned around. Errol felt a quick acceleration and next he knew they were charging full-on. He could have jumped off the back of the animal. Could have let himself sprawl onto that scriptorium roof and face Utlag on his own. The stag jammed his back hoofs against the edge, set himself back like a coiled spring, and they shot into the sky like an arrow out of a bow, up and out over the black abyss. Errol was expecting to fall, to go down in a long arc, as they had at that waterfall from gaol. And then he was afraid that they would overshoot their mark. But they slammed down onto the roof of Gamalama House with such crashing force that the famous cubeb cakes, which were baking in the kitchens of that guild tower, fell flat.

PART III

Ready

IT WASN'T A SLOW NIGHT for me, either. Mildenhall had come for Marek, to install him for his guild apprenticeship. We numbered fifteen now, left behind on Thebes without Emem or our roof master. No one cared whether I came or went in the direction of trouble. And, despite the fact that Marek had left instructions with us for a celebration, everyone forgot that this was my birth-night. I was seventeen.

I ran the lines to Lascaux House and pulled Terpsichore from where she was making rags for the new pelts on their roof with a crew in her yurt. I was in a hurry. Why? Did I intend to stay the night with her? No. I don't know. Yes. We took a swim at Teifi. We went to her tent and talked about nothing. She showed me a list of ship names and said she wanted a fleet of ships and a crew of kelps. She told me about the strata full of younger brothers and sisters she had left behind. I wasn't really listening. I didn't think she meant real ships or her own kelps. Everybody has their idiot dreams. Hers sounded fine with me and I told her that. Here's all I could think about: I knew what she looked like without a shirt on.

"Are you ready now?" she said.

I looked behind me. It was a small tent, and there was no one in it but the two of us. Still I said, "Me?"

Border Crossing

I HAVE WONDERED what my twelve-year-old self would have thought of the night we were about to have in that city. Errol Thebes was crossing the sky, leaping from tower to tower on the back of a furred projectile that had entered this world through his ribs. Meanwhile, I was finding my way with the muse of the dance.

My twelve-self would have loved this.

The year I was twelve I used to lie in my sack every single night, thinking the same grand things. Soon I will be splendid, I thought. They'll send me early to the roofs like the best of all the pelts in this guild. I will be wild up there and run faster than everyone. Roof masters will refer to me behind my back as indispensable. Everyone will love me like men love Arthur and Beowulf and Odysseus, the way they love my cousin Errol. I will be perfect. I'll not have any time to think about life after the roofs. All the kelps I once knew will wish they were me. And while I am in high places I'll find a girl so enticing she will take all of my attention. She will be so beguiling, every runner, especially Errol, will writhe with jealousy when they see her with me. And on some night when I have chased her around the roofs all night I will take her clothes off, first her tunic and then her leggings.

That is as far as I ever got, when I was twelve and alone in my bedroll.

And then I was thirteen, and fifteen, and seventeen. Not a kelp, not a guilder: a *mearc-stapa*, in our grandmothers' tongue. A haunter of the borderlands. And it was tonight: the tenth of Rhagfyr of the fabricated year of DCCXIII. My roof master was gone. And my birth had been forgotten. And I had garlic breath from the soufflés Ping had made us for supper, and I was wearing my red wool tunic with the torn armpit, and I had brought with me a pack of cards, and my old flat pillow I've had since I was four. Was I staying? Was I going?

It was a blur. I was seventeen, but I was my twelve-year-old idiot self. This runner with her hands on me, she was infinitely unexplored, a world outside my walls. Her hair was still wet from the swim. I could feel her pulse behind her ears and in her chest, and then she put her fingers in my mouth and on my hip bones and pulled up my tunic and found my belly button and kissed me on my mouth while she touched me where only my own hands had ever been. I smelled her sweat and tasted my tears.

I HAVE THE SCRAP OF PAPER in my tellensac. This was hastily scrawled:

To the runner from Thebes. I remember Shirazad's tale exactly as it was told to us by a foundling from Bamako House. You told it wrong. The queen didn't do laundry. She took a bath. The thief was not a crow in a tree. It was a magpie whose nest was behind a tile. At first I thought you to be a braggart from the roofs who didn't know what he was telling, and then I realized you told it wrong on purpose. We have such a tile in the baths of the scriptorium, with a magpie painted on it. I have just now pulled away that tile and found the spican. They are not safe here, so I am leaving them with your fylgia. I wish I could send the sheath—we know from experience that the spikes are mayhem without it—but I must assume you are about to present the empty sheath to the abbot. I fear Rip will be in gaol before this night ends, and I dread to imagine what will happen with the street cat Jago, but somehow you must escape. You have seen the monstrous labyrinth that exists below the earth in this city, or you wouldn't have asked me about the foundlings in gaol. You are clever. Here, all we have been able to do is feed the foundlings who live and breed on the streets and wait for their days in gaol. You, from high places, can do more. If you need help, contact me, but take caution. We are watched.

In the tradition of scriptorium monks, the writer had inked an elaborate *N*.

Darkness

ERROL THEBES STOOD NEXT TO A SMALL TABLE—it was more of a desk, really—squinting into the light over a bed, waiting for His Honor the Chancellor Regnat of this vast quarantine city to stop snoring.

The chambers spanned the top strata of Fremantle. The bed was huge, boxed off with curtains that had been tied open. The air reeked of war, as the regnat's lamps were forged of iron, like the bed was, and like the armor and the weapons and nearly everything else here, and the lamps were fueled with sulfur powder and saltpeter. There were hundreds of them, sputtering along the walls in blinding blue-white pulses of light.

The regnat was an inexplicably large mound under a mountain of skins and furs.

Errol cleared his throat.

"Not guilty!" The regnat startled. Some coins fell from the bed and Errol realized the regnat was sleeping on his gold.

"It's Errol Thebes, Your Honor. From Thebes." The regnat sat up. He was wearing some sort of eye protection, which looked like twin lenses of black in a frame that fit over his head. He glanced at the door.

"How did you get in here?"

"Through a window," Errol said.

"Why aren't you dead?"

"I survived the drop. And the streets."

"This is a nightmare."

"No, Your Honor. It's real. I've come to request your help. To report that finally someone has survived the streets and can tell you what is really happening there. The streets are overcome with"—Errol looked around the bright room seeking a word with relevance—"with darkness."

I cannot explain, even now, why Errol didn't see what he didn't see. Over the course of the next half uur, he fervently requested, obstinately demanded, shamelessly begged, and finally attempted to bribe the regnat to lead a high army to the streets to rescue Rip, to save Arthur's life, to pull those foundlings out of pits. What did he think? He thought the regnat would leap from his bed and ring the bells all over the city, and do what honorable kings do in books and scrolls.

"The spikes are attached to the leg of my stag, waiting on a turret down the hall out the window."

"Your what?"

"A stag, Your Honor. It's a deer. And I understand now why Your Honor had me dropped from the roofs. You were protecting the city, keeping the black-iron needles safe in a lit room in the guarded tower of Fremantle."

What can I say? Errol thought the regnat was clean. I imagine he had to ignore the truth because it was getting in the way of the regnat he wanted to believe existed.

"Absolutely." The regnat struck a match to ignite a lamp. The lighting of a flame of a lamp in such a bright room had the effect of holding a candle to the full sun.

"Your Honor, the prisoners are pitted against one another. I have seen cats, sheep, deer, rats—"

"Nothing better?" said the regnat.

"Better?" said Errol.

"Nothing rare?" The regnat drummed his fingers on the mantel.

Errol laughed. "A fox is rare, to me. A dog is rare."

The regnat kicked a log into his fireplace. "No kardunns?"

Errol felt a chill on his neck. "None that I saw."

"Good."

"I did meet someone obsessed with rarities."

"Utlag. You have met Utlag."

"Aye."

"Then you have crossed paths with the abbot."

"Aye."

The regnat lit another lamp. "A freak, Utlag."

"It was hard to look at him," Errol agreed.

"He used to be something to look at."

"I don't understand his relationship with the abbot."

"They work at cross-purposes. It can happen that way."

Errol felt relief wash over him. So the regnat knew everything. Of course he did. This was why he was the leader of this city. Finally, Errol thought, he had found his way back to the roofs and into the guild towers, and had told the regnat all of it, and now he could leave the work to the one who knew how to wage war and make justice pour over this city. He was tired. He didn't want to think about the streets or about what it meant to be the son of a freak. (I could have told him a thing or two about that.) There would be good food in Fremantle and a bath and a room in this most heavily guarded of guild towers. And he could sleep.

"Your mother is an embarrassment," the regnat said.

The remark took him off guard. Errol could only think to say, "I can't imagine what she saw in Utlag."

"He was 'different.'" The regnat laughed. So did Errol. "Utlag was a mistake. But Margaret Thebes wouldn't listen. I suppose you don't want to think—nobody wants to think about the bed life of their parents." The regnat was studying him now, his eyes flat and cold. He said, "You are here to kill me."

"No! I'm a runner! You're the regnat!"

"You're an outlaw."

"I just hoped you'd bring an army. Just your presence on the street would bring hope. I'll go with you."

The regnat poked at the fire again. "Your brothers never amounted to anything."

"I'm not them."

The regnat set down the poker and crossed his arms. He said, "It's time for you to go. To sheath those iron spikes and hand them over, and to get out of my quarters. You're a sickness in this city. You're Rip and you're Fenn and you're that foul mother and you're Utlag."

Perhaps what blinded Errol was that he already believed what the regnat had said. He turned to go, then turned and thanked the regnat and reached for his hand.

"Do you really think I'll touch you?"

"I apologize."

"I wanted you gone. I always have. When Utlag told me years ago that he threw you over the roof of the guild, I thought we were done. The two brothers were gone, and now so were you. But I realized he had done nothing more than throw off a foundling he mistook for you, and you were plenty alive in that guild. There you were, winning the Long Run. And then in Ganso, you were fool enough to defend those two pelts on your roof who stole the iron spikes, to tell me to my face that you had stolen them from these very quarters. I had my chance then and missed it. It took that foul cousin of yours to give us the best advice we'd gotten. Put a foundling on the cut line, he said. Why hadn't I thought of it? Any damsel in distress would bring you in."

"I don't understand." Errol was backing away. "I was an innocent kelp in Thebes. I only wanted to be a runner. Why would you want Utlag to kill me?" His words sounded to him like tiny letters falling out of his mouth. He fell backward over the regnat's footstool and got up. "Ow."

The regnat came toward him with sudden speed, calling out for the guards.

Errol turned and ran into the wall, knocked over the globe of one of the wall lamps. Hot glass exploded on the floor and the light hissed and went out. The regnat hesitated for a moment in the sudden, lesser brightness.

Errol saw that.

He ran, crisscrossing the wide hallway, toppling hot globes on the walls while the regnat screamed, until the tunnel was a wreck of broken glass, sulfur reek, and darkness.

A Ghost

WE WERE INTO HER TENT and out of a high percentage of our clothes when there came a low bellowing from the abyss off the south side of Lascaux.

"Here's to the maid with a booo-sums of snow! Now to her that's as brown as a berry! Here's to the wife with a face full of woe—" (loud belch, long silence) *"And now to the damsel that's merrr-rrry!"* Thud, as though someone had thrown something at the tent. I looked at Terpsichore, too alarmed to move. *"Let the toast pass! Drink to the lass! I'll tell you she'll be an excuse for the glass—"*

"Don't move," I said to Terpsichore. "Please. Don't move."

———

He was gaunt. His hair was matted to his head. In one hand he held a flask high. In the other he wielded his navaja. He came toward me unsteadily across a plank from Gallia. The plank bent absurdly under his weight. He appeared to have antlers growing out of his head.

I should have been glad to see him. Beyond glad. My cousin! My best friend! Back from the dead! But, for one thing, I thought he was a ghost. And then I hoped he was, for guilt rose in my gut like bile. With him gone, I had been able to hide from what I had done, that I had been the cause of his end. But here he was, the exact size and shape of my fear. Maybe he didn't know—

"Parsival!" he said, slashing the air with the knife. "My arsh enemy."

He knew.

"Errol Thebes! Cousin!" I whispered, feigning calm. "I, we, thought you were dead."

He thrust the tiny knife forward and went low, en garde. Now I could see why the plank bent under him: An enormous antlered beast, easily the size of seven of us put together, followed him, tethered to a line in his hand, its hoofs delicately balanced on the plank. The stag moved his head to study me with one eye.

Errol's finger went up on the hand with the flask in it. As if to tell me a secret. "Ish a stag," he said.

"Let me guess," I said. "The black-iron spikes?"

"Yes! Thash right! How did you know? Here's to my friend Odd Theebsh, who knows everything!" He bowed to me, but the motion set him off-balance. He stepped into the air, tilted off the plank, and made a jackknifing motion to steady himself. My hands dripped with sweat.

"What are you doing here?" I said.

"Hiding from the regnat. Also! I've returned with Bayard to slay you—"

"Bayard is the stag?"

He held up his navaja and said, "Bayard the Blade."

I crossed my arms. "You named your knife? Feh. Get off that plank. It isn't safe."

"Safe! Ironic, coming from you. I'm here because"—he had to stop to think—"because I had one question for you."

"A question," I said, full of dread.

"Why did you hate me?" And there it was. "The regnat said you shugges—shugshet— The regnat said you put that foundling on the cut line and said I'd get her safe off it. So now I know it wasn't the foundling. It was you, Oddly Enough, who wanted me dead." He pointed the knife at me from twenty feet away and thrust it. He lifted one leg and turned himself around on the plank, as if he had meant to find me in the opposite direction. A drunken fight, alone. All the while he was saying, "I felt the earth come at me like a sledgehammer because of you! And then all kinds of horrors because of you, and then—" He paused so long I thought he had forgotten me.

"Then?" I said.

"Then I was unwelcome even in the low places. Irony! The guildmaster's son—an exile from heofon *and* hel. How much did you hate me, Odd Theebsh?" he yelled. "More or less than your father did?"

"My father wasn't who we thought he was. You dropped because you stole the black-iron spikes. I didn't steal them. I didn't bring that on you."

"Maybe I did." He looked at the knife in his hand.

"Get off the plank, Errol."

"But the plank is the only place for me. *Betweonen*. In between. I am unwelcome everywhere. Come out here, Odd Theeebsh. Throw me off. But I should warn you. I am"—he pitched sideways—"I am a felon now. A murderer. And a fool. I trusted Rip and he lied to me." Here he took a long swig again. "He didn't tell me Utlag is our father till the end. Or what gaol was."

"Rip who? Are you talking about Rip Thebes?" I said. Even under these circumstances I could be caught by a story. "And who's Utlag?"

"I don't know what he is. He does this thing with his throat." He opened his mouth like a gaping hole and exuded a strange clicking sound at me. "And the regnat is as foul as anyone—"

"You've been to see the regnat?"

"Don't worry. The regnat won't find us," said Errol. "His guards went to Thebes." He looked at the flask thoughtfully, and then at me. Now his eyes were running with tears. "They tied that cat down, Odd Theebsh."

"What are you talking about?"

"How can you stand to exist, knowing what we know about the streets? How much has to be ignored just so we can live here in this high place?"

"You're bringing me down. Just get off the plank."

He was silent for a moment.

"There's a girl in that tent, isn't there?" he said.

"None of your business."

"Don't spend the whole night in there. What's her name?"

I hesitated. "It's Terpsichore."

"You don't know her real name, do you?"

"Shut up."

"You love that foundling."

"I said, *shut up*. I'm not spending the whole night with this one."

I couldn't solve him. I turned and walked away. Went to the door of Terpsichore's tent and crawled into the sack with her.

She said, "Who was that?"

"No one."

"You're not staying."

"Of course I am. Not. I don't know."

I forgot about my not-dead cousin out there on the plank, who would return or fall. One or the other. I forgot about the foundlings in the morgues, the regnat, my insane father, the horrors of the streets, the date, the year, the city, my name. And the time.

SOMEWHERE IN MY BONES, I knew the sun was rising. But the muse's kisses were an elixir, and after I had pulled off her leggings, desperate to climb onto her, it would have been easier to stop two falling bodies in a screamer than to stop us. I had waited my whole life for the relief of that moment. And then, without much warning, I would never be twelve again.

There was no yesterday. There was no tomorrow. There was now.

———

It was impossible to miss the silhouette of the roof master from Lascaux, his hair tied in elaborate knots. I could tell from his shape that his arms were crossed. I felt like a kelp caught stealing.

"She likes Parsival," I said stupidly, realizing I was wearing the helmet.

He invoked, as he was obliged to do, that law of prudes and scriveners: "Should the night meet the dawn while two are together alone, they shall be bound as one, as the woven rays of sun and moon."

Like everything else that begins as poetry and ends in paperwork, this law was written to ruin lives. Mine, specifically.

Her parents were brought up, though they would not look at me. My own mother was carried over the lines, wiping her hands from kitchen work, fussing about my dirty tunic and leggings. Why hadn't I written, and no one had told her I was with a girl or such a beautiful one.

None of my friends were there. All of Terpsichore's were, almost as if they had been expecting this.

What was her real name?

They bound us facing each other around the hips and chests. Wound the lines around the dropping apparatus. Terpsichore insisted on tying the actual knots. The brakes lifted and we heard a loud chunk, like a gallows. My stomach hit the top of my throat, our heads flipped back, and we fell: stones plummeting into the fog. Nothing was in my mind all that way. No hope of dying, no fear I could name, not even the song I had always planned to sing when I was dropping. I wrapped myself around her so that it was my ribs that broke in the bindings and not hers. I was the Grail knight, Parsival, after all. It was the least I could do.

Her real name was Leah, but I had never yet called her that.

Master Guilder

ERROL HAD ENOUGH EXPERIENCE carrying body bags across the roofs, in his years as a runner, to know he was in one. There was an occasional "Heave!" It was a command his stomach was obliged to obey.

They dropped him, and somebody unstrapped the bag and opened it. A furred muzzle punched his jaw and, behind the muzzle, three foundlings stared down at him in overbright lamplight.

"Leave him be," said a man's voice, and a big plate-sized hand pushed the stag and the foundlings away and shielded Errol's eyes from the lamp.

"Woody Thebes," said Errol.

"Errol Thebes."

"Where am I?"

"Fiftieth strata of Thebes Guild. My quarters. You're a lucky one, runner. The list of things that happened to you last night would fill a kelp's diary."

"Aye. Lucky. That's me." Errol's head felt like someone had set the bog pots in it and was exploding them one by one with fireworks. "Oh no—"

Woody put a pot under Errol's chin.

" 'Twas a long night," said Woody. "I believe whiskey was involved."

Errol fell back on the bed while Woody went to rinse the pot. "I'm so sorry for this." Woody turned in surprise. He had known a more arrogant pelt once. "I dreamt I fell from a plank."

"There's not so much cleaning up to do, in dreams."

Errol looked at his hands, which appeared to be made of wax. "I hope nobody saw me like this."

"Just us. Jamila Foundling, of course. I doubt you know her. She's accustomed to foul things, though, being a foundling. She—acquired—your tellensac for you, from Margaret's quarters. Here."

"What did I say to it?" said Errol, reaching for the sac. "To the foundling."

Woody raised an eyebrow. "How much time have you got?"

Errol groaned. He drew himself back into the body bag and held the flaps together. "An eternity."

Errol had gone on at length about the quality of his private parts. He had tried to show Jamila all his scars and had talked about a fight he lost against a pack of street runners, and was more upset about a fight he had won.

"There's more, isn't there?" said Errol.

Woody scratched his chin. "You said the foundling reminded you of the guildmaster, who was lonely and spiteful and had bound herself to a monster. And then you tried to kiss her. That rather killed whatever festivity was left."

Errol remained in the bag till noon.

———

When he woke again he was alone in the room. He was able now to move his eyeballs.

The bed was made of cedar planks. The pillows and blankets smelled of pine; the dressers and desk and chairs were maple. Tables, bowls, spoons, cupboards. Pencils. Everything had been ornately hand-carved. A spike of heartwood had been left on the desk in the middle of becoming a pair of knotting spikes. Errol picked one up and saw that Woody had carved a minuscule cage, and in the cage, an ironwood cricket.

Woody came from the hall and handed him a cup of tea.

"I thought you lived in the workshop," said Errol.

"In another place and time, the forest would be home for me," said Woody. "This is the irfelaf of a forest. I smell the woods in the wood."

"Right now I just smell this foul bag and the stench of my own self. So you met Eikthyrnir, I see," said Errol. The beast was sprawled on his back by a fire in the hearth. "He's a stag."

"Aye. Well. He barely fits in the guild tower. I had to bind him in ropes to lower him through the hatch. He'll have to stay here in my quarters. Fremantle is searching for the spikes again and surely would be interested in finding you here."

Errol sat up fast. The last time he saw the iron spikes they were unsheathed and strapped to the stag. They were gone now and he had lost all memory of the night.

". . . thought you were gone, Errol Thebes," Woody was saying. "It's an uncommon thing, to have you back in this guild. Aye, but I must be off to work or Margaret will come find me, and she'll find you. I'll be back at midday. By then some toast will go down all right. No one but the foundlings knows you're here. And the hatch-guilder." He paused with his hand on the doorknob. "By the way, it was a drop for your cousin Odd today, as well. He was bound this morning to the runner he calls Terpsichore."

Errol lay back and put his hands over his face. "What a fool."

"Don't be iron on him. 'Twas noble. He didn't argue or dispute the dawn the way some do."

"I didn't mean him. I meant me."

———

Errol slept fitfully until all that was left of the whiskey was the headache.

Woody had rigged up a rain shower from black leather sacks of water suspended by a wire bucket outside the vents of the tower, heating in the winter sun. Errol scrubbed himself and his wounds clean under a pure rain of hot water. When he got out and dressed in the foundling's gray tunic and leggings Woody had left for him, he turned to look again at that water system. Guilders took only cold baths. Where had he seen such a device before? Next to this contraption, there were a dozen tiny trees growing in the band of light from the air vent. Trees? He spun around. On Woody's desk he saw a rolled quill holder made of wool felt. Next to it, a fan spun in the heat from a tiny fire fueled by wood shavings, warming the room. Woody's quarters were full of things Errol already had seen somewhere. He laughed suddenly, for it came to him. These were ideas he himself had sketched as a kelp on scraps of paper and tacked to the walls of our room.

WHEN I SAID "GOOD MORNING" to my bound-wife, I tried to hide my panic at having such a thing. The weight of her hung on me like a stone. Could I step out of her tent without telling her where I was going? What if I met some other girl right away who was better? Terpsichore sat in her bedroll watching me dress, taking a handful of the beads she had from the apothecary. I missed my own tent, my books, my roof. She gave me a long list of the things I would have to do today to satisfy her guild's requirements for apprentices. I would not have to take exams to be accepted, she said, because I was wed to her, as if it were some great honor to make rags and flies. On and on she went like a roof master. Had I said I would apprentice here? Had I agreed to subject myself for life to the infinite ropewalks of Lascaux? Feh. Was I to provide for her or was she able to make her own work? Could we stay on the roofs? I went dismally with her to breakfast in Lascaux's yurt. She and I looked like guilders now, rumpled and committed.

The girls elbowed one another and flirted with me. They were safe, now that I had a bound-wife. The boys stuffed their shirts with two buns each and rolled their eyes at me and winked. Idiots. I'd have done that myself the night before.

And then, worst of all, they all picked up their plates of breakfast and left us alone. They thought what? That I would undress her here and now if I could. But I wanted the opposite. She was attractive enough. However—oh, I could fill a book with *however*.

———

When I passed Grid later in the morning on the plank at Thebes, she looked me over and said, "Congratulations?" She asked me if the muse was happy and I shrugged, and said, "Of course she is. She has me." But the joke fell flat. Truth: I didn't know how my bound-wife *was*. Parsival might have checked in to see how his new bride felt after such a hasty binding, whether she looked at him and felt her spirits rise. But I was not, in fact, him.

The Apothecary

ERROL STARED, agitated, at the apothecarist's door on the eighth strata of Thebes, wondering how an apothecary could be closed for business during the day in a busy guild.

"Pull the string" came a voice from the other side of the door. Errol reached over his head, found a string in the air and pulled it. He heard a bell tinkle just behind the door. The door opened immediately and a wiry man in a red apron stood in front of him, pressing his fingertips together in the shape of a tent.

"And?" he said.

"I must have something for an unrelenting headache," said Errol.

"'Unrelenting.' That's new." The man spun on his heel. Errol ran to keep up with him, immediately lost in a maze of hallways, each hall lined from floor to ceiling with shelves; each shelf organized with crocks, tins, and jars. The air smelled thickly of reeds and earth. It reminded Errol of the river, where he had been washed of the blood of a street fight, and of Dagmar's yurt, where her boiling salves had killed the infections in his wounds. He was surprised to feel a longing in himself to be back on the streets, on the riverbanks where he realized, at this random moment, he had felt at home.

The apothecarist led him to a room with a high table, a stool, and wood burning in a hearth in the wall. Behind the table were a dozen barrels, covered with slate lids. Errol took the stool while the apothecarist produced a mortar, which he rubbed with the corner of his apron.

"I find myself thinking, a whiskey headache," the man said.

"That's remarkable. How did you know?" said Errol, wincing at the volume of his own voice.

The apothecarist shrugged. "The pallor of the skin. The distended veins in the eyes. The restlessness in the legs. Also the flask in your tunic pocket." The man opened a barrel marked KASTE OP. Inside was a mound of thousands of tiny, waxed beads, a dozen of which he expertly flipped into the mortar.

"Take six now and six more in six minutes." He covered a yawn with the back of his hand. "Relief comes in twelve minutes." He tapped rainwater from a steaming pot in the fire and set a cup of it on the table. Errol poured the first six beads into his hand and swallowed them with the rain. The apothecarist reached into the drawer under the table, took out a pair of sand timers, and set one of them on end. He and Errol watched the sand flow through the tiny funnel.

By and by the apothecarist yawned again. He pulled a thick leather logbook from under the table and opened it. "The apprentice's name?"

"Uh. Bayard. That is, Bayard Phrygia. Bayard Thebes," Errol said. "It takes a while to get used to the name change."

The apothecarist studied him closely, then returned to the page. "You're not registered here."

"Registered with an apothecary?" said Errol. "For what purpose?"

"For your ration of these," the man said, tapping his quill on another barrel behind him, labeled SIS. "We give them to all the new apprentices, the runners coming down off the roofs. They call them 'sissies.'"

"What are they for?" said Errol.

The apothecarist shrugged. "After three years on the roofs, all runners have trouble living in the guild houses. Restlessness, wanderlust, a longing for high places, et cetera."

"I won't have those troubles. I'm glad for the safety of a guild tower."

"Just wait. You will have trouble. And when you do, these will make you forget the things that you wish you had: the roofs, the sky, your old friends, the exuberant work on the lines, all the exciting things you used to do on the roofs. They ease the transition." The apothecarist put up his hands in a gesture of surrender. "Otherwise you're up all night roaming the hallways, carrying on about a kind of homesickness you can't describe. Spending all your money on whiskey. Frightened of the infinite thirty or forty years ahead of you in a quarantined guild." He patted the barrel with his hand. "Unless I give you these beads, no one in this tower will get any sleep."

"Keep them for someone else. I don't need them," said Errol.

"You are all, I think, like wild animals, discovering the bars for the first time, of your cage."

"'Sissies' sounds like an insult of some kind," said Errol.

"I suppose. The apprentices gave it that nickname. The original name had to do with an arrogant king."

Errol paused. "Sisyphus?" he said.

"One and the same. Pushing the stone up the mountain every day for infinity."

Errol thought of the foundling Jamila. She had said she would prefer to be Sisyphus. She would never agree to take these beads, Errol thought. Stubborn. He pointed to the next barrel. "And what are those?"

"Pasione Ritorno? The Return of Passion. For falling into love."

Errol laughed.

The apothecarist tipped his head. "Is it funny? Perhaps laughter is assent. Perhaps you need them already?"

"I think I can manage to fall in love on my own, with all due respect to your beads," said Errol.

"I'm sure you can, the first day. And the second. But a year later? Or two? Most often they're used for falling back into love."

The sand in the first timer ran out, and the apothecarist flipped the second one. Errol swallowed his next six beads. "Do they work, those passion beads?"

The apothecarist bristled. "This is not quackery, Bayard Phrygia. Or Bayard Thebes. Let us say your wife is bored of you. *Are* you bound? Not yet? Well, imagine a wife, then. She once loved even the way your breath smelt after sleep. That same wife, five years later, is tired of the annoying way you assume she wants breakfast in bed. There is nothing for the two of you but the same four walls, nowhere to go in this iron tower, nothing new to discuss. Perhaps you married her when the sky was your world. But now"—the apothecarist shrugged—"perhaps you come down to see me, and I put two of these beads on the guild's tab. You melt them in the bottom of her tea cup and I don't see either of you again for weeks, except maybe walking the guildhalls at night making eyes at each other. Maybe she even pinches you in the backside when she thinks I am not looking." The apothecarist tipped his head to the side. "Just be sure not to put it into another woman's cup, by accident. Then, instead of love, we've got theater."

"Was that humor?" said Errol.

"I find myself laughing."

"What about that one—Taedium Absentis?"

"The remedy for boredom. An uur after taking one of these beads, you will find that even congealed eggs are fascinating. *The History of Head Lice*, volume four, exceeds, in pure excitement, the tales of Virgil." The man put his hand on his stack of books, which included all four volumes on lice.

"Why don't people just find something to do? Play games, like we used to when we were kelps? Act at theater?" said Errol.

"Right. And after four decades of theater, you'll come see me, too, for a few of these beads."

"I won't."

The apothecarist contemplated Errol's face. "No. Maybe you won't. You are, no doubt, made of stronger iron than everyone else in the history of this city."

The apothecarist put his fingers on the next barrel. "These evoke memories of glorious things in your life, things that perhaps never actually happened. Take two and you've been a warrior; five, a victorious one. Ten, you're bound to Helen of Troy."

"Why not take the whole barrel?" said Errol.

"Everyone says that. When it comes down to it, no one dares. These," the apothecarist continued with his fingers on the next barrel, "make for long, glorious dreams. Those? Are for removing fear. And those—"

"Stop," said Errol. "I don't want to know any more."

The apothecarist paused in mid-sentence. "I see." The two of them were silent for a long while. "I cannot lie," the man said quietly. "It is not a high life, in Thebes House, but it is a middling good life. The work can be interesting if you put yourself into it. Beautiful things are made here, and the world waits for them with anticipation. You live maybe four or five decades out of the sunlight, and if you are restless during those decades, or bored, or afraid, or devoid of certain necessary feelings, I am at your service."

The sand on the second timer ran out. Errol stood and drank one more cup of the rain. "Thank you," he said. "My headache is gone."

"It is nothing," said the apothecarist. "Literally. In faith, the water was the cure. Whiskey dries you out."

Errol laughed. He turned to go and then turned back. "I have a question of a personal nature."

The apothecarist was writing something with his quill in the logbook. "'Confidential' is my middle name."

"I wonder what the remedy might cost, to cure a case of the ague."

The man did not stop writing. "Quinine and artemisia are easy enough to come by. Inexpensive. I find myself wondering, why do you ask?"

"I have a friend with it," said Errol.

"Ah. A *friend.*" The apothecarist put down the quill. "Who is your so-called friend?"

"It's not me, if that's what you mean."

"I know it's not you."

"How do you know?"

"Where to begin? The ague, known also as malaria, is an illness borne in the spit of insects of swamps and lowlands, and we have few swamps in the guilds, or lowlands. Or, for that matter, insects. Occasionally we have the rumor of head lice."

"I have carried tons of beads, including artemisia and quinine, from the ships to Raepteek House, from Raepteek to other towers of our district," said Errol. "Are you telling me we have none of those beads, here in Thebes?"

"Do not insult me, apprentice. Follow me and I will put my hands on the bottles of those beads before you can forget your name again."

The apothecarist stopped abruptly, lit a lamp, picked up a thin white bottle, and dusted it with his apron, although it was already clean. He poured a formula of five brown beads and two green-and-white-striped ones into Errol's hand.

"Artemisia," the apothecarist said. "And quinine. I didn't say we don't *have* them; I said we don't *need* them. We don't need ninety percent of the medication in this apothecary. We're quarantined." He patted the iron wall.

"Aye. Well, a kelp would require a great deal of this remedy, more than we have here, am I right?" said Errol.

"I have enough for sixty-five or seventy children here, and can order more from Raepteek. How is it that you know a child with the ague?"

Errol stepped back. "Pardon me. Did you think I said ague? It must be the accent I carry from Phrygia House. Not ague. Ache. Sorry." Errol poured the beads back into the bottle and wiped his hand on his leggings. "Ache," he said again.

The apothecarist studied Errol closely, his forefingers tapping his apron. At length he said, "I am just as interested in helping people as you are. And I am obviously better at it or you wouldn't be here, planning to steal what I myself have made and can prescribe. I would find a case of the ague fascinating and would be honored to treat a child. Shall we continue this ruse, or do you want my help?"

A Contract

MY BROTHER HEIMDALL was out of place in the yurt on the roof of Thebes. "So," he said. "Bound are you, then? May as well be dead."

"What of it?" I said. "You don't belong here. A nightmare, come to summon me."

"You don't belong here either, *Parsival*. Time to come down, now you're wed."

"I belong now. And I'm not dead, brother. Only bound." I lit a lamp on the table and watched the shadows play off his face. "Bound pairs are allowed to stay high."

"I give you nine months on the roofs and you'll be down there with the rest of us, tending a skinny, puking baby. Can't raise a kelp on the roof. It'll slip right over the edge."

"Did you come up here to practice your soothsaying?" I said.

I hadn't seen him in two years. In that time I had grown lean and strong. He had grown thick pads of fat on his shoulders and black stains on his teeth. We sat at the table across from each other. He ran his fingers over three pieces of parchment before him, neatened them into a squared stack and stared at me.

I said, "Did you need to borrow money from me?"

"You'll be the one needing money, now that you're bound to Leah Lascaux," he said.

"You don't know anything about her," I said, aware that for all I knew she was probably waking up at Lascaux right about now and wondering where I was.

Heimdall slid the top piece of paper across the table and I looked at it from a distance.

He said, "If I don't know anything, then I don't know Leah Lascaux is in debt twenty-three thousand uurs. And I don't know that her parents were paying it off. But debt, as you know, is transferred to the bound pair on the day of the binding. I wonder if she chose you for this reason, so she can buy shoes and festive things to put in her hair. In any case, I'm afraid you will not be able"—here he grinned lecherously—"to satisfy her. You don't make anywhere near enough money."

"I'm well paid and so is she," I said, although I had no idea how much money she made, and this was the first I'd heard of her debt. Twenty-three thousand was a staggering amount, more than I could earn in any apprenticeship I was considering.

Heimdall pushed the second piece of parchment across the table.

He said, "If by 'well paid' you mean that you earned a thousand three hundred thirty-two uurs since you rose to the roofs, you are correct. Except, as you must know, the money you earn before you are bound, everything up until this morning at dawn, returns to your family. I have had it transferred to my accounts."

I steadied myself with a hand on the edge of the table. "How did you gain access to my accounts without my consent?"

"I'm family." He tapped his fingers on the third piece of parchment.

"What is *that*?"

"This document once belonged to Errol Thebes." I felt my jaw tighten. He slid the page over to me. It was an apprentice's contract. I ignored a hundred *hereafters* and *whenceforths* in the language of Virgil and dropped to the end. There was an offer: "An apprenticeship in the documents room in the Guild House of Fremantle on a per annum salary of twenty-five thousand uurs with the expectation of guild work for the duration of: One (1) Lifetime."

The regnat had signed the bottom of the page with a flourish.

"I don't understand. This is a contract Errol received, to work in Fremantle. But someone crossed out his name and wrote mine."

"Not someone. Heimdall Thebes. I wrote your name there today after the regnat came to see me."

"Why? Why would the regnat come to see *you*?" I looked at the date at the top of the contract. "This contract was not written today. It was written two years ago. Errol and I had just come up to the roofs."

"Aye. Look at the date. It was a big night for Errol Thebes." I stared at the page, drawing a blank. "Think about it. It will come," Heimdall said. "It was the night he had done that Big Run, and suddenly he could have anything he wanted—"

"It's called the Long Run."

"Aye."

"He won it. The prize was anything he wanted, anything at all. He never told me what he requested. He wanted to go to Fremantle?"

"Aye. And read the small print," Heimdall said, a grin spreading on his face. Several boxes had been *X*-ed in the Addendums section, entitling Errol to huge food allowances, access to the libraries of all the guilds, a room in his quarters just for card games. There was a diagram of the floor plan of his quarters, which would make his mam's at Thebes look like a broom closet.

"Read the last bit," said Heimdall.

I dropped to the bottom. Someone had handwritten: *The apprentice is permitted to bring a single foundling to Fremantle. The foundling will be Jamila Foundling, Thebes House.*

I looked up. "He didn't even know Jamila. Why would he bargain to take my foundling with him?"

"I can't imagine," he said, playing with me.

My mouth opened and closed in surprise and pain. "He found out about her somehow," I said. "And he realized that I had kept her from him. This is why he never told me the prize he had chosen—"

Heimdall chuckled. "Well, but think of it now. Now you can take it all back. Even the foundling can still come with you, as she has no choice in the matter and she can—shall we say?—read to you, even if you're bound to someone else." My heart was starting to race at the thought of a life near Jamila.

I stared at Heimdall, trying to find the card trick he was playing on me. "Did you pay to put my name on this contract, with my money?" I said. It was all I could think of.

"Don't be ridiculous," he said, putting out his thick hands in a gesture of good-will. Then his eyes shifted and there was a shadow in the pale flesh at the sides of his face.

"What's in this for you?"

"Nothing! You fooled yourself to think that Errol, or any guildmaster's son, would have anything to do with you. I have just showed you how a family truly watches out for its own. When the regnat visited me today, I urged him to put your name here."

"The regnat," I murmured. The pain obscured the fact that the contract made no sense. Errol had won the Long Run. He was the star of the roofs. Why would he ask for something he was going to get anyway? All I could think was that Errol struck that deal with the city in order to take everything I had.

". . . I would do this because I am your brother," Heimdall was saying. "But the regnat is not so generous. Errol Thebes is back in the towers."

"In Thebes," I said, before I had a chance to keep my mouth shut. In a split second I realized what was going to be demanded of me.

"It's a small exchange for what I've done for you today. Lure him in with a girl, like you did the first time."

"That was an accident," I said.

"Have another accident. When you bring him to me, all of this will be yours. You'll have uurs coming out of your—"

I raised my hands to stop him. I stared out the door of the yurt, into the night. "What has Errol Thebes ever done to you?" I said.

"Done to me," Heimdall said. "Do you have any idea what it is, to be the son of Slyngel and Gudrun Thebes, when your aunt is the guildmaster?"

"I have some idea," I said, under my breath.

"Fenn and Rip—they had everything. I was an obscure kelp in their kingdom." He paused, remembering. "You are aware of the boredom contained in this tower?"

I nodded imperceptibly.

"But those two didn't care for the kingdom. They showed no interest in running their mother's guild. So, what does Heimdall Thebes do? He watches. He waits. He is between the two sons, agewise, and invisible to both. Their mother will not speak to him. She tracks her own two pelts, trying every night to get them to come back to their quarters, to do their work. She longs for their father, a creeping bound-husband who comes and goes at night and climbs walls. Heimdall Thebes thinks to himself: Margaret Thebes is a rising guildmaster in this city. Even the regnat comes here to meet with her, to seek her council behind closed doors. If her sons are fools, Heimdall Thebes will step in and run the guild. He will rise."

"All you've ever done is stoke furnaces," I said.

He flinched. "I came to Margaret Thebes with calculations showing how much better the guild would fare if we opened the flues to capture the winds outside the tower. She liked that. Then I found a clever way to store extra firewood, to hang it from the rafters so we could forge at full capacity straight through Beklemek."

"And she fell in love with you."

"One day Margaret takes Heimdall into her quarters. She teaches him the books. Just the books for the furnace rooms, but a month later she puts him in charge of the disposal of the ash, through pipes he has commissioned, which dump directly onto the street instead of into the earth as the old ones did. The old ones clogged with the sewage, and overflowed."

"Lovely," I said.

"I was rising. But then, one day and without warning, Margaret Thebes is thick with child again. Our uncle, the air-licking freak, has not been here for seven years, and I suspect every man in the guild. How can there be a third? But sure enough, she is in labor. And there comes of her a third son. And now I, I who have already been patient, I have to wait while that kelp grows up. And as luck would have it, he grows up more arrogant than his brothers. And perfect in every way—agile, inventive, calm, attentive to detail. When his brothers go to the roofs, he looks like the young prince. Perfectly suited to the work of running a guild. I hated him."

I said, "Errol Thebes's mother didn't even like him. And his brothers left him. And he had no father. How could you be jealous? He was more miserable than any of us." I already knew the answer to that question. Heimdall had not been the only jealous one.

Heimdall slumped. "When Margaret sends Errol to our quarters, tells our mam to raise him, I think to myself, 'Good. As long as he's with us, he'll become nothing.'

"But I didn't factor in Woody Thebes. One afternoon Woody and Errol come to look at the books. I am working now in the guildmaster's offices, but Margaret asks me to step away from my desk. Remember, I am eighteen times now around the sun, and the young prince is eight. When he is done with the calculations she gives him, using my pen, Margaret says five words to me: 'Return to the furnaces, Heinrich.' And when I steady my knees, I find the words to tell her my name is Heimdall." His jaw twitched. "Which means I will strive for my entire life in the low places of this cold guild tower, scraping the stink out of the pipes I myself have invented.

"What do I have against Errol Thebes?" He spit, a brown gob slipping down our yurt wall. "When the regnat contacted me this morning, I leapt at the chance to find Errol. For once, one of us should rise."

I pulled the papers closer to me on the table, stared at them. Errol had planned to leave me behind. What kind of a friend would take what little I wanted and have it for himself? Would leave me behind with a wife and her debt?

"What will the regnat do to Errol?" I could barely hear my own voice.

"It's unlikely they will let him wear a drop-line this time." A grin played at the corners of his eyes. "You know this will happen with or without you. You may as well profit."

A Stranger

ERROL CLIMBED OUT of the foundlings' wall through a hole under the stairs at the thirty-fourth strata. He stood at the shadow of the arch to the Great Hall, smelling root stews in the midday kitchens. He had not expected to hear the workaday chatter of the first lunch shift. Some kelps ran past him on the stone stairs, charging into battle with their wooden swords.

"I em Beowulf! Heer me RAAAAR!"

"And I em Grendel, so ye should watch your hind parts!"

A voice behind Errol made him jump. "That game was my son's favorite."

Errol said nothing.

"Are ye deaf, foundling?"

"I'm sorry," he said, putting his hand up to his neck, to cover the lack of a mark. *"Wil ye wesh my to mak the kelpies te halt spillen pain on ye?"*

"Nay. If I wanted the game banned, banned it would be already. Do you know who I am?"

"Aye. Mam. Margaret Thebes, guildmaster of this very tower." He kept his back to her still. He saw her move in the corner of his eye. "I am sure that son misses you," he said.

"Are ye besting me? In what square inch of your foundling head did you find that idea?"

"I miss my own mam, is all, and she had nearly as many concerns as you do."

"I pity her. Let me guess. A man is the cause of the trouble?"

"Aye."

"'Oft hath even a whole city reaped the evil fruit of a bad man.'"

Errol nearly turned to her. "Are ye quoting from Hesiod?" He had never known his mam to read.

"Aye. And how would you know that? Apparently I've met another scholar taught to read by Jamila Foundling."

"Aye, Mam. I'm sorry to be so well-informed. If it relieves you, I cannot read the crisis in this city."

"What do you mean by that?" Margaret said, drawing nearer to him.

"Which one is the bad man in this city: the fiend who lived here once, or the regnat who cannot exist apart from bright light?"

"Who are you?" she said. "How do you know that?"

"No one. But rumors spread in the morgues. How far does the evil spread, Mam?"

"The whole city pays taxes in foundlings. That cannot be stopped. And the streets are foul. But this hardly concerns you, foundling. I'll not pay the tax in foundlings till my body is cold. When the regnat came last week and did not find the particular knotting spikes he wanted, I gave him gold. He cannot take his eyes off gold."

"I would prefer to fight the regnat."

"Too many of the guilds would take the side of Fremantle. To keep the regnat in office, to keep the guild exports leaving the city. Guilders fear even good change."

"Why did you let a creature so foul as Utlag into the guild in the first place, Mam?"

She raised her fist, as if to strike him, but withdrew it and wiped at her eyes. "Remember who you are, and who I am."

"I remember," he said.

"I had no idea he would turn the city upside down, seeking something he digs from our ribs. Feasting on us. A predator."

"Could you not tell from looking at him that he was foul?"

"He was far from foul when he was young. He was uncommon."

"As hel is uncommon."

She stiffened. "You are too bold, foundling. Show me your face."

Errol turned slowly. She eyed him as she would a sack of wool she was considering for purchase.

"Well, my son was a far better-looking thing than you are. Beowulf, as I told you, they made him every time, and not just because he was mine. There was the noble in him, and something else as well. A rare thing. Not anymore, but he was."

"He misses you, Mam. I am sure of it."

They were quiet for a long while, and Errol realized how often he had seen Margaret in the company of foundlings. Her secrets were safe with them. She shook her head as if to shake off all they had just said to each other.

"Flattery will not free you from rubbing the stairs, foundling." She pulled herself up to her full height, and still looked up at him. "Didn't you have something to do?"

"I lack a rag," he said.

"We hide them in that bin over there, says *rags*. You might be done now and onto some more useful chore if ye didn't waste my time carrying on about things that'll not change."

Knotwork

JAMILA LIFTED HER HAND to cover the glare of a stranger's head lamp at the foot of her makeshift bunk in the morgues of Thebes. This one smelled of cold fur.

"Foundling," he said to her.

She put down her knotting work and reached out. Errol thought she was going to strike him; he caught her wrist.

"Outlaw," she said. "It's a good thing I can read."

"Ah," Errol Thebes said. "A past insult returns, that I may regret saying it again."

"What do you want?"

"Woody said I had to—or rather, I myself *wanted* to—apologize. I said things last night that were foul. I am not accustomed to whiskey. I didn't mean at all to—I must have sounded like a fool—"

"You're not doing much better this time," said Jamila.

She twisted out of his grip and pulled him up as if he were a kelp. Her strength surprised him. He knelt at the end of her high bunk, aware that dozens of foundlings were sleeping around them in warm bunks, with tiny lamps over each of their heads. Bunks? These were coffins, stacked along the walls, and Errol had the fleeting realization that there were twice as many bodies in the room as the live ones he could see. So small, these foundlings all were, under the crushing weight of the iron tower that was Thebes.

She had a scroll on her pillow. A worn fiddle and its bow hung from a hook. A rag tunic lay folded at the foot of her rag blanket. *This is everything she owns*, Errol thought, and then realized he now owned even less. Next to her lay a small heap of knot work, still on its spikes. He picked it up.

"What are you doing back in the guilds?" she said.

"I came to teach you to knot," he said, holding the edges of her handwork. "Aye, word reached the streets that you were trying to knot some sort of a blue question mark with lips, and I was the only one who could help. *This* is a disaster. Comes of working in the dark."

"I can hardly knot in the light," she said.

"Then it's lucky for you I'm here." He sat next to her and turned his head lamp so he could examine the knotted thing. He felt the edge of the spike in it and saw blood on his finger. "This is Banhus-theof," he said under his breath. "Where did you get these spikes? They're without their sheath and yet you were just knotting with them, in the darkness."

"Yes," Jamila said. "I have lit the foundling kelps, so they will be safe."

"But what about you? Have you already met the knotting spikes in the dark?" Errol could see now she was bandaged under her thin rag of a shirt.

"Aye," she said.

He spoke slowly, as though waking. "You were there at Lascaux House last night. I remember it now."

"Somebody has to protect Odd, with you gone to the streets."

"I wish you had done your job better. Why didn't you keep him from meeting the dawn in that tent with that girl?"

"Why didn't you help him?" Jamila said.

"He told me to go away. The whiskey blurs it. Then I was talking to that muse. I was on a plank and I saw you. I yelled out. I—"

"You threw the spikes at me."

Errol cringed. "Aye. And then I was falling. How is it, then, that I am alive?"

"It's best if you don't remember."

"No. It isn't best. The parts are coming back to me. When you saw me fall, you dropped off the plank. You were reaching for the spikes while you fell."

"The spikes were also coming for me. Luckily the abyss is dark."

Errol furrowed his brow. "This can't be real. Somehow you knew that whatever was going to happen to you, with those spikes, would happen on the fall from that plank—"

"I didn't *know* it would happen. I thought it might."

Errol felt the sensation of falling, even now. "How did you know it would happen before you hit the earth?"

"It was a guess," she said.

He reached up to touch her bandage.

"It hurts," she said.

"Of course it does. How on earth could you have known that whatever came from your banhus, from your ribs, could catch you and me in the air?" He shook his head in disbelief. "And that it could bear the stag as well?"

"That wasn't a guess. I've smelled the beast for years, in my palms and fingers. Hoofs and feathers, both. Of all Pliny's animals, what else could that be?"

"The winged horse. A rare beast." Errol felt a thrill in his ribs at the bravery of such a leap.

He considered now his history with Jamila. His meeting her at the tufuga's and the way he had grabbed her that night and told her she would never amount to anything. At the party on Al-Razi, accusing her of collaborating with the regnat.

"Why would you ever save me? I have never been anything but foul to you."

"It was an otherwise dull night," she said. He laughed. And then he pulled up a corner of her blanket and looked under it. He shone his lamp around the room.

"And where is that beast of yours now?" he said. "No doubt he, or she, wants to be with you. My stag is likely thrashing Woody's quarters as we speak."

"She could not be contained by a tower. Or a wall. She is gone. Safe, elsewhere."

"Jamila Foundling. You are a whole city unto yourself."

He picked up her knotting again. "Well, and who is this half-knit beast taking up precious real estate in your sack?"

"He is a wyrm I'm making for one of the foundling kelps."

"Name of the dragon?"

"I haven't named him yet. He isn't done."

Errol winced. "There are *rules* concerning this, Jamila Foundling, and you are in flagrant violation of them. You must name all wyrms before their heads are knitted, or incur stiff penalties."

"No name fits him."

"Don't be ridiculous. Wyrms are the easiest beasts to name. Ask anyone."

"I'm asking Errol Thebes," she said.

He caught his breath when she said his name. "And Errol Thebes shall reply," he said. "There are the traditionals: Fafnir. Bullar. Tiamat. Kukulkan. Ying-long. Also one cannot forget Lagarfljotsormurinn or the Laidly and Lambton Worms."

"Those are not names," she said. "The Lambton Worm was just from Lambton. Same with Lagarfljot. And laidly means ugly. The Ugly Worm."

"Then you could call him Saint George's, after the famous dragon by that name," he said.

"I protest," she said. "That's is not a name, either. It's the name of the slayer of the dragon. Hardly an appropriate name for the dragon himself."

"I beg to differ. When that little dragon was born, just a tiny wyrm scorching his cradle, and long before his neck started to fall over like this one's, his mother named him Saint George's. Can you believe that he was later slain by Saint George? Huge coincidence, really. I mean, what are the chances?"

Jamila petted the dragon's half-knit head. "I thought Flicker would be good," she said.

"You must be joking. How can he hold his head up at dragon gatherings—how can he hold up this head at all, really?—when all the other fanged fire-breathers are going around as, you know, the Dreadful Biter. Listen, this is simple. What is your nightwatch's name, that small fellow sleeping over there, shirking his duty to protect you from me?"

That foundling was a tiny kelp, who sat asleep on the floor under the dim light that burned in the tunnel. He had a book open in his lap.

"He's Hrothgar, named after the king in *Beowulf*," said Jamila.

"There's the perfect name," said Errol.

"Well, you could give Hrothgar a blanket so long as you're planning to steal his name."

Errol dropped to the floor and carried the kelp to an empty bed. He pulled a blanket over him, lit the lamp with a flint that had been left next to it, and set the kelp's book next to his hand.

"Did you teach him to read?" Errol said, returning to her.

"Aye."

"Did you teach them all?" he said.

"Anyone who wants to know," she said.

"And dance? Do you teach them that?" he said. "The rumor of you is circulating on the streets of this city."

"It's not much of a story," she said.

"I do wonder if you ever have danced the gavotte in the guild kitchens," he said.

"Nearly every night, when you important guilders go to sleep. Listen, why did you come here, back to the towers?"

"To forget what I've seen," said Errol. "The repair of this blue dragon is all I'm prepared to think about at this moment. That, and eyrouns. Let's go steal a pair of real knotting spikes from somebody's workbench and get something to eat, and I'll teach you how to do the one thing you can't seem to do."

Waiting

A SHORT LENGTH OF STRING slipped through the bars in the overhead disk in the mines of gaol and fell to the floor of the mine shaft.

"What's this for?" yelled Rip.

"You're trying to climb out. That should help," said Utlag. "That, and a thousand more like it."

Rip slumped on his knees in the dirt. The stone walls were marked where he had tried to climb. He, and a thousand before him.

"I feel sure the spikes will come back to us soon," whispered Utlag. "The regnat is searching the guilds for that runner who has them. I look forward to knowing what beast lives in you."

"I am an empty banhus like Fenn. Thanks to you."

"Well then, a half beast will be of interest, too. A curiosity."

"In the interest of fatherly love, could you show some mercy?"

"In retrospect I probably should not have been a father."

Mine

IF ERROL'S FYLGIA was that gawking stag Eikthyrnir, with its antlers raking every wall it passed, certainly I had to be something. Something that could sign a contract with Fremantle. Something that would appeal to the foundling who was about to be mine. Something that could turn on a friend who had turned on me.

My bound-wife, who had witnessed a rescue on the planks, told me Jamila had caught the iron spikes.

For the third time, I broke into my own guild and slipped down through the walls to the bottom of the tower. Right in front of a dozen foundlings, I pulled the needles from Jamila's bunk.

The iosal hatch-guilder made me pay this time, to *return* to the roof. I crossed the lines to Corinth House, as far as I could get from Thebes and Lascaux, and checked the log to see which runner would be gone for the night.

It was someone else's tent, someone else's sack, someone else's life. I sat in it for a long time, before taking the spikes from my pack and waiting for something I didn't believe would happen. When the moon went behind the clouds, I extinguished my lamp.

A Question

ON THE PLANK FROM TEIFI HOUSE TO SHOU, on the east edge of the district, Errol took off his boot to show Jamila how Dete had pinned him to the street. He lifted his shirt to show her where Clegis had stabbed him. He told her of the pub squall and what he had done to Dete. And how the bear came, that fetch. And how Dete had wanted a going-story. Here, high off the streets, checking constantly for the regnat's guards, it was hard to believe Dete had been anything more than a pelt, just someone as surprised as anyone by what was happening to him. Errol told her of the cold thickness of the winter river. He told her of Rip and watched her face broaden in a grin, that the wild second-son of Margaret Thebes was yet alive. He told her of the first appearance of Eikthyrnir, of Dagmar and the wolves who went out to catch arrows. He described The Bluebird and the kelp Arthur, who lay dying not so far from where they now sat. Last he told her of Utlag, who lacked a reflection, and the abbot. And of Jago's cat. And despite all of that he said, "I miss the streets and the life around that river. Curiously, the stag is at home there."

They sat out on the plank for a long while, watching new stars rise.

"I had thought the regnat would lead an army into gaol, so sure hope would come in the form of a great leader. I'm a fool. Nobody believes the stories you and I do. When you have nothing to eat, when your children are dying, when evil is at large, a story is irrelevant."

"Take it from a foundling, the stories are relevant. Perhaps only your choice of leader is wrong."

"Who else could lead this city, but the regnat?"

"The leader sits on this very plank."

He shook his head. "I am an outlaw."

"See it a new way. You're a guildmaster's son who knows the streets. You love these towers. Think of it as your duty, not your decision."

He picked at a plank splinter in the palm of his hand. "Someone once said I didn't know anything of love. Someone also said I was not fearless, and there was truth in that, too. I'm afraid now, even of running into a mirror somewhere and seeing myself half gone."

"Then let's get that over with," said Jamila. "First, I have a question I cannot answer. I understand that many are perishing in gaol, victims of the pits and the arena. But where do the survivors go, the ones who win the fights?"

Mercy

THE PAIN WAS A SURPRISE. It was a sharp cut to the chest at first and I tried to spread my arms to face it. One spike ran up the center of my ribs, the rough edges of it worked like serrations of a knife. And then I felt as though someone were grabbing the two walls of my ribs and pulling them open like a book. I begged the sky for mercy. I screamed for my mam. I felt myself falling. Just before I left the world, something vast and magnificent convulsed and exploded from my split ribs.

Mirrors

THE GUILD HOUSE AL-HAZEN kept a storeroom on the roof, of silvered glass plates—mirrors that its guilders cut and angled in the making of telescopes. Errol stood in front of one of those now.

"Open your eyes," Jamila said from the other side of the storeroom flap.

"Your eyes would be closed, too, if you had seen what I've seen. Utlag cast no reflection. Imagine if you spoke and no sound came out. Or if you weighed nothing. The only worse fright was to see the reflection Rip cast: half there, half gone."

"Just look."

"Half eaten. Like a man dying of gaping battle wounds but still wandering about the field."

"Sh."

"When we first met, you and I, in the tufuga's tent, you said my mother had had another man." Errol put his hands to his face. "Was that true?"

"Yes."

"The first was Utlag, was it not?"

"Aye. Utlag was her bound-husband. He came and went at night when your brothers were young, and then left altogether. Before you were born."

"How do you know that? You can't have been born either."

"It's common knowledge in the morgues. Foundlings depend upon the business of the guildmaster's family."

"But Utlag is iosal. How could she bind herself to him?"

"Look around you at this city. Tell me you don't see similar mismatches."

"If he was her husband, he was Fenn and Rip's father and likely my father as well. You do understand what that would mean. I would be unfit in every way—"

She was standing with her forehead on the flap. "Do you want to know who Margaret Thebes went to, when Utlag left her?"

"Yes. No. I don't know. I'm not ready. Is there a chance that second man was my father? I am hoping for someone old and dull and thick and *human*. I want to be something worth seeing."

"There is one way to know."

He put his head back. "I have a feeling you already know."

"I saw you in a mirror, when you were small. Fighting with Odd."

"Then let's have it," he said, and opened his eyes and saw himself. He turned. There were his wounds. The soles of his feet. His own back. He opened his mouth.

He pulled his eyelids away from his eyes. Ran his hands through his hair. Studied his nethers. His armpits. His fingers.

"I don't look like anyone I know. But I am all here . . ." he said, his voice trailing off.

"While you're at it, can you see now why everyone made you Beowulf all those years?"

"Insane in the eyes. Torn to pieces. Wounded in every quadrant. Aye, I look exactly like Beowulf."

She said, so quietly he barely heard her, "You are beautiful." He leaned against the flap from its other side. No one had ever said such a thing to him. Before he could reply, she said, "And to lead is in your blood."

"I'm nearly out of blood, Jamila. And I can't manage even to lead myself."

As Errol dressed himself, he felt so tired he had to sit down. She went in and stood facing him. He said, "I am done in. I need to sleep somewhere and this is as good a place as any. I think no one will find me here. I won't be angry if you go." But she pulled his shirt on, over his head. And he laid his head on her shoulder and then on her lap and fell asleep. Once that night he stirred in his sleep and said, "I'm sure you know him, as you seem to know everything else. Tell him that I am relieved to be his son."

Gallus

A JAB TO THE FACE WOKE ME. I put my arms over my head. "Stop it!" Something grabbed a piece of my hair and yanked. It spat at me. Up and down, its voice rolled. *Hawwwww!* while it pinched me. It smelled of closets full of must.

I found a flint to strike, lit my lamp, and lay on my back, too sore to roll over. The fylgia bent over my face and eyed me with a red eye, its pupil dilating and contracting. *Hawwwwww.*

I reached up to touch its bony white face, its warm beak, the flap of skin hanging from its chin. At least it was not a rat. There were wings involved. An eagle? A swan? I grabbed it swiftly by the legs and it fell over and hung upside down in my grip.

"No," I said and groaned. I stuffed the chicken into the laundry sack of the runner whose tent I had occupied, and pulled the ties tight. The bird stormed in the bag, flinging itself at everything, finally collapsing in a heap.

I put my head out and found the tent surrounded by runners. I didn't know the roof master at Corinth, but I felt sure she was the burly one with her face a finger's length from mine.

"This is not your tent," she said, jabbing at me. "Are you alone in there? If not, you know the rule. It's dawn."

"I am already bound. So I'm punished enough. Anyway, I'm alone." I stuffed everything in my pack and hit the lines before anyone could see the mess I'd made of the bedroll.

I returned the spikes to the morgues. While I waited, I gave a name to the raging he-chicken. "Come on, Ovid," I said. "If I'm going to turn on him, let's get it over with."

"WHAT IS IT?" Errol said, his voice full of interest. Jamila had brought him here, to the south edge of Marathon, and had carried a telescope from Al-Hazen. "I see ships," he said. "Easily two hundred ships, by the light of a fire on the banks. What is the power of this lens?"

"They're two miles downriver."

He was silent a long while, his eye to the lens. Then he said, "Those are our ships."

"Aye."

"They are supposed to be long gone."

"Look at the riverbanks."

Errol moved the telescope slightly. It jerked widely across the range of mountains. He moved it back and found the banks. A bonfire blazed on the riverbanks, flames as high as the ships' masts, sparks swirling in the sky overhead.

Jamila said, "They have been there, burning, since Ship."

"What are they burning?"

"Look."

"I can't see anything. It's an inferno. Certainly more than the heat to keep the crews warm. A furnace. Are they burning firewood?"

"Nay."

Errol watched as the one of the men on the banks flung a giant blue bowl across the banks and onto the blaze. He cried out, "No! Why would they—?"

Errol thought of two thousand coracles, and the incense burners, the fletched arrows, the vihuelas, the thousands of knotting spikes his own guild made: a year's work of a whole guild city, of thousands of men and women who thought the world was waiting for the things they had made. "Why on earth would they burn our work?"

"Think about it."

"I don't want to think about it. I want to stop them! Did thieves attack them? Are thieves burning the work? I don't understand! Why would they keep us busy, sending us food and supplies, only to burn the exports and send the ships away with empty hulls?"

"The hulls will not be empty. Those ships are waiting for something."

"What? What are they waiting for?"

"You know the guilds are taxed—"

"I know. In foundlings."

"And you have the iron spikes. Which has halted a process."

"What process?"

"They use the foundlings and those black-iron spikes to produce something the world wants, from the pits of gaol."

"Beasts?" he said. "The beasts who fight in the arenas?" He looked again through the lens. "Are you suggesting that we export animals to a world that already has beasts of its own?"

"No. Not exactly. I realized it when you described the pits and that arena. They put foundlings and beasts into those shafts. They let them hear one another be killed. Most are victims. But a few go mad with fear. In the arena they win, and win again. And again. Monstrous. Like that one you told me about."

"Jago."

"Ready to kill anyone for any reason. Or for no reason at all. Where are those winners? There would be hundreds of them. Maybe thousands, from a year's worth of production. Some human. Some beasts. The ships are waiting for this year's shipment of Jagos."

"What would the world want with Jago?" And then he remembered the abbot's quarters in the scriptorium and the display of brute power, of armor and weapons, and an irrelevant obsession with war.

"They use the spikes to make monsters."

"Aye."

"We are a war machine."

I DON'T KNOW HOW LONG I had been asleep in someone's little bed in the morgues but the chicken woke me in time to watch Errol untie his tellensac and re-tie it to the loop of Jamila's belt. I watched his ease with her hips. She put her arms up to make it easier for him. He held his breath, no doubt feeling the quarantine of her foundling beauty. He unbuttoned her tunic and put his hands on her ribs. "I live here," he said. "When everyone forgets me, I live here in this banhus."

I was seething with anger at him for taking her from me, and for writing the contract to take, officially, everything else I wanted. Soon that would all be reversed. He would be gone and she would be mine.

But I had to hand it to him: He had memorized the hero's script. He lived in her banhus. He gave her that tellensac, which was everything.

What are we, really, but a sackful of our own tales?

Mearc-Stapa

THE CHICKEN CAREENED BEHIND ME, pecking and clawing at my ankles, trying, I think, to stop me. I was running, frantic, searching for my cousin where I had watched him disappear into the morgue tunnels. Backtracking, turning into dead ends, until I smelled a bucket fire.

"—and the fear is insurmountable," Errol said. I backed away fast, thinking he was talking to me, that he had heard me sneak up on him.

There was no bucket. No bucket fire. The tunnel rustled with the petals of a thousand yellow flowers blooming on the walls. I squinted, for they were moving. Not flowers but winged insects clinging to the stone and iron. Pyrallis? Glow worms? My mind raced through the pages of Pliny. Silk moths? The slow beating of their wings fanned a thousand tiny flames on their backs.

"*Ond se sy a?*" A voice rustled among the wings, in the ancient tongue of our mothers. "And so you will give up? You'll die here, in the morgues."

"Why not?" said Errol. "What use am I on the streets?"

"*Why not?*" The voice mocked Errol. "Let's start with Arthur."

"Irrelevant," said Errol. "Arthur is a tale from outside our wall. Achilles. Arthur. Beowulf. The Robbing Hood. That sort of heroism is extinct in this city."

"Not *King* Arthur. That was a different book. I'm speaking of the kelp you left behind. You told him you would come for him. You promised the same thing to a girl dying in gaol. No doubt your brother Rip is also waiting for you."

"The kelp is certainly dead of the ague," Errol said, his voice barely audible. "Utlag will have put an end to Rip. A public drowning makes monsters of everyone who watches." Something alarmed the insects and there was a panic of fluttering that moved through the tunnel.

"Don't presume to know who's been fetched. Otherwise I would have to hand over my office keys. Here."

"What's this?" Errol reached out.

"Kahve. You have a great deal to do tonight. This will help."

A red cup appeared. Errol took it out of the air and drank from it. "How did you make kahve in a tunnel of the morgues? And I taste butter in it."

"Not butter. Fresh cream. From roan shorthorns."

"There are no cows grazing in this city anywhere."

"Ah. Well then. You must be right."

"Who *are* you?" Errol said. Even in the wing-light I could see no one in the tunnel but Errol, who said, "Anyway, if I bring beads to the kelp Arthur, he will only die of some other malady next week. Everyone is sick, in the streets."

"True enough. Consumption could get them," said the other. "I put my money on leprosy."

"Is this sarcasm?"

"I thought I was helping you come up with excuses."

"I'm nothing. That's the best excuse of all. I am a runner thrown from his own roofs. How could I even begin to fight against the forces of the abbot, the regnat, and Utlag? Even one of them alone would be too much."

"I thought your advice to the regnat was sound. Even if you do not prevail, you can be a symbol of hope."

"That sounds absurd now." Errol brooded for a long while, drinking the kahve. Then he said, "How would it end?"

"That depends. How good are you in a street fight?"

"Insufficient," Errol snorted. "As you already know. And terrified."

"Really? Terrified of what?"

"Of *what*?" Errol laughed. Again there was no levity in it. "Where to start? I am afraid they will drown me. Or starve me into subjugation. Or some beast will eat me alive or the stag in that arena. I fear my own blade, that it will kill again. I fear being eaten alive—"

"You said that twice, being eaten alive."

"I fear it twice." Errol paused, took a long swig from his cup. "And I fear bad kahve, if I return to the streets."

"Was that humor?"

I was bitten with a new jealousy, of the camaraderie Errol had with that voice.

"I'll tell you the surprise. I hadn't anticipated falling in love. Now I do not want to die."

"Aye. That was one of our better ideas. Here's a thought. Has it occurred to you that strength of combat is only one of your strengths?"

"Skills of the mind are of use only in the guilds."

"I see. Well. You would know. What with thousands of years of experience on the streets."

"Why do you say things like that? Who *are* you?" Errol said, impatient now. "I demand to know."

"It's better for us all if you don't know my name."

"No. Think about it. I could fight in your name, as armies do in the library scrolls."

"Men haven't done all that well by my names, outside the wall. And they find plenty of names for one another as well. *Zwerver, paria, satan.* Any excuse to make a foundling, or an enemy."

"I'm different from the others. I'm better."

"Yes. That's exactly what they say, right before they hunt one another down. No, let's see what you do with your own name first."

The insects were silent, their flames low.

"Here, you'll need another cup of this kahve."

"If you won't admit a name, that's what I will call you. The Kahve Maker. No matter what tunnel I find you in, or what street or pit or roof, I'll know it's you." The other was laughing. "Or, no." Errol was serious now. "You're mearc-stapa. Haunter of the borderlands."

I still could see only Errol. The smell of the kahve made my stomach churn.

"What was that sound?" said Errol.

A FORCE THREW ME AGAINST THE WALL of the tunnel and I was gasping for air. A head lamp went on.

"Who were you talking to?" I demanded. The insects were gone. Errol threw me down to the stone floor and bound my hands and feet with the rope I myself had brought. I struggled but his knots were certain. "Who was that?" I demanded, my face pressed into the floor. "Is it Zeus? I'm not joking. Did you see those butterflies on fire?"

"I don't know," Errol said, panting from the exertion. "I haven't seen whatever it is." He fell back against the wall and we sat facing each other. "Why are you stalking me?"

"Heimdall is working for the regnat. He made me come."

"Since when did you do anything Heimdall says?"

"I'm not," I said. "I came to warn you."

"Why did you bring the rope, then?"

"So Heimdall would take me seriously. I said I would bind you."

"Really. And he believed you could do that?" We were both breathing hard. I hoped my red-faced panting would cover the red-faced lies I was telling. "Is that bird your fetch?" he said. Ovid looked up at me, as though to see what I would say.

"Who knows? It follows me everywhere."

"You're an idiot. It's a chicken. It's your fetch. So you stole the needles from Jamila?"

"'Stole' is such a complicated word."

"Well. You're lucky he can go everywhere with you. Eikthyrnir can't be with me inside this guild tower without thrashing everything."

"That sounds about right," I said. "What are you going to do next?"

"It would save me a fair bit of trouble to go with you to the roofs and turn myself in to Heimdall. A quick drop for me and it would all be done. And I bet it would be worth a few uurs to you."

I hadn't expected him to come so close to truth. I looked down at the ropes cutting into my wrists. "I'm bound, did you hear? I have a bound-wife."

"Woody told me. And how is it, to have a wife? To be wed?"

"Like drowning and a fall from a great height all at once."

He laughed. "What, are we out of arsenic?" And I had to laugh, too.

"Don't you love her?" Errol said.

"No! No, I don't love her. Yes. I do. I don't know. She was kissing me and taking all her clothes off. I didn't have a chance. Do you have any idea what it is like?"

"I need details," he said, grinning.

"Shut up." I kicked him with my bound feet. "I was naive about the possibilities."

"Tell me everything." This was jovial.

"Get your own wife!"

"I'll take yours!" Errol said. I shuddered and was sober again. "And what about this rooster?" When had the bird climbed into his arms? "Harbinger of the dawn. Why didn't he warn you the sun was rising when you were in that tent with the muse? You would be a free runner still."

"Do the math, Errol Thebes. I didn't have the rooster yet."

"Still, from inside your ribs, you felt the warning." He was right about that.

The chicken murmured while Errol scratched its neck absentmindedly, and it eyed me while it drank from Errol's kahve cup.

"Even my own espiritu prefers Errol," I said under my breath.

The tunnel filled with another wave of the thick smell of kahve, and Errol reached into shadows and said, "This must be for you." I stared at the wall in astonishment. From it tumbled a white linen baker's sack. "It's sonhos," he said, as if the delivery of pastries through a stone wall in the morgues were a common event. "Will you attack me if I untie your hands?"

We ate in kelp-happiness, the sonhos filling our mouths with clouds of fruit and powdered sugar.

He was licking his fingers. "Odd Thebes," he said. "You have to find some way to love your bound-wife."

"This is excellent advice from the one who steals other men's women."

"Steals? When have I ever stolen?"

"Anyway, I hate the iosal rule," I said. "You spend the night in a tent together, east meets west, and the next thing you know you're bound. Nothing but paperwork. And why don't you find *yourself* a girl? What about that foundling you just left in the morgues?"

He made a face. "Were you following us?"

"I know everything. *Everything.*"

"Tell me this, then. I'm confused, Odd Thebes. I thought you loved that foundling. I once thought you loved her in a binding way." I felt my chest tighten. If he was so sure I loved Jamila, why would he have written that contract to take her away? "But then I discover that you have bound yourself to this runner whose name you don't even know. And then you ask me why don't I take the foundling. An Odd question. Which do you love, the wife or the foundling?"

I spat against the wall. "The foundling belongs to me."

"She didn't mention belonging to anyone."

Panic rose in me. I suddenly remembered I had fallen asleep, back in the morgues. "Was that a whole night?" I blurted. "Did the moon and the sun meet for the two of you?"

He took another pastry from the bag. "I thought you said it didn't matter. *Paperwork*, you called it. If I did stay a night with her, maybe it was nothing."

I glared at him. "Did you or not?"

He stared at me, toying with me. And then: "No. I left her." He leaned his head back and rubbed his face with his hands. And then he began to talk about what he had seen. About the streets and gaol and Jago and Arthur. He drew his knees up to his chest like a kelp, hiding, and he wept.

I had no solutions to offer, but I wanted to possess some knowledge of equal gravity. So I told him that I was seeing beasts, as my father had.

"You really are the harbinger of the dawn," said Errol. "The one who sees what no one else sees." He sat up quickly now and looked at me with interest. "In that case, tell me this. Have you seen the regnat lately?"

"Not since Fremantle. That night of Al-Razi."

"What beast did you see when you looked at him?"

"I don't know," I said, agitated. I didn't want to be seeing beasts.

"Say it."

"You won't believe me."

"I always believe you."

That stunned me, for I knew it to be true. *Three of spades*. "The beast was unmistakable. Wings, scales, a whiptail. A filthy trail of coal smoke shooting from the sides of its fanged mouth."

"A *wyrm*?"

"Aye. A reptile drooling vitriol. A dragon."

"You're sure? How big was it?"

"Big. The size of a yurt. If it ever did come through his ribs, it wouldn't fit in his guild quarters."

"Excellent," whispered Errol. "I wonder how it would like a vault."

The Prize

"I WON'T TURN YOU IN TO THE REGNAT, on one condition," I said as Errol was binding my hands again. We both knew I was in no position to bargain. "I'm serious, Errol Thebes. I *must* know what you asked for when you won the Long Run."

"It's a stale subject, Odd," he said.

"You, who already had everything. What was it?"

Errol cinched the knots. "I never got what I asked for. Anyway, it was a fool's request. It was nothing."

"Nothing?" I said. "I doubt that." I knew what it was. I just wanted him to admit it.

"It will only be painful to tell you."

"I demand to know."

He studied my face. "I'll tell you, but only after I bind your mouth. Otherwise I'll have to listen to your protests."

"You're no friend!" I blurted. "I already know what you did. You were going to get your own place in Fremantle and leave us all behind. My mam. My family. Me."

He gagged me. He extinguished his lamp and stood in darkness. His voice was quiet. "All right, Odd Thebes. You've been wanting to know this answer for two years. But you're not going to like it. I asked them to draw up a contract for an apprenticeship for me, at Fremantle."

"Hmph."

"I requested a good job, fine quarters, food, good money. I told them if I had to live in Fremantle, I wanted to be set for life." *There it was! He admitted it!* "They asked me if there was a love interest. I asked them to include a foundling. Your mam gave me her name. I hated foundlings but I thought you loved her. The contract was standard issue. They drew it up, signed it, and handed it to me. They were happy. It was what they all wanted me to do anyway—Fremantle, Thebes, the whole city—so why not give it to me for a prize?" *How could he just stand there and revel in this?* "And then," he said, "while they watched, I crossed out my name and wrote yours."

I convulsed.

"Don't get excited."

"WHAT?" I said from behind the gag.

"They wouldn't do it. I told them it was my right to choose my reward for the Long Run, and it didn't have to be for me. But they said no. They said you were unsuitable for the work." I could have broken my wrists, I was pulling so hard to free my arms from behind my back. "I didn't want to tell you all this," he continued. "Because they're wrong. All those languages you know, the barding, the things you see—you're brilliant. But they couldn't see it." Behind that gag, I cursed in every language I knew. "They said the prize had to be for me. I argued that it would be. We all knew I would end up in Fremantle in the end, so you and I would be near each other, we would be bound, you to that foundling and me to Kitchen Girl, and we would live together. And I told them that would make my life in Fremantle bearable. The regnat offered me anything or anyone else in exchange. I was angry, but I didn't know then that the regnat was iosal. Or that he hated me before I even met him. I still thought he was to be respected. *So what did he ask for in the end?* In the end I requested a fresh pear, which is, as you know, an impossibility in a walled city with a thousand locked guild towers. As impossible as kahve with cream."

Why had I been so quick to doubt my cousin, who had never once lied to me or let me down?

Errol put his lamp on and turned to go. The chicken's beak was raised; he was proudly holding a feather from his own tail. It was such a silly gesture, but Errol bent and took the feather. He stuck it into his thick mass of hair.

I struggled to get the binding off my mouth, to warn him that my brothers were waiting fifty yards up the tunnel. But I was bound in every possible way, and useless.

Brother Enemies

I KICKED HEIMDALL when he came down and cut the gag from my mouth. I kicked my brother Ragnar, who was with him. The tunnel was filled with guards from Fremantle, all in armor. I ran up and down their ranks, kicking them all.

"You lied to me!" I yelled at Heimdall. "How could you lie to me?"

But Heimdall had something else on his mind. "Where is he?" he said. "You warned him off!"

"What are you talking about?" I yelled, pointing down the tunnel. "He walked right into your arms!"

Heimdall grabbed for my eyeballs. Such fury I had never seen. "You warned him off! He never came out."

"What?" I said. And then I burst out laughing. "You idiots. Of course he came out!"

Heimdall and Ragnar exchanged looks and their faces fell. They had seen him, all right. They had parted forces in the tunnel and let a stinking, ragged foundling pass through while they waited expectantly for the Errol Thebes they knew, the conquering hero.

They beat me up. They kicked the chicken and me all the way down the hall. I deserved it. Foundlings carried us up, inside the walls, and passed me back to the roofs. Grid carried me to my new bound-wife, who bathed me and washed my wounds and bandaged the chicken and me and made me tell it all, even the parts about Jamila.

ON THE GUILD HOUSE SAMOA, Errol crept among the tents, opened the flaps until he found the tufuga. The thick little man came out with his wife, who was, to my surprise, tall and agile, with a thick mass of red hair. She was covered entirely by tatus. Her belly was as round as the tufuga's paunch, although, based on my scant knowledge of human reproduction, only one of them was bearing a child. Errol and the tufuga disappeared into the box tent. Half an uur later, Errol emerged with his arm wrapped in fresh bandages. He ran the lines to Peste House, stole some ma'amouls for himself and the stag, and returned one last time to Thebes, marked, as any third-year runner, with the symbol of his resting house.

———

Ovid and I trailed them, keeping our distance. The city had slipped without notice into the icy month of Hornung, and we had cold-finger winds on our necks. I could hear the sounds of runners stirring in their sleep in their tents. The only light was starlight.

Errol removed one of two packages from his belt, climbed the mast, swung down under the crow's belly, turned the lock, and opened the door. The crow contained various contracts and objects of importance to Thebes's roof masters. He added a single long, thin package, the length of a knotting spike.

When he dropped to the roof, he set the other package into the bin of outgoing mail in the yurt. It looked like all the other long, thin packages that would be leaving the busy spican guild that morning. Anyone who saw it would assume someone at Strael House had ordered a set of knotting spikes to get some winter sweaters made. No one would guess it was an iron shaft that bore a set of instructions for the fletcher.

Chicken Drama

WHEN TERPSICHORE CAME TO MY TENT THAT NIGHT, the chicken pressed himself into the corner and issued a furtive growl. When she tried to throw him out, he staged a crowing fit, throwing his head so far back he looked like a man having his lungs removed with a fork. He fell over backward and lay spasming on my pillow. Later that night I found three quills, a handful of apothecary beads, a piece of pie, and the relics of Grid's tellensac in his corner. On my bound-wife's orders, I locked Ovid out of the tent, where he crowed along with every bell. I went out to remind him that roosters were, in certain parts of the world, sacrificial birds.

THE APOTHECARIST TOOK HIS OLD RUNNER'S PACK from its hook by his door. It was leather, embossed with a firework display known in his birth guild as "the peony." He had saved it for thirty-six years, dusted and oiled it and hung it next to the hook where he hung the apron he wore every day. Even in his quarters on the eighth strata he could hear the sound of the runners on the roofs singing. And he heard their thundering feet and banging pots, shaking the tower with sound in their long-standing good-night to the guilders below, at the uur of tumultus. He kept it ready.

He had packed in a hurry: his mortar and pestle; sand timers rolled in oil cloth; his original copy of *Materia Medica*; his lunch. Six strapping foundlings arrived to haul sacks of beads to the roof. He paid them well, as much for their discretion as for their effort. He was violating so many guild laws tonight, he had lost count.

"And?" the apothecarist whispered to Errol.

"And the roofs are quiet."

"One thousand, three hundred, forty two," the apothecarist whispered as they watched the foundlings come up.

"Pieces of luggage?" said Errol.

"No. Stairs. I find myself winded."

"*One pack*, we said. You were supposed to bring what you could lift and haul on your own."

"If one kelp has the ague, then others do. You should see what I had to leave behind."

"I hope you packed those Taedium beads, in case you get bored."

The apothecarist stopped short, for a huge, antlered beast had come around a tent. He raised an eyebrow.

"It's a stag," said Errol.

"Specifically it is *Cervus elaphus*," said the apothecarist. "Maybe even *Cervus elaphus hanglu*. Though of course I have never seen either alive, only in the form of powdered antlers. Will it bite?"

"No."

The apothecarist reached up to touch the stag's broad neck. Eikthyrnir swung his head around to see who was touching him and knocked the apothecarist flat onto the landing.

"You said—"

"I said he doesn't bite," said Errol.

———

There were warm breezes, which my bound-wife would record later that morning in the roof log at Thebes as "perhaps enough to lift Odd's spirits." The smell of breads rising across all the roofs and the early sounds of runners stirring in their bedrolls flooded the apothecarist with memories. He took out his clean rag and unfolded it and dabbed the corners of his eyes.

"I beg your pardon," he said.

"Not necessary. I feel it, too," said Errol.

Errol strapped him into a harness and onto a drop line and attached the sacks to the line. He hooked himself onto the end of a line as well and gave instructions to the foundlings who would control the drop that he had no intention of dropping like stones. The apothecarist stood at the edge.

"Don't look down," Errol said.

"I find myself wondering about the lines. Are they fresh?" he said.

"They could hold you, me, your luggage, the stag, and the contents of this tower."

"The stag? Surely we are not taking that behemoth with us on the same line?" The apothecarist reached for a bottle of beads in his pocket.

Errol put his hand on the man's shoulder. "You are brave. I cannot think of another guilder who would do what you are doing today with me."

An irritable voice behind them said, "And what am I then, a piece of cheese?"

Errol knew before he turned around who it was.

"What are you doing here?" he said.

"I'm going with you. Obviously," said the tufuga.

Errol felt an idiotic sense of excitement. "What about your bound-wife?"

"It was she who sent me. Threw me out on my"—he looked at the tidy apothecarist—"on my welcome mat. She heard you telling me about that kelp who wants a tatu and said she would go herself if she wasn't about to deliver a child. Where's my harness? Otherwise I'll have to jump to prove I'm half the man she thinks."

"I find myself wondering *which* half," said the apothecarist, looking over the grimy little tufuga. "Why do we need a tufuga on the streets?"

"Everyone wants to be marked," the tufuga said. "More than they want your beads, they want what I have."

———

The tufuga had jammed his gear into his old runner's pack in such haste that bits of rags and tools jangled from it and had to be taken out and repacked.

The stag pranced impatiently while Errol strapped him into a sling. When they were all four harnessed into the drop lines, they stood all together at the edge of the plank.

"Think on this," said Errol. "There is a kelp. His name is Arthur. He has a child's interest in archery and beasts, and he misses his dead mam and his sister. You must get to him soon or he will not live."

"*We* must get to him," corrected the apothecarist.

The tufuga leapt off the plank and was gone. The apothecarist sat down and lowered himself into the air below him. Errol jumped with his arms widespread. And then the stag leapt, and the other three were thrown into the sky, like underwear on a clothesline on which a three-ton weight had fallen.

The apothecarist yelled, "I find myself needing to change my pants."

Finally steady, they dropped side by side, turning in the wind, the lines spinning out in the hands of the foundlings.

"May I ask your name?" Errol shouted to the apothecarist.

"Bede."

"An apothecarist named Bede?"

"It's a coincidence."

"And you, tufuga? What may we call you?"

"Chaunce!" He was thrilled to be falling so fast.

"And you are Errol Thebes," said Bede. "Margaret's son. When I return, she will flay me for this. There is no safe place to hide from her."

Errol laughed. "Did you know who I was, all along?"

"You're the talk of the guilds. I put two and two together when you showed up at my door and said you were Bayard. The name of your legendary knife."

The foundlings lowered them the last few yards. Errol unclipped the harnesses and tugged on the lines, which snaked slowly away over their heads, out of the shadows into the light of the sun.

"Remarkably steady under the feet," whispered Bede.

"Smells like my wife's cooking," said the tufuga. "I have the sense we're being watched. Can we move fast enough to avoid detection?"

"Make as much noise as you can," said Errol. "We're depending upon being caught."

By a Thread

I WONDERED THAT NIGHT what I would have done in Errol's situation. The City of a Thousand Guilds was under siege. Frozen in winter, frozen in fear. Thousands of guilders toiled in the towers, their work burning upriver on the banks. Fear prevailed in the streets. Under the earth in a maze of tunnels and cells known to its inmates as gaol, beasts and humans huddled together in cells waiting to be pitted against one another, all their dreams reduced to the single hope for a quick end. Those who lost were devoured. Those who won? They were shipped out to make mayhem in the world outside the wall. Monstrous wares. Assassins. Warmongers. The regnat was corrupt. So was the abbot. The fleet captain. And that twitching creature Utlag. A pair of iron knotting spikes, the only uncommon items anyone had ever seen our city's wall, had been turned to foul purposes. And in the middle of everything else, Errol loved a girl.

———

He'd put a single iron spike in the gut of Xerxes. He'd sent the other to the master fletcher at Strael House with a note (yes, I read it), in which he instructed the fletcher to split the enclosed chicken feather, the one my fetch had given him, and tie it on the spike—like any other bolt—and send it to Fremantle for testing. It was an idea, the note said, for putting flawed knotting spikes to use. He signed his mother's name.

That night I rigged a long line off the south edge of Mildenhall and dropped sixty strata to the twenty-third. A kelp at the vent was surprised to see me there, staring in at him like Zeus. When he finished screaming, I sent him to find Marek.

I couldn't remember a day when Marek loved me so much as this moment. We talked at length through the vent about Errol's situation. I asked him what he would do, if he were Errol. He sucked his teeth.

"Press for war," he said. "The roofs are one commander shy of an army. And every kelp in the city is trained. Wrestling. Archery. Blade work. Ten thousand runners, as strong as the warriors in any scroll. I myself would return to the roofs if Errol called for help."

I gave him the bad news, that Errol had left his blade behind in his tellensac, that he had told Jamila that he himself had been wounded by it more than he had wounded anyone. "You would have to convince the general of the need for weapons," I said.

"If I know anything about Errol Thebes," Marek said, "the hardest part will be to convince him of the need for an army."

When Marek was called back to his work, I knotted a hamac to the fly outside Marek's tent and fell asleep, dangling in the wind in a gossamer cylinder. I wanted to be part of something bigger than myself—a war, a city, the work. I wanted so much to know how it felt to be Errol. Instead I awoke to nightmares of being stalked by a bogle. The dreams were a kind of tax I had to pay, for doing nothing.

A Delivery

WHEN I RETURNED TO MY TENT the next morning my bound-wife was in it, reading. She was more beautiful than I remembered. I sat across from her on the bedroll and stared at her. She was mine. I had a right to look.

"A foundling was here, to deliver this," she said, tossing me a copy of Homer. "It said the book was a binding gift to us from Slyngel Thebes. Who's Slyngel Thebes?"

I cringed at the thought of Jamila actually meeting Terpsichore. "Slyngel was my da," I said. "He's dead. Did you speak with the foundling?"

"It offered congratulations. I thanked it."

" 'It,' " I repeated, flatly defensive.

"Yes. It. What do you call your foundlings?"

I would be hard-pressed to explain the mind of the human male, even my own mind. I longed for Jamila. So I put my hands on Terp. She turned her back on me and I came around and kissed her, harder than I should have. I grabbed at her shirt and pulled it off her and kissed her, and she pushed me down on the bedroll and took off all my clothes. I wonder, as I tell this, if she was trying as hard as I was to forget someone. As we lay next to each other afterward, she reached for her pack and took her beads from it.

"What?" I said.

"It's nothing," she said.

Feh. I am a translator. *Nothing*, in the dialect of bound-wives, means "everything."

I was relieved when she spoke. She asked me about Errol, what I thought he would do next. I told her what I knew—the two spikes, the apothecarist, and the tufuga. I said that if Errol's strategies were anything like his card playing, he was in trouble.

"Maybe you underestimate him," she said. She was playing absently with the loop of junk line she carried around with her. "As he has no army and no power of his own, he has to find a way to set his enemies on themselves. I imagine he will reunite the spikes at the moment when they'll do some damage. The foundling thinks the same thing."

"Feh," I said. "That's *dyslic*. I thought you said you didn't talk to the foundling?"

"I said no such thing."

"I know Errol better than either of you. *Dyslic*. He could never think of such a strategy."

She stuck her tongue out at me in a way that, although I doubt she intended this effect, made me need her again. But she was getting up to leave. "I speak your guild's tongue, Odd Thebes. If you want to call me stupid, find a language I don't know."

When she left, she left the junk loop on her side of the tent. She had made of it a trefoil knot that, technically speaking, was impossible.

An Odd Letter

HOMER'S WRITINGS CONTAINED WITHIN ITS PAGES a torn bit of parchment. I could smell the whiskey on it. Here it is, in my tellensac:

"od. theebes," it begins, *"wantin and rekless men now posess the citee, the werst of them al crawls up our tower en drags me from my sack. opressing me to tel him wat i see, wether i see a grefin any where or a feenix or a rosinol. i see everything but cannot hide from the feend anyware. with wiskie i cannot see beests. he leves me alone wen i am on the drink. nobodie wil help slingl theebs. i well die this nite for the feend put vitriol en my wiskie and made me drink befor i new wat it was. od. theebes, ye must do wat i cannot. i cannot protect the geld master an yore cuzin wen the crawling feend finds out she es alive. ye alone see whet i see. eevin as a wee kelp ye reeched for something behined my sholder an i no ye saw my byrd, as shore es i see yors. i wil leeve this note in homer and i no ye wil find it wen ye rede. win the cittee bak. protect yore cuzin. i cannot. thiss is from slingl theebs"*

I was shaking. "Wanton and reckless men," I repeated. Where had I read that before? I had read it *here*. The very book was in my hands.

I flipped through the pages of the book and came to the near end, where the old King Laertes tells Odysseus, the son who's been gone twenty years, the son he does not yet recognize, "Stranger, verily thou art come to the country of which thou dost ask, but wanton and reckless men now possess it."

There was a hole in the page. I turned the page to see what had been torn from it. The name Odysseus had been hollowed from a line on the other side. My heart seized like a fist. I dropped the book on the roof, pressed it open hard. In the gutter of the book there was a tiny mark, a mere smudge of dirt in the gutter of the page. *Gal.*, it said. *Gallus. Gallo.* The cock of the yard. The harbinger of the dawn. I had been reading Homer for years. I was not an *oddity*, as my brothers had told me, some freak in a long line of rats. I was Odysseus, the hero of the greatest tale I knew.

If one man can be the ruin of a city, one could be its victor. That is what my insane father wanted when I was born and he named me, and he wanted it again the day he wrote this note as he lay, murdered, and put it in a book I was sure to read.

PART IV

Regrets

"WE ARE FOLLOWED," whispered the tufuga.

"There is no way out of here," said the apothecarist.

They had come to the place where Errol had first met Jago, Dete, and Clegis. And now they faced a ragged gang of rogues. A voice called out, "Why would you ever return, outlaw?"

"We came to help, Jago," Errol yelled.

The mob parted and the taut, pale, black-haired figure of Jago came at Errol. He looked like a corpse. Vacant. Someone grabbed Errol's shirt, kicked the back of his knees, and took him down.

"Lovely to see you, too, Clegis," Errol said. He turned his face in the muck so he could look at Jago. "You're alive. I'm relieved to see it."

"You can't be serious," said Jago.

"I thought the cat was dead. I thought you were gone."

"Don't ever mention her again."

"We're here to help."

Jago's head jerked back as if someone had swung at his face. "You're late," he said. He held up his hands, crudely bandaged.

Errol thought he would vomit. "What happened?" he said.

"You happened. When they were done with me in gaol, they brought me up to the scriptorium. When you disappeared from there with the iron spikes, they extracted this fee from me. It was a long night."

"I had no idea," said Errol.

"Exactly," said Jago. "You have no idea."

"Where is your cat?"

"I told you never—"

"The abbot wants you all to be afraid," Errol interrupted. "So does the regnat. They want fear to rise in all of you so they can keep this city nameless and quarantined, so that you and your fylgias, your *others*, will all be monsters they can load onto the ships, to sell outside that wall."

Jago kicked him. "Do you actually believe you discovered all that? That none of us know? Look at me, outlaw. I am fear risen. I am the monster."

"They took the cat," said Clegis.

Errol gasped. "She can't be gone. Where is she? How can you bear it?"

"Bear it? Look at me. What are my choices?"

Clegis blurted out, "The farther she gets from him, the worse off he is. She's in gaol."

"Shut up, Clegis," said Jago.

"Or she's on the ships," Clegis said.

"How did you get away from the scriptorium?" asked Errol.

Jago reached a finger in to pick something from the back of his teeth. "Suffice to say they created a monster. Possibly they regret that now." Jago saw Errol's horrified stare. "There's an abyss between us, isn't there, runner?"

"Where is my brother?"

"Rip is in gaol. So I've heard."

"If we work together, we can take the streets back. We can empty gaol. We can find your cat."

Jago knelt next to him. Errol glanced at the apothecarist, who was staring wide-eyed at the stolen tattoo on Jago's arm. "Work together? Ah. If only I had thought of this years ago, it would have saved me a lifetime of trouble." The mob behind him was silent.

"I have a plan," said Errol.

Jago pulled Errol's hair so his neck bent back and his throat scraped the ground. "Your plan is nothing. Less than nothing. You cause more damage."

The tufuga cleared his throat. "We came to help a sick kelp. The three of us did. Four, with the deer. Let us help him. We won't bother you."

From where Jago dropped his face on the street, Errol saw the group's attention turn to the bizarre form of the tufuga, tatued as he was even on his bald head.

Jago stood. "What are you?"

The tufuga drew himself up. "I am the lead apprentice from the guild house Samoa. A kelp named Arthur Bluebird wants a tatu. And I, like my colleague the apothecarist here, make house calls."

Jago said, "You came to help one kelp? *One?* And how will you choose which one of all the kelps on the street to help?"

The apothecarist said, "I brought extra beads."

Jago looked at Errol. "That's your plan? A tatu for a kelp? Some beads?"

Out of the corner of his eye Errol looked up into the planks and lines a mile over his head. There was safety, if he'd only stayed high. Instead he was going to die a fool's death. Embarrassment first. Then pain. Then death. And the stag would die, too. And the apothecarist. And the tufuga, with all of those marks they would take.

Errol heard the apothecarist saying frantically, "Now look here! No one needs to harm anyone! I have enough beads for everyone." Clegis had pulled a knife from his pocket and was carefully unfolding it. He handed the knife to Jago, then cleared a place in the muck of the street and held Errol's fingers down on the cobbles.

Jago knelt down and pressed the tip of the blade into Errol's longest finger at the knuckle joint. Errol could feel it scraping the bone and saw his blood running onto the street.

"The streets are not for heroes, runner. And if they were? You would not be one of them. There are children here who are more heroic than you are, who rise against me every day. You save a snake and you think you're a hero. You draw a knife across Dete's ribs and think you know how to do it. Let's see if you can withstand any of the pain we know here."

"I'm sorry," said Errol. He watched the knife on his hand.

"Shut up."

"I'm sorry I killed Dete," Errol said. He held his hand still. The stag moved closer and laid his great muzzle on Errol's shoulder.

"If you're begging in hopes of pardon, that only proves you are a coward," said Jago.

"I'm not begging," said Errol. "And I'm not a coward or I'd have never come back. I'm telling the truth and you know it. What do you want? You said I left you here, and now I'm back. We both know I'm a murderer and I will never be free of that."

"Shut up," whispered Jago. "If I say you're a coward, you're a coward. These are my streets."

"Cut my fingers off," said Errol. "What are you, afraid to do it? *Min utlagend handa.*" This was his mam's tongue, the ancient tongue of the guild, and tears were running, falling into filth of the street. "I am begging you, cut my hands off. For I cannot get Dete's blood from them."

"I could do better than that. I can kill you for it. Everyone here would see that as a fair exchange."

"Do it, then! I sent him, unsafe, to places unknown. His beast came to fetch him. I was there, remember? And I can't think who to tell of my regret, for where is his mam? Where is his da? I have only you, Jago. And you were a foul friend to him, and you know it. You cheered me on in that pub. I will never cease to wonder what Dete might have been, nor fail to meet him in my nightmares. My hands are bloody with him. I will be glad to have them gone."

Jago took the knife away. The mob had wanted to see a runner bleed, and they saw it. But it was not the pain of knife in muscle that affected them. They all knew something of regret.

"Clegis," said Jago. "Do we know this kelp Arthur?"

"He's my cousin. The archer."

Jago turned in surprise. "This is that Arthur? With the dog fylgia?"

"That's him."

"A pit cur! If I had an uur for every arrow that kelp and his men, and Sitembile, sunk into my men—"

"Men?" said Errol. "He fought real men?"

"Fought, killed, maimed, blinded, unmanned—there's the hero you've been looking for, right there. An eight-year-old kelp."

"Nine," said Errol. He could not help but smile at the thought of little Arthur, with his dirty fingernails and that cowlick, fighting real monsters with a real bow.

Jago closed his eyes and threw back his head to think. "Does Arthur live, still?"

"He was no longer waking," said Clegis.

The apothecarist cleared his throat. "I can still save him."

"No one is going to save anyone," said Jago. He shifted his gaze to the tufuga and said, "But before that kelp dies, you'll put a mark on him, if that's what he wants. And you?" he said to Errol. "Get up. I'll do you a worse favor than taking your hand. I'll set you free on the streets, and Utlag will come for you."

"AND?" whispered Bede.

"And what?" said Errol.

"You're not going with us, are you?" said Chaunce.

Errol watched Jago, readying his mob to move toward The Bluebird, heaving the sacks of the apothecarist onto their shoulders, reining in the stag. The stag would be safer with Jago. *That* was irony.

"No. I'm not," said Errol.

The tufuga said, "Everywhere you go, they perforate you. You need us."

Errol raised his eyebrow at the tufuga. "That's an odd thing for you to say, as Chief Perforator."

Errol had business with Utlag. When it was over, he said, they would all meet at Thebes and rise together on the foundlings' ropes.

"If anything happens to you, I will be alone with this pill-monger," Chaunce said. "I would follow you to heofon and drag you back to this city."

"And if Errol is in heofon," said the apothecarist, "he would smell you coming from ten fathoms."

Errol felt his chest swell with admiration for these two guilders who had risked everything to come to the streets with him. He watched as they set off without him, all the way down the street with Jago and his mob. The great stag was with them, for the mob had him by ropes. He reared up and turned and stood staring at Errol.

Errol said, under his breath, "I am ready."

The Gauntlet

AS ERROL MOVED ALONG THE RIVERBANK, a man came toward him with his head held forward and down like the ram at his heel. A woman had the same restless eyes as her ferret. An old toothless woman limped along, with a disheveled starling hopping on her shoulder. More than before, he was aware of the similarities in the eyes, gait, and the sounds between the people he saw on his path and the beasts who trailed them.

"I have a pair of iron spikes in my pack," Errol said, as he had said to everyone he had seen.

"Who cares?" the starling's woman said.

"I'm sure you know someone who cares," said Errol.

He saw her twitch. He left her and walked to the riverbank. He sat in the grass and waited for news to travel.

As he waited, he played with something in his pocket. He took it out and saw the shatranj piece—the faras, the horse—the one he had given to the kitchen girl. *Who had put it there?*

Out of nowhere he was hit from behind. He spun around. He had known this was coming. He was curious to see who they had sent.

"Pollux." Errol could hear himself talking as if his head were underwater.

"Why didn't you stay on the roofs? You are nothing but one runner against a whole city." Errol felt himself drool. He tried to wipe his mouth but missed. "You've got what Utlag wants. And the regnat. And the abbot."

"They have my city. And I want it."

Pollux charged at him again, and this time Errol took the force straight on, then watched his fingers twitch as his body folded up and sank to the dirt.

THE ABBOT PAUSED THIS TIME, before he stepped into the pantry, and went for a lamp. The lamp flickered, spat, and went dark.

"I'd be grateful if you wouldn't haunt my borders with that question, like this."

"I'm not here to ask the question," the voice said.

The abbot reached for a cup. "All these years and we're finally going to change the subject. Should we discuss politics, do you think? Or matters of the soul?" He reached for a chair he couldn't see and sat down on it.

"An adversary is coming for you," said the voice.

The abbot ran the flat of his hand across the table and wiped a crumb away. "Politics, then. Who is it this time?"

"A worthy adversary."

"I see. Well, I have wondered about that fleet commander. He has always thought the gold was brighter on my side of the wall."

"If you think I am speaking of the fleet commander, you and I have a different definition of 'worthy.' Why do you hoard all that gold, anyway? You and the regnat."

"I have the world's attention. I'm what they refer to as a player."

"That is not a good reason."

"Yes. Well. You wouldn't know how it is." The other was silent. "So, who is this adversary?" The abbot's voice fell to a conspiratorial whisper. "It isn't Rome, is it?"

"You jest. Does it not occur to you that this opponent could mean your end? That I am here to warn you?"

"Others have tried to do me in. Remember Rip Thebes. You used to say he was worthy."

"I haven't changed that opinion."

"I won't end, and you know it. I am forced alive by desire. I live for ships, for the promise of war, for the surprises my Banhus-theof brings."

"We've seen more surprises than we should have, on this bit of earth. Abominable surprises. That creature Utlag, for example."

The abbot toyed with his spoon. "Yes. Well. I was curious to see what would happen if I let the needles have their way with my ribs. I had hoped for something more. One of those great dragons would have been nice. Bit of a mistake, Utlag was. I had hoped I was more than that."

"He is not your original fylgia and you know it. A parasite."

The abbot slumped in his chair, a rare breach of posture. "What *was* I, before he infiltrated? A lion, I imagine."

"You'll never know. You shouldn't play—"

"I will play with the sawols of men, if I so choose. Even my own."

The kitchen grew colder.

"If," said the other, "if you had spent any time at all in those ancient texts in any of those languages you destroyed on your shelves, you would know the difference between the thing you call a sawol and the espiritu your needles dig from rib cages. The spirit."

"They're dull books," the abbot said.

"The adversary coming your way understands the beasts who inhabit the bone houses."

"Oh, good. I could use his advice. For example, how to get the vipers not to attack their keepers for the duration of a ship's journey? Logistics. One bear is worth twenty dogs, so we feed the twenty to the one. One bear in chains and terrified is worth eighty dogs, so we set all those beasts together in the pit and anything standing at the end will make me a sack of gold. More gold if it is a man who can handle a weapon."

"A foul system."

"I don't care. I don't care at all. I am a merchant tired at the end of the day and unwilling to consider whether business is worth doing. Unready, as you may have guessed, to leave my city just because of some book-learned snot of a foot soldier coming my way."

"Very well. *Fiat justitia ruat caelum.*" Try as he may, the abbot could not get the lamp to light without calling for Nyree.

ON THE FLOOR OF A SHAFT, Rip lay. A day had been lost. The cover above his head scraped open.

"Did you bring the iron spikes?" Rip called.

"Spikes are gone. Runner stole them. We don't have time for that now. Nigh time to set you in the pit. Are you weak?"

"You tell me." Rip stood in Null's lamplight.

"You're half gone, but we already knew that," Null said.

Iron scraped on iron again and the cell went dark.

"How long do I have to wait?" Rip yelled. He lowered himself to the floor again. The tunnel above his pit was silent. Rip gave up any thought that the ending was going to come easily. He gave up the hope of seeing his brothers—the younger one who aggravated him and the older one who came to him every night begging to have his teeth filed, who haunted the mines of gaol and slept somewhere deep in the earth, who brought him broken things he had found in the streets in some tender, useless gesture.

"The wild animal wants to come home now," Rip said, his face swollen with dry tears. "*Oth ure feldhus. Oth ure banhus. Oth min heofon. Infaer ic.*"

To your tent. To your ribs. To heaven. Let me come home.

Null was still there. He scraped an old piece of skin from the mine floor with his fingernail. "There, now." He tasted it and put it in his mouth. "Nobody cares." He was accustomed to the habits of caged things, their tendency to commit poetry near the end.

Suspicions

THE ABBOT WAS RELIEVED to hear Nyree coming down the hall. He did not wish to be alone, although he was suspicious of her. He had seen her near the vault, and she shouldn't have been there.

"A test of your knowledge," he said. "*Fiat justitia ruat caelum*. What is the meaning?"

She lit the lamp he held out to her, and bowed. "Its specific interpretation is 'Do justice. Let the sky fall.' But in practice, it means something more like 'In order for justice to prevail, all hell will have to break loose.'" The abbot shifted uncomfortably. "It is an unsettling phrase, found in the ancient texts," she said. "Has the abbot been reading?"

Lugius said, as offhandedly as he could, "Yes. As usual." He paused and added, "I read that in Sophocles."

"But Sophocles did not—" Nyree began, and then thought the better of it. "I mean to say, Sophocles is tumultuous for this time of day."

"I am aware of that. This stove needs cleaning. Send up a housekeeper."

Nyree left in a bow, for she did not want the abbot to see her face. An abbot in a scriptorium should know the difference between the language of Sophocles and the language of Virgil.

ERROL THOUGHT AT FIRST that he was blind. He lay on his back. He could feel his eyelids open, but there was nothing to see. He felt cold water along his spine and stone chafing his shoulder blades. Water soaked the backs of his leggings and the hair on the back of his head. A drop of it fell on his face and his hand jerked up involuntarily, but he could not reach his face, for the bedrock in which he lay could fit no more than a body.

"Steady," he said to himself.

Beyond his feet, there came the sound of iron grating on iron, and Errol saw lantern light playing off a pair of eyes in the barred window of the door to this chamber.

"I thought the climax of the story always came in a high place."

"Shouldn't you be hibernating, Utlag?"

"You let yourself be caught. And yet you haven't got the iron spikes. A crypt of sorts seemed convenient. Less of a disposal issue, at the end." Errol lay silent. "A last request is traditional."

Errol tried to remember his plan. But he was thrown. For one thing, he was wounded, yet again. For another, he had not expected to be in a crypt. A shaft, yes. Or the arena. But not a tomb. "I want to speak with the regnat. Alone."

"The regnat? Curiosity!" said Utlag, holding the lamp up to the vent. "Why?"

"I want to know about gaol and the pit. He knows everything."

"I know everything."

"I doubt it—"

"Ask your questions!"

"I'm merely curious to know how the foundlings in gaol's prison cells, those shafts, are turned into beasts of war."

"Why?"

Errol shrugged. "I'm a guilder's son. I'm interested in how things are made."

"I am not permitted to say—"

"See? I thought as much. As I said, I will need to speak with the *regnat*."

Utlag hissed. "We pry the foundling from his herd, his flock, his pack. Drop him in a pit."

Errol's head throbbed in the cold water but he made as if to yawn of boredom. "And then?"

"Introduce him to his nightmares." Utlag threw open his mouth, which unhinged at the jaw with a sick sucking sound. A series of long teeth unfolded from the roof of his mouth. Errol rammed himself so hard away from the door that he hit his head against the back of the crypt. "Like that," said Utlag.

"Is that all?"

"All? No. I wake the foundling in the night. Even the sound of my fingernails on his door will drive him insane. I take away everything he has carried in with him, even his clothes. I wound whatever lives in the cell next to his and let him hear it begging for its life. *Clever.* He will do anything I ask after only five minutes of that."

Errol gritted his teeth. "That's what you were doing to Jago, when you were threatening to drown Rip. You were trying to make a monster of him."

"I don't *try.*"

"What comes next, after that?"

"The foundling will be unsettled in a day. So frantic not to be alone that he will beg even for my company, which is"—Utlag clicked—"ironic. He will either be submissive or wild with rage. In either case he is ready to meet the iron spikes. We throw them in the pit. The beast extracted from his chest will be the same species it would have been—a jackal is a jackal—but the fear will have made it mad. In the best cases it will tear the flesh from a creature four times its size. I'm sure you know the regnat and the abbot have found a market for such beasts."

"And you? What is your market?"

"I have higher purposes. An object of desire—"

Errol interrupted, "Would the jackal have attacked the very man from which it came?"

Errol heard that clicking sound. "I see what this is all about," said Utlag. "You're afraid that stag will attack you. No. Certain predators will do that. Spiders. Jackals. Not a stag."

"A relief." Errol feigned sighing. He had known his stag would not hurt him.

"Have you seen a jackal?" Utlag said.

"Not yet. I imagine you'll make that happen, sooner or later."

"You see? I hadn't even thought of that. Imagination works better than reality in tearing a man apart," said Utlag. He clucked and went silent, waiting. "I know more."

"Mm," Errol said. "I don't imagine you know what evil is happening in the guilds, on the roofs."

"Insulted!" Utlag hissed. "Ask me anything."

"Is the regnat aware the guild work is burning?" Errol said.

"He orders it," Utlag said.

"And that guild foundlings are being dropped at night?"

"By the hundreds, at his command. They come through the tower Fremantle."

"Why foundlings? Why not runners or guilders?"

"Exasperation! If we took runners or guilders, the towers would come out in force. Do you see? No one will ever fight for a foundling."

"Why don't the streets rise up and fight? The streets are full of foundlings."

"Actually the uprisings are many. The abbot rounds up the mutineers. Also their friends, their families, their beasts. It doesn't go well for them."

Errol swallowed hard. "How hard is it for you to climb the towers?"

"What?"

"You heard me."

Utlag licked the air. "Look." He put his fingers through the bar of the cell. "Touch them," he said.

"I can't reach—"

"Touch them!"

Errol twisted his body in the tomb. Utlag's palms were covered with tiny, stiff hairs. "I go anywhere I like. I also have skills with locks." Errol yanked his hand away.

"Is that why the regnat mocks you? Because you're"—Errol let Utlag wait—"extraordinary?"

"He hates me. I took what he could not have."

"He has a whole city."

"I took the bound-wife he wanted. I fathered the sons."

"How the hel—I mean, what are you, exactly?"

"Alone."

"That must be terrible," said Errol. He was surprised that he meant the sympathy in his voice.

"It's impossible," whispered Utlag.

"And the sons?" said Errol. "Was it impossible for them, too?"

"No one cares. Rip is a disappointment, as you saw. Fenn is frightening even to me."

"*Is?* You mean *was*," said Errol.

"How do you know Fenn?"

"I am from Thebes. Have you forgotten? And was there not a third son?"

"No! No third son. Not of mine. But the bound-wife was unfaithful to me." Utlag's mouth constricted on the words *bound-wife* so that they sounded like a belch. "She cast me out. I returned the favor. Haunted that third son, threw him off the tower."

Errol cringed. "Why wound a kelp?"

"Why? So she would pay attention. You should have heard the kelp screaming—'But I am the guildmaster's son!' As if that would save him."

Errol's stomach heaved. Poor Feo. "I see. I suppose it's only fair that the kelp should suffer for what his mam had done." Errol felt sure anyone could tell he was lying.

"There. See? *You* understand."

"Who was the father of that third son?" said Errol, wishing as he said it that he had not.

Again it came as a belch. "That regnat."

Errol blurted, "No!" He pressed his fingernails into his palms, determined not to lose control of himself. "The regnat is foul."

Utlag showed his face again. "We are in agreement. You'll be glad to know I spend my time frightening him." Utlag leaned against the cell door now, like a man coming to visit a convalescing friend. "Without the iron spikes, the abbot can't make his fylgias, and the ships leave empty. So I keep them, to get his attention. It makes it difficult. He hates me. Meanwhile the regnat mocks me. So I must terrorize him. I leave the spikes where he doesn't expect to see them. In his bog. In the bedchamber. He cannot lock his doors sufficiently or move high enough in that tower to escape me."

"He fears the pain of the spikes," said Errol.

"It's not that," Utlag hissed. "He doesn't want to meet his beast."

"I thought a man's beast was his companion. His friend."

"There are exceptions." Utlag's voice dropped to a whisper. "Do you mind your beast trailing you everywhere?"

"I love it. I love the stag."

"Yes. Yes. That's what it *should* be." Utlag put his forehead on the bars.

"So all those lights of Fremantle are kept lit so the spikes cannot work on the regnat."

"He is a coward," said Utlag.

"Will every beast you frighten become a raging thing, driven by fear? Are your methods reliable?"

"In every way," Utlag said. "And yet? No. For we find bits of nobility or courage here and there among the beasts."

"I'm relieved to hear it."

"We feed the noble ones to the others."

Errol kept silent again for a long time.

"What about *your* ideas? The kardunns, the bonnacons, the rossignols?"

"Why do you want to know?"

"How many have you found so far? Centicores? Or yales?"

"Not one," Utlag said. "Yet. But I have many foundlings waiting in the cells and I'm sure one of those will be rare. You will be interested to know there was one guilder in Thebes who could see a man's beast."

"Slyngel Thebes," said Errol. Then, quickly, "He died."

"He didn't die. I ended him. He wouldn't help me. It was easy to find a poison for a thirsty guilder." Utlag wiped a thin black line of drool from his chin.

Errol wasn't sure he could keep going. But he had to. "Still, like you, I am irritated that no rare beasts exist yet in this city."

"Irritated?" said Utlag.

"Of course. Is this city deficient?"

"Exactly! I feel the same! I wish I could read the signs as Slyngel Thebes did."

"I wish I could help you. There are foundlings I suspect are rare." Utlag was watching him closely. *Suspicious!* "So many of them are sheep, you know? Or houseflies. But a very few have a way of moving or some uncommon skill. I'm sure they're rare."

"Yes. Yes! That's what I mean."

"I assume you keep records in the vault. We could go over them together—"

"Yes. Of course."

"Oh, but you don't have access to the vault."

"Oh yes. No. *Confusion.* I *can* open it without the abbot's key but he threatens that—" Utlag paused. "So he is the only one. I will ask him—"

"I would be honored."

"You're lying to me. You wish me dead. You are tricking me."

Errol paused. "My stag is waiting for me at Bluebird's. You can check if you don't believe me. I trust you with that information."

"I trust you too. I do. Excitement," Utlag said. "Wait for me here."

———

Of all that had been said in this exchange, here are the three answers Errol needed:

No one in the streets was strong enough to lead an uprising.

A predator could turn on itself.

The abbot had sole access to the vault.

A Fool

LUGIUS DID NOT LOOK UP FROM HIS DESK. He said, "Don't talk. Just yes or no. Do you have the iron needles?" He was speaking to neither the fleet captain nor the regnat. He was speaking to Utlag, who was hiding outside the closed door. The abbot could smell him.

"Why was I not informed of this meeting?" Utlag hissed, moving into the room with a hand clenched. "Agitated."

"You're here, aren't you?"

"I came with news."

The abbot was filling out a shipping form. The fleet captain stood watching. Already he had been in this room since sundown, and his ships had been anchored downriver for more than a week, burning the guild trinkets and waiting for the true exports. The regnat sat in a far corner of the office, his body appearing as a mass of shadows at the center of blinding lamplight.

"I am interrogating that runner, to see what he knows about the spican. Meanwhile he has provided information I'm sure the abbot will be interested to know." The abbot sighed. "Listen! This runner knows of foundlings whose beasts are rare!" The abbot's pen stopped and his shoulders slumped. Utlag wiped the spittle from his face. "Bonnacons. Wyrms. I came here to get my records from the vault, to compare them with his information. He is going to give me names. I am sure we have something worth more than all the ships you three have filled."

The abbot said, "How many times do I need to tell you? There are no rare beasts in this city. Least of all, yourself."

Utlag hissed, "Then why does the regnat over there stay in the light? What rare thing is he afraid of?"

The abbot was half out of his chair. "Sit, Utlag. Sit *down*."

"Listen! The runner said there is no sheepness to these foundlings he knows. They are not houseflies or rats. He is sure of it."

"Sheepness," said that abbot flatly, putting down his quill and staring at some point on his desk. "That's what we have, to go on? A lack of sheepness? I, too, lacked sheepness and look what it brought me."

A pool of black fluid filled Utlag's lips. "Unkind," he whispered.

The regnat spoke: "We must fill two hundred ships with exports by tonight, but we cannot, for you cannot produce the iron spikes to finish that work. You are a waste of time."

Utlag backed away. "In that crypt below the earth I finally have someone I can trust."

The regnat laughed. "Let me tell you something about that runner. He's Errol Thebes, third son of Guildmaster Margaret Thebes." Utlag was down on all fours now, at the sound of Margaret's name, his back arched. "He is the one you thought you threw off the roof. You threw the wrong kelp off the roof, Utlag. Margaret tricked you. Now he has come and tracked us here. He's not a kelp anymore. He's a rising guildmaster. And he has come to finish us."

Math

THE TUFUGA HAD SET UP A TATU BENCH BY THE FIRE, and a long queue wound around the room. Trula was making potato soup. The apothecarist was treating Arthur and a roomful of others whose symptoms were the same. Jago stood in the middle of the room, the center of a kind of chaos that was new to him.

Will Bluebird yelled out, "Who can it be, banging at the door, that isn't here already?"

Two men stood there with hatchets and ropes. Behind them stood so many more that Will Bluebird could not see where the crowd ended. Utlag had sent for the stag, they said. Will Bluebird closed the door. Jago went to a crack in the wall and looked out.

Utlag had sent a hundred. Jago had sixteen, plus Arthur's five. If Arthur had been well and fighting, or if they had Jago's cat, they could almost have called it even. Jago was at the wall a long time and finally said, "Give them the stag."

"No, we can fight," said the apothecarist.

Jago raised his eyebrow. "A tufuga and a formidable apothecarist. Right. Listen, if you don't give up the stag, we'll be bloodied, and Arthur and these kelps will be taken anyway." The two of them crossed their arms and stared at one another, until Jago said, "You know what your noble runner would say."

The stag rose when the mob came for him. For a long moment the men all stood back, in awe of the great creature he was, his face noble, his body powerful even in surrender. Then? Then they threw a set of ropes around his antlers and another set around his legs and yanked one set to the right and the other to the left, and he went down so hard the pub shook.

The tufuga followed at a distance. The hundred men dragged the stag down into the earth, pushing and folding his great bulk into the tunnels and finally forcing him to get up and lie on a cart they could pull. The tufuga crept after them. When the stag's antlers jammed up against the tunnel walls, the men got out their hatchets. When they reached the depths of gaol, they prodded the stag with spears to force him through the gate of the arena. A crowd cheered when he looked up at them. He struggled to stand.

ERROL HAD BEEN SO SURE Utlag was going to return. But now the back of his head was underwater, and the back of his legs and his shoulders. His lips were frozen hard. The spray of the drops falling on his chest had made a wet bib on his shirt, like a baby's. It frustrated him that he could not remember the guild word for "baby." He felt for the bars in the door with his foot, tried to think how to slide the window open so the water would run out of it before it was over his face.

A knock echoed in the tunnel, and Errol thought it was Utlag returning but it was the pinging of the stone of the earth under pressure. It was nothing.

Errol was nagged by the disparity between the stories he knew from the tales told high in the guild tower and his own story playing out here, in this low place. The men and women in the scrolls he knew did not die this way, losing whatever sanity they had because water was dripping on the same sore bit of skin. When they died at all, they died in the great heave of battle, or arm in arm with their compatriots, in a towering wall of salt-sea water. They did not vomit or relieve themselves in the water in which they lay, as he had done, or spend the last uurs of their existence in a tomb no one could ever find. He had never thought of the thousands of people whose stories went untold, whose ends were small and frightened and far away, who were never found. He cried out for mercy, and not for himself.

He heard a tentative try at the bolt. It must have been only his imagination again. There it was again.

"Let me out!" he said.

"You are still alive," a voice said.

Errol jerked at the sound. "Utlag? Yes! Yes! I am alive! Let me out!"

"That will come later." It was not Utlag. Errol could not place it. He was breathing too hard to hear or think.

"*Later?*" Errol yelled. His ears were below the water, so everything was distorted. "Later? Then you are about to hear me drown!"

"Yes. You smell of panic."

Errol laughed and water washed into his mouth. "Give me soap and I'll wash! Just open the door!"

"I'm not complaining. The scent of you is a pleasure. The salt sweat in your hair. And something musky, animal."

"What sort of man are you who would torment me with this, while I drown?" He held his breath, waiting to hear the lock turn.

"A hungry one."

"Yes. I am hungry, too. At least you are free to get yourself a meal."

"My meal is here."

"Open the door and give me some of it? Please. I need the strength. I am freezing."

"A frozen meal, then."

Errol felt the hairs on his arms stand up, his chest tighten hard on his lungs. "What?!" He wedged his feet against the door.

"There is no need to worry. I shall wait until you are dead or nearly so. I need something of a chase, but it will be quick."

"You don't have a key—" Errol said, knowing already that he was wrong.

"Utlag gave it to me. Found me. Said there was something in here for me. Traitors are particularly savory, those were his exact words."

So Utlag had found him out. "I will not be murdered twice in the same night. I will not!"

"Ease yourself. You sound like a *lytling.*"

There was the word he had wanted. *Lytling.* Who was this, who spoke in a Thebes House dialect and knew the word for "baby"? "Rip? Rip! Is that you?"

"Who is that?" demanded the one outside his door, striking a flint in the window.

"Rip, open the door. This isn't funny," Errol said. "I regret all I've said. Let me out."

"Who is that?" said the stranger outside the door. "How do you know my brother?"

"Your brother?" Errol gasped. "How could Rip Thebes be *your* brother? He is mine—"

THE TUFUGA'S HEART POUNDED, his pulse in his ears. He heard something breathing. He lifted his hands to his ears to stop it all, to calm himself.

From their shafts the prisoners listened to him move. He could sense their presence. And they could sense his. He had lost his way, lost the stag.

He touched the stone wall and felt along it and turned up a tunnel, silently.

He stopped again. He was unnerved by an essing sound that followed him. It had not been there before, but it was now: *sssSSSSsss*. His neck was a cold sweat. He turned to get away from it. Again it was at his heels. Something grabbed his ankle and he shouted out. He wrenched his leg away, turned, ran, crashed into a wall. The sharp grip came again from behind, and he flung his arms behind him wildly, slapping it. Now it leapt upon his back and held him until he stopped yelling.

A voice whispered in his ear, "Are you the tatu man?"

Chaunce nodded.

A lamp went on. "I am Sitembile. I am here to guard your back."

"Guard it or break it?" Chaunce said, shielding his eyes from her light. She got down and slung her bow over her shoulder. She was a mere kelp. "Did you make that sound? That *hissing*?"

Sitembile's eyes darted down at her feet, where a red asp was stretched around a curve in the tunnel, its head raised and bobbing. The tufuga jumped on the wall and clung by his fingers to a tiny outcrop of granite.

Sitembile shrugged. "I'd like to tell you he's more afraid of you than you are of him, but that would be a lie."

Sacrifice

"THIS IS THE PART OF THE TALE," Errol said, straining for breath in the wet space in the rock, "where I should be overjoyed to find that my long-lost brother has arrived to open the door of my tomb. You have to admit this is awkward. Here you were going to devour me, and now you find I am related. What are the manners for this?"

Grunts and shifting.

Errol yelled, "Say something! At least keep me company. Tell me how all of this happened to you. To me."

Fenn must have set his hand on the bolt. Errol heard the latch move. "Simple," said Fenn. "Our mother fell in love with an apprentice ironsmith."

"Simple," said Errol.

"Margaret was rising. People warned her away from him, but you know how that goes. They were bound and dropped before she realized he had not come from anywhere. He was something other than human. Perhaps your sharp teeth have come in as mine did, or your appetite for flesh."

"I don't have that."

"Rip didn't inherit it either. Like his mother, he eats from the table. But if he doesn't wash, he reeks of hides. You have that same aroma."

"No. It is a stag you're smelling. I am not the son of Utlag," said Errol.

Fenn paused. "You have a fetch? Can you look in a mirror?"

"Yes."

"You're lucky."

"Everyone keeps telling me that," said Errol. "See me here, drowning three feet from my brother who plans to eat me? There's luck for you. Worse, my plan has been thwarted."

They both heard the sound of footfalls in the tunnel and the voice of another man, echoing off the walls.

Errol said, "Fenn?" but there was no answer. Errol could see the flickering light of his brother's lamp through the barred window. He wanted to yell out, to be freed. But he was aware that Fenn was hungry, and he feared for whoever was coming down the tunnel. The man called out, "I am in the wrong shaft of this foul place," and turned to go, when Errol cried out, "I am here! Save me!" He listened. There was only the dripping.

"Where?" the man asked. The word did not have time to echo before Errol heard a scuffle, a scream, and frantic chase. It was Pollux, the henchman. When it was over, Errol heard Fenn outside of his door, sobbing.

"Go on," said Fenn.

Errol swallowed and said from a dry throat, "I can't remember what I was saying."

"You had some sort of plan."

Errol moaned. This was too hard. "My plan depended on too many things. On living, for one thing. And on Rip, who, if he is alive, is too much a coward to do what is required."

"You could be kinder to him."

Errol laughed. "Does that seem at all ironic to you?"

"I know what it is to be human. Half, half. In that fraction is my dilemma. Rip has cared for me all these years, knowing I have no fetch in my chest. I am a monster. His ribs are empty as well. He fears that truth more than he fears death itself."

"He is nothing but fear."

"This is how I know you are fully human: You are fully the judge. Tell me the plan you had."

It took only a few sentences to lay out the whole idea, for it was a simple one, juvenile really. When he was done, Errol laid his head back in the water.

"And what would you do with the iron spikes, in the end?" said Fenn.

"Destroy them."

"And have you given some thought to what your plan would mean for Rip?"

"Obviously he and you both would be free of Utlag."

"I'm afraid it could be more complicated than that."

"Afraid?" It was a strange idea, that such a monster could be afraid. "I have a question for you now. Were you afraid, to be dropped?"

"Of course."

"I was never so afraid in my life. I broke my ribs," said Errol.

"You chose the right line, then."

"How else would I be here?"

"I did not."

Errol inhaled fast. "What?"

"What hurt more was that the regnat said he was dropping me for our mother's sake. Rip had done nothing. Gut runs. That was all. I was becoming my father."

"Mam grieves, still," Errol said.

Fenn paused. "No."

"She was never the same after it. But how did you survive the drop?"

"Look at me," said Fenn, striking the flint again and putting his face to the vent. Errol gasped. "Do you call this surviving? Destroy the spikes. Destroy Banhustheof. No one should be playing with the irfelaf. Make this half-life worth something." The flint light went out and Errol heard Fenn shuffling down the tunnel.

LET ME TAKE STOCK NOW, for even I have forgotten where I have left all the players in this tale. The main actors are offstage: two black-iron knotting spikes. Divided. One lies in silence in the belly of a crow on the roof of Thebes; the other, in a pile of test arrows at Fremantle.

Errol Thebes waits deep in the earth, entombed alive among the dead in a chamber filling with water. His fylgia, the great stag Eikthyrnir, has been dragged into the arena where his nightmare awaits. The tufuga is trying to find the stag before it is too late, but he has no idea what he or Sitembile can do to stop what is happening.

Rip waits, languishing in a cell, afraid to be cast in the dark with the black-iron spikes, which will crack open his ribs and find nothing but an empty bone house.

The apothecarist is with the kelp Arthur, hoping the second dose of quinine and artemisia will take effect.

Jago, lacking his fetch, is wandering the streets alone, well aware that a battle is about to begin and that he has no real part. His allegiances are to himself.

The abbot, the fleet commander, and the regnat are in the abbot's quarters. The fleet is waiting to leave.

Utlag is running to the tombs. It has only just occurred to him that he had sent Fenn to devour the one player who knows where the iron spikes are.

Dagmar is digging clams in the mud with her wolves.

Terpsichore is packing.

Jamila Foundling is ransacking the closets of Thebes.

———

Errol heard the vent slide open. The water was high.

"You lie," Utlag said.

"If you want the spikes, you'll have to listen to me," he said hurriedly. "We'll need Rip."

Utlag spat, "Rip is in the pits of gaol, Errol Thebes."

"If he dies, you and I will have to knit all our toques with one needle."

Utlag held up the lantern. "You lie."

Errol closed his eyes. He was unaccustomed to lying. "Rip didn't trust me with both the spikes, when we brought them in from the street. He said I was an arrogant line-runner. He took one. I kept one. Go to him first. He'll say he doesn't know where it is. You can understand why. He doesn't want his ribs broken. He'll carry on about it and yell and lie. He'll tell you he threw it away. But he knows. Tell him for me that he can rot in hel if he doesn't give you the spike. No. Wait. Tell him he can go to the crow." Errol paused. "It's an expression from Homer's tongue." Errol was confident Utlag would deliver his message if he soaked it in venom. "I do, actually, have one last question.

"I know from your iosal instructions how to take a foundling and subject it to so much fear you cause it to turn into a warmongering thing. But tell me this, Utlag. How do you take a foundling and make it noble, so that it will sacrifice its life just so you can live?" Errol gritted his teeth against the cold. "Which is to say, how do you cause it to rise?"

Utlag was silent.

Errol whispered, "Aye. That's what I thought."

RIP GRINNED, at the bottom of the shaft. So, Errol did have a plan. "Fine. Is that what he said? 'Go to the crow'? That arrogant runner. Let me out and I'll get you the spike."

The Crow

"THE CROW," yelled Rip. "Why did he have to put it in the crow?" He was running hard along the river. He found Dagmar digging razor clams with her wolves.

They ran together, while she tied a silk line to the nock of one of her arrows. She had rehearsed this a thousand times. At Thebes she released the arrow. It soared up and over a fly-line and arced down again to earth.

Rip took the two ends of it in his hands, struggling to walk up that tower. He felt like a fool to be so uncoordinated. And, oh, it was a thin, thin pair of lines. Thread, really. After ten minutes he had risen three strata up the side of Thebes House. He was panting with fear. He could already feel the swaying of the towers. In an uur he was only halfway.

Why, of the infinite hiding places in the city, did Errol choose the highest point on Thebes? And look at me. I am drenched with sweat, my hands are soaked, my heart pounds in my chest, my knees are shaking so terribly I will fall before I get anywhere near the top. I cannot believe she still has this effect on me.

IT WAS DARK WHEN I RETURNED to Thebes. Terpsichore had gone to Lascaux. I searched half an uur for the chicken and finally heard its clucking overhead. He was perched on the roof of the yurt.

"How did you get up there, you flightless bird?" I climbed up and sat next to him. The night breezes played with the feathers of his chest. For a long while he watched the shimmering lights of the aurora borealis. I attempted to pick him up, but he stabbed at my arm. He looked at me, then down below him into the abyss between Thebes and Bamako, then back at me, then down.

"It's a long way down. Is that your point?"

And then I saw the fly was vibrating. Someone had managed to get a line over it, and they were coming up even as we watched. A man appeared, swearing, soaked in sweat. He flung himself onto our roof and lay there on the edge, filling his lungs with high air.

He turned to look at me, and his face was as full of daring as I remembered it.

"Who are you?" he said to me, and I felt the thrill I had always felt as a kelp when Rip Thebes noticed me.

"I'm Odysseus. Your cousin."

Ovid, his harbinging complete, scratched the back of his neck with his foot, slid off the yurt, and dropped with a thud to the roof, reassembled his feathers, and disappeared into my tent.

Irfelaf

NYREE HAD NOT FELT IT NECESSARY to tell the abbot that she had received a delivery from a woman in the company of wolves. It was a piece of burlap, wrapped around a black-iron spike. The wolf-woman said the spike had been shot at her by archers on the roof of Fremantle. She had eyed Nyree, as if to decide whether this monk could be trusted, then had pointed to the word *irfelaf*, which had been scratched into the iron.

"For the vault?" Nyree had said.

"I believe so. Yes."

The tale was rising.

RIP OPENED THE HINGED DOOR in the crow's underbelly. He removed the package Errol had put there. He was suddenly aware that all of Thebes's runners stood on the roof around the mast, looking up at him.

"The infamous Rip Thebes," said Grid, from far below him. "Odd Thebes was right."

"We need an army," Rip said.

"There are thousands of us, prepared to fight," Grid said. "Although we lack weapons and armor."

"I've brought the armor." We turned to see who spoke. It was hard to tell, since the speaker was standing under a cloak of fur.

"Who are you?" Rip said.

"Nobody in particular."

"That's Jamila Foundling," I said.

A Roof Master

HIS EARS HAD BEEN UNDERWATER for a long while now, and he could hear only muffled sounds from the tunnels, and the pingings of the towers as they swayed in their foundations above him. He was trying to think of that kitchen girl and what she would do in this situation. The foundling. Sure of herself, even unto death. He would try for that.

The water amplified the sound of the lock barrel turning and there came the slide of the bolt and the door burst open. He grabbed for the walls but the water swept him with it. He fell to the granite floor of the tunnel, too numb to feel anything. He lay sprawled, helpless, sopping, frozen, blinded by the light of a head lamp.

He felt fingers moving across his shoulders, air moving in his face. He braced himself and wondered whether his cold body would feel the pain, or what it would be that Fenn would take first from him. But from the other side of the light came the sound of someone sucking his teeth.

"I wonder if you remember how to call for help," said Marek.

RIP WAS THINKING TO HIMSELF that there were always three brothers, in tales from the world outside the wall. The first two were useless fools; the third was always the hero. The regnat sat across from him, a shadowy figure in the glare of the light of his lamp bearers. The fleet commander circled the table. The abbot stood by the fire holding the single spike Rip had brought.

The doors of the vault room were suddenly thrown open, and monks ran every which way to grab blankets and towels.

Utlag swept into the room, followed by a rare sight on the streets of a roof master carrying upon his back the body of one of his runners.

Errol was swollen and shaking and blue from the ice water. He stared at Marek with blank eyes as monks wrapped him skillfully in blankets. "Where are we?" he whispered.

"The scriptorium. As you asked."

Errol turned to study each of them and then to stare into the light that was the regnat. "I thought we might find you here."

"Where is the second spike, Errol Thebes?" said the regnat.

Errol furrowed his brow. "You'll need the sheath."

The monk Nyree was standing next to the abbot. She bowed slightly and said, "I believe you put the sheath in the vault, Your Grace. The last time the outlaw was here." The abbot turned to look at Nyree, and held his eyes on her long and hard, a feeling of suspicion blooming in him.

What happened next occurred within a fraction of a minute, but it will take more than that to describe it. It was a round of thimblerig, the shell-and-pea game. There was a pair of iron needles hiding under various cups, and I myself, skillful though I am at thimblerig, did not see them when I first heard this account.

On the abbot's orders, Utlag took the abbot's key and unlocked the vault hatch, a heavy iron door in the floor. The iron was kept searing hot by internal fires; Utlag lifted the hatch with a wad of his robe, propped it up, and disappeared down the ladder. After a while he came halfway up the stairs, his eyes shifting. "The sheath isn't there."

"Ridiculous," said the abbot. "I put it there myself. Look again."

Utlag disappeared again. The vault was large enough only for a few shelves and trunks. He came up the stairs and stood next to the abbot and handed the key to him. "Nothing."

The regnat said wryly, "Shall I ask my guards to retrieve what your pet cannot fetch?"

"It is my vault. They would be trespassing," said the abbot.

"This is my city," the regnat sneered. "That key is mine. That vault is mine. This scriptorium is mine." He started down the ladder.

Nyree looked over at Errol at that moment and saw his lips curl in a grim, fleeting smile.

"I forbid this!" yelled the abbot. But the regnat was already in the vault. His light guards made as if to follow him but there were too many of them and he waved them out of his way.

There was a great deal of crashing and heaving. "Nothing! There is no sheath here! Where have you put it, Lugius, you fool?"

"It's right there!" said the abbot. He shoved his monks out of his way and flew down the stairs, turning, with the spike in one hand, to grab a lamp from Nyree with his other. Nyree pulled the lamp away from his hand.

"I'll hold this for you," she said.

He looked at her oddly, and well he should. "I'll deal with you later," he said.

He was all the way down the stairs before she murmured, "I doubt it."

At that moment, with the abbot and the regnat in the vault, Errol heaved himself out of the blankets off the floor and stumbled toward the red-hot hatch. He threw himself upon it, to close it.

Rip's jaw dropped open. "What the—?" he said.

Errol had wagered everything on an arrogance so complete that both the regnat and the abbot would ignore the enormous likelihood that he was lying to them, in particular that he was lying about the whereabouts of the second spike. It was in the vault, marked *irfelaf*. Not only would they both go into the vault, but they would charge into the vault. Not only would they charge, but they would not see the spike, because they were competing to find the sheath.

Utlag's eyes darted back and forth between Rip and Errol, and then he screamed, "Fright!" He lunged for the hatch but Rip got to him first and pulled him away. Utlag bit him.

One would think the battalion of light guards would do something or that the monks would. But none of them understood why it mattered so much that two men might be closed in a vault that contained a few contracts and a knife sheath.

There was one flaw in Errol's plan: The abbot was a warrior. He did not lose. He had reached up to stop the hatch from closing and taken the full weight of it on his fingers. Errol grabbed the hatch with his shirt, burning his hands, and slammed it down again. The abbot reached up and around the hatch and grabbed Errol's wrist. The regnat, too, reached out for him.

In a moment that seemed to stand still in time, Errol took one look around the hall. He knew the abbot and the regnat would never release their grip on him. The door would remain open, the city in a balance. And so the bee wolf threw himself around that hatch and into the vault, grabbing the inner handle as he went in. He kicked at the regnat and the abbot and let his hanging weight pull shut the vault.

———

There was a pause and then an explosion within the vault, blowing bright smoke from the seams of the hatch and filling the scriptorium. A froth of hot amber oozed from under the hatch. Something not human screamed from within.

Utlag tore himself from Rip's arms and threw himself down next to the vault, licking at the hot hinges. He slipped his fingers into the lock in the door, prying at it, shrieking.

The fleet captain was pale. "Could someone explain?"

"I believe the abbot, the regnat, and that runner have met the regnat's beast," Nyree said. "And it wasn't a sheep."

In the smoke, Utlag turned to face the room, searching for a way to brace himself. While he stood, his skin tore off his muscles, his muscles off his bones, exposing raw nerves. Aside from the pain of it—the gums pulling back from his teeth, the throat vibrating like a live bird, the blood spraying from veins that unraveled in his hands—besides all that, there was a wasting-sorrow, as a solitary creature writhed in pain while the members of another species looked on. Rip reached for Utlag's hand, but the hand undid itself and Rip was left holding nothing but a stain. The last organs left were a pair of lungs, which lay whinnying on the floor. A thin red bit of thread was visible from the spot where Utlag had been. The other end ran under the door into the vault to the abbot. And then the room and the vault were silent.

"Come away," said Nyree, reaching down. She wiped Rip's bloody hands on her tunic. She looked at him and said, "Oh."

Rip wiped his hands on his tunic, then on his leggings. There was more blood on him than he could wipe off. "Where are my fingernails?" he said. When he turned, everyone was staring at him.

One monk had his hand to his mouth.

"Give me a mirror," Rip said, reaching up to touch his face. His voice sounded strange to him.

"Maybe not just now—" said Marek.

One of the monks ran to the hallway and pulled the iron-framed mirror from the wall and turned it to Rip.

THE STRONG SPINE RIP HAD INHERITED from his mother held him up, and the rest of what he'd gotten from her kept his heart beating and his vision. But the parts that were from his father, the other with no shadow and no reflection, were gone.

Together the monks tore linen towels and wrapped him in long strips, which gave him a form again that was human. Nyree reminded him the apothecarist was still on the street and could help.

Rip didn't seem to hear her. "There's a chance Errol is alive in that vault," he said.

"Of course. We'll take care of him. But where are you going?"

"To my brother."

Done

"SABA," the regnat gasped. "Saba. Sabasababa." He flung himself onto the table, rolled onto his back, and arched in a spasm. His eyes were wide-open in surprise—although there was no surprise about it—for he had finally met the beast he had known all along was in his ribs. He spat a mouthful of venom onto his chest and watched as his skin blistered in the acid of it. The monks who had opened the vault and carried him out of it now covered their faces for the scriptorium was ripe with a smell of reptile. They had seen many things but never a man dying crushed and scorched by the flail of his own fylgia.

Marek yelled from inside the vault, and the monks came running.

When Marek put his hand to Errol's face, the water of his own sweat boiled at the touch on Errol's skin. The monks ran for kitchen potholders to carry him to a quarantine room in the scriptorium, and they set him in a trough of water and watched the water roil and his body seize.

Nyree retrieved the leather sheath from her quarters, uncurled Errol's fingers, took the spikes. She slipped through the halls to the abbot's office and set the sheathed spikes in a box marked CHARITABLE GIVING.

She used a fireplace shovel to scrape what was left of Utlag into a bucket and put the bucket behind the abbot's stove in the kitchen. She followed the red thread of his remains to the abbot's scorched body, pressed up against a wall. She carried the abbot out of the vault and laid him next to the regnat. And it was done.

"I AM CONFUSED," the tufuga whispered, standing on the ledge. "First I thought you attacked me. And second I thought we were getting out of the mines."

"You said," said Sitembile, "that you wanted to save the stag."

"So you're helping me?"

The tufuga looked down at the stag, leaning against the wall of the arena, his legs folded under him, his half-sawn antlers swinging from the stumps. Then the tufuga turned and stared at Sitembile and at her snake until she shifted uncomfortably and said, "What?"

"Snakes are wicked. Everyone knows it. You can read it in books."

"If I was working for Utlag, you could call me wicked. In your service, however, I'm more of an asset. Like the snake, I thrive in the dark. I strike accurately but without what you might call excessive forethought. I lack fear. Errol Thebes saved my snake and me from Jago. He was a fool. But that's the nature of stags and, on merit, I owe him."

"I see. What is the name of your snake, by the way?"

"Snake."

"Sentimental," said the tufuga. "I do wonder what beast lives in my ribs. In a moment like this I can't help but want to know."

"Something about you says warthog to me," said Sitembile. "I mean that as a compliment."

It was the same arena Errol and Rip had seen: the oval pit with an earthen floor and a stone-and-iron wall and bars surrounding it. There were a half dozen gates in the wall, cells, with starved predators panting behind them. Rough-hewn stands gave a restless mob a place to sow disorder. Men stood on the wall, taunting the crowd and jabbing down into the arena to stick the stag with prods. More of them stood in the stands with bows and full quivers.

The crowd wanted the stag to rise. A man on the wall slid one of the iron gates open on its wheeled track. They waited.

"That's Null," whispered Sitembile. "He works for the abbot. He is unsurpassed in gaol for staging such matches. Anywhere he goes he has a ring with a fight in it."

A flat, broad, reptilian snout appeared from behind the raised gate. Null prodded the beast with a hook till it roared out of the cell. The reptile was twice the size of the stag. It tore about the ring on thick, squat legs, its tail whipping, swinging its head with its jaws open in a joyless grin.

"Don't move," whispered the tufuga, as if the stag could hear from that distance.

The stag knew to keep his head still, but his eyes followed the reptile circling the arena. Finally someone in the stands threw a rock at the stag, which caused him to flinch. The reptile shot at him like a projectile, throwing him into the air with legs splayed.

The tufuga opened his eyes. The reptile was writhing, its jaws clamped on the stag's ear and what was left of the antler, yanking while the stag struggled to pull away.

"You must do something!" the tufuga screamed. "Do something or that thing will tear the stag apart!"

Sitembile took an arrow from a quill over her shoulder and set it in a bow. Her snake essed between her feet. "The best I can do now is make it quick for the stag."

"No!" said the tufuga. "That will be the end of Errol Thebes as well. Kill the predator!"

"You're serious."

"Yes, I am! Why not?!"

"Because it's a risk. It will bring the attention of Null's men. It will bring their bolts."

"We can't just sit here! Do it!" said the tufuga.

Sitembile was talking to herself now: "If this is the absurd heroism of the roofs, well, all right, then." She pulled back on the bowstring, exhaled, and let fly the arrow. The arrow sang through the dead air of the pit, through the crowd, past the stag and past the monstrous reptile, through the clutch of men who were standing at the wall, and into the navigable center of Null's chest. Null looked up in surprise and his eyes settled on Sitembile. For a moment the two of them considered each other. His entire existence depended upon fear. She was unafraid. He put his hands to the shaft of the arrow, fell over the railing, and into the pit.

"You missed!" yelled the tufuga. "You hit that man Null! When the reptile is right there with the stag in its jaws! I thought you were an archer! How could you miss the reptile?"

"I haven't missed a mark since I was four. You said to hit the predator."

The reptile in the pit had caught sight of Null, who was dragging himself toward a wall of the arena. In a blur of red, Null's name became more fitting that it ever had been.

"Shoot the reptile now!" the tufuga squealed. He reached for Sitembile to drag her forward and aim again. She was not there, and so he turned and saw. Sitembile lay on the stone ledge, her hands to the nock of the bolt in her chest. The asp was curled up her hands, its weight slack, its eyes warmer than they had been in life.

WHEN I ASKED HIM LATER, the tufuga was unable to explain where the bolt had come from. He hadn't even *seen* it. In his grief, he thought the whole thing could *un-happen* if he only did not move. He stood watching the stag, lying now in the dirt, and watched the reptile turn to face the tired deer and then trot toward the animal to finish it off.

A hopelessness pervaded the arena.

And then? Then. There came a rumble from the shafts and tunnels of the mines. Stone and gravel rained from the ceiling of the arena. The tufuga later remembered thinking the city was falling into the earth, crushing them all. From the wings of gaol came a stampede. An insane wild herd of steeds, hares, satyrs, rossignols, wildcats, crickets, foxes, peafowl, bears, bulls, mountain goats, wildcats, werebears, bonnacons, minotaurs, oxen, unicorns, eels. Eels. All pouring out of the tunnels and into the stands, one on the heels of the next, as if a river of fur and scales and feathers had burst the walls.

The stag was pulling himself up, trying to run. The reptile, riled by the fury of the sound, threw open his mouth. Pliny's army, that mob of field-guide beasts, had charged over the iron wall and were coming into the arena itself. They were led by a strange stag who moved with awkward gracelessness, as if its front was trotting and its back was galloping. Its white tail hung off to the side. It came to stand next to Eikthyrnir, and the rest of the animals surrounded the wounded stag.

———

If I am to be accurate, none of the animals were exactly beasts. In a reversal of the strange truths of this tale, here were the skins of animals inhabited by humans. Skins formed into costumes and masks from Pliny House, from Beklemek, for the high parties of Winter Ship.

The reptile took one look at the huge, bizarre herd, roared into its lair, and the tufuga leapt from his ledge and rolled shut the gate.

Rest in Peace

RIP STRUCK THE FLINT OF HIS LAMP. He had never come so far into the earth, to where his brother had gone to hide. He found tracks in the gravel. Bits of wood stacked in the shape of tiny towers. He pushed his lamp through the pinch, ducked, and pressed himself in. There, among the discarded remains of abacuses, barrel staves, torn fishing nets, locks with keys broken in them, and vihuela strings, he found what remained of Fenn.

He cleared a place to sit, reached into his pocket, and uncorked a flask.

There was a time when he and Fenn had raced the halls of Thebes House, wild in the eyes and not yet sharp in the teeth, when they won all the races and knew all the hiding places, when they taught each other to make knots on pairs of spikes. Before they realized who they were and what Fenn had to do to stay alive.

Then there was that day. The regnat and one guard. No witnesses. The choice of three lines. Rip pointed, and the guard strapped both brothers to the end of it. Just before they neared the earth, they realized it was the wrong line. Fenn wrapped himself around Rip. Held him in his arms. Fenn was the elder, after all.

Rip raised his flask. "Stay high."

IT WAS AS THOUGH some fiend had gotten into Errol's lungs and was scraping the walls of his chest with shards of glass. When he opened his eyes in the evening, he was in the middle of a convulsion.

He saw Marek and said only, "Mercy." When the convulsion released him, he said, "Tell it."

"The regnat and the abbot are gone," Marek said. "That creature Utlag is gone. The fleet commander ran from the city to meet up with the fleet. He was empty-handed. That monk Nyree has brought the iron spikes to safety."

"Where is Rip?"

Marek hesitated. "He went to see Fenn."

Errol convulsed and his body arced; every muscle in it pulled taut. The long bones in his thighs and arms bowed so hard Marek thought he would snap.

"It was a wyrm, was it not? The regnat's beast?"

"Aye, a dragon," said Nyree, who had just come in. "It was bigger than the vault. We found scales, claws, teeth, whatever was not consumed by the fire. Everything is scorched and the walls of the vault were ruptured. You survived because, we think, the regnat was between you and the beast."

"I will die, too, from the venom. We've all read of wyrms."

"You're improving by the uur," she lied.

"Take me to the river."

She shook her head. "There are riots, now that the people have heard a rumor the regnat and the abbot are gone."

But the two of them carried Errol to the river and pitched a tent for him on the bank. The rains were coming down hard by then, with winter thunder. Errol felt the steadiness of the earth under him.

The Double

NYREE WAS NOT REQUIRED TO CLEAN. She was the director of the staff of the scriptorium, and now the staff was treating her as the new abbot. But she had to think about that bucket she had set behind the ovens. She had to do something about it.

She resolved to take the bucket outside and light a fire, set the whole thing ablaze. She would gather a few of the monks to do it with her. No one should pass from the earth, even such a creature as Utlag, without being mourned. She went to the bucket and braced herself to do this work. But the bucket lay on its side, empty.

NYREE RAN TO THE FLAP of Errol's tent on the riverbank and stopped, breathing hard. She overheard two voices from within.

"—but the abbot is dead," one of them said. That was Errol. "Are you not gone, too?"

"I am not exactly what you think," said the other. "It's a relief Lugius is gone, actually, for he despised me. I will only have to look five minutes to find another banhus. I just find someone who's miserable, as the abbot was. I dig out his spirit and replace it with me. I will need those iron spikes—"

"If you are not a fylgia, what are you, Utlag?" said Errol. "Some sort of parasite?"

"A freak. I am one of one."

"I am in the presence of a double walker," said Errol.

"*Doppelganger, jawohl!*" said Utlag. "That's one name they've given me, outside the wall. More ancient? *Ka.* Move to the north? *Vardoger.* Sooner or later, everyone tries to name the thing. A man and his double."

"What do you call yourself?" said Errol.

The other paused. "I am a lack."

"I see," said Errol. "Well, you managed to wound my mother, Margaret Thebes. There's more than one way to inhabit someone's banhus."

"That was different. I thought it was possible—"

"You thought it was possible someone could love you?"

"Be careful, runner. What you think you know is not even half of what's needed. I was rare."

"Which explains your search for the rossignol or the bonnacon, in a city of bone houses," said Errol.

"We all long for something."

"I don't."

"What a fool. You above all. You want to be the one hero. You, who sacrifices the men closest to you."

"Sacrifices?" said Errol, leaning back into his bedding. "What have I sacrificed? I don't feed the weak to the strong."

"Not even your brothers?"

"My brothers are better off today than they were yesterday."

"Ah. So no one has told you." Outside the tent Nyree cringed. "They were my sons. Their lives depended upon my life, and I came undone, as you arrogantly chose. It's not so easy to rebuild them. Suffice to say, you are a worthy adversary, but as a friend, you are truly dangerous."

Errol felt a convulsion slipping into his muscles. "Tell me again. Did you ever even once get what you were trying for, using the iron spikes?"

"You know I didn't."

"Not a griffin? Bonnacon? Caladrius, winged horse, yale, manticore, rossignol. Not a wyrm?"

"Nothing. I fed the refuse to the rest of the—"

"The beast that attacked us in the vault was a wyrm!"

"We couldn't even get a ram with one horn in the middle of its head—" Utlag stopped. "*What* did you say?"

"It was a dragon. The regnat's beast."

Utlag faltered. "I knew it. No. Yes. False! You weren't there!"

"Oh, I was definitely there. It came after the abbot like a fiend from hel's own furnace."

"It was a gharial. People with no experience often—or maybe it was a crested newt. For sure. Was it the size of my hand?"

"It was as big as the vault. Scales. Venom. Speed. Smelled like a bonfire. Screamed like a hundred men burning in its innards. Spat flames. The regnat was trapped in his own blaze."

"How did you escape the vault?"

"Irfelaf," said Errol. "I shielded myself beneath the last regnat of this city."

Utlag's neck pulsed. "I must see go and see what's left of it," he said, rising again to his feet. "There must be more of them. I can begin again. Tear open some banhus and start over."

Errol gasped now, overcome by the seizure. "You will find no banhus in this city to inhabit. We are strong now."

"That is a pretty sentiment. But I can always find some miserable, jealous wretch." Utlag turned again to go and stopped, for he saw me coming toward him.

I felt danger but Utlag shifted his gaze, for directly behind me came Marek and Dagmar with Dagmar's fleet of wolves, then the apothecarist and the tufuga, and finally Jamila. The foundling was wearing Errol's coat over a black tunic and leggings, her night-black hair let out of its braid. She reached up to put her hand on the muzzle of the stag, who limped next to her.

Eikthyrnir's antlers were gone, and his fur was caked with blood where his left ear was gone as well. His head pulled up hard with every step but he moved with purpose.

Utlag's eyes shifted to a huge black creature behind the stag, a beast so large it looked like a turret of an iron tower. Its hoofs were feathered with hock fur; it carried its beautiful head at the girl's neck, watching her face, its broad wings drawn back against its sides. Behind the winged horse came a slew of kelps from the street.

"Outnumbered," Utlag whispered, and was gone.

In the Balance

DRAGON VENOM WAS NEW TO US ALL. Errol's pulse was weak, his breathing erratic. I talked to him all night, told him every story I knew, from when we were kelps. Every bit of news from the guilds. It was the reverse of a going-tale: any tale to keep him here. We called in Dagmar and the apothecarist to apply whatever seeds, pulp, pith, scale, bark, or spit they could extract from the winter earth.

At midday Jamila came into the tent and took off his blankets, wrung out a camphor rag and heated it in the iron pot on a cookstove Marek had set up in the corner. She washed his face, his shoulders, his chest.

She stopped to look at his arm. There was his guild mark—the crow, with its wings. And the brand above it, marking him an outlaw. And there was his third-year mark, his resting house, the one he had gotten when he visited the tufuga on his way off Samoa. It was the shatranj faras, the chess piece, the horse that he had given Kitchen Girl. Errol opened his eyes.

"Stay high," Jamila whispered.

"Is this heofon?" he said. "Am I gone?"

"I had heard you were improving."

"You were misinformed. Where did you come from?"

She turned her head to the door, where the stag had pushed his head into the tent.

"What happened to him?" Errol whispered.

"The antlers will grow back," said Jamila.

"No. They won't. We're dying." His back arched in a spasm. "Jamila, don't stay on the streets, when I'm gone. Go high."

"You may not leave."

Here he grimaced in pain. "I'm not at my best." He cringed and roared, and put his hands on his skull. "You should go."

A High Meeting

THERE WAS NO HANDRAIL. I had seen the narrow, tiny spiral stairs that led from the street to the pinnacle of the scriptorium roof. But I had seen them from my own tower and now I was climbing them, wishing for a handrail. I was tailed by the feathered harbinger of the dawn, clucking his disapproval as he flapped to keep up.

"Are you here?" I yelled at the top. My clothes were soaked with sweat. "Where are you?!"

"Gea." The voice sounded like a voice muffled by a rain. Yes.

"I've been looking for you everywhere," I said.

"I was there."

"I've come to demand answers. Why don't you just step in and save Errol Thebes? We both know he deserves it."

The mearc-stapa was silent for a while. A roosting stick appeared and Ovid hopped onto it.

"You want him fixed, like he's a frayed line."

"Yes. I do. I can even get down on my knees if you want. If that's protocol."

"Cliché."

"What, then?"

"A small exchange."

"Excellent. Where do I put the money? Is there some sort of cup or an account or what?"

"A different exchange. But I am obliged to warn you that Errol Thebes will only be getting into more trouble with the ships after that. Which means that if you want the job done right, I'll also need to slip upriver where the ships are anchored and draw up a wind to send them home."

"Yes. Good point. Do that."

"While I'm at it, I might as well fix the whole situation on the streets. Disease. Death. Felonies. Otherwise Errol will be getting involved with that again. And let's make it so everyone gets along. While I'm at it, I'll bring Fenn back from the dead. And a handful of others. Sitembile. Feo. Durga. There's a start—"

"I suppose."

"Might as well bring back the abbot, too, and the regnat. Let's make it so they get along with everyone. I mean, as long as I'm doing this."

"That's too much. Just save Errol. What do I owe you?"

"We can make it an even exchange; let's say you fix Margaret Thebes."

I hesitated. "What do you mean, *fix* her? She isn't broken."

"Talk to her. Persuade her to fall in love with better men from now on, instead of Utlag, who cast the city into despair. Get her to be—how would you say it?—*frugal*. Uninvolved. Celibate. Unambitious."

"That's not fixing her, it's ruining her. Margaret Thebes is the guildmaster. She's tangled. Complex. A mess, really, but Thebes wouldn't be Thebes without her."

"All right, then. Let's try this offer: Instead of actually fixing her, just tell this story as if you *did* fix her. As if she'd never got involved with Utlag in the first place. In exchange I'll save Errol Thebes and everything else."

"This is a waste of time. You know that story would be untrue and untellable. Without Margaret, it would not have happened."

The mearc-stapa sighed. "All right. So, let's say, then, that you fix Jamila instead. She's naught but a foundling, right? So you have unlimited power over her."

"Have you met Jamila?"

"Tell her to be indifferent from now on. Malleable. Teach her to cook. Yes, that's it. Because if you could just get her to stay in the morgue and cook, and stop jumping from roof to roof like that, we could all sweat a little less."

"I would hate Jamila if she stayed in the morgues."

"Well, of course. But if you don't fix her, then you and I will just have to meet up here next week, because you'll be demanding that I save her from some new trouble she's gotten into. Your friends are a handful, really."

"No they're not. It isn't fair what happened to Errol," I said. "The dragon. All that. Errol didn't ask for that."

"On the contrary. Errol Thebes specifically asked for it. 'What beast did you see when you looked at the regnat?' he said to you. Remember that conversation in the morgues?"

"I remember."

"And did you not say, 'It's a wyrm'?"

"I did. Yes. So your point is that he brought this on himself. But what about the things he didn't bring onto himself: I'm speaking of gaol."

"I wasn't necessary there. Marek found Errol. Sitembile saved Eik from the pit with Jamila Foundling and a thousand beasts. And that tufuga turned out to be useful. I didn't do any of that. Listen, if you want me to fix Errol Thebes, I will. If you want me to fix everything, I will. No exchange required. But you'll hate me when it's done."

I sat sulking. Finally I said, "If you fixed everything, you would be like one of those guild mothers running around making sure nothing happens to her kelps."

"Yes, or like a bard who won't let the story unwind."

"What is that supposed to mean?"

"I think we both know."

"Jamila punched me when I kissed her at the party on Al-Razi. I admit I left that out."

"That will not surprise anyone."

"All right. I caught my hair in the line and lost the Long Run."

"Everyone knows that already."

I sat brooding.

"Fine," I yelled. "Fine! Slyngel's letter to me said *she. 'i cannot protect the geld master an yore cuzin wen the crawling feend finds out she es alive.'* In the common tongue: 'I cannot protect the guildmaster and your cousin when the crawling fiend figures out she is alive.' *She.*"

"There you go. That's the bit you've been avoiding."

"Because I don't want to tell it."

"Characters are not puppets, Odd Thebes. You're bound by this, and so am I. They own their scripts. If I get involved in the plot, what chance does the apothecarist have of being heroic?"

"He's not going to be heroic. He's going to prescribe dittany, which will cure Errol of a werewolf bite, which he does not have."

"I just saw him digging madder root in the mud flats, with Dagmar."

"Is that the cure?"

"Do you want me to kill the plot for you?"

"No," I said sullenly. "No I don't."

"This place, this city, this map contains everything you need. That was the last-minute agreement. In the attics, the cellars, the fields, the rivers, the mines, the streets, the guts of plants, your hands, your minds, your banhuses—"

"To save Errol?"

"Gea. To save everyone. I don't do things healf-ears, as your mam would say."

"Wait, you know my mother?"

The other paused, waiting for me to catch up.

"I have to go," I said.

"I, too. How are we leaving this? Am I fixing anyone?"

"No. But it was a long way up here. I have to warn you. Did it ever occur to you that, if you don't fix things, people will stop coming?"

"Did I say that I never fix things?"

"All right, then," I said. "Because what good would you be? In fact, what are you at all?"

"I am a bard. I carry their tellensacs with me." The mearc-stapa paused and I felt, in that pause, the weight of all the tales we two carried. "You tell me. You're a bard. What purpose do *you* serve?"

I had no other answer to give. I thought of Errol, Jamila, Margaret, Rip, Fenn, Sitembile, Dagmar, my mam. "I love them," I said.

"Bingo," the voice said.

"What in hel is *bingo*?"

JAMILA HAD WRAPPED HERSELF in the blankets with him and was telling him tales from the foundling passages of the tower. My ribs ached. I loved them more than anything in the city. I sat outside the tent flap to hear her talk to him.

Just after midnight, Errol cried out so loudly that I woke up confused, thinking that his screams were my own night terrors.

Marek came running with Nyree.

"This is all," said Nyree. "He's done. Rip should be here for this." She looked at me. "You're his cousin, right? You should go in there with him."

I opened the tent flap. Jamila was kneeling next to him. His eyes were closed.

"Stay," she said to him.

He waited so long to speak, I thought he was gone. Finally he said, "Why?"

"Why? A thousand reasons."

"One."

"Because you're in love. That requires your presence."

He could barely speak. "I am. Yes. But with whom?"

"With a foundling."

"No. No. I love someone who keeps a feathered horse in her ribs. I met her in a dark kitchen."

"I know her."

"I bet you do."

"Also, Rip needs you. Odd needs you. The city does."

He rolled his eyes and smiled. "I don't care about them right now. You," he whispered. "Do you need me?"

"That will depend upon who you become."

He smiled.

As she leaned over, reaching to push the hair from his face, his hand came up and he grabbed her wrist. I stepped back at the force of it. He pulled her to him and sat up at the same time, his mouth open as though he would devour her. He held his mouth to hers and one hand behind her neck while he got up and came over her, and was on top of her, reaching around her to hold her hips, her ribs, to him with this press of strength. I watched her pull him to her with her hands on the bones of his hips. He was hungry for her, like no one I had ever seen, certainly no one I had ever been.

He paused finally to breathe and said to her, "Aye. This is heofon."

I whispered, "Stop committing poetry."

He did not have to look to know who was behind him. "Stay high, Odd Thebes."

"Just wondered if you need more madder root," I said. "Or anything."

When I turned to go I bumped into Chaunce, the tufuga. I was far from home and couldn't place his face at first.

"Ovid, isn't it?" he said.

I FOUND JAMILA sitting outside his tent. The stag and the winged horse were sleeping in the riverbank grasses with their muzzles in each other's shoulders.

"Have you seen the chicken?" I said.

"He's in Errol's sack," she said. "He snores."

"Why aren't you in that tent, Jamila Foundling? Get back in there and get what belongs to you. Make Errol commit to this. Happily bound and dropped."

She studied me as if to solve some puzzle. She said, "I'm not ready. And Errol is barely bound to his own stag. Why would we want to be bound?"

"Move over. Let me talk sense into him."

"He's not in there."

"You're false." I pushed away the flap of the tent and found only Ovid. "But I thought that's what you were doing last night? All that kissing."

"Why does this matter to you?" she said. "You were ready to be bound. I'm not."

"No," I said. "I wasn't ready. If I'm bound with this noose, so should you be, the two of you." Jamila was looking at something over my shoulder. I turned to look. I put my face in my hands.

"Are you coming to our tent?" Terpsichore said.

"Do you still want me?" I said, unable to look up.

She sniffed, as if she was thinking about it. "I have a noose your size. Be a shame to waste it."

Gauntless

ERROR RETURNED LATER and fell asleep in his tent. He awoke when a dog was licking his face.

"Arthur?" he said.

"Of course it's me. How are you? Are you recovering?"

"Aye. And nay." Arthur wore one of the tufuga's red bandages, all the way up his arm.

"What guild house did you choose?" Errol asked.

"I thought of outlaw, of course, or the crow of Thebes, to be even more like you. But then the tufuga said the choice had to be true, and I am not from a guild house. And the opposite of outlaw, really, with all due respect. And I miss Sitembile. So."

The fire-colored snake was wrapped from his wrist to his shoulder. When he held his bow-arm straight, an arrow, under the snake, aimed straight off his arm.

"She would love it," said Errol. "It captures her great skill."

"Sitembile was gauntless," Arthur said.

"Dauntless," said Errol.

"That's what I said." Then, soberly, "My sister also died. In gaol."

"I met her there. She asked us to care for you," said Errol.

"I see."

"My brother Fenn also died," said Errol. "And I cannot find my brother Rip."

"I'm sorry for your losses."

Errol considered the face of this kelp who had inspired so much of what happened in the days that just transpired. It was a good face, strong and friendly and ready.

Errol said, "I must apologize, for I underestimated your valor, Arthur, and that of Sitembile and your men. You've been fighting for years all of the foul business of gaol. You should have heard how Jago feared you. I misunderstood."

Arthur took out his bow and a cloth to wax the bowstring. "You thought we were kelps. It was an easy mistake to make." It will be another five years till Arthur is old enough for his voice to crack.

DAGMAR FLOATED IN THE RIVER, out in the middle, her wolves sprawled in the usual heap on the far shore.

"I know you're there," she said.

"I'm hardly here," said Rip, from the shadows on the riverbank.

She ran her finger at the surface of the water like the fin of a fish, and watched the moonlight gather in its wake.

"There's nothing I can do about this now," Rip said. "But I loved you once. Fenn and I both did." He adjusted the bandage on his hand. So much pain.

"That cannot be true," said Dagmar. "You've ignored me since we met on the roofs, and avoided me for years on the streets."

"How could you understand?" Rip said. "You, with an entire pack of wolves, and me, empty." She could see in his silhouette, as he paced, the remnant of his swagger. He would be gone soon, as Fenn was gone. From the darkness Rip threw something. Dagmar caught it before it hit the water and sank.

"Which story can anyone tell, from an empty tellensac?" she said.

"There's one story to tell," said Rip.

"What about all your other tales? What about the roofs? And Fenn's gifts. And all these kelps you feed. Your friends at the Bluebird—where are those relics?"

"My one relic is the weight and shape of a quarantined city. What my father did. I'm sure you know the tale. Everything we need is here. Right? Tales included. I know you've asked every denizen of this city. I must hear the story before I go."

Dagmar did know the tale. Bored sailors gossip from ship to ship, is how she knew it. She lived on the bank of a harbor and listened, once a year. She didn't speak their language when it first happened; she did now. They feared a blade of iron so aggressive it leapt from the forge to attack its own smith. That was its origin, a thousand years ago. Or ten thousand, depending on the sailor barding. What is a calendar in a quarantined city? The smith had gone too far, wandered the mines and descended into the shafts in a restless search for irfelaf iron. A pair of eyes looked out from the gashes the knife made in the smith, and from the cut in his apprentice. Cuttlefish, the both of them. He used the blade on everyone. Sheep. Loons. Cattle. The wall was thick but the word got out and the world had to have this blade. Nothing was left of the city, after the invasions. A remnant population, not even a name. There are gaps after that. Some say a sailor or a petty officer visited the city a decade later, or a century, seeking line from Lascaux for rigging. Some say she climbed light-footed it to the roofs. Others add that a parasite had by then invaded the smith's bonehouse, that the blade was reforged and lines were rigged across the abysses, and ships came every year to take the assassins. And one sought rare things. But Dagmar never spoke of any of this—not before now, and not now.

"A pair of rare sons," she said aloud.

"*Rare*," Rip snorted. "You mean half human. That's all you'll tell?"

"I never speak it, so you will never leave."

"Look at me. I'm leaving either way."

An ancient presence moved over the surface of the river.

"*Tila hami*," it said, in the language of Bamako House, whose mark Dagmar wore. "Stop crying."

"You first," Dagmar said. The thick fragrance of tuberose filled her nose. She slipped underwater and came up for air. "I cannot help him. I can do anything in this city. But I can't help him."

"But you are *kunna*, then. This is what I do."

"*Kunna?* I am many things, but not lucky."

From the shadows Rip demanded, "Who is there, in the water with you?"

A voice startled him. "Let me see you."

He turned fast, his bloody hand already raised.

It was Dagmar, standing next to him, with the river running off her. Her wolves nosed at his bandages. "You should go away," he said to her. "I am the dying son of a parasite. I have no fylgia in my rib cage. Remember me as I was on the roofs. There is no cure for the vacant thing that I am."

But Dagmar ignored him.

All his life Rip had longed for this, longed to be known, even for the diminished thing he was. Now, finally, he let her unwrap the linens and let her see.

PART V

WE HAULED UP JAGO on a drag line a day after we ourselves had returned to the roofs. He was blinking in the bright light of the setting sun, pacing and agitated. He was sure we had lured him up here to punish him in some guild court for war crimes. But curiosity about an invitation from the high roofs had snared even him.

When his gaze fell on me for a moment in the yurt, I could only think about what his hands had done. Foul with mud and sewage and all his clothes fitting too tightly, he was out of place here. He had brought a piece of junk rope with him that he'd found in the streets, and I realized he'd brought it up on a kelp-like impulse to seem like one of us, to appear that he knew what he was doing. I didn't have the nerve to tell him he had found that rope in the streets for a reason, that some runner had dropped it because it was frayed, and it was fatally dangerous. It would drop him.

We rang the bell to tell Errol that Jago had arrived; from his errands, Errol and Eikthyrnir came back to Thebes. The two of them, Jago and Errol, stood facing each other. Errol absentmindedly rubbed the stag's nose.

Jago spit off the edge. "So this is where they store all the heroes," he said.

" 'Tis a rare privilege for us, your visit," Errol said. "We will do well by you."

Jago lifted his chin, defiant. "I see for myself the hatches into the guilds have been locked in preparation for my visit."

"The guildmaster has kelps to consider, and elders. However, as you can see, we are neither kelps nor elders here on the roof." Jago did take a look. We were a strong lot and sky-worthy and we outnumbered him, ten thousand to one. "Also, we thought you'd like the sky."

Jago looked at him sharply. No doubt he wondered what Errol could mean. I wondered the same thing. Errol reached for something from his pack, and Jago braced himself, expecting to be pushed off the edge. Instead Errol handed him a package wrapped with the striped twine from Lascaux House. It was perhaps the first thing Jago had acquired in his life without first knifing its owner and stealing it. He barely knew how to open a gift. He chewed through the twine and ripped the papers.

"Is it a flying line?" he said.

"It's a rag. For twelve stones' weight. That's what I use. You and I are the same."

"This is for me?"

"I thought you would like to run the lines."

Jago looked out across the city, at the roofs of a thousand towers' banners furled in the sunset as far as he could see, vihuela music drifting from the edges, lights hanging on strings from every yurt, the fragrance of steaming tagines rising from the roof kitchens. These were the silk-lines he had had to watch from a mere mile away all his life. They were our roads, as strong as iron; they were our seaways, as mysterious as the curve of the earth. They were soaked now in red light from the setting sun. I knew Jago missed his fetch, the streetcat, and could barely stand to live with her wounded and trapped somewhere on a ship heading downriver. Still, some light went on in his eyes.

Second Sight

RUNNERS SURROUNDED US at every bucket fire Errol visited, to hear the stories again, whatever he was willing to tell of the streets, the vault, the mines. I found myself complaining to Jago about it.

"It was always this way. And now, again. They can't even remember my name now that he's back."

"Which one of your many acts of self-sacrifice did you want to be remembered for?"

———

One night at Thebes, Errol and I sat along at our own bucket fire.

"What?" I said.

He pointed to Faisal, who was gnawing on a piece of bread over by the yurt, and said, "I'm guessing a rodent."

"Ha! Indeed. *Sorex*," I said. I could see the shape and fur of a shrew, gnawing on Faisal's pack laces. "And Seppo? What's your guess for him?"

"He doesn't look like much but he has courage."

"*Aper*," I said. "Wild boar."

"Grid must be something that soars?"

"*Aquila*." I pointed to the sky over our medic's head, where I could see an eagle circling. "Do you really not see that?"

"I sense it but I can't see it. You are the seer, Odd Thebes." He lowered his voice. "What about Marek? Some edge beast. *Capra*? The goat?"

"No. Can't you feel it? The predator? *Panthera*. Which, interestingly, is the same as your new best friend, Jago."

Later that night I overheard Errol talking to himself at the fire. "Same beasts. One raised high. One, low." As if this explained a great deal.

Scars

THERE WAS REVELRY ON THE ROOF OF THEBES. Bowls and platters appeared out of Ping's kitchen, heaped with hand pies, pickles, cheeses, drageoirs, and we built a bonfire and stoked it all night. I watched the girls talking with Jago. Grid. Talwyn. Siwan. Even Terpsichore, nauseous with a stomach complaint, came out of my tent. Was it not enough that I was raised in Errol's shadows? Now here was Jago to take their attention?

Rip came up on the same line that had brought us Jago. He and Errol left us to sit on the plank between Bamako and Thebes.

"You are somehow unafraid of the heights," Errol said.

"Look at me. Is heights what I should fear?"

Errol laughed.

"However, I should shove you off this plank for sending me up to the belly of that crow. It was an insane plan."

"If you're going to shove me off, make it for something I deserve. Try this: I didn't stop even for a moment to think what would happen to you when the abbot died and Utlag came undone."

"Someone had to put an end to it."

"Then you could throw me off for the insults I leveled at you in front of your friends at that pub. The Bluebird."

"What you said was true. I am low."

"I didn't understand that you took care of kelps on the street, or Fenn. I wouldn't have cared for him. I'd have hunted him down."

"That's what he wanted you to do."

———

Later I was next to Jago around the fire. He was staring at Grid.

"Get in line," I said.

He didn't hear me. He said to her, "How did you get those scars on your neck and arms?"

She lifted her shirts and showed him the rest of it. He touched the scars and I could see that he knew his way around her. He had never seen a lightning wound, though. Such things did not happen in the streets. What did it feel like to be hit? He wanted to know. How had she gotten over her fear of the sky? Was this in her tellensac?

I was irritated that I had never asked her these questions.

Of course, once anyone shows a scar, all the scars have to be shown. Seppo held up his hand so we could see the absence of the small finger he lost to frostbite. Faisal had broken his nose and teeth. Ping had scars from the hot ovens. Among us there were rope burns, tower collisions, marks from kelpish blade work in Thebes's workrooms. Jago was responsible, I knew, for the stab wounds his men had inflicted on Errol; Errol was responsible for the finger subtracted from Jago's hand. Neither of them mentioned these stories or the irfelaf scars, but Grid pointed to white slashes on Jago's neck and shoulder that looked to me like scrawled fragments of some mad alphabet.

"From the last fight I lost," Jago said. "A knife. And I was held down in a fire."

"Who was your opponent?" Grid asked.

"My da."

Her eyebrows went up. "How old were you?"

"Five or six. I don't know. No one keeps records."

We all fell silent at the thought of a kelp treated in such a way.

Rip was healing, but his scars ran across his face and down his neck and chest and to the nether reaches of his body. I watched the girls look him over. I, too, looked him over. He was half gone. What was there to say? Grid said she could rub oil into him to relieve the pain. He said that any remedies so far only added to it.

"There's always me," I said. "If you're looking to rub someone."

"You have Leah," she said, nodding at Terpsichore, who had fallen asleep behind me with her head in her folded arms.

"All she does is sleep," I said.

"What did you expect?" said Jago, as if he knew something I didn't. He leaned over and whispered in my ear, "I have beaten my own men and murdered others in their sleep, whereas you call yourself the bard. Does it concern you at all that I, and not you, have heard the stories from your bound-wife's tellensac?"

"Are you threatening to take my wife?" I whispered back.

"If I was threatening you, you would already be gone."

"Are you showing off, then?"

"Don't be ridiculous."

"Tell me what you know about her."

"Ask her yourself."

"I will. When I'm ready." I couldn't stand it. "Tell me the relics at least."

He made a sound of irritation but he whispered: "A scruple weight. A cube of sea salt. A piece of hemp twine tied in a boiling knot."

"Bowline," I corrected him.

"A black feather, this little piece of stag fur. A seed. A diagram of a court game on a scrap of paper. A notebook of the names of ships in a fleet."

CHAUNCE, THE TUFUGA, sat with us for an uur to bring news from the streets. He had stayed long enough there to tatu anyone who had an idea of their mark and would return to do more. He said the most common request was to finish, or to *correct*, the naught brand on the foundlings' necks, by adding the directionals of a compass or astrolabe, the rings of Saturn, the rays of a rising sun, the workings of a gear, the spokes of a ship's wheel, a crown, a bloom, the strokes of an alphabet letter from one tongue or other. It was not uncommon to see people walking the streets with the mathematical symbol of infinity on their necks.

Bede the apothecarist had refused to rise. Instead he had sent for a tent and sacks full of beads and barrels of food and teas, and one of the guild flags of Raepteek House. He opened a sick house for the streets on the banks of the river. The last Chaunce had seen of him, the apothecarist was sitting at his tent flap with a line of malignant life-forms, human and animal, stretching down the riverbanks and through the streets, farther than anyone could see.

"And Arthur?" said Errol.

"We brought him up. My bound-wife has taken to him, and to his men. She sent them down into the guild for baths and bed, where they've slept since yesterday without waking." The tufuga looked at the clock tower. "My bound-wife gave birth while I was on the streets. We have named the child Sitembile."

The monk Nyree came up the lines and appeared in the yurt, where we all sat around the fire. She laid the sheath in front of Errol. He opened it and removed the iron spikes. Who would think such plain tools could do such damage to a city?

"I promised Fenn I would destroy these," Errol said.

"It's impossible to destroy them," said Rip. "And they cannot bear to stay hidden."

"Listen to yourselves. We're talking about two bits of iron," I said.

"With an iron will," said Rip.

"An equal will was required re-forge them," said Nyree. "You've heard that on the streets some speak of an ancient boatswain."

"What did you say?" said Terpsichore. "Pass those to me." I had thought she was asleep. Errol passed the spikes around the circle to her. She rolled them in her fingers and held up to the light of the fire. "These aren't precisely cnyttan spican," she said.

"What else would they be?" I said.

"Hold them to the light. Anyone can see they each have a tiny hole bored in one end. For stringing a lanyard through the iron, so it won't get lost at sea. This hangs round the neck of a sailor, for the constant knotwork of rigging."

Errol laughed. "How did we miss it? These are marlinespikes."

———

I left the yurt and went to the edge of the roof. The flies appeared to me now not as just a web of lines that could carry us to the edges of this city, but as the riggings of a thousand ships in the vast harbor of an abyss. Pulleys and chains clanked against the iron masts. I had the sensation that someone or something had long ago imprisoned us in guild towers; someone else, perhaps that boatswain, had given us a glimpse of freedom by rigging a high world. I shivered. Till that moment I had not noticed in my own tale the repeated appearances of ropes and masts, knots, splices, bells, or my bound-wife's obsession with a fleet. For a fleeting moment I could see a larger tale rising, like a ship surfacing from under the sea in a gust of salt spray, shimmering with light. That glistening ship slipped back under the waves and left me alone with the tale I knew.

A Binding

THE BRIDE KEPT A THOUSAND WITNESSES WAITING.

I could name names from the roofs and the streets, and from the guilds, but the most remarkable guests were the beasts: Eikthyrnir the noble stag; my gallant rooster, Ovid; the winged horse Jamila had named Tulak; Arthur's little dog, whose name was Arrow; and of course Dagmar's Roban. All of them sat waiting for the binding, their feathers and scruffs lifting in the warm westerlies, as if they had spent their entire life politely attending bindings and funerals.

I stood next to my bound-wife, wondering why she had chosen to wear a gray dress, a sack really, to the wedding. She was thick, and rashy around her mouth and on the back of her neck, and she ran her hands over her belly as if to soothe her intestines. She met my eyes, but I turned away from her. The rooster pecked at my foot, siding against me in this minor marital standoff. I was at odds with myself.

And then came Jamila. Errol had not seen her since they'd risen, and he pushed through the crowd now to get to her. She was barefoot, in a thin red silk gown with a damask belt slung around her hips. Red roses had been embroidered on the belt. When she passed by Terpsichore, they clasped hands and spoke for a moment, out of earshot.

I barely noticed Dagmar had come out of Rip's tent, in gossamer robes of white, green, and brown and a crown Rip had woven for her of river grass. The two of them stood in front of us all, wild creatures, uncomfortable with the attention. Marek read a few words about the laws of bindings, official jargon that no one ever bothered to listen to at bindings, and the two of them stepped out on the plank. Roban pinned himself to Dagmar. Marek shrugged and bound the three of them together. Noticeably missing from the plank was any beast of Rip's.

I thought for a moment that Rip would reconsider, given his terror of falling. But instead he turned to Errol.

"That foundling met the spikes in the abyss, did she not?"

"She did," said Errol.

Rip reached out his hand. "I'm ready," he said.

"If you're sure," said Errol, who took the sheath from his pack and handed it over. Rip tipped out the spikes, handed the sheath back. He kicked the release on the plank and the threesome dropped out of sight.

First, silence. And then there came a piercing scream from the abyss, as though a firework had been shot off Bian Pao House, and a streak of red light burned up through the darkness and over our heads and exploded in the sky. From the center of the fire rocketed a spray of crimson and violet flames, with a ragged tail and wings *whomping* big and hard at the smoke with gale force. The bird steadied itself in the sky, as hot and bright as a fragment of the sun, then dove down to return to Rip.

Errol laughed. "Of course. What else would it be?"

"See," I whispered to Ovid, "I told you there would be other birds."

ERROL AND HIS STAG were summoned by the assembly of the guildmasters, held in the Great Hall at Fremantle. The regnat's guards were now following the orders of a council led by Margaret Thebes. Errol was made to give an accounting of himself and all he had done. A great many subjects were gone over, particularly the burning of the guild work, whether the ships were still downriver waiting for beasts, and how the city had come to be under such a state of siege. The meeting ran on while the guild towers slept.

In the small uurs, Errol spoke his mind, telling what he had known and seen of the streets and the scriptorium and gaol. The guildmasters wanted to know whether it was the knotting spikes that had caused the quarantining of the city. Errol did not know. But he said the spikes were uncommon, which meant they had the capacity for great ruin or great good, depending on whose hands they were in. They asked after the double walker, Utlag. Errol said his whereabouts were unknown. Then Errol described the great emptying of gaol, the release of the frightened, worn inhabitants of the pits.

"I am nagged by a question," he said. "I asked it of the double walker, and got no answer. I ask it now of you." A thousand guildmasters held silence, waiting. "What makes us rise?"

"Lines, of course," said one of the guildmasters.

"I don't mean it literally, friend. What makes us people of high thought, high action? Rather than low."

The guildmasters conferred among themselves.

"A steady balance of work and sleep," called out one.

"Festivities, to break up the work year," said another.

"Meat pies."

"The presence of children."

"Private bedchambers."

"Praise for work well done."

Margaret Thebes, who led the assembly, remained silent as she had been through it all, neither joining the rising support for Errol nor detracting from him. When the room was done, she asked, "How do you answer your own question, runner?"

Errol said, "It is all new to me. I am far from understanding."

"Tell what you know," said Margaret.

Errol put up his hands in a gesture of resignation. "I believe a stag will fail to thrive under the same conditions in which, for example, a snake will flourish. A stag cannot do a snake's work, or a snake a stag's. Or eat what a snake eats. Or live where she does. Or spend his day in the same way. Or learn what she learns, not even how she learns it. But under the right conditions for each, in the right habitat, they both thrive."

Someone said to go on.

"I have seen that any beast can be turned low by fear, or rise with courage, if—"

"If what?" said Margaret Thebes.

Errol hesitated. "I don't think I know," he said.

"Tell it," called out a guildmaster. "Don't keep secrets from us."

"It is not stubbornness that keeps me from saying it."

"Think in a new way."

"All right, then. I am thinking of Theseus and the labyrinth, and the Minotaur and the ball of string. The thread saved Theseus, for it led him back out. I, too, was saved by a thread."

"The thread to your stag?" a guilder asked.

"Yes and no. I could not live without the stag. But it was another thread, a binding thread as strong as silk rope, a thread to someone else—" He hesitated. "There are no words to describe this, none that I know. It was uncommon. It was a pulling force." He seemed now to be talking to himself. "I felt pulled by her, somehow, pulled home like I had never been before."

"Ha! The word you're looking for is *love*!" roared a guildmaster, and the room burst into laughter and hoots of appreciation and calls for the name of the runner he loved.

Errol met Margaret's gaze. He thought he saw anger in it, and dislike. He wondered what he could ever have done that would make his own mam find him so repulsive.

"How could such a small thing as knotting spikes be such a great force?"

"The tiniest thing can carry great power," said Errol. "It is what we do, when we come upon something that has uncommon power, which tells us who we really are. This is not confined to the knotting spikes. Or to the uncommon objects in the tales in our libraries. It is also true of the uncommon powers of invention, of work, of the written word."

"Of love!" a young guildmaster yelled out. This was Cwym Teifi, the coracle guildmaster.

"It seems to me the high triumphed this time," said a guildmaster standing in the doorway. "Thanks to a runner of skill."

"If I understand your remark, then I must thank you for the compliment. But I am reminded of lost men and women who might disagree with you."

When it was over, the assembly asked Errol to wait on the roof. In less than a quarter uur, they called him back to the hall, and offered him a position in Fremantle. *The* position in Fremantle.

She

ERROL AND I RAN THE LINES TOGETHER after that meeting and took our breakfast to Al-Hazen, where he could borrow the long lens of that telescope to see what the ships were doing. From the roof of Marathon, he pointed the lens south and let me look first.

"There are no ships," I said.

I have known Errol all my life but had never seen that expression on his face. One part fear, two parts anger, and three hundred parts responsibility. If he were to be regnat, the gone-ships were his problem. Someone was waiting at the other end of the river, expecting a delivery of *monstrous wares*. Nothing would arrive but ships with vacant cargo holds. Surely that someone would be angry enough to come at us for a reckoning. If so, then a thousand guilds in this city would depend upon Errol to know what to do.

I took a piece of parchment from my tellensac and handed it to him. "Maybe this is the right time. Probably not."

He read it aloud. "wantin and rekless men now posess the citee." He looked up at me. "Homer?"

"By way of Slyngel Thebes."

It took a long time for him to read the whole letter, for the grammar was insane, the spellings were inconsistent, and there was that reference: "i cannot protect the geld master an yore cuzin wen the crawling feend finds out she es alive."

"It's always about a girl," I said.

He rose to go, then turned to me. "Clearly I have business with Margaret Thebes. But first, it's not a coincidence, is it? That this reference—'wanton and reckless men'—is from the bard Homer and that tale of a great odyssey. Which leads me to believe your da, who wrote it to you, was also revealing your real name. I am pleased finally to know you, Odysseus Thebes."

The Guildmaster

HIS MAM WAS SMALLER THAN HE REMEMBERED.

"I must know the truth," he said, standing in her door in the guildmaster's quarters of Thebes. "If I am to answer the request from the guilds, I must know who I am."

"And have you forgotten all your manners, in this quest for truth?"

"I'm sorry, Mam," said Errol. "Greetings and I wish you good work this day."

"Aye, and the same to you. Tea?"

"Nay. It is too much trouble for you."

"And have you forgotten who I am?"

Errol smiled at her ease with power. "I'll have tea, then," he said, and watched while foundlings materialized to fill the table with cloths and teas and cakes. Margaret poured his cup and put sweets on his plate, and he was surprised she remembered how much sugar he liked, and that he preferred walnut ma'amouls over fig or date.

"All right, then," said Margaret, setting down her spoon and picking up her cup. "See if you can find the thread that unravels the knot."

"My questions will cause pain," Errol said.

"We'll see."

It was the first time in his life he noticed how red her hands were from the work of running this great iron tower, this small city unto itself, which teemed with activity even now while the two of them sat at a linen-covered table. There was beauty in those hands, and in her strong bones and in her tired eyes and even in the way she tied up her hair. She put her hands around her hot tea, aware that he was taking her in. He was wondering, and he had no guess, what beast prowled her banhus.

"Were you not bound to the creature Utlag?" he asked.

"Aye," she said. "Five years."

"Did you know who he was when you were bound, that he was the parasite, the double walker of the abbot Lugius?"

"Of course not. I thought he was a runner, or later an apprentice."

"Did you never wonder why he removed the mirrors from Thebes?"

"There are more fears than can be counted in this city."

"Fenn and Rip: Were they your sons and his?"

"Aye." She set her cup down. "Wild kelps, like their father."

"And yet I am the son of another."

She paused. Then: "Aye."

"You had another man."

She hesitated again. "Aye, I did. But I was not unfaithful. Utlag was long banished."

"Banished by you."

"Aye."

Errol knew she was more serious now than she had been at first. That she was waiting for the next question. He said, "The new man was Utlag's opposite. Not a wild beast but a steady one. Not an outsider but an insider. One you could and can trust."

"Aye." Margaret stirred her tea. "You can put it that way."

"In choosing him, you didn't choose the one who publicly wanted you, who wanted you more than anything he owned or ruled. And everyone knew it."

" 'Tis true."

"He was not the regnat."

She spoke low now. "Nay, 'twas not. And I have paid for the error. I should have allowed that binding."

Errol leaned over to her. "I have met the regnat in low places and high ones, and I promise you, you made no error. You chose one who could remedy pain, instead of inflicting it."

"Aye. Except I didn't choose him. He chose me."

"It was Woody Thebes, was it not?"

"There you have it." Margaret put up her hands and moved as if to rise.

Errol said, "Woody wasn't the beast Utlag was."

She sat again. "You would think. But he was wild in his own way." When Errol put up his hands, Margaret quickly said, "Of course you don't want to know the private details."

"I definitely don't. But you had a child together."

"Aye. A beautiful—kelp."

Now Errol rose from the table and began to walk around his mother's sitting room. He stopped in front of the fire. "After the birth, you presented the guild with a third son." She looked up at him and waited. "There is more to be said about that third son. But we must go back in time first, again to Utlag. You expelled Utlag from the guild three years, or maybe four, before you took to Woody. Even so, Utlag was angry. He came for you, did he not? He haunted this guild with the intent of ruining everything that meant anything to you."

"Aye, he did."

"And yet it was the regnat who came for your sons. It was not Utlag. It was the regnat who dropped Fenn and Rip from Fremantle." Here, Margaret put her face in her hands.

"Aye."

"The regnat did this to punish you."

"He had no kelps of his own."

"The regnat is dead, Guildmaster Thebes," said Errol. "I have killed him."

Margaret breathed deeply and said, "I know. It will take time to feel the relief in that."

Errol nodded and went on. "It was nothing to the regnat to drop two runners when his regular business called for dropping foundlings to the streets, dead or alive. To be preyed upon. To be sent to gaol and trained in the ways of monsters. Assassins." Margaret nodded. He sat down across from her.

"What?" she said.

"I met Fenn."

Her mouth fell open. "How is that possible? You mean Rip. Rip is the one who's alive. Not Fenn."

"I met him when I was in gaol, in the mines below the streets."

"Tell it," she whispered.

"The fall didn't kill him."

Margaret put her hands up yet again, let them fall, took her cup. Errol refilled the cup for her, and said, "Fenn was damaged by the fall but survived it. Even in the streets, life was impossible for him. He was never one thing or the other. He had an insatiable appetite for human—"

"His father was the same."

Errol stared at his hands. "Rip took care of him. They were tender with each other. Fenn brought absurd bits of scrap to Rip every day from the street. Gifts."

"Did Fenn—" Margaret faltered. "Did he know that I didn't request his fall? That the regnat lied?"

"I told Fenn you missed him. I took this liberty. It mattered to him."

Margaret crossed her arms, as though to keep herself in one piece. "I thank you," she said. "I didn't know how to be his mam."

"Don't thank me. I'm not done. The regnat did not have to come after the third child, the son that, to the regnat's disgust, *also* was not his. All he had to do this time was wait for Utlag to discover there was another son, and Utlag himself, assuming the regnat was the father, came for that one. Utlag was the bogle who haunted me all through my kelp years." She would not look at him now. "You knew that would happen," he said.

She stared at her cup. "Aye, I did. But I didn't know it *was* happening until you came into my quarters one day with the report of it, and a list of suspects."

Errol inhaled slowly, his breath catching at the idea of a small kelp positioned to take the full force of the double walker. "So let us clear the records of innocent men," he said. "Slyngel Thebes, my cousin's father, was not my bogle."

"Nay. He watched you like you were his own son. Lived in constant fear of Utlag, who threatened him at every turn. Even fought with Utlag to keep you safe. Lost his thumb in the fight and died of poisoning. The third of Faol."

"I wish you had told me this before Slyngel died. I wish I had thanked him, rather than hated him."

"None of us thanked Slyngel Thebes. He was an embarrassment."

"Also, that foundling Feo was not my bogle." Margaret put her head back and swore. "Even with your love of foundlings, you sacrificed him to save me."

"Not only you."

"And it was not the first time you sacrificed a foundling kelp to save your own." Margaret flinched. "You have found the thread. Yank it out, will you?"

Till now, Errol and Margaret had been speaking in the dialect of the guilds. His mother's tongue. His grandmother's. The ancient tongue of Thebes House, for the ancient words were always used to discuss such powerful things as were at play here. But Errol ceased now and spoke in the common tongue, for he had already begun to feel like an intruder in Margaret's guild.

"Here is what I had to ask myself," he said. "What would I do to protect my third kelp, after the first two were thrown from a mile-high tower? My answer? I would do anything. I would build another tower on this one, to keep Utlag from that baby. Aye, but towers do not keep Utlag out! So I would keep the child as far from me as possible, while keeping it near enough to watch and to love. Perhaps I would have it raised by another—say, by my sister Gudrun. Aye, but a guild house knows no end to gossip, and everyone knows the guildmaster was pregnant and the sister was not. That would not be enough, would it?"

"No it wouldn't."

"So where do I hide that baby? In my quarters? In the morgues? Utlag can open locks with his fingers. He can move without footfall. A baby would never be safe." Margaret was biting her lip. "No, I would hide the baby in a ruse. I would hide the baby in a ruse that only I and the midwife would know. Not even the father."

Margaret turned her face, unable to look at him. "But the father found out," she said. "He found me in the morgues holding my own baby."

"He was suitably enraged at what you had done."

"He left me because of it."

"I know," said Errol.

"Oh, just say it!" Margaret snapped. "*I'll* just say it. I exchanged my baby for the baby of a foundling mother who had died in childbirth. I did it. Yes. I paid the midwife to keep the secret. I didn't drop her, you'll notice, which would have been easy. And I gave the foundling infant a chance to rise to guildmaster."

"Or to die, which was far more likely. Especially if he—if *I*—ran the roofs."

"Aye." Margaret stared at her fingers.

Errol pressed on: "The bargain Woody would make was that he would stay away from his own child, his daughter, to keep her safe. He would do it only if he were allowed to train the boy, who was me, with everything I needed, to prepare me for what trouble would come my way. He had a conscience."

"Aye. Woodwork was his idea. Archery and wrestling," said Margaret.

"For your part, you had to pretend to dislike me," said Errol.

"I wasn't pretending. I hated you as I hated everything I had done, all the trouble I had brought on this guild, on this city."

Errol winced. This was more than he wanted to know. "I see. Well, suffice to say, you began to pay Thebes's taxes yourself, rather than in a count of foundlings, to protect your daughter."

"Aye. I pay in gold."

"That is a great deal of gold," he said.

"I run a guild frugally. And I have the respect and gratitude of the foundlings, so they work harder than the foundlings in other towers. They don't know what I did to Feo."

Errol said, "And they don't know what you did to me. Utlag made me something of an experiment, really, to see if he could make fear rise in me to create some rare beast."

"You are rare," she whispered. Errol put his hands up. He neither wanted the compliment from her nor could he live without it.

He continued, "I'm very much afraid that Feo was my brother. The only family I had left."

"Your mam died incoherent in childbirth and took her secrets with her. But yes."

"I thought there were no secrets in this tower, kept from you."

"You were mistaken."

Errol moved Margaret's cup and his so that nothing sat between them. "Have you never told Jamila Foundling who she is?"

"I have not and I will not." Margaret wiped tears away.

"I will tell her."

"She'll certainly die, if she knows. If she appears to be anything but a foundling, Utlag, wherever he is, will come for her. And you won't know what form he will take or how she will die. And that will haunt your nightmares forever."

"Her choice, not ours."

"Don't talk to me about choices. I have lost sons. I can't bear to lose her. And while we're declaring such truths, you can't be foolish enough to think that the guilds will let you rise, if you're just a foundling. You now have a secret to keep as well."

"I didn't ask to be regnat. I have no such lack."

"Then you must weigh the third risk, that Jamila will not love you, if she rises and you fall."

Errol drew back in surprise. How did she know anything of his relationship with Jamila? "I'll be gone in any case, before she has a chance to leave me." He closed his eyes and breathed in the sweet smell of tea in the guildmaster's quarters. It was the last time he would be here, he knew. "If you will not tell her, then I will."

"I forbid it."

"I'll take that into consideration." Errol stood and put his napkin on the table. "Incidentally, I noticed you abstained from the vote in the guildhall. I wondered why you were not chosen to be regnat."

"I had already written to the guildmasters to say I would not take the position. There are too many skeletons."

"Why not Rip?"

"Utlag's son? The guilds would never permit it."

"Would you want me to rise over you, when you knew in truth who I am?"

"I was the one to bring the discussion to a vote when I did. I know my fellow guildmasters. I knew they would choose you then and there. We none of us know what to do with those black-iron spikes that burgle the rib cages. You do seem to know." She looked around at the empty remains of the tea they had drunk. "And now you're leaving yet again and where will you go?"

"To make a tellensac for your daughter."

"Here, then," she said, pulling her own tellensac from her belt. It was heavy with relics. She picked out a wad of paper and handed it to him. "This belongs to her."

Errol kept his hands from shaking as he read. Afterward he said, "I respect what you've done for Jamila, and even for me. You have been her mother and mine as well. Now I must bind myself to the work of the city for I am at the very least this city's son."

Margaret stood. "You've brought honor to this guild, runner."

"Foundling," he corrected her, and left.

Paperwork

I MET JAMILA in the kitchen in Thebes House after midnight and pushed the tellensac across the table to her.

"This is from Errol," I said. "It's yours."

"Foundlings don't have tellensacs."

"Like I said. Yours."

Errol *had* made it for her, with an ornate carving of the winged crow on one string-pull, the winged horse on the other. When Jamila tipped it over, a tiny wad of paper fell from it. She peeled it open.

"A page from the midwife's book," she said.

"Aye."

"It gives the date, DCXCVI viiiR. It says, 'Born to unknown foundling, a son, at four bells. Mother perished. Father unknown.'" A crease formed between her eyebrows. "Here it says, 'Born to the guildmaster, Margaret Thebes, half an uur after dawn, a daughter. Father: Not given.'" She looked at me and said again: "A daughter." I waited for her to take it in: A boy, born to a dying mother. A girl, born to the guildmaster. She inhaled, fast. "Errol was sacrificed," she said.

"No! You were sacrificed! And, here's something else."

It was another scrap of parchment:

Jamila Thebes—As it happens, you are a high creature living in low places, and I am another lie told in a city of secrets. I must leave the wall and will head downriver. My stories are half-truths, except those that are between us. You will rise, and I wish you a tellensac full of marvels. I cannot hope you will remember me, but I will remember you forever and am in your service, and in the service of your city, always.

Signed, Errol Foundling

I expected her eyes to be red with tears. Feh. *Mine* were. But she said, "Who does he think he is, writing a letter like this?"

"What do you mean? He's sparing himself the embarrassment of being sent away."

"But I may do what I want!"

"Don't you understand, Jamila? You have everything now. You can choose *any-one*. Anyone! Why would you choose a foundling? Anyway, Errol is dropping to the streets. He's nearly gone. What is the point of hanging on to the idea of him when I am here? *What?* Cousins have wed! You might remember I was willing to wed you as a foundling. Why are you making that face? Certainly Terpsichore would not stand in our way, given your newfound status. And you could—"

"*Nearly* gone?" she said. And then she ran, up the stairs, up the ramps, one hundred sixteen strata to the roof. She leapt from the edge of Thebes, soared across the abyss, slammed against the side of Bamako, turned, and sprang back toward Thebes. Down, down, she went, zigzagging across the abyss, dropping into the fog. I flung my pack onto my back, clipped my long-line to the fly, and dropped to catch her.

Errol was still lowering himself from his long-line when we reached him in the abyss. He put a brake on his line and the three of us, four, with Eikthyrnir, dangled thirty strata over the earth. My chicken stuck his head out of my pack.

"Préférerais tu," Jamila said, breathless. "Which do you prefer, to be trapped here with your friends forever or escape and never see anyone here again?"

"I have no choice but to go," he said. "And you have no choice but to stay and lead."

"I don't want to run a guild tower."

"Not a tower, Jamila. A city."

"I don't want that. I live with foundlings. I steal food and work gossip like a puzzle while nobody sees me. I dump bog pots. I wear an invisibility cloak."

Errol stared at her, a grin spreading on his face. "See it a new way. You're a guildmaster's daughter who knows the morgues. You love these towers. It is not a decision. It's a duty." Jamila dismissed him with a wave. He said, "When I thought the regnat would lead an army into gaol, I was wrong. You led the army."

"A herd."

"So? An army with fur. You went to Al-Hazen, with its thousand lenses trained toward the sky, and turned one lens downriver to find that the ships were burning our work. Plus, think of it, Jamila. You have the devotion of a city of foundlings. You believe in the tales of the library. You are fearless. Disciplined. Enduring. You tell only the truth."

"I'm not permitted to lie."

"That's a ruse. You tell the truth because you believe in it."

"Margaret Thebes can lead the city."

"When you come out of hiding, she will forward your name to the guilds. I know her. Despite what she said, she would do this. There would be strength in her recommendation."

Jamila was silent for a moment. Then, "I would move the regnat's quarters. I hate Fremantle."

"Where would you go?"

"To every guild. I would build a yurt and live at one guild and then another. A moveable yurt. I would begin in the streets."

"And what would you do about the foundlings?"

"Imagine a city where the regnat is marked with the naught and everyone wears a tellensac. We all have some deficit. We all have tales to tell."

"And what about the ships?"

"A large-scale attack on us will take them some time. We need a scout."

"Dispatch a scout, then."

"Fine. But I would want you to take Odd with you," she said. "He would learn their tongue in five minutes."

"But he can't go."

"Wait!" I howled. "Since when is my life in your hands? Either one of you!"

Jamila continued as if I were not there, "Take Jago," she said. "Jago needs to find the cat of his. She is on the ships. He is worse off, the farther she goes from him. Odd will go back down into the guilds with Leah."

"Jago!" I yelled. "Jago! The felon! Why Jago? And why do I go down into the guilds where Errol Thebes won't go? I am *gallus*! Harbinger of the dawn? And anyway, you are nothing now, Errol Thebes! A foundling! Why should you go downriver on the first expedition out of this city while I stay here and rot in a tower?"

Errol said, "Odd, I would go anywhere with you and that would make a heofon of any hel. But you have spun your own line and bound yourself with it." I swung at him hard, but he ducked and I bloodied my fist on the side of a tower instead. He kept talking. "What kind of a bound-husband would leave—"

This time I did hit him, hard enough to feel my bones crack against his jaw, and we both spun wildly. I was punching and kicking, and I grabbed his pack and yanked it off him. Was I trying to kill him? Of course not. Yes. He grabbed the stag's line to keep from falling.

"Damned arrogant foundling!" I yelled. "You! *You* are the Banhus-theof! You stole Jamila from me, and now you steal yourself! This is a perfect city. Nothing needs changing! All you do is leave!"

"What is this about?" He grabbed my line and held me at arm's length.

"Nothing." I was holding his pack behind me. "Nothing. I'm not you."

"Who are you, then?"

"I'm Odd. I tell your tale. That's all I ever do." I put my head back. "I'm odd."

"Odysseus."

"Yes." I was defeated. "Ironic. I'm Odysseus who can never leave home."

"Go to your bound-wife."

"She can't bear the sight of me. She has to take beads just to spend the night with me. And don't look at me that way, Jamila. That pity is iosal."

Errol's expression changed as if a lamp had turned on. "Wait! Jamila! Odd doesn't know—"

"Know what?" I said.

Jamila reached for him. "Stop, she's not ready for him to—"

"Know *what*?" I shrieked, petulant.

"Your bound-wife is thick with child."

"*What?*" I flailed. I yanked my line away from him. There was a high-pitched screaming in my ears and my line was spinning out. I was falling out of the sky. Ovid squeezed himself out of my pack and gripped my shoulders, flapping and flailing as if he were my wings.

Opening Lines

I STAGGERED BETWEEN THE TOWERS, disoriented. Was this Thebes or Bamako? Had I come so far as Pliny? I could hear the great hero Errol Thebes calling my name, trying to find me before some ill could befall me. The last thing I wanted was to be rescued by him, hauled back up the lines to my guild roof, to my bound-wife. The streets were less terrifying to me, at the moment, than the thought of returning to the guilds, only to become a father and to rot in a furnace-room job for fifty years. I tore around street corners, the chicken flapping and sliding behind me. I slipped into an alley, down a stairwell, sliding on slime-covered steps, losing the two of us in one of a thousand underground tunnels.

Preoccupied with getting the rag over my nose, I misjudged the size of a rut in the tunnel floor. I thought that I would hear the slap of my hands and knees on the ground. Instead, I felt air in my hair and my stomach in my throat, for I was falling. I slammed against the walls of the shaft, my head lamp flashing wildly on the surfaces of stone for what must have been a mile. Or fifty feet.

I passed out. When I came to, my lamp was still pulsing and Ovid had fallen in with me. I felt sure Ovid was thinking that Errol would do better, but in fact Errol had made all the same mistakes. The floor was piled high with femurs, kneecaps, skulls, teeth, fur, shreds of clothing.

Whether I slept next or lost consciousness again, I don't know. And for how long, I don't know. When I came to, my lamp was still pulsing.

I dug through Errol's pack and found all manner of useless paraphernalia: brake clips, his navaja, the wrappers from ma'amouls, his tellensac, his copy of the book of laws.

"No quill," I growled. "Of course not. Never, ever does a hero write his own tale. Leaves the telling to the lowly bard. My plight, to scratch and jab at the truth. *Jot it down, Odd. Get a quill, Odd. Empty our tellensacs. Tell us our tales.*" The feathered dawn-bringer eyed me, for I was eyeing him. I grabbed a feather from his wing and yanked it out. He shrieked and jammed his beak into my hand. I used Errol's blade to cut a nib in the quill. There was no paper. The only thing I had was the parchment of the scroll. I scraped the ancient ink off the first section, using the blade, and I spit into the handful of scrapings, to sop them and reconstitute from them a dark-enough liquid. I dipped the nib of the quill in that salvaged ink and began my going-story.

I will never be Errol Thebes: hero, foundling, outlaw, guildmaster's son,

Banhus-theof. I will never have Jamila, the winged horse, the likely regnat. Already I hate the facts of this tale. I spit into the ink supply again and wrote: *I am nothing but a chicken. And my bound-wife, I've seen it, is* cattus. *A house cat. Orange with black stripes. What hope is there, for that kelp of ours?*

I put the quill feather down and sat with my face in my hands. What was I doing? I was wasting my tiny palmful of ink, the irfelaf, in a fit of whining. Out of nowhere, a single thought occurred to me: Did she ever wish she was not bound to me?

My head ached as I picked up the quill again.

"Sing, Muse!" I yelled. "Sing, that I may tell my city glorious, that I may—I don't know—not come out of this looking like a complete idiot."

Be warned. A fragrance rises off this ink. The recipe is equal parts blood, gall, sewage, tears, the spit of a dying bard, and the soot from a sputtering head lamp. This day has not gone well.

These words felt to me like a tiny pile of wool from which I could pull and spin the long thread of a tale. After these I wrote of a near fall of two pelts, and of a girl with a crow tattoo, and using every drop of spit-ink, of a city under siege, of the herd in our rib cages, of the quarantined lives in a thousand iron vaults, of an uncommon thief and the fiends who sought rare things or made monsters of us, of a runner who dismantled the power of fear, of a foundling who held the welfare of the city above its own.

My spit made more ink. Ovid's blood made more ink, for I needed five more feathers to finish the tale. My tears made more, when tears came. In the telling of that season of Beklemek, in the tale of that beast in our room. Finally, because the chicken and I could not weep enough or spit enough or bleed enough, I added seepage I found in the skulls and kneecaps and foul, stinking liquid I squeezed from pieces of frayed clothing in the pit. The attarh would certainly have a name for such a gangrenous concoction.

I realized, as I wrote, that I had spent this whole tale obsessed with a rare thing who did not belong to me.

How different was I from that fiend Utlag?

I had a choice to make. I preferred to rise on a line right now and return to Terpsichore. I preferred to ask, as I should have asked a hundred times by now, how I could bring cheer to her. How she feels about that kelp of ours growing in her belly. And whether I can get her a little plate of ma'amouls and some tea. I prefer to teach her my strategies in games of cards and assure her that I would pull us out of debt and, on hard days, I will ask what is troubling her.

I will even find the courage to go back down into the guilds, to make a living, plying silk lines, in Lascaux House, so that Terpsichore—no, *Leah*—can live with her family.

The rooster, in many parts of the world, is a sacrificial bird.

Someday, when we are very old, I will remind her of her days on the roof, when she herself forgets them, wildly embellishing the night we met, so that our kelp will believe it was love that bound us from the start, and not blinding lust on their father's part.

Speaking of fathers, I prefer to not be a drunk. Just because I see beasts when I look at people, I would not do to my kelp what my da did to us. A righteous chaos he was, and we suffered for it. I would be better. I would read the poet Ovid to Leah and dance with her in our guild quarters. I would be her Parsival.

How many more pages do I have, of unrelenting self-interest? None.

I am dying in a pit alone—which, I admit, is iosal timing, for I am finally ready.

Signed,

Odysseus Thebes

THIS IS LEAH LASCAUX, alias: Terpsichore.

I found the bard here on a ledge near the bottom of one of these shafts in the place they call gaol. I've covered him with a blanket, him and the chicken, and given them water, and I've read his going-story from beginning to end.

It took me three days to track him here. The mines are worse than I thought. Like everyone else on the roofs, I am accustomed to the heady life of high places, surprised by the mayhem of low. But tracking is a skill of mine—many siblings, many hiding places in a guild tower—and so is stealth. I make rope. That, too, came in handy.

Three corrections, where my character is concerned:

Orange feline with black stripes: yes. House cat: no. I have the banhus wound and a big cat by my side to show for it.

Shoes: yes. Debt: no. I work hard and there's a stash of gold in my accounts that the guild banks say is uncommonly large. I *know* Heimdall said the opposite. Tell me: Why does anyone believe Heimdall Thebes?

And third: the very idea of Odd and me staying in Lascaux House for seventy years is enough to make me take a screamer. A fleet of ships. A crew of kelps. A map. Those are my ambitions.

In Lascaux, the master guilders speak of a boatswain who left the sea to find a dark city. They say she taught our kelps to trust with fearlessness the fly, the knot, the rag, the sky. I am a skeptic. If she is so important to us, what was her name? Who are her children, her grandchildren? Where is the written record? Sometimes, though, I do feel her ideas in my hands, when I am tying her knots and running the rigging of a city. When I dream of a fleet.

Jamila has returned to the towers to lead—Jamila, who says I smell of starlight, bowline knots, and feline, and who knew before I did that I was to bear a kelp. Errol is waiting for us at the south wall, building a raft with Jago, urgent to find his cat. We'll need Odd for his skills with the word. He wants to be my Parsival but I don't need a knight. I prefer Odysseus Thebes: translator, bard, seer. A player in his own tale. We are citizens of a thieved, burned, gutted city; we are bound with the sinew of uncommon wounds. I've packed our tents, bedrolls, tools, boots, gold, navajas, ma'amouls for Errol, eyrouns for Odd, the twin marlinespikes, beads for myself, which our medic gives me to cure aazein. Aye, we all have something that unsteadies us.

I'll need a midwife by summer. This kelp of ours will come when we're on a ship somewhere. If Odd can run the lines and win at maw and bard in pit-ink across thirty yards of lawless parchment, he can probably catch a baby.

Enough. There's an Odd runner who needs to rise: a quill for his tellensac and this tale is done. We have a fleet to catch. I'm ready.

Leah Lascaux

EX LIBRIS LB:
Notes on the Library at Thebes

The author is indebted to librarians from ancient Alexandria to the ethereal stacks of Perseus and Gutenberg for safeguarding the books and scrolls of the 151st strata of Thebes; to the skilled bards of the Aegean Sea for detailed reports of the Muses, the Argonauts, Achilles, Penelope, Theseus, Ariadne, Sisyphus, and on; to Publius Ovidius Naso aka Ovid, for love and all the gossip, even from exile; to Hesiod, for the dark side; to Homer, for the travels of the magnificent, flawed Odysseus; to Edith Hamilton, who threw the ancient myths in her pack and carried them over the lines to us; to the bard of Avon, whose line 70, spoken by Mercutio in Act I, Scene 4 of *Romeo and Juliet*, is delivered in this book by Talwyn Thebes; to Pliny for his roving (that is, *insane*) *Natural History, Book VIII,* quoted by Odd Thebes on the night of the striped infant bear; to the anonymous writer whose description of Beowulf's arrival to kill the monster provides a tellensac tale for Dete; to Shirazad, whose incidental tale of a magpie and a beaker of jewels supplies the elements for an urgent encodement at the scriptorium; to Luo Guanzhong, aka Luo Ben, whose massive *Three Kingdoms* includes a frightening line redirected in this book toward Slyngel Thebes; to the collectors of the tales of sugar houses and infinite bean plants, of princesses who lose their shoes, sleep ten decades late, complain about small vegetables in their beds, and double as pond birds; to the writers of the Narmada River, who left us the Markandeya and a name for Durga; to the bards of the northern sagas who stoked the fires of Yggdrasil, Valhalla, Eikthyrnir, Bjarki, Uxafot, Gylfi, and gave us the recipe for the chain of Fenrir; to von Eschenbach, Malory, and T. H. White for their reports of King Arthur's nights and the road trips of the self-involved Parsival. The author would also thank the poet who wrote the six lines of Sanskrit Jamila Foundling reads exclusively, but the author has no idea what that text was; such is Jamila. Many thanks, though, to the collectors of the ancient hymns, publick house cumulatives, rambling ballads, nursery rhymes, and sailor shanties sung or in some cases screamed in this book; to Lully, for Errol's favorite gavotte; to Ajam, whose "Bandare Landan" is a close approximation of the first song on the set list on the night of Ship; to the obsessed guilders of every world who publish, for example, the complete rules for extinct card games, the specific colors of a thousand particular seas, the slander of medieval bestiaries, the ingredients of ma'amoul, the record of occurrences of animal others, the names of constellations nobody on earth can actually identify, the parts and function of ancient timekeeping devices, the odd practice of filing teeth; to Turin and Sanchez, whose roving (that is, *brilliant*) reviews of perfumes would be of keen interest to the attarh; to Lindahl, McNamara, and Lindow for the chilling concept of the outlaw; to Ashley, for 3.2 billion knots and the mention of a sailor who knit a hammock on two broomsticks; finally, to the deranged among us, and before us, who conjure uncommon things in order to explain the news on any given day.

ACKNOWLEDGMENTS

Most of a writer's life occurs in isolation. This has been truer than ever since March, with the world locked down in a global effort to contain a pandemic. We are now also in the throes of a Civil Rights uprising in the United States: a mighty roar of outrage against acts of racism we witness daily in our Instagram feed. Masked, gloved, six feet apart, we protest in the streets. In the middle of an epic reality, I pause to remember the work behind me and to raise a Beklemek glass and say thank you:

To the people who do the real work of rescue in a dark world, by saving the victims of sickness and sorrow, the real foundlings and discarded animals. I am a fan of the organizations Partners in Health, for people, and Best Friends, for animals. A percentage of the profits from this book will go to them.

To the librarians and booksellers, particularly at Broadside Bookshop and Meekins Library, who are my 151st strata.

To Craig Davis, Professor of English Language & Literature at Smith College, who helped me develop what he calls a "middle backwater" guild tongue for Thebes, suggesting words that were themselves fully packed with plot, and he straightened out my Welsh too. All mishaps and contortions of language in this work are my own.

To my colleagues at Signature Sounds, who could settle a deserted island and throw a music festival that weekend, and to the two bands I manage and adore: The Suitcase Junket and Twisted Pine. To the A-Team: Georgia Teensma, Abbie Duquette, Kelsey O'Brien, Kathleen Page, and Emily Woodland, for devotion beyond all call of duty.

To Sam Stein, Chris Jerome, Max Wareham, Jeff Lewis, Ali Telmesani, Laura Lefebvre, and Brie Sullivan, who've actually or metaphorically driven across the country listening to ideas or chapters long into the night on dark highways.

To Rick Beaupre, who tatued the guild mark for Thebes on my arm.

To my agent, Melanie Kroupa, who believed in this manuscript long before I did, and despite the fact that it's not her usual cup of tea but rather a weird and horrifying tale that arrived in her mail in "tiny" 500-page installments. She made it possible for me to do the work I love. And to our agency chief, Rubin Pfeffer, who treats his writers like family, and found this book its home.

To the team at Dutton and Penguin Random House, for taking this book into their care and giving it a glorious life. To Julie Strauss-Gabel, publisher; Melissa Faulner, publishing manager; Anna Booth, designer (her many ideas included scrubbing the pages to make them appear as palimpsest); Natalie Vielkind, managing editor; Rob Farren, copy cheef (jk), Anne Heausler, coppy editor (ditto)— imagine the trouble Odd Thebes gave the copy department; Kristin Boyle, cover design (who hid the spikes in front of our eyes); Lizzie Goodell, heading publicity; to AJ Frena for the thrilling cover art (I carry that first draft of the cover around with me everywhere); to Francesca Baerald, for the breathtaking maps and borderwork. I wrote this city and yet, when AJ's art and Francesca's maps arrived, I could no longer navigate without checking first with those images and maps. And especially to my editor, Andrew Karre, who uses every skill in his possession to understand and forward the causes of others, who holds the city's interest above his own, who knows the time to leave so-called safety and drop to the streets, and who makes, of all that seems impossible, a festival on the tower roofs.

To my family: George and Shirley Bertrand, who are righteous and taught me love; Henny and Eddy Teensma, who survived the war and Nazi occupation with sturdy splendor; Ton, Pablo, Kymo Vermeulen and Ingrid DeRaat, my beloveds; Peri Hall, Janet Street, Carol Boyd, Emma Rodrigue, and, from long ago, Shosh Marchand, Kathy Smith, Emily and Eleni Dines, sisters of an only child. To Nick Teensma, who drives the backroads and listens to the tales and is the closest thing to a runner I know; and Georgia Teensma, who is my first reader and is as dear to me as the girlfriends of my childhood. Most of all, to Hans, who never flinches when I buy printer ink when what we need is milk, who loves even the parts that freak him out, who shows up every morning for coffee and makes that my favorite time of every day, and who is the city in which I live.

Stay high.

Lynne Bertrand

JULY 1, 2020